William Al-Sharif is a British philosopher, scientist, historian, and author of over 80 books and 300 articles. He and his family live in Scotland.

https://willalsharif.com

THE
DIVINE FAMILY

WILLIAM AL-SHARIF

Chiteki Books
47 Fa side View
Tranent, EH33 2NS, Scotland, the UK.

ISBN: 978-1-7394959-0-9

For Cat Hen (Caitlyn), with much love and admiration

Chapter 1

"What a fool! They will kill him." Maria Wyatt stood amidst the tranquil beauty of her front yard, with a gentle breeze caressing her face as she surveyed her cherished garden. Her blue eyes settled upon a white rose, its pristine petals glistening under the warm rays of the sun. She reached for a pair of sharp shears, their blades glinting with a polished gleam. She positioned herself beside the rose and guided the shears toward the brown stem. As the blades closed in, severing the connection between the flower and the plant, a sense of furious resentment washed over her. "They are vicious. I cannot believe they closed the bridges. For what? Do they think New York is Sicily?"

"But he made a big mistake. He should not have agitated them with his foolish remarks."

"Yeah, he is stupid, but his stupidity does not justify burning government offices and closing the bridges. And what about the Irish goons who want to chop off his head because he made a funny joke about the Pope?"

"The Catholics in the city are horrible. Nobody feels safe with them. Last week, an Irish guy shot his cousin in the face because she loved a lesbian Chinese girl. Disgusting."

"They are hypocrites. They say homosexuality is a sin, but shooting people in their homes is good. You know what happened in Vinegar Hill because of their drugs and murder. The neighborhood now is a ghost town."

"Thank God, it is peaceful here."

"Speaking of the devil. Here is the king of kings and his scary boogeymen. Do not say a word about Italians."

A man halted his steps on the opposite sidewalk. His gaze shifted, drawn toward the presence of the two women. Curiosity sparked within him, causing his face to turn left and gaze at the pair. His features evinced intrigue and empathy. His restless mind wove stories, conjuring narratives to explain the social dynamics he perceived. Were they close friends sharing a heartfelt conversation? Sisters exchanging intimate secrets and laughter? Strangers who found an instant connection? The possibilities swirled within his imagination. "Wait here," he said to two companions. He crossed the quiet, tree-shaded street and rested his fingers on a black metal fence. "Hello, Maria. How are you doing today?"

"Doing fine and enjoying the warm weather."

"Yeah, it is a lovely day. Who is the other lady?"

"This is Jennifer. She is a friend from Queens. Do you like a cup of tea?"

"No, thanks. Need anything?"

"Nope. Everything is OK." She gave him two roses. "Your family has many guests today."

"We are expecting something in the house." He smelled the roses. "We will tell you the news. Catch ya later. Thanks for the flowers. Have a good day. Ciao." He waved his Borsalino and recrossed the street.

"Who was that hunky man? I like his black hat."

"Don't you know him? He is Sandro Lucciano, the godfather of the Italian Mafia."

"My God. Do you feel safe living here alone?"

"Yeah, I feel all right with the Luccianos. Sandro and his guys can kill a hundred men, but they will never beat a woman. That is a part of their creed."

"Does he live in that building?"

"No. He and his wife come on the weekend to see their two sons and daughter."

This conversation was on a Friday afternoon in the middle of September. A golden gleam of sunlight slanted over Brooklyn, and residents enjoyed the bright, balmy weather. Locals strolled and chatted at the bustling corners of the vibrant streets. That calm ambience had eased the communal tension after the murder of a Gambino crime boss, whose mutilated body the police found in a car trunk with multiple shots in the head and the chest.

A breath of wind blew in from the east, and gray clouds swept across the blue sky, casting a volatile atmosphere over the bright cityscape. But amid the subdued tones, a magical transformation took place. A burst of color appeared, stretching across the western horizon - a dazzling rainbow. The vibrant curvature, painted with nature's subtle palette, arched against the backdrop of the darkened clouds. Its radiant hues illuminated the sky, emitting a spell of awe and wonder. The colors danced in harmony, weaving a symphony of blues, greens, reds, oranges, yellows, indigos, and violets, creating a breathtaking spectacle.

In public parks, people paused in their activities. The sparkling skyline had captured their intrinsic attention. Conversations dwindled, and wandering individuals drew phones from pockets as they sought to capture this extraordinary moment. Smiles graced their faces as they aimed their cameras toward the resplendent rainbow, eager to freeze this supernal display in time.

Laughter and whispers filled the air as strangers bonded over the shared experience. Children pointed with excitement, their eyes wide with wonder, while couples leaned closer together, their hands entwined, marveling at the magnificent arc of colors before them.

The city's rhythm slowed, as if the celestial show had seized the entire collective consciousness. The colorful rainbow painted a vivid contrast against the setting of the gray clouds, serving as a reminder of the beauty that can appear even at the darkest times. Rapid snapshots captured the transient dramatic moments, preserving the memory of this ephemeral beauty and sharing the joy of witnessing nature's enthralling artistry.

As the dark clouds continued their grim march

across the sky, the dazzling rainbow faded, its colors growing fainter with each passing moment. The attractive spectacle, which mesmerized the onlookers, had receded into the scenery of the ever-changing sky. At this time, four clean-shaven men, exuding an air of controlled confidence, ascended to the flat roof of a four-floor building at Third Place in Carroll Gardens. Clad in tailored, double-breasted pinstripe suits, their smart attire radiated a timeless elegance that reflected their wealth and social milieu. In their hands, they grasped automatic rifles, symbols of danger, power, and influence.

With concurred movements, their eyes scanning the surroundings, they positioned themselves on the roof. The urban landscape sprawled before them, a maze of streets and buildings that held secrets and challenges. The men's facial expressions remained stoic, their focus unwavering, as they prepared to receive an order and carry out their mission.

Cool wind rustled through their groomed dark hair, offering a brief respite from the intensity of the moment. Their sharp eyes took in every detail of their locale, assessing potential perils and vital points of interest. They calculated every step and made each decision with the precision of adept experts who had honed skills through countless trials.

Whispers of communication crackled through the black earpieces and the mini microphones they wore, exchanging information with relatives in the city. Their whispered messages embodied order, mystery, and alertness, a potent combination that alluded to a clandestine world concealed behind closed doors and general rumors. To certain Italian men, the automatic rifles symbolized the complexities of their existence, which obscured the line between law and lawlessness.

When the armed men's left feet touched the thick brick parapet, Sandro looked up at them and wagged two right fingers. They raised their heads and fired shots for twenty seconds. The piercing sound of the tracer bullets had shattered the atmosphere of the hectic borough. Maria and Jennifer dashed into the kitchen and took shelter behind the breakfast bar. Their bodies trembled, with the fast adrenaline moving through their veins, causing them to shiver with fear and exhaustion. "I told you the Italians are insane."

Young and old pedestrians and shoppers panicked, yelping and scurrying to convenience stores, bars, and sheltered places. They used cell phones and called relatives and police departments. A lame man hunkered beside a green hedge, clamping a phone to his ear. "The Mafia guys are shooting in Third Place in Brooklyn." Three police cars, loaded with armed officers, rushed to the street and lined up in front of the brownstone house. After hearing the blaring sirens, a boy wiped his runny nose with his fingers and stood on the doorsill of his apartment. "Mom, look over there. The cops are at that big house."

His smoking mother peeked out and nudged him back. "Stay inside the house. These are the Italian clunks who make trouble every day."

With tight grips on their holstered pistols, six police officers advanced to the guarded, fenced house and met

Sandro and his second son, who stood on the bottom step. An officer relaxed his facial muscles, and a faint smirk tugged at the corners of his lips. "How is everything, Mr. Lucciano? What's going on today?"

"Hi, John. Today is a time of delight and joy. My family is celebrating the birth of my new grandchild. I assure you, my dear friend, everything is fine and under our full control." After stepping forward and adjusting his black necktie, he patted the head of a curly-haired boy who came out to watch the dialog. "Franco, bring cookies to the cops."

"Thanks, and congratulations to the family. We must go now. But, please, no more gunfire in these residential neighborhoods. People get scared when they hear gunshots."

Sandro wiped his wide lips with a cotton napkin. "Wait. Come on. We are one family in the city. You and your officers should taste our Italian cakes."

Franco brought a decorated Florentine tray of stuffed cannoli cupcakes. "Please, help yourselves. Don't be shy."

Each officer got a cupcake and thanked Sandro. Three FBI officials and a half-dozen news reporters hastened to the jammed street. The officials stood at the center, sensing the gazing eyes fixed upon them. They exchanged brief glances, communicating their shared purpose. The news reporters, equipped with cameras, microphones, and notepads, jostled for the vantage points to capture every detail of the scene. Eager to uncover the truth and deliver the news to the public, they brimmed with avidity, ready to document the unfolding narrative. Sandro rubbed his right jawline. "Why are you here?"

An agent pouted with displeasure. "You know why we are here. Your buses and trucks are blocking the city's bridges. Please, we do not need more troubles."

"We also do not need troubles. But the indecent mayor says we exploit Italian women and kids for drugs, arms deals, and prostitution. Are our women prostitutes? Are we pimps and dishonest people? Answer me."

"No. But, please, commuters and students are not responsible for what the mayor says about your folk. Please, ask your drivers to end the blockage."

Sandro stared at a male reporter carrying a Sony shoulder-mount camcorder. "Put the camera on and come here." He snatched a microphone and focused on the camera lens. "Listen to me, dirty mayor. I say simple words. You must apologize in public before noon tomorrow, or you will face our Italian rage. You have no place to hide or run, and there is no other way. Resign now. Now. New York needs a decent man. The guy who says obscene words about Italian women is not a real man. This is my last offer, or hell will wait for you." He made a call. "Leonardo, ask the guys to leave the bridges and come back soon. Your wife has given birth to a boy, and we are having a dinner party." Sandro put his phone in his jacket pocket and gestured for the officers and the journalists to go away. "Please, leave this place and respect our privacy. God bless you."

He touched his son's shoulder. "Marco, let us see the family and the baby." They leaped up the exterior stairs and moved into the house. "He is a magnificent boy. His eyes are of gold and his soft hair is brown." Isabella, Sandro's silvery-haired sister, said.

"Great. Can I see him?"

"*Sì.*"

He tapped his son's back. "Go to the kitchen and help your mother and sister."

Isabella knocked and opened a brown door. Sandro entered a bedroom and approached a woman lying on a bed and holding a swaddled baby. He wiped her sweating face with a bandana. "How are ya doing?"

"Fine. It was a long labor. I felt I delivered two big babies."

"You had after-birth contractions," Isabella said.

"Anyway, I am doing well now. Thank you."

"God bless you. You have done a fantastic job." After kissing the woman's forehead and covering her pale feet, Sandro lifted the baby and crooned. "Look at him. He is God's angel. He looks like a cherub angel. I should call him Angelo. Yes. Angelo. Angelo. Long ago, high on a mountain in Mexico, lived a young shepherd boy, Angelo...." A series of piercing detonations stopped his singing, and an outburst of wind rocked the building and rattled the windows and doors. The baby's mother stared at the dancing chandelier and covered her ears with pillows. "*Mio Signore. Gesù Cristo.* What are these loud sounds?" Sandro placed the baby on the bed and opened two taupe drapes. Bolts of lightning flashed like fiery spears across the dark sky. Swirling gray clouds blackened the turbulent troposphere, and the constant cacophony of rain had startled drivers and strollers in the borough. "It was a nice sunny day. What happened to the crazy weather? Hailstorms in this month?"

After closing the drapes, he lifted the baby. "Oh, my God. Your son is happy and smiling. He didn't cry or feel afraid of the blasts." He shifted his face to the left and called out. "Where is Giulia?"

"She is in the kitchen."

"Bring her here."

Giulia Mugavero, Sandro's sister-in-law, entered the room. "*Sì*, Sandro."

He wobbled his heavy head and pointed his right forefinger at the baby's mother, trying to convey his understanding of cultural practices and the depth of attachment and emotions that come with the new experience of motherhood. "Bella, I know how you feel about your first baby. You are his mother, and I respect that with all my heart. But you know, we follow our southern Italian traditions. You nurse him, and Giulia will breastfeed him. The baby needs our intelligence and strength."

Feeling powerless, Bella crossed her arms over her chest and tilted her head. "As you wish, uncle."

Leonardo arrived home and placed his umbrella in a wooden basket beside the main door. After taking off his navy raincoat, he stormed into the house, kissing his father's and mother's hands and his wife's lips. "Your face is white and cold. You need a shower and food. Where is my boy?" He hugged, kissed, and swung the baby. "Have you chosen a name for him?"

"I wish you name him Angelo. He is like an angel."

"*Perfetto*. I like the name Angelo. It reminds me of

Michelangelo and his splendid work. Did you see the mad lightning and hear the thunder? The streets have flooded with a foot of water."

"Weird weather. The thunderstorms shook the entire house."

"Where is the wine? Who is making dinner?"

"Viola and Fernanda are cooking maccheroni and chicken cacciatore. Your mom is making cannoli."

After a long, chatty dinner, Leonardo, Bella, and their baby moved up to their house on the second floor. Marco Lucciano and his spouse Fernanda Orsini and their daughter Celia occupied the fourth floor, while Viola Lucciano and her partner Carlo Stellino and their son Franco lived on the third floor. The other relatives stayed on the first floor.

In the morning, the city's mayor resigned and apologized for saying the Italians employ sex workers and teens to smuggle narcotics and handguns. The Lucciano family gathered at lunch in the dining room on the first floor and gloated over his forced resignation. Sandro stood and raised a glass of red wine. "This quick victory is for all of us. Real men make genuine families. The guy who doesn't love his family can never be a real man. Don't do anything against the family. I have never doubted your honest affection and loyalty. Do not tell anybody outside the family what you want to do. What we say to each other in the house stays confidential in the family."

In this household, Angelo grew up with affection and love from his family, and his composure and joyful nature had astonished everyone around him. In

February, high sustained gales and persistent snow squalls struck the northeastern states. Twenty inches of snow blanketed New York City. The snow closed the parks and clogged the streets, forcing the Lucciano family to remain indoors in their Carroll Gardens building. One night, Leonardo and Bella watched Clint Eastwood's *The Bridges of Madison County* in their bedroom and slept buried in their thick bed covers. A brief, howling tempest pounded the frontage of the house and shook the windows. In a surreal moment, a white, radiant light descended upon Angelo, casting a soft glow that permeated the essence of his being. As the light enveloped him, he felt a surge of energy moving through his body.

With each passing moment, the light intensified, illuminating his room and banishing any remnants of darkness. Angelo was too young to understand or feel the connection to something greater than him, a force of pure energy and enlightenment. The light seemed to choose him, igniting a spark in his being to guide him toward a path of growth and discovery.

As the light faded, leaving behind a lingering sense of its energetic presence, Angelo awakened and stood, looking at the bed of his parents. "Mama. Papa. Mama. Papa." Leonardo wiped the lid of his right eye with the back of his hand and opened his eyes to the sound of Angelo's soft voice. "Mama. Papa. Mama. Papa." Leonardo rose from his bed and plodded to Angelo's wooden convertible crib. With a flash of joy and energy, Angelo bounced on the balls of his feet, his hands gripping the rail for support. Each bounce propelled him higher, a momentary suspension of gravity that brought a smile to his face. "Papa. Dad. Daddy. Love you. Love you." Leonardo held him and kissed his face. "Papa loves you too."

Bella switched on her beside lamp and raised her head. "Was he crying?"

"No. He jumps and speaks like a tween. Do you believe that?"

"Mama. Mommy."

"This boy is a miracle. Bring him to me."

She dandled him on her knees. His body slid down and nestled against her, finding comfort in her warm embrace. As they swayed together, her motherly care and affection enveloped him, soothing any worries or fears. He crouched on her abdomen, muttering vague words. "What did he say?"

"I don't know. He said mama and papa and love you."

"Mama, mom. Daddy, dad. Love. Love. Cold. Cold. Snow. Snow."

"Oh, my God. He said nothing before this night. How does he speak at this age? How does he know about love and snow?"

"I do not know. Maybe he heard us talking about love and the snowstorm. He is a smart boy. Let him sleep with us."

Angelo pressed his mother's left breast. "Milk. Milk."

She removed her linen sweatshirt and bra, and he sucked her pink nipple. "Our son is a work of God."

At eight o'clock, Leonardo got up from his bed and opened the opaque curtains. "Look here. Who painted the heart shape on the window?"

Bella put on fluffy slippers and a white bathrobe. "It was not here yesterday."

Leonardo's fingers touched the colored window. "Someone painted it from the outside. Who would do that?" He opened the window and looked out at the snowy front yard. As the soft snow blanketed the ground, a trail of footprints appeared, their presence marked by a subtle glimmer, which reflected the light of a rainbow, bouncing off the snow particles and creating a spellbinding effect. "Somebody was here."

Bella placed her forefinger on the window. "My God. This is the first letter of Angelo's name. He is the only person in the family whose name starts with A."

"I know." Leonardo brushed his teeth and went downstairs to talk to his parents in the living room. "Did anybody come to the house to see you?"

"No. Who would come? The city is closed."

"There are unusual footsteps outside the house."

"Where?"

"Under the kitchen window."

"Let us see."

After wearing a winter coat, boots, and a wool beanie, Sandro opened the front door and shuffled on an icy flagstone walkway. A flashing rainbow hovered over the house, and footprints shimmered with a fusion of colors under the kitchen window. "Weird. A guy and a dog were here. How could they jump over the fence and come to the window in the early morning? Why didn't the family see them?" He inspected the prints. "This is odd. These are not boot or shoe prints. They are ballerina slippers." His right palm touched a footmark and glistened. "It is soft. A light-weight kid came here to get a toy."

"I am not sure about that. Look at your hand and behind you. There are only six footmarks. No one came from outside, and one person walked three steps. Look up at our window. Someone drew a heart and a rainbow tree on it."

Sandro wiped his hand with a napkin and lifted his head. "Who could do that without using a ladder and making a noise? I will ask your brother to check the security cameras."

"I have good news for you. Angelo talks and walks now. He is awesome."

"That is wonderful to hear. It sounds like he has reached an exciting milestone in his fast growth. His ability to talk and walk opens a whole new world of adventure. He is a blessing from God to the family. Ever since his birth, everything has been going well. We finished the Irish morons and made excellent deals with other Italian families, and our businesses are flourishing. Is Angelo awake? I want to see him. He brings joy to my heart. Wait. Maria is coming."

Maria stood at the fence gate. "Morning, Sandro. Hi, Leonardo."

"Morning. Why are you out in the cold?"

"I saw a glimmer of light entering the second floor of your house. After that, I saw a white angel walking and flying over the house."

"You are lucky to see an angel. When was that?"

"After one."

"Are you sure?"

"Yeah. Why would I lie?"

"I believe you. Join us for breakfast."

"Thanks. I have some laundry to do. Take care of Angelo. A holy angel came to see him."

Leonardo hurried upstairs, and Angelo sprang up on the bed. "Dad. Papa." He jumped on his father.

Leonardo kissed and lifted him. "Grandpa wants to have breakfast with you."

Angelo clapped. "Yay."

They went downstairs to the kitchen. Leonardo put Angelo in a highchair and sat across from his parents. "How is my favorite boy? Kiss me." Sandro stood and kissed Angelo's face. "What is grandpa's name?"

"Sandro."

"Who is this woman?"

"Grandma Oriana."

"What is this thing?"

"Teapot."

"And this?"

"Eggs."

"And this?"

"Cornetti."

Marco came down and greeted his parents and brother. "Good morning."

"Good morning, Uncle Marco."

"Jesus Christ!" Sandro kissed Angelo, gazing at his eldest son. "Your child is a divine marvel. He got our brains and something else from heaven. Take care of him. He will be a great man." He sipped black coffee and paused for a moment. "Marco, can you check the security cameras? I want to know who came to the house when we were sleeping."

"OK, dad. After I get my breakfast." In the afternoon, he called his father. "Come with me. I want to show you something."

Sandro stomped into a small room equipped with computers and flat-screen monitors. Marco pressed two keyboard keys. "Look at these infrared images. A tall woman, holding a girl and wearing a long dress, and a dog or a wolf landed here."

"From where?"

"From the air. Seven seconds later, they jumped up and entered Leonardo's bedroom from the wall. Fifteen seconds later, the woman and the animal left the bedroom and disappeared. The girl remained upstairs."

"Doing what?"

"I do not know."

"How did they move through the wall? Didn't they make a noise and awake your brother?"

"No. They are like ghosts. That's why we don't see their physical bodies. The lack of visible features means we are dealing with different beings."

"So, Maria was right."

"Maria was right about another person." He pressed the right arrow key. "Fourteen minutes later, a ghost with little clothes and long hair fluttered in front of Leonardo's bedroom window. With a paintbrush in her hand, she painted the window for eighteen seconds. After that, she escaped. She looks like the mysterious hooded woman who carried a baby and left the house from the back door before Angelo's birth."

"Bella said she gave birth to two babies, but your mother and my sister had denied that because they were with her."

"We were in the house, and I still don't know how we didn't see this woman."

"Is she who painted the heart and the rainbow tree on the window?"

"Yeah, though I don't know how she painted all that in eighteen seconds and without a palette. These two women are not people like us because they fly and do not have bones and blood. They are aliens, ghosts, or angels."

"What was the time?"

"Between one thirty-seven and one fifty-eight."

"My Lord! Angelo got up and talked at two o'clock. Is he related to them?"

"Ask my brother and Bella. Viola thinks Angelo is the new messiah."

"Why does she think that?"

"Because he was born without the placenta. An invisible person washed and perfumed his body and brushed his hair. So, my sister thinks he is the anointed savior who will bring salvation or a divine message to humanity."

"Jesus! Who is this boy? Does your brother know about his son's birth?"

"I don't think so. He had never talked about Angelo's unusual birth."

"Your brother is a gentleman. Don't mention the flying aliens to the family and leave his son out of the conversation until we find out the truth. Monitor the girl who stayed upstairs. We don't need a creepy ghost in the house."

In the next six months, Angelo amazed his family with his reading and writing skills. He pronounced and wrote extra words every day. By one, he spoke fluent English and Italian and predicted political events and natural matters. "She talks to me" was his answer when people asked him about his knowledge and predictions. They thought he meant his mind because he pointed at his head. At three, he and his parents left Brooklyn and moved to a luxury home at Park Place in the Financial District. Bella set up a fashion company on Broadway and women's lifestyle magazines. One day, she sat with her British parents to divulge her deepest emotions and plans. She expressed how she longed for a tranquil place where she could thrive and pursue her aspirations without the constant pressure and judgments of the extended family members. As she continued, with her voice filled with warmth, she expressed her joy to be close to her friend Nina Seneca, an interior designer, and a member of the indigenous tribes in Cattaraugus and Erie counties. She told them how Nina had been a pillar of strength and support, and how their close friendship brought immense happiness to her heart, when Leonardo worked fifteen hours a day and six days a week to manage the family's diverse businesses in Brooklyn, Queens, Manhattan, and New Jersey.

At four, Angelo joined a private school on Broad Street and earned the highest marks in all subjects. One day, Bella informed Nina about his eloquent speech, encyclopedic knowledge, and weird conversation with an imaginary girl. "The other day, he asked and answered complicated questions about the earth and the universe. He talked to an invisible girl and said to her he likes girls because he is a girl. Once he said to her, 'Do you like my toy? Let me show you this game. Do not be silly.' I do not know why he gossips with a ghost and thinks it is a girl. When I asked him about his natter, he said he speaks to a clever girl who sits in his left ear. Do you think his behavior is normal?"

"Yes, it is normal. His super intelligence makes him imagine things in his head. He is cute. How is his reading?"

"Incredible. He reads Isaac Asimov's books and fantasy stories. His English and Italian vocabulary is amazing. Do you remember when he recited 'The Last Word of a Blue Bird'?" She gasped and closed her eyes, placing her hands on her abdomen.

"What's wrong?" Nina touched her shoulder.

"My tummy is sore. I get stomach cramps."

"Where is the pain?"

"Here. Below my belly button. I did not get periods for six months. There is something wrong with my gut and reproductive organs."

"Do not tell me you got menopause at this age. How is your sex life?"

"Terrific. Leonardo is like a horny stallion. We have sex every three or four days."

"What did you eat in the morning?"

"I had an English breakfast. Sausages, bacon, baked beans, fried eggs, and grilled tomatoes with a glass of milk."

"Honey, do not drink cow's milk and eat processed meat on an empty stomach. It is not good for you. Have a fruit and vegetable smoothie before you eat heavy food. Show me your belly."

Bella doffed her tunic blouse, and Nina touched her vertical navel and flat belly. "Ouch. There is pain down there, right above my vagina."

"Love, you need to see your doctor. I will take you to the clinic. What do you say?"

"That's fine. I am not working today."

"Call the clinic, and I will get Angelo." She entered Angelo's carpeted bedroom. "Put on your shoes. We are going out."

She drove her car, and Angelo chatted with himself. "Wow! Did you see that fat guy? ... Look at this huge bus? ... Hot dogs. Do you like hot dogs? ... Do you wear shorts like her?"

Nina rested her right hand on Bella's left thigh and winked. "Your son will be a talented actor."

"Or a Mafia gangster like his grandfather."

They visited a medical center at Maiden Lane. After abdominal, blood, and urine tests, a doctor gave Bella four bottles of pills for pain relief, hormonal imbalance, nausea, and constipation. The drugs worked well and eased her intestinal pain, but one day, Angelo opened the column fridge and chewed a handful of her pills. He tramped to her bedroom with bare feet and an empty bottle in his hand. "Mom, do you have more chocolate?"

"Chocolate? What is in your hand?" She shouted and nabbed the bottle. "Where are the pills?"

"What pills?"

"The pills in the bottle."

"I ate them. They are yummy."

"Oh, my God. How many pills did you eat?"

"Maybe twenty. They are small." After shutting his eyes, he passed out and fell on the floor like a crumpled rag. "Angelo. Sweetheart. Angelo, talk to me. Do you hear me?" She stormed out of her house and banged on Nina's apartment door.

Nina gaped at her face. "Love, what is going on? Why are you shaking?"

"Angelo ate my pills and conked out on the floor like a dead body. Please, take me to the hospital."

"Did you call nine-one-one?"

"No. Please, honey, help me. I am scared. I want to kill myself."

"Hold Angelo and control your emotions and stop crying. He will be all right. He is our special boy." They hurried to NewYork-Presbyterian Lower Manhattan Hospital's emergency entrance at Gold Street. Angelo vomited on his shirt and defecated in his pants. Nina parked the car and galloped into the hospital. "Please, we need help as soon as possible. The boy in my car has gulped down his mother's drugs."

Two nurses put Angelo on a gurney and pushed him into a solitary room. Angelo convulsed, retched, and excreted with his eyes closed, and the nurses cleaned his naked body and bed. A doctor entered the room. "What happened?"

"He... My son swallowed my... my prescribed pills." Nina embraced her shoulders.

"Which pills?"

"Premarin. He thought they were candies."

"When did he take them?"

"Thirty minutes ago."

A nurse brought an IV bag and injected a needle into Angelo's left wrist. The doctor slid a plastic tube into his mouth.

Nina sat and stayed with Angelo, rubbing his left fingers over her mouth and mumbling words. Bella exited the room into a quiet hallway and called her husband. "Come now to the Presbyterian Hospital. Angelo is sick, very sick. I am stupid. I hate myself."

"Don't panic and calm down. I will come soon."

Leonardo arrived at the hospital ward, and his wife leaned on a wall. "What happened to Angelo?"

"He ate my pills when I was in the bathroom. He thought they were chocolate."

"How did he reach them?"

"He used a bar stool."

"Where is he?"

"In this room."

He trod into the room and stared at a doctor. "Hi. I am Leonardo Lucciano. I am Angelo's dad. How is my boy?"

The nurses raised their eyes, and the doctor took two steps back. "We still do not know. Your son's heart, kidneys, and liver are doing well, but we may transfer him to an intensive care unit if his health deteriorates further. I assure you we have excellent physicians and equipment, and we will do our best. Please, come back after an hour."

"I want to stay with my son."

"I understand how you feel. But, please, you don't need to see his feces and barf."

He stared at Nina. "What about her?"

"I will ask her to leave."

For an inscrutable reason, the doctor didn't ask Nina to leave, and Leonardo squeezed his fingers and left the room without speaking. His eyes glared at his wife. "I don't know what to say about our son, but if he dies, you will go back to England for good. I am serious this time." She inclined her head and capped her mouth with an index finger.

Leonardo tramped to a noiseless corner and called his father. "Dad, sorry to bother you, but Angelo is in the hospital in a serious condition. Can you come? I need you to be with me. Please, don't tell the family."

"I will come. Which hospital?"

"The Presbyterian near Pace University."

"What's going on?"

"Angelo swallowed his mom's drugs. She didn't keep them in a locked cabinet. I am worried about him. He is in a coma and like a corpse."

"*Mio Signore.* You should teach your little English woman a lesson. Jesus! I will come soon after I talk to your mother and brother."

Twenty-five minutes later, Angelo jiggled his head and breathed out. His slim fingers wiggled and touched Nina's hand. "Hey. Where is mom?"

Her lips kissed his hand, and her hand caressed his perspiring forehead. "Your mom will come back soon." She called Bella. "Angelo is awake."

His parents raced to the room and stood on the right

side of the bed. Angelo closed and opened his drained eyes. "Mom. Dad."

His parents cuddled him, weeping. "Son, do not worry. We are with you, and you are in an excellent hospital."

"Dad, don't cry. I am sorry for eating my mom's drugs. This will never happen again. I swear." He put his finger in his left ear. "She said I won't die because I am a good boy."

"Who is she?"

"My buddy. She is...."

A nurse interrupted his chatter and checked his pulse, temperature, and blood pressure. "Positive news for you. The danger is over now. Your lovely boy lost plenty of liquids and nutrients, but his immune system is impressive. Is he vaccinated?"

"No. Angelo didn't need a vax."

"He must remain here tonight so we can watch his recovery. You can go home now. Come in the morning, and your child will be fine. Get clothes for him."

A girl's voice hissed into Angelo's left ear. "No worries, my love. I will not let you die. I am always with you because I love you."

He turned his head to the left side. "I love you too."

Leonardo put his phone in the inside pocket of his jacket after talking to his father. "Son, what did you say?"

"I said, I love you."

"I love you too."

"No. I talked to my friend."

"You are dreaming. Nobody is there."

"No. She is here in my ear, and I love her."

"We love her too. See you in the morning. Nite, nite, sweetheart." Bella kissed him.

Nina placed a kiss on his brow and left the hospital. In the morning, Sandro, Oriana, Leonardo, Bella, and two bodyguards visited the hospital. An eerie silence prevailed in the long reception corridor when Sandro waddled to Angelo's room. Doctors, nurses, and local visitors had avoided him, fearing his fickle anger. A receptionist mumbled to her colleague. "Oh, my God. This big man is the Italian Mafia boss who bought the luxury hotel near Rockefeller Center. What is he doing here?"

"I guess he knows the Italian kid who came in yesterday."

"I should go somewhere else in case he shoots at us."

After entering Angelo's room, Sandro removed his felt fedora and kissed his grandson's face. "How is my favorite boy?"

"I am good, grandpa."

"Never be afraid of anything, for all things are in God's hands. Love nobody more than the family." He turned his face to the right. "Where is the doctor? Call the damn doctor."

A female doctor came into the room and spoke to Leonardo. "Your son is doing well today. You can take him home. He needs fresh and juicy food and water. After a week, bring him back to the hospital to ensure everything is all right."

Angelo and his family and the two bodyguards exited the hospital and returned to the house at Park Place.

Sandro entered the family room and placed his hand on his son's shoulder. "Call Riccardo and tell him we want stuffed flank steaks with fettuccine for lunch at one o'clock. Angelo is weak and needs healthy food."

At ten to one, they entered an Italian restaurant on Wall Street. Four waiters and a chef welcomed them and kissed Sandro's hand and face. "Uncle, sit here. The food will be ready in two minutes."

Sandro, Oriana, Leonardo, and Bella sat at a round table, and Angelo rested between his father and grandfather. A waiter put silver forks and steak knives on the table, and two other waiters brought the food. When Sandro spread a cloth napkin on his lap, Angelo dragged his chair back. "Angelo, stupid boy," Leonardo yelled and wanted to spank his son. Angelo jumped five feet above the floor and flung a steak knife at a man with a gun up his sleeve. The blade entered the man's right shoulder, and his pistol fell to the floor. Angelo ran and hammered the man's chest with his open hands. The man leaped ten feet before collapsing on the wooden floor.

Angelo gawked at his hands. "Oh, my God. Who made these hands?" His right hand covered his right ear. "Who are you? How did you make me strong?"

"Little bastard. You fecking prick." The injured man leaned on his left arm and pushed himself up. A waiter kicked his handgun away, and two others thumped his face and back and pointed their guns at him, waiting for an order from Sandro to shoot.

Leonardo embraced Angelo. "Are you OK, son?"

"Yes, dad. How did I get this power? Who am I?"

"You are our angel."

Sandro got up after throwing his napkin on the table. "*Fermare.* Leave the jerk. I want a word with him." He smacked the man's face. "Don't you know who I am?" He pressed the man's jaws and turned his face toward his nephews. "Isn't he a jackass? What do you want me to do to him?"

"Let me kill him in the kitchen and burn him. He is an Irish pig."

"Feck off, dirty bastard. Your fecking father killed my dad and dumped his body in the river. And you crook waged a bloody war against my Irish people and murdered my cousin Mickey Spillane."

"Irish people? Who was your father?"

The man wiped his mouth with his left sleeve. "Cian McManus."

"How dare you come here to spew your filth? Unlike you, coward shit, your father was a real man. Yes, he supported Mickey's crap, but he loved his family and respected his enemies." Sandro paused for ten seconds. "God bless his soul. What have I done to you? My dad died in Italy fifty years ago, and I didn't kill Mickey. Mickey died thirty-six years ago, and your stupid people killed him. So, why did you want to kill me?"

"Because you are a big gobshite. You killed my son and brothers and ruined my family's life."

Sandro gripped the man's throat and batted his nose. "Train your foul tongue to respect the Italians. Are you blind? Don't you see where you are? Where are your folks?"

"You know we are in Hell's Kitchen."

"Hell's Kitchen is peaceful now after I cleaned your trash. I opened superb restaurants and a plaza in your hood. Many of your people work for me. I thought the Irish were the good Catholics in the town. I prefer peace, and you piece of waste should have treated me with respect as a real man. But you are a blockhead like your filthy Westies and Irish goofs. Call the cops and the ambulance and remove this garbage out of here."

After hiding their handguns in their dark pants, Sandro's relatives dragged the Irishman out of the restaurant and pitched him on the busy, adjacent sidewalk. Strollers panicked and scurried for cover. Three ambulance paramedics arrived. One of them checked the wound and pressed his fingers on the neck. "He is still bleeding, and we can't remove the knife here. He needs an operation."

Four police officers and two FBI agents entered the restaurant and circled the Lucciano family. An agent twisted his lower lip, staring at Sandro's stern face. "Hello, Sandro. When will the fighting stop? I thought the Italian war was over."

Sandro's left forefinger rubbed his chin. "This is an Italian restaurant. Ask everybody. We got our dinner when the Irish hitman wanted to kill me."

"How do you know he wanted to kill you?"

"He pointed his gun at me. The gun is over there. You can check the fingerprints. I don't know why the Irish folks hate me."

"Don't you know why?"

Sandro lifted his arms and huffed. "Come on, officer. I say what I mean, and I don't lie. Do you think I would hurt an Irish guy when my wife and English daughter-in-law are having lunch with me? My family stopped the revenge business when my father left the country sixty-seven years ago."

"Revenge business or crimes?" The agent turned his face around and glanced at walls covered with photos of Italian boxers, actors, and soccer stars. "Who threw the knife?"

"My grandson."

"Your grandson? Do you mean this grandson? How old is he?"

"He is seven. Come on, man. For God's sake, look at his innocence. Do you want to arrest a seven-year-old child for defending himself and his family? Yes, this was self-defense. The people here saw what happened."

"Yes, the people here saw your little grandson acting as your bodyguard. Interesting." The officer brought a chair to the table and sat beside Angelo. "Hello. What is your name?"

"Angelo."

"How old are you?"

"Seven."

"Who taught you to throw knives at people?"

"No one."

"Did you throw a knife at the white man?"

"Yes. I threw the knife."

"Why did you do that?"

"He wanted to shoot grandpa."

"How did you know that?"

"He carried a gun, and I see what you can't see."

The agent beamed. "What cannot I see?"

"You cannot see your girl, who is watching *Clueless* in her bedroom, and you cannot see your son, who is eating a cheese and pineapple pizza in the living room. You also cannot see your wife, who is ironing clothes in the kitchen."

The agent rubbed his jaw. "Impressive. How do you know I have a wife, a daughter, and a son? Do you know their names and age?"

"Yes. Your white wife Rachel is thirty-nine, your son Tom is eleven, and your blonde daughter Amy is thirteen, and her birthday is after six days."

"Oh, my God. Unbelievable. Who are you, little man? You should work with the FBI."

"I told you I see what you can't see."

"How? Are you a wizard?"

"The words I say come from my mind, and I hear faraway voices you cannot hear. It is like a magical vision from a crystal ball."

"Incredible. Your English language is grand and flawless. My kids should join your school. Finish your lunch and go home. Good boy." The officer turned his face to Sandro. "Your grandson is a miracle. Please, do not give him a gun when he grows up. He won't need it."

The officers exited the restaurant, and Sandro held Angelo on his knees and kissed his hands. "Bravo. Bravo. You are our hero. The whole family is proud of you. You have saved our lives." He wiped a tear.

"Grandpa, why are you crying?"

"I am not crying. I remembered my dad, who put me on his knees when I was your age and said I would be the greatest godfather in America. Someday, you will be the best leader in our family. I wish to be alive when you become a big man like me. I will take you to my new hotel tonight, and we will sleep there." He gazed at his son and Bella. "How did you make this boy? He was sick in the hospital. How did he get that superpower in four hours and at this age? I am two hundred forty pounds. How did he push me back? He is our savior. Do what he wants and never defy him. I say this to the whole family." He exhaled, and his right hand thudded on the table. "Where is the steak? Where is the wine?"

Having savored a grilled steak and relished a glass of rich red wine, Sandro ventured into the restaurant's bustling kitchen. As he entered, a feeling of suspense and provocation had prevailed, drawing the attention of his eager nephews. They flocked around him, their eyes wide with admiration and enthusiasm. "You need to fix the restaurant's security, and I want you to teach the Irish nerds a hard lesson. Leave the guns and take the rods. I want to see broken arms and legs. I also want you to protect Angelo. You will need him, and he will be your savior."

Two days later, Marco took his father to a private room. "We did what you asked us to do, but Carlo made a big mistake."

"What did he do?"

"He killed a boy."

"Why? I said no guns."

"The boy tried to stab me."

"How old was he?"

"Fifteen."

"God. Did anybody see your faces?"

"No. We wore masks. But the boy's little sister was there."

"Jesus. Who is she?"

"Cian's granddaughter. She is nine or ten."

"What happened to the boy?"

"We threw his body in the Harlem River."

"I see. We will condemn the killing in public and donate money to the poor girl. But before we do that, I want a word with Carlo. He needs discipline."

Five days later, Bella and Angelo returned to the hospital for a health update. Dr. Jonathon Hagen fixed his stethoscope and examined Angelo's eyes, mouth, heart, back, and abdomen. "Please, go to that corner and get a story. I want to talk to your mom." Angelo selected a book and sat on a chair. The doctor turned his face toward Bella. "Your son is doing well, but there is something I could not figure out. I mean, I have seen nothing like it in my whole professional life. Your son has a penis but without a scrotum or testicles."

"What does that mean?"

"That means your son's male genitalia will not produce sperm, androgens, or testosterone, which is an essential male sex hormone for developing masculine voice, muscles, and body hair. Instead, he has a girl's body and a functioning female hole."

"A female hole? Where?"

"Between his penis and anus. It is a perfect vagina."

"You mean a girl's vagina?"

"Yes. He has labia, a cervix, a uterus, and a clitoris. We could not detect ovaries because of his age. Do you know that? Didn't he tell you anything about his body?"

"No. Will Angelo become a woman?"

"That is possible. However, I cannot say your son is intersexual or epicene because his body comprises two opposite sexes."

"Oh, my God. Does he have a twin inside him?"

The doctor adjusted his glasses and smiled. "No. That is not possible because a twin needs normal organs to breathe, eat, and live. As an anatomist, I cannot explain how your son has a boy's face and penis, female legs and arms with complete bones and organs, and a hidden, boneless body with a vagina. I am not saying he is a hermaphrodite." The doctor opened a folder and showed Bella an x-ray image. "This is his midsection, and this is the groin. Look here. If this outer layer of the skin is the boy who has the penis, this interior skin is the girl who has the vagina and the kidneys. Look at the waists. There are two epidermises, and there is no hair on the body. Apart from his head hair, his arms and legs have no hair at all. The urinary tract connects to the female genitalia, not to the penis. His penis will not erect, ejaculate, or urinate. The other organs, such as the liver, the stomach, and the heart, are parts of the boy's body. That's why I say he is a boy and a girl. A nurse told me he says he is a girl and speaks to a girl inside his head. I have never come across such a case."

"I am amazed. What do you want me to do?"

"Nothing. You cannot change your child's biology and sex hormones. I suggest you allow him to explore his sexuality and gender identity without fear. Was he born with a birthmark on his leg?"

"No. I don't think so."

"There is an awkward scar on his left leg. A nurse told me that the scar appeared after he came to the hospital, but I don't think that is possible." He paused and looked right. "Angelo, please, come and sit here." Angelo rested on a bed, and the physician rolled up the left leg of his pants and placed four fingers on the shin. "This mark looks like a cat's eye and a micro camera. How did this happen? Did he injure himself or fall on his leg?"

"No. I am not sure. This is the first time I have seen it. Angelo didn't let me bathe him or change his clothes in the last week. What do you suggest?"

"Nothing. Just leave it. It will not harm him and will fade when he grows up."

Bella returned home and told Nina what the doctor said to her. "What do you mean Angelo is a boy and a girl?"

"The doctor says he has two opposite sexes and a separate vagina with a urinary tract. His penis is defective and has no testicles. How didn't I notice that in the last seven years?"

"This is weird. Angelo always says he speaks to a girl inside him. He has smooth skin, and his voice displays a gentle tone, while his behavior and speech align with feminine characteristics."

"And his hair has become smooth like yours. I wonder if Giulia has something to do with his body. I was not happy when she breastfed him for a year and fed him stigghiola and animal guts. She is the scary witch of the family. But what about the creepy mark on his left leg?"

"Let me see it."

Angelo came to the room, and Nina inspected his scar. "It looks like an eagle's eye. The eagle is a sacred animal in my Seneca culture and religion. We should visit my tribe and see a noblewoman who knows about spirits and skin marks. Her name is Colestah Blueskye. My people call her the medicine woman because of her healing and psychic power. I am sure she will tell us something about Angelo's body and mark."

Bella told Leonardo about Nina's suggestion. "Go after three days when I am in New Jersey. Keep a gun in your bag."

With Bella in the passenger seat and Angelo behind her reading a story and tattling with himself, Nina drove seven hours to Cattaraugus County. They made their way to a two-story white house near Front Avenue in Salamanca. An elder woman appeared, her tresses cascading in a fluid motion of darkness, akin to the long shadows in the forest. Adorned with beaded earrings, shimmering like fragments of captured moonlight, she welcomed them with an expansive smile, her arms outstretched in an embrace of warm generosity. "Hello and welcome to Onondowahgah, the People of the Great Hill, or the Seneca Nation." She clasped the hand of a woman adorned in delicate braids; their elegant strands entwined, portraying the artistic finesse of their maker. Around her sleek neck, a coral crochet necklace beautified her upper chest, with its vibrant chroma mirroring the beauty of her flawless face. Together, they stood in a humble, imposing communion that transcended the welcoming words. Their connection alluded to the unspoken threads that bind souls. "This is my daughter, Talisa. She lives with me."

"This is my English friend Bella Lucciano, and this is her son Angelo."

After a dinner of bean soup and grilled fish and vegetables, Colestah asked her daughter to stay in her upstairs bedroom. "What can I do for you?"

"It is about Bella's son. Weird things happened to him in the last ten days. His hair has become girlish and glossy, and there is a spooky mark on his left leg. He says he talks to a girl inside him."

"Angelo, come here and sit on the table."

With an amused face, Angelo sat on the edge of the dining table. Colestah lit smudge sticks in an abalone shell and murmured foreign words. "Keep your head up. Open your eyes and do not blink." Her gaze lingered upon his eyes, her scrutiny delving into the depth of his being. With gentle intent, her right hand grazed his silken hair, as if seeking a tactile understanding of his essence. It traversed further, grazing his forehead, as if tracing the contours of his deep thoughts and dreams, a subtle exploration of the mysteries concealed within his mind. "These are a girl's eyes. Open your eyes wide." He extended his gaze, stretching his eyes wider to encompass a new reality that evolved before him. In response, she halted her steps, and a shiver moved through her body like a fleeting tremor of bafflement. The intense pause epitomized an unspoken realization, as if in that suspended moment, a profound connection had forged a bond between them. The delicate thread of their joint experience had trembled under the heavy weight of unspoken options, implying the intricacies that lay hidden beneath the surface of their first meeting. "Holy Mother of God. A miracle is unfolding before my eyes. Who are you, our beloved one?" She gazed at Bella. "Is he your child?"

"Yes."

"Where are you from?"

"From England."

"Your child carries the divine light. How could a human like you give birth to this unearthly miracle?"

"God knows. What do you mean he is a miracle?"

"In your child, there is an incomplete girl because of his divine and human nature, and there is a beautiful girl goddess inside him. She is swinging over a floating bed made of white fluffy clouds and decorated with twinkling stars. Her name in English is Hintocha." She placed her right hand on Angelo's head. "Bless you, our bearer of God. How did she enter your body?"

"I don't know. She has been with me all the time. She didn't say she is a goddess."

Nina gaped at them. "Who is this girl goddess?"

"She is the goddess of love. She is stunning, and her charming eyes are dancing with a sparking fire."

"How do you know her?"

Colestah opened an antique cabinet and selected a file. "This is her picture with her mother."

Bella held the picture. "She is pretty, and her mother looks like a queen. How do your people know their profiles?"

"There are paintings of Jesus and his mother. Did any painter see them? Drawing and painting express what people feel and imagine."

"She talks to me every day. I like her, and she is funny."

She patted his left shoulder. "Yes, she speaks to you because she loves you."

Bella moved her fingers to her face. "How there is a goddess in his body?"

"Like your God Who incarnated in Jesus Christ. We believe every person, animal, tree, and rock has a spiritual soul. Your child has more than a holy soul. His soulmate is the immortal goddess of love." She brushed Angelo's hair. "Take off your shoes and socks and put your legs on the table."

Colestah cast her gaze upon his left leg. As her eyes traced the contours of his limb, a quiver coursed through her being, and her hands found their way to her face. Their delicate touch couldn't conceal the unstoppable tremors of emotions that danced upon her mien. In this moment of intense examination, her essence had vibrated with a mixture of surprise and apprehension. Her crinkled hands trembled in a symphony of nerves, mirroring the ripples of her innermost thoughts, as she delved deeper into the enigmatic tale that had happened before her. "Oh, Gitche Manitou. She is alive. She is alive. What a joy!" She moved with a soft blend of nimbleness and heaviness, her toes touching the ground as she danced around the table. Her emotions, unbridled and raw, had manifested in the warm tears that streamed down her bronzed face, creating rivulets of passion. Amid her tumultuous dance, she sang an enchanting melody, an ancient hymn that resonated with esoteric words, carrying an air of mystery and wisdom. In this intricate interplay of movement and sound, she embodied a tapestry of emotions and incantations, a captivating spectacle that held in her presence spellbound. "May the Great Spirit bless you forever. You are the Chosen One. I don't believe my eyes. The eagle's eye on the leg is the ultimate hope that our goddesses had promised us. The Great Spirit has blessed me with His divine love. I can't believe it." Her head descended upon the table's surface, her forehead finding solace in its cool embrace. Tears, like the bittersweet droplets of a grieving widow, flowed from her eyes, tracing brooks upon her cheeks. In the depth of her sentiments, her weeping became a poignant lament, echoing the anguish of a wounded soul. The weight of her dolor bore upon her, casting a shadow over her countenance, as she sought relief in the release of her tears, allowing the pain to find expression in this cathartic outpouring of agony.

Nina stood, moving her hand on Colestah's back. "What do you know?"

Colestah wiped her tears with a shawl and placed her palms on Angelo's head. "Do you remember how you got the eye on your leg?"

"Yeah, I remember. When I slept in the hospital, a woman kissed my head. I opened my eyes, and she smiled. She wears a short dress, a black hood, and a head chain and has red hair. Brown cuff bracelets cover her forearms. There are black lines on her face. I saw a short sword in her hand. She said she is a sky warrior. There was an eye in her other hand. She said the eye would make me strong and make her commander see what I do. After that, I heard a woman's voice in my right ear and dreamed I was a flying girl like an angel."

"You are very intelligent." Colestah shut her eyes and shed more tears. "Blessed is she whom the Eagle Goddess loves. Our liberation is near. The holy mark on Angelo's leg is Anna Awehitecha's eye."

Nina stared in astonishment at her watery eyes with a feeling of surprise and disbelief. "Awehitecha? Who is she?"

"Awehitecha is the Supreme Eagle Goddess of war and wisdom. We call her Awehitecha because of her fearless spirit. Our legends say she came down to earth on the back of a female eagle. The eagles and the animals are her friends. The First Nations do not know why she left her house in the sky or where she lives."

Bella placed a forefinger on her lips. "What is the bond between this goddess and Angelo?"

"Our sacred legends say Awehitecha had vanished after leaving the third sky. But her eagle's eye on your son's leg proves that this goddess is in America, and she has chosen Angelo to protect him and hide the greatest secret code of Gayadosha."

Nina stretched her back. "What is that?"

"Gayadosha is a divine cryptogram preserved in a golden box over the highest sky. It recorded the past and future events of the universe and all existence. Its greatest secret code is about the final apocalypse of the universe and the earth after the return of the Eagle Goddess and her divine family, who will rule the world when it is full of corruption and crimes. Their eventual return is far greater than the second coming of Jesus Christ. They will defeat the falsehood and fill this land and the universe with justice and usher in a golden age before the Merciful God of humanity reigns over the world."

"What else you know?"

"The eagle's eye tells us that the Eagle Goddess will bless and lead our nations when Angelo is forty."

"How do you know that?"

"Look in the eye. You will see a countdown timer and the number thirty-three."

"Why forty?"

"Forty is when the divine revelation manifests its truth among people. God talked to Moses when he was forty. An angel talked to Muhammad when he was forty. In my religion, a goddess appears to a blessed woman when she is forty."

"Do you mean Angelo will be a woman when he is forty?"

"He will be a full woman when he is twenty-one, and his male characteristics will go away."

"Why twenty-one?"

"Look at his palm. There are twenty-one lines."

"Why did the Eagle Goddess choose Angelo?"

"Because your child will be a special woman and the mother of a special son." She touched Bella's hand. "Be proud of bearing such a child. Your child is sacred."

"I feel that. He has done amazing things in the last

few days. His intelligence, memory, and strength are extraordinary. He even predicts the future.”

“That is because the High Divine has given him supernatural powers and wisdom. Do you remember what happened when you gave birth to him?”

“I felt I gave birth to two babies who had never cried. Angelo was born unblemished and with no blood on his body.”

“That means a goddess had bathed him. Anything related to the weather?”

“Yeah. Appalling thunders rocked the house, and heavy rain flooded Brooklyn.”

“That is not pleasant news. Someone had committed a grievous mistake, and a supreme goddess was angry. Did anything significant happen in the first year?”

“Angelo started talking to himself and us when he was five months old. He said a girl sits in his left ear and tells him stories. I remember something else. There was an image of a love heart and a rainbow tree with the capital letter A on our bedroom window. We don’t know who designed it after we slept. My husband told me there were sparkling footprints in the snow and under our window.”

Colestah sobbed and covered her eyes with her hands. Bella hugged her. “I am sorry. We haven’t come here to make you sad.”

“I am not sad. I am happy.” She rose from her seat with a graceful movement, her spirit stirred by a surge of tenderness. Drawing near, she pressed her lips against Angelo’s head, a gesture infused with affection and warmth. Her touch conveyed a myriad of emotions, a silent reassurance, and an unspoken connection. "The colorful heart shape meant a family of goddesses had celebrated Angelo's birth and connection to the divine. A goddess painted the heart shape and the rainbow tree as a sign of her love for him. The capital letter A is the signature of a divine family of goddesses, not the first letter of Angelo's name. The names of this family's members start with the letter A." She rolled up Angelo's sleeves and rubbed his lanky arms. "These are a girl's arms, and these are a girl's legs. Your child has a girl's heart, mind, and soul. Someday, he will be a divine woman and rescue her lovely son from a great danger. Does he have a girl's genitalia?"

"Yes. Angelo has functioning female genitalia. The male part is dysfunctional."

"That proves your child will become a real woman. Please, cover the eagle's eye all the time because the evil gods and the chief devil, Tawiscara, and their demons are Awehitecha's arch enemies. They wish to hunt her down because they don't want her and her divine family to liberate our people who lost their lands and freedom. They may seduce Angelo and make him a swindler or a hoodlum to steal and decipher Gayadosha's sacred code. Do not worry. Awehitecha's warriors will fight them." In a gesture both tender and reverential, she kissed her right palm and bestowed a touch on his forehead, her hand cradling his brow with a gentle grace. Through this act of intimacy, she sought to convey a feeling of protection and solace, an offering of comfort in a world that appeared unfathomable. "Say Awehitecha when you are in trouble. As you grow and wherever your path takes you, she will give you strength and protection. I will print her name for you."

After that unique occasion of affection and trust, Bella hugged Colestah and, with earnest conviction, had made a solemn vow, pledging her complete silence, an unbreakable oath to protect the sanctity of Angelo's secret, shielding it from the prying eyes and judgmental tongues that loomed in the periphery. This act was not a casual promise; it held the weight of unspoken struggles and unwritten chapters, a testament to an enduring bond of love that transcended societal expectations and norms. When Leonardo inquired about her trip, she met his gaze with an unwavering resolve. She spoke, in a measured tone, of Angelo's future, weaving a medley of hope and prosperity. Her words, imbued with an unshakable stance, had painted a pleasant picture of a destiny untainted by affliction or misfortune. In this moment of exchange, a delicate balance teetered upon the precipice of truth and fiction, as she shielded Angelo from the burden of distrust and fear that threatened to engulf everyone's heart. She showed her resolve to shield Angelo's dreams from reality through a self-imposed act of courage. "The Seneca medicine woman says Angelo will be like Superman."

"Do you believe her superstition? Our hospitals and psychologists are the best. Do we need to send Angelo to a Native American woman who tells fairy tales about gods and ghosts?"

"Our physicians won't know how and why Angelo predicts events or why he has supernatural powers. Our son is a wonder of wonders. I told the Seneca woman I became pregnant after we visited Our Lady of Lourdes." She caressed Leonardo's hand. "I believe God and the Virgin Mary had blessed our lovemaking and son. I feel Angelo is the new savior and redeemer. See how he saved your dad from the Irish hitman."

In the depth of Angelo's consciousness, a disrupted elation surged, for he realized that within the confines of his body, a divine being had dwelled. This revelation had ignited a fervor within his soul, casting a light on the agitation that lingered in him. In this profound awakening, he saw himself not as a mere mortal, but as a vessel for an ethereal entity, a conduit through which a mysterious goddess might manifest. That realization had transformed his feeling of himself, infusing his existence with a sense of purpose and grandeur. This recognition of his nature had let him embrace the boundless possibilities that lay before him, reveling in the divine splendor that lived within the margins of his earthly repository.

One day, he sat on his bed, staring at his bare chest. "I know your name now. What does Hintocha mean?" He shivered when tiny, red lips appeared in the middle of his torso. "Hintocha means the spirit of love. So, I am the one who loves you. Let me kiss your hand." He put his hand on his chest. When she kissed it, he jumped off the bed, quivering like a wet hound. "Breathe and do not be afraid. I am your love and goddess. I can make you fly and see the world."

After drinking a glass of mineral water and collecting himself, he gazed at a tall wall mirror and rubbed his slender arms. "How do you breathe?"

"I have a nose, and I breathe your air."

He closed his nose and mouth with a hand. "Oh, no. I cannot breathe. No. No. I am dying. I want air." She laughed. "Goddesses do not need air to live. We do not rest and sleep, and we do not eat to live."

"How do you live in my blood and veins? Don't you feel bored?"

She giggled. "Do you think I live in your blood and veins? No. I live in a castle floating on a cloud people cannot see. I am like a dream. The people and places you see in your dreams do not live in your blood and flesh."

"How do you look like?"

A vision materialized before him, as if it had come out of a fantasy world. In an elegant Native American dress, a girl appeared in his bed. She seemed to hover at the edge of reality, a shimmering apparition that defied the boundaries of time and space. Her attire spoke of antiquated traditions, evoking a sense of ancestral wisdom and a profound connection to the land. In this enigmatic encounter, she lifted a veil, revealing a glimpse into a realm that obscured the boundaries between the tangible and the intangible. "This is how I look like."

He yelped, placing his hands on his face. "Love, don't scream. Come and sit beside me." She uttered in a tone that held kindness and reassurance, urging him to forsake fear and embrace the desirable haven of companionship.

He sat beside her and touched her hand. "Your eyes

are honey. I like your brunette hair.”

She fondled his hair. “I also like your soft, light-brown hair. Please, do not cut it until it reaches your shoulders. I want to feel you are a girl like me. What do you think?”

“I am a girl. I don’t know why I look like a boy. This body is not me.”

“There is a cosmic reason for being half a boy now. Don’t worry. I will make you look like a girl at the right time. But now, I don’t want your family to punish you and think you are a trans girl. Your grandpa and dad have plans for you. One day, you will be the godfather of the Italians in America.”

“Italians are weird people. I wish to live away from them. Why did you choose me?”

“I didn’t choose you, but love brought me to you.”

“Where was your house?”

“In the second sky.”

“Do you know the Eagle Goddess?”

“She was a friend for a while.”

“But you are a girl. How was she your friend?”

“I was not a girl. My mom made me a girl to be with you. We will grow up together.”

“Do you speak Red Indian languages?”

“My people are not Red Indians. They are not Red or Indians. They are the First People or the First Nations.”

“Sorry. I didn’t mean it.”

“I know you didn’t mean it. I will teach you Seneca and Mohawk. Say *skat*.”

“*Skat*. What does it mean?”

“It means one.”

"How do you say I love you?"

"*Gonoohgwa.*"

"*Gonoohgwa*, Hintocha."

"I love you too." She gave him a kiss on his face.

"When can I see you?"

"Call my name when you want to see me. You are the only human who can see me. Tell no one in this world you speak to me."

Angelo discarded the limitations of societal norms and allowed his hair to grow unabated, cascading down his shoulders in a pretty display, and transcending the rigid boundaries that controlled him. His tendrils became a clear indication of his refusal to conform, an outward sign of an inner rebellion against expectations imposed on him by his family and traditions. With each passing week, he restyled his hair, a silent challenge to the constricting notions of conventional male beauty. Thus, his body, behavior, and feelings had become more feminine and averse to boys and boyish manners. On one occasion, he entered his mother's bedroom, brushed his hair with a paddle brush, wore a white miniskirt, and put on red lipstick and nail polish. He touched his male genital organ. "Why are you here? I don't like you. I will cut you off." He looked in the wardrobe mirror. A woman beautified her face with a gentle smile, the curve of her red lips conveying a subtle radiance that illuminated the room. With effortless grace, she raised her right hand in a fluid motion, offering a wave that was both a greeting and a gesture of love. "Hello, my sweetheart. Do you remember me? You will be the most beautiful girl anyone would see."

Angelo yelped and plunged into the bed, embracing Hintocha. "Who was that?"

"That was your beautiful voice. Don't think of your looks. You are a girl and have a girl's voice."

"Not that. The warrior in the mirror talked. Who is she?"

"I didn't pay attention. Look again."

They glanced at the mirror, and a flow of emotions rocked their beings, manifesting in a shared outcry that reverberated through the air. "My Goddess. She is a warrior goddess. I don't know her name."

"Hello, Hintocha. Are you having fun here?"

"Who are you? How do you know my name?"

"I know you and know your mom. Did your mom punish you and make you a little girl?"

"How can you see me?"

"I can see anything." She gave them a kiss in the air. "Bye."

Angelo covered his body and half of his face when his mother opened the door. "Are you OK?"

"Yeah, I am OK."

"Why did you scream?"

"I saw a woman in the mirror."

Bella looked around. "Why are you in my bed and hiding your face?"

"I used your lipsticks."

"Why? Let me see." She removed the bedspread. "Don't use my makeup and clothes when your dad is here. I know you are a girl, but we don't want trouble with your dad and his family. Go to the bathroom and wash your face and hands and wear your pajamas."

He covered his face with a cushion and ran to his bedroom. He stood beside Hintocha and looked in the mirror. "Where is the woman?"

"I don't know. Maybe she is a ghost."

The enigmatic woman materialized, appearing from the mirror's reflective surface. Like a spiritual being traversing the threshold of realms, she stepped out of the mirror into the room, her presence imbued with an otherworldly allure. "Hintocha, please, go home."

"Go away. I am a goddess, and no one can ask me to go home."

"I can." She blew and made Hintocha disappear.

Angelo shivered. "Where is she? Please, don't hurt me."

"I will never hurt you. Don't you remember me?"

"I saw you in the hospital. Who are you?"

"I healed you when you were sick. I am your real mom."

"Don't lie to me. Bella is my mom."

"That's not true. They took you away from me. You were a girl. What happened to your body?"

"I don't know what you are talking about. My body has female and male things."

"You are like twins in one body. Say *yayksahuh*."

"*Yayksahuh*." He gaped at his body. "Oh, my God! I am a girl. How do you do that?"

She smiled. "Say *hahksah*."

"*Hahksah*. Oh, my God! I am a boy."

"You know the secret now. Say *yayksahuh* when you want to be the girl and say *hahksah* when you want to be the boy. You can be a full boy or a full girl for a couple of hours every day. Do not tell anyone about this secret or about me."

"You have orange-ginger hair and six abs. You look like a fantasy warrior."

"Yes, I am a warrior from the sky, and this is my sword." She looked at an American football on a shelf. "Ask that ball to come to you."

"Come here." The ball flew and landed on his lap. "Wow."

Her glowing hand touched his forehead. "I give you the power to protect yourself. Use it when you need it."

He gazed at her thighs, belly, and breast cleavage. "You are beautiful. Don't you feel cold?"

"No. The weather doesn't affect me. I am a divine fighter and the queen of beauty. OK, honey, Bella is coming. I will see you later." She kissed his forehead.

Angelo harbored the secret of the charming and mysterious woman who entered his life and shielded the captivating enchantment that had taken hold of his heart. However, his biological and behavioral changes had incited school students to bully him and call him a femboy and a tomgirl. One day, four students had targeted him with taunts and torment as they loomed outside his classroom. Like vultures circling their prey, they reveled in their collective power to inflict pain on him. Their words lashed out, sharp and biting, aiming to diminish his spirit and shutter his resilience. One of them sneered. "Hi, tomgirl. Show us. Do you have a weenie or a vag?" They sniggered.

"You are nasty boys. Stay away from him," a female student said.

"Shut your hole, tomboy."

"Dinah, come here." Angelo turned his face toward them. "We are in the school, and decent students do not behave like that. Please, stay away from me. I do not wish to hurt you."

One of them snickered and jeered at him. "Did you hear that? Come and give me a slap in the face."

Angelo pursed his lips, creating a subtle crease that displayed a multitude of tacit emotions and brought forward a sense of contemplation, as if he was trying to hold back a torrent of thoughts and words. "You asked for it, dummies." He spread his fingers and pointed his hands at them. The students slipped to their knees, and one of them moved his jittery hands on his legs and squawked. "What happened? Help! I can't move my legs."

Angelo smirked. "I asked you to stay away from me, but you disregarded my request." He widened his eyes, transforming them into white orbs, and causing a feeling of fright that permeated the enclosed corridor. His mouth twisted, emitting a horrifying sound that made the students shiver. "I am the Omen. The Scream. The Vampire. Get up, buffoons, and do not make me angry again, or I will kill you." The students got up and fled.

Dinah clapped. "My hero. They deserved it."

Angelo gaped at his hands. "How did that happen? How did I get that power?"

Dinah held his hand. "You are a superstar."

On another day, Etan Stormer, a chubby, short-haired student, chased Angelo after leaving his car and cornered him near the stairs of his building, smacking his arms and groins with a hickory stick. "Show me your boobies. Are you a boy or a girl?"

Angelo extended and poised his right hand, as if he was preparing to weave a variety of magic. He trembled with suspense, ready to unleash the incantation that formed on the tip of his lips, but his father showed up and hoisted Etan with a firm hand around his collar. "Hey, boy, what are you doing? What did you do to my son?"

"Dad, leave him. He is a jerk. The goddess will beat him up."

Etan dropped his stick, and Leonardo put him down. "I do not want to see your face here again. Do you understand me?" Startled, Etan nodded and retreated, his features etched with surprise and fear, receding from the scene. Leonardo hugged Angelo. "Are you OK, son?"

"Yes, dad."

"Don't walk alone. Ask the driver to walk with you. You said the goddess. Who is she?"

"She is my invisible friend."

"I see. Did the boy hit you? You should be a fighter and...."

A car screeched, its tires squealing against the asphalt as it came to an abrupt stop. Leonardo and Angelo hurried outside the building and saw Etan groaning and sprawling on the street and in front of a taxicab. Leonardo embraced his son's shoulders. "Your goddess was here."

Etan pointed his finger at Angelo. "He did it. He is a

witch. He is a witch."

Angelo raised and lowered his right forefinger. A dozen pigeons landed on Etan's face and chest and excreted on him. Etan palpitated and screamed, and Angelo laughed.

Leonardo held his son's hand. "How did you do that?"

"I am a magician."

"Let us go home."

Angelo walked seven steps before turning his face back. He saw the orange-haired warrior standing on the sidewalk and waving to him. He smiled.

At home, they met Nina, who had a cup of tea with Bella. Angelo ogled her refulgent hazel eyes and went to his bedroom to talk to Hintocha. "What do you think of Nina? I feel I have known her for ages. I wish to spend more time with her."

"I love her and like her decorated home. To be honest, I am not too fond of your house when the Italian men visit your family and say rude things about everyone. Sometimes I wish to kick their butts."

Angelo requested his mother to allow him to do homework, watch TV, play games, and read books in Nina's next-door house. She agreed.

One day, Nina entered a bedroom and sat on a hassock. "What are you doing?"

"Playing a *Ticket to Ride* game."

"I heard you singing."

"I sang 'Just a Boy and a Girl in a Little Canoe'."

"Does Hintocha like your singing?"

"Yeah. She also sings for me."

Hintocha chuckled. "Ask her to take you to the town. You should see more people."

"Can you take me out to the town? My mom doesn't allow me to walk on the streets, and she is always busy."

"OK, sweetheart. I will take you out, and we will walk on the streets. What about Times Square?"

"Good. I have never been there."

"I am off tomorrow. We will go there in the morning and get delicious pizza and ice cream." The next day, she took him to Times Square and Seventh Avenue. When they roamed around hand in hand, he noticed a silver tabletop telescope in a department store. "Get the telescope so you can look at people and distant things," Hintocha said.

"Can I have this telescope?"

"Why do you want it?"

"I love to look at the sky and stars."

"OK, darling. I also like to watch the sky." She bought the telescope and moved out of the store. He grabbed her left wrist with both hands. "Come with me. Come. Hurry. Go here." They rushed into a café. "Wait here." He darted to the sidewalk, and his open hands halted a speeding double-decker bus, averting a potential disaster that threatened the safety of pedestrians and vehicles in its path. The bus driver fixed his gaze on him, with his frozen eyes filled with astonishment and adoration, as he made the sign of the cross on his chest, admitting the fortunate intervention that had unfolded before him. People applauded and surrounded Angelo. "Are you OK?" "How did you stop the bus with your hands?" "Who are you?"

Nina ran out of the coffee bar and cradled his head. "Please, leave him alone."

A woman clapped. "Your boy is a superhero."

"Thank you." She and Angelo scuttled to a car park and sat in the back seat of their car. "Oh, love, thank you for saving many lives. The bus could have killed a hundred people. Let me see your hands."

He opened his hands, and she rubbed and kissed them. "How did you know about the bus?"

"My eyes see the future, and the goddess talks to me. Good that nothing happened to us."

"You mean Hintocha told you about it?"

"No. Hintocha speaks in my left ear, but the Eagle Goddess talks in my right ear. I don't know how to see her and talk to her. Can you keep the telescope in your home?"

"Why, honey? I bought it for you."

"You know my family. I do not want my dad and granddad to know."

"Know what?"

"Know my behavior. Look at my hands and hair. I am a girl. I love girls and don't feel I am a boy."

Her fingers touched his pinkish cheek. "Colestah said you are a special girl, and there is a beautiful girl goddess in you. You will always be a wonderful and precious girl, and someday you will be like a gorgeous model. But tell me, why did you ask me to buy the telescope and keep it in my house?"

"I don't want my cousins to play with it. You are a girl, and I love girls."

"I also love girls. Girls are cute."

In the morning, Leonardo, clutching a copy of the *New York Post*, stood beside his seated wife in the kitchen. "Who is Angelo? I want the truth."

"He is our kid. What do you mean?"

He dropped the newspaper on the dining table. "Look at this picture. Angelo stopped a fast bus with his hands. How is that possible? Is he a human?"

"Oh, my God." Her fingers played with her lips, and tears moistened her eyes. "He told me nothing about the accident. He is a human like us. I was with your family when I became pregnant and gave birth to him when your mother and sister and aunt were with me. The only thing I can say is our son has been a sign of God's grace since he started talking. He sees things we cannot see and hears voices we cannot hear. His personality is out of the norm, and his power is astonishing."

"Did he tell you anything about his power?"

"He says a goddess talks to him."

"He told me that. What about Nina? Is she a witch or something?"

"No. How do you say that about her? She is an amicable friend and a normal person like us."

"Why does she live alone in an expensive house? Does she have a family?"

"She has never talked about her family, though the Native Americans love her so much."

"Please, ask her not to take Angelo to outdoor places without a bodyguard. We don't need troubles and the media attention."

Bella visited Nina. "What happened yesterday? How

did Angelo stop the bus?"

"He used his hands."

"How could he do that?"

"Colestah said there is a goddess in him. I think the goddess gives him power."

"How? Why him? Why did this goddess choose him?"

"How would I know her intention? It is hard to know what she has in mind for him. I think Angelo will tell us the truth when he becomes an adult."

Later, Leonardo took his father to Italy and called his wife from Naples. "My big man is lucky to be here with the family. Talk to Viola or Marco if you need anything. Look after yourself and Angelo. I will call you every morning and before I sleep. Bye, darling." Bella took advantage of his vacation and asked Nina to live with her. Angelo got his father's house keys and kept them in his school backpack.

Two days later, he was in the school classroom. "Teacher, I need the toilet."

The teacher sank his jutting chin on his chest and checked his wristwatch. "You can wait ten minutes. Why didn't you go to the restroom during the break?"

"I don't know."

"Wait until the class is over."

Angelo crossed his legs and could not control his bladder. A rowdy student saw Angelo's stress and wet pants. "Teacher, Angelo is peeing and shitting in his pants. Yuck!" Unruly students guffawed, and the teacher asked Angelo to contact the office and leave. When he reached the classroom door, a menacing glint filled his eyes, fixated on the unsuspecting teacher. He flicked his right hand, a sinister gesture that signaled impending danger, and unleashed an implicit threat lurking in the shadows. The impact was swift and brutal as the teacher's head collided with the solid desk, a resounding thud echoing through the classroom. His chair skidded to the left, as if pushed by an unseen force, intensifying the sense of disarray and chaos. The teacher's body crumpled to the floor, his back making a sickening impact. A malignant silence fell upon the room. Students, with their eyes gleaming with mischief, suppressed their laughter with sniggers. It was a chilling display of collective amusement at the teacher's plight. "Angelo is a warlock."

Angelo exited the school and asked his driver to take him home. When the driver stopped the car at his building, Angelo hurried to his house, hiding his upper legs with his jacket and bag. He picked up his father's house keys and opened the main door without making a noise. Bursting into his mother's bedroom, he paused, gawking at Nina's topless body and bare thighs on the lower back of his naked mother. Nina bawled and covered her breasts with a pillow.

"What are you doing? Why are you naked?"

Bella glowered at him. "I have a sore lower back, and Nina is fixing it. Why are you here? Why did you leave the school?"

"Look. I peed in my pants."

"Why didn't you go to the toilet?"

"The crabby teacher didn't allow me to leave the classroom. I don't like him. He is ignorant."

"How did you get into the house?"

"I have my dad's keys."

Nina covered Bella's lower back with a towel. "Stay here. I will bathe Angelo."

She filled a freestanding tub with tepid water and liquid soap and took off Angelo's clothes. They rested in the foamy tub, playing simple games with plastic toys.

After the bath, Angelo wore a white robe and scampered to his bedroom, and Nina pecked Bella on the lips. "Angelo got his first period. I saw blood on his underpants."

"You mean menstruation?"

"Yes. Shocking."

"Oh, my God. That means he is a girl with ovaries. What should we tell him?"

"Nothing about his sex, but we need to show him how to use the menstrual pad."

After that day, it became customary for Nina to wear a triangle bikini, strip off Angelo's clothes, and bathe him when his mother was at work. She became his helper.

One day, Angelo muttered obscure words as he stood behind a curtain and peered through the telescope. Nina stood at a window and spotted a young woman wearing a pink monokini and sunbathing on a balcony. "Honey, what are you doing?"

"I am using the telescope."

"I know you are using the telescope. But why is it down? It is not good to peek at women in their homes. Do you like a guy to look at your mom's underwear?"

"What can I do? I am a girl and love to look at girls. Why don't I look like a normal girl?"

She cuddled him and wiped a tear. "Honey, you told me about your girlish feelings many times. God made your body in this shape for a reason. What would you do or say if all Americans were blonde girls? Imagine all flowers are red and all fruits are green. Beauty is in assorted colors, shapes, and sizes. Love who you are, and you will be happy. I am sure God has a plan for you and will make you a lovely woman. But, love, it is bad to stare at women's bodies. Don't worry. I will take you to the beach and the swimming pool to see the girls there."

She took him to hotel swimming pools when she was free. He felt happy to swim with her and see nubile girls. However, he became introverted, reticent, and bookish for an unknown reason. With the help of Hintocha, he excelled in the school and got the top grades. By the pubescent age of thirteen, his body desired Nina with an intensity that overwhelmed his love for her. As the tantalizing allure of their connection grew stronger, he faced the dilemma of conducting an intimate affair without arousing his family's suspicions. Thoughts raced through his mind, strategizing ways to navigate this treacherous path, careful not to leave a trace of his secret desires. One day, Hintocha asked him to creep into Nina's bathroom and peep at her body when she stood in the shower. "I cannot do that. She may kick me out of her house and tell my mom."

"I will not allow that to happen. I am with you. So, be strong. Nina loves you and hides her true feelings for you. She always calls you sweetheart and honey and touches your hands and face.”

With a furtive glance, he slinked into the steam-filled bath. His eyes darted, unable to resist stealing a forbidden peek at her alluring body. The rising steam added a surreal quality to the lustful scene, concealing his presence in a veil of secrecy. Every stolen glimpse had intensified his carnal desires, igniting a dangerous flame that flickered between temptation and guilt.

Nina stepped out of the shower room and wiped her face and arms. As she wrapped herself in a towel, her eyes saw Angelo sitting on the floor. “Honey, what are you doing behind the basin? Were you looking at me? That’s not a respectful manner.”

“I love you. You are my best friend.”

She embraced him. “Sweetheart, I love you too. But please, do not come here again when I am in the shower.”

“Why? We swim together and sleep in one bed. Don’t you remember what you did with me? You took off your clothes and bathed me thirty times, and I saw your breasts and legs.”

“That happened when you were a little kid. You are a big boy now.”

“Why do you call me a boy? I am a girl.”

“Sorry, honey. You are a cute girl, but please, don’t come into my bathroom when I am naked.”

“Why do you say that? You were naked when you bathed me. You wear a bikini when you swim with me. Why did my mom allow you to bathe me and take me to the swimming pool? I spend more time with you than with my mom and dad. Why?"

"Your dad and mom are always busy with their business and family. They trust me and want me to care for you until you become an adult."

"But why do you kiss my mom's lips when my dad is not with her? Why do you sleep naked with her in her bedroom when she is alone?"

"Gosh. I am an adult. I love your mom, and you know she is my best friend."

"Do you have an affair with her?"

"I am a free, mature woman. Why do you ask me this question? Ask your mom."

With fondness and lust, he toyed with her fingers, tracing invisible patterns across her delicate skin. Each touch carried an electric charge, a silent language of desire. "You have a perfect body, and I feel attracted to you when you wear a bikini and swim with me. All my dreams are about you. My genes and DNA scream for you. I love to touch you and look at you."

A subtle flicker of vulnerability crossed her face as she swallowed her saliva, with her throat tightening with an unspoken tension. "You are thirteen, and I can't have sex with you. Sex with you is child abuse and crime."

"Who says love is sex? I need affection or a kiss. Please, let me kiss you if you love me."

"Hmm. OK. You can kiss my face." She closed her eyes and turned her face to the right.

He kissed her silent lips and made her weep. "I wish you understand." She tapped his head.

His hand touched her face. "I am sorry. Please, don't

cry. Why are you crying? We are alone in the house and can do anything we like. I love you, and you love me."

"Gosh, you have a girl's beautiful lips and voice. I know, sweetheart. You are an angel from heaven." In an act of uninhibited desire, she pressed her lips against his, with the world around them fading into nullity. The erotic exchange of their kisses carried the magnitude of their hidden connection. With a silent understanding, she led him to the sanctuary of her elegant bedroom, an inviolable place where they could release their free desires. Behind closed doors, they surrendered to the flame of their passion, indulging in the fruits of their affair. In that romantic space, time ceased to exist, consumed by the raw intensity of their shared desires, as they embarked on an amorous journey where ecstasy and secrecy converged in an explosive culmination of their yearnings. He stood hushed when she wore a thong and lay topless on the bed, marveling at her body.

She waved her hand. "Come here. Come and sleep with me." She covered her breasts with a bedspread.

His head rested on her right shoulder and upper chest. "Take off your top. I want to feel your back. You can touch me, but do not make intercourse, or I will ask you to leave my house."

He rested his hand on her left breast. "Are you afraid of my dad and granddad?"

Her fingers danced across the smooth skin of his back. "No. I am not afraid of them. But you are still a kid. Besides, I am a strict lesbian and will never have sex with a man."

"I am not a man." He mumbled an ancient word and

made himself a girl, breaking his promise to the woman warrior who taught him how to change his body. "You see. I am a girl."

She quivered and rolled herself off the bed. With her left hand covering her mouth, she wept. "Oh, my love. Come here. Come here." She kissed his face and lips and pressed her breasts against his chest. "How do you do that?"

"I can change my body when I want."

"Tell me more."

"I discovered a secret."

"What is it?"

"If I say *yayksahuh*, I become a girl, and if I say *hahksah*, I become a boy."

"Who taught you these extinct words?"

"A friend. I don't remember her name. I am afraid."

"Sweetheart, don't be afraid. Hintocha and the Eagle Goddess protect you."

"I am not afraid of the outside world, but I am afraid of myself, of being intersexual. I feel there are two people in my body, and I don't know how to get rid of the boy and keep the girl. Who made me like this?"

"God made you like this." She opened a drawer. "Wear this bra. You need to get bras to cover your breasts. Be a girl when you are with me and be a boy when you are with your family. Your granddad will kill you if you say you are a girl, or if you make yourself a girl. Forget your sex now and relax." She twirled his hair and gazed at his glimmering eyes. "Honey, are you happy now? Do not tell your mom and dad about our love. This love is a private matter between you and me.

Do you understand what I mean?"

"Yeah, I understand."

"Why don't you get a girlfriend? There are many gorgeous girls in your school."

"I am confused."

"Why? What happened?"

"I love Hintocha, and a Swedish girl loves me."

"Who is she?"

"Her name is Dinah Hansson. She likes to talk to me, and I like her. She kissed me two days ago."

"Why don't you ask her to be your girlfriend?"

"My Catholic family will never allow me to have a Mormon girlfriend. What should I do?"

"Ask her to come over to my house so you can have private time together. Keep your spirits up and be kind to her, and don't propose anything until you trust her. Did you tell her about your body and feelings?"

"She told me she is bisexual, and she thinks I am intersexual. I didn't tell her I can make myself a girl."

"Interesting. Don't tell her about the girl thing. Invite her to my house to get to know her better and hide nothing from me. I am always here for you. We will talk about your emotions later, but now, close your eyes and sleep." With a gentle touch, she placed her fingers over his eyes, inviting him into the realm of dreams. The moderate weight of her touch brought a comforting darkness, soothing his weary mind and lulling him into a peaceful slumber.

The next day, they went out to Chinatown for lunch. After eating chicken fried noodles in a restaurant, they strode through a lonely alley to get their car. A man pursued them, with his heavy footsteps echoing in the air. With each fast stride, he shortened the distance between them until he grasped Angelo's shoulder, his grip like a vise. In a swift, instinctive motion, Nina spun around, with her eyes flashing with anger. Without a moment of hesitation, her hand shot forward, touching the man's face in a resounding blow. "Leave him, you son of a bitch."

The punch knocked him down. He rubbed his bristly chin and drew a dagger from his pocket. "Stay away, slut. I just want this fecker who tried to kill me."

She kicked his midsection. He fell to the ground and placed his left hand on his belly. "You bitch. I will kill you." He got up and wanted to slash her face, but she twisted his arm behind his back and pitched him up against a wall. He fell to his side, cursing and staring at her. "Who are you, hoor?"

"Shut your mouth, bastard." Angelo turned his face and recognized the raging lout who wanted to shoot his grandfather in the Italian restaurant. "The Italians will kill all the Irish if you hurt me."

"You know how to talk, little kid. Come with me, or I will slaughter you, scut." He got a gun out of his jacket pocket and pointed it at him.

Nina seized Angelo's hand. "Run with me."

"I am not afraid of him. Hey, come and fight me like a man."

The Irishman rose to his feet with a malevolent glint in his eyes as he brandished his pistol. Nina tugged Angelo behind her, and a heavy ceramic pot flew into the air and cracked the man's skull. He died, and his blood scattered on the tarred ground. Nina enfolded Angelo and covered his eyes. "Honey, don't look. He is dead." She picked up her cell phone and called nine-one-one.

The screech of sirens shattered the silence as a police car and an ambulance raced toward Cortlandt Alley. An officer collected the Irishman's folding pocketknife and gun with a pen and put them in a plastic bag. "What happened?"

"This plant pot fell on his head from this building."

The officer looked up at the building and saw two pots on a windowsill. "How did the flowerpot fall in the middle of this backstreet?"

"I don't know. Someone pushed it."

"Did the guy hurt you?"

"No. Maybe he followed us to snatch my purse."

"Do you live in this area?"

"No. We live in the Financial District. We had lunch in a Chinese restaurant, and my car is over there."

"What is your name?"

"Nina Seneca, and this is Angelo Lucciano."

"Lucciano? Are you related to Sandro Lucciano?"

"Yes. He is my grandpa."

The officer smiled. "You can go. Take care."

Nina and Angelo sat in the car. "Who killed him? Who threw the pot on his head?"

"I guess your goddess is protecting us."

"You are strong. Where did you learn to fight?"

"In a martial arts club."

The local news said the dead Irishman was Patrick McManus, a fugitive member of the Irish Mafia that terrorized the state. Angelo told his family about the incident and how Nina had protected him with her martial arts skills. His grandfather reacted. "There are multiple ways to destroy a family. The senseless Irish played with fire and burned themselves and ruined their families. Next time, listen to your father, who asked you not to go out without a bodyguard. I admire your bravery. Your enemies will fear you when you fear nobody."

Angelo invited Dinah Hansson to Nina's house and asked her to be his secret girlfriend. She agreed, though Nina's love for him, pure and unfaltering, had surged through her with intense force. It consumed her every thought, every breath, as it wove its way into the very fabric of her being. The challenges they faced and the obstacles they overcame had strengthened the depth of her affection. It was a love that defied logic and reason. She allowed him to sit on her thighs and kiss her lips when Dinah was not with him. They pursued their platonic love until he was seventeen, when his powerful grandfather died of a heart attack. Thousands of Italians and dignitaries had attended his televised funeral ceremony at St. Patrick's Old Cathedral. The Lucciano family buried him beside his father's grave in St. John Cemetery in Queens. Angelo sensed his community's immense influence and saw Leonardo's private appointment as the new head of the Sicilian Commission and the Lucciano family.

Chapter 2

As they sat together in the head office on Wall Street, Leonardo and Angelo had engaged in serious, private discussions about the family's wide business ventures. Angelo, filled with ambition and resolve, expressed his candid thoughts. "We need to expand the family's businesses. The opportunities in the market are vast, and I believe it is the time to take calculated risks and grow our enterprises."

Leonardo listened to his words and appreciated the drive and ambitious spirit his son showed, traits he had instilled in him over the years. He acceded, admitting the rational validity of the proposition. "I agree, my son. Expanding our businesses is a natural process. We have built a solid foundation, and now it is the time to explore new horizons while preserving the core values that define our family. What do you suggest?"

"There are a half-million Italians in Toronto, and there is a district in the city called Little Italy. There is also Little Italy in Ottawa. Canada is a vast country, rich in oil, timber, minerals, and other natural resources."

"Why Canada?"

"I wish to study and work there to depend on myself and get a new life experience."

"What? Do you want to leave the family?"

"No. I can't leave you and the family. I want to rely on myself and extend your company's business in Canada."

"But we do not deal with minerals and timber, and you don't have much experience in our business."

"You know, I see the unseen future. The future will be for digital information and artificial intelligence technology. Besides, I got the best marks in the school and have a superhuman mind. I asked grandpa to invest in real estate in Manhattan Valley. We got over fifty million dollars last year."

"I know that. But you spend your time at home. Anyway, we need a proper arrangement if you want to study and work in Canada."

"Don't worry about anything. I have a plan and enough money to set up a business. Please, let me go to Canada."

"As you like. You know I will never stop you from doing the things you love. You are my special child, and I will never let you down. But, son, I want you to be more honest with me. What do you hide from us?"

"Nothing. I live with you, and you see me every day."

"What about your androgynous body? Do you feel comfortable with it? Do you need surgery?"

"What can I do? God made my body. Surgery will leave scars and won't change how I feel about myself. I feel shy to go out in the city. The media may say you have an outlandish child."

"The media is not my concern. You are the main thing. What about the girl you see?"

"Which girl?"

"The tall blonde girl you see in Nina's house."

Angelo blushed and swallowed his saliva. "She was my classmate and closest friend in the school. She supported me when students mocked me and called me femboy. There is nothing serious between us. She is a Mormon, and her parents are from Sweden. Her father owns a travel management company, and her mother is an actor and a model."

Leonardo interlocked his fingers and smiled, proud of the person his son had become. "Fine. Let us make it happen. We will have a party before you go to Canada. Good luck, son. I will always love you."

After leaving his father's office, Angelo visited Dinah, who lived in a posh house on Warren Street. "I am going to Canada to study and work. Do you like to come with me?"

She listened, her expression reflecting a mix of emotions. "Sorry, love. I want to go to college to study journalism. We will be together after graduation." She filled her response with plain honesty, emphasizing her commitment to pursuing her dreams and aspirations. While she cherished the fond bond they shared, she recognized the importance of personal growth and persuading individual goals.

"Study journalism in Canada."

"I can't leave my mom and dad and my young sister. We can see each other on the weekends and holidays. What do you think?"

The prospect of being apart during their studies, hundreds of miles away in different countries, might have been daunting, but their love and support for each other remained steadfast. "I believe in you, and I will root for you every step of the way. Our dreams might lead us on separate journeys for a while, but I know our love will endure, and we will reunite and be together. You have my phone number. Call me when you want to see me."

She reached out, placing her hand on his. "Thank you for understanding. I will think of you while we are apart, and we will make it through this stronger together."

Angelo traveled to Toronto and bought a four-bedroom house in West End. "Hintocha, I feel happy to be free and away from my family's hierarchy and Mafia networks. I wish to be a lesbian like Nina. Do you know how I can get rid of the boy's parts?"

"Why do you want to remove the boy's parts? How can you do anything to the boy when you are a woman and when you can't see him? And if you kill the boy when you are him, how would you become a woman and be alive? The half-boy lives with you, and you may die if you change your biology."

"But I cannot have two distinct personalities and two

opposite genders. I wish to be one person."

"You made love to Dinah. What would you say to her? Do you want to tell her you became a woman and your penis turned into a vagina? How will she recognize you when she sees you as a female with red hair and gray eyes?"

"But I want to be a lesbian."

"You can be a lesbian with me and heterosexual with Dinah."

"Are you a lesbian?"

"Yes."

"How? I have never heard of lesbian goddesses."

She rubbed his right thigh and caressed his breast. "There are lesbian goddesses, and I am one of them. Do you like to be my human girlfriend?"

"Yes. But what about the male thing inside me?"

"I love you and don't care about the things inside you. Be a woman with me and be a boy when you are with your family and Dinah. Your dad and family will disown you if you say you are a woman. So, what do you want to do now?"

"I am confused. I will order hormone-feminizing pills from online retailers to turn the boy into a girl."

Angelo embarked on a lavish quest to create an abode that reflected his unique feeling of feminine decorum and sensuous fantasies. With a discerning eye and a free spirit, he bought exquisite garments, crafted furniture, sensual portraits, and delicate statuettes that displayed his deepest desires. Each item spoke volumes about his complex inner world. His clothes draped his body, transforming him into the embodiment of his most cherished fantasies. The furniture invited languid repose and secrets of intimacy, and the glamor and surreal portraits mirrored his yearning for elegance. The statuettes served as tangible manifestations of his carnal desires. In this realm of curated opulence, he found sympathy, a sanctuary where his authentic self could unfold and celebrate. Each piece in the house was a testament to his unapologetic embrace of his identity, an ode to the fluidity and depth of his human desires.

Hintocha slipped into the role of his devoted helpmate and lover, a constant presence by his side, keeping him engaged and enthralled. With tireless dedication, she dealt with his every need, predicting his desires before they arose. Her commitment was not born out of obligation, but from a genuine love that radiated from within her spirit. She became his emotional coach and intellectual confidante, as they embarked on exhilarating adventures. Her charm and wit kept him entertained, and their laughter echoed through the rooms. Together, they roistered in the felicity of companionship, their bond unbreakable. She was the anchor that steadied him, the flame that ignited his passions, and the muse that inspired his creativity. In her presence, he found inspiration and liberation, knowing that with her by his side, he could conquer the world.

One early morning, he woke up at three o'clock, feeling invigorated and appreciative. Hintocha fondled his hair. "Where are you going?"

"The Eagle Goddess has asked me to get up and go out. I feel someone needs my help. Come with me."

After wearing tracksuits and brushing their hair, Angelo and Hintocha jogged in High Park for ten minutes. "Do you hear that whining sound?"

"What did you say?"

"Remove the headset. Someone is crying."

As he turned his face to the right, his ears caught the sound of a low, wailing cry. It was a sad sound that moved his sympathy, a mournful lament that seemed to reverberate through his being. He tried to decipher the origin of the anguished sound. Was it a cry for help, a voice of hapless despair? He made his way toward a sequestered spot nestled amidst a dense thicket of towering trees. The interlocking branches overhead created a canopy of shadows, casting a pallor over the secluded spot. He caught sight of a forlorn figure, a young woman huddled in distress. Her body trembled, and her muffled sobs carried through the air, veiled by the curtain of her long hair that concealed her face and hands. A shroud of mystery enveloped her, leaving him concerned for her well-being. With each step closer, the woman's cries grew more audible, piercing through the silence of the surroundings. As he reached out a hand to offer comfort, his heart swelled with empathy and a burning desire to unravel the depth of her suffering. What lay behind the veiled curtain of her hair? What secrets did her trembling hands hold?

"Hi. Why are you crying? Why are you grieving here? Can I do something for you?"

"I am sure my life is not your business. Please, leave me alone?"

"But you are weeping outside your home."

"It is not your problem."

He sat next to her. "For the sake of our shared humanity, I will cry with you."

"Dammit. You are crass. Leave me alone."

"Do you like a dirty-water hot dog? Poof. I will not leave you. It is four o'clock. Let me take you home."

"Feck. Why are you grilling me? Do I know you, man? Leave me alone."

"Oh, boy, I love it. I like your Irish New York accent." He clapped and sang. "I've been a wild rover for many's the year. And I've spent all me money on whiskey and beer."

She raised her head as tears streaked down her face. "How do you know that song?"

"My mom introduced me to Irish singers and folk bands. I love Enya's 'Only Time'."

"Your mom? Is she Irish?"

"No. She is a Roman Catholic from Cornwall in England. She supports the Irish nationalists who want Northern Ireland to join the Republic."

"It is the North of Ireland, not Northern Ireland."

"I agree. I am Angelo from New York."

"Angelo? Are you an angel?"

He giggled. "Yes, I am an angel sent down to save you from the wild beasts. I am the bread of life. I am the true vine. I am ...."

"Blah, blah. Are you a joker?"

"Come on. Let me take you home. Italians do not leave women crying alone in the jungle. Get up before the hungry dinosaurs and tigers crunch you." He chortled. "Please, I am a decent guy. Stand and let me take you home. Both of us are from New York.”

“OK, Italian Rambo.”

In silence, they padded down Garden Avenue until they reached the outer stairs of an apartment. She smiled at him. “Thank you.”

“Welcome. Do you know Toronto?”

“A bit. Why?”

“I am new here. Can you show me the city?”

She hesitated for a moment. “I came a couple of weeks ago. Where do you live?”

“I own a house on Indian Road.”

“I will meet you at the corner of this road at twelve o’clock. Is that OK?”

“Great. Thank you so much. Glad to meet you.” At five to twelve, he waited on a sidewalk. A woman in jeans and a black-pink checkered flannel shirt came to him and shook his hand. “I am Caitlyn.”

“Cat Hen?”

She chuckled. “Cat Hen? You are funny. No. I am Caitlyn. It is an Irish name.”

“I am Angelo Lucciano.”

Angelo’s family name resounded in her head like a tolling bell, filling her with a sense of trepidation. Her body recoiled, her hands clutching her arms, though his visage had enthralled her gaze. The allure of his face, with its enigmatic features and captivating skin, had held her in a mesmerizing spell. Her gaze swept across his fashionable attire, taking in every detail of his trendy clothes and brown polished shoes. The way he presented himself spoke of a meticulous attention to style, an epitome of contemporary fashion. “Gosh! This is a shocking surprise. Are you related to Leonardo Lucciano?"

"He is my dad."

"Are you serious?"

He pulled a wallet from his pants pocket and gave her a driver's license and a photo of him with his parents. "How do you know my dad?"

She examined the license and the photo. "Wow! I don't believe it. Your mom is very classy." She looked again at the picture. "I am lucky to meet you. Wow! All New Yorkers know your dad and family. I like your layered hair. You look like a model or an actor. Come on. We will take my car instead of the bus."

"She is gorgeous," Hintocha said.

"Quiet," he said.

"What did you say?"

"It is a quiet hood."

"Yeah, I like it here."

He sat in her car. "You have a superb whip."

"Thanks. I got it four days ago." They moved to downtown Toronto and explored the Royal Ontario Museum, Kensington Market, the Art Gallery of Ontario, and Yonge-Dundas Square. They savored their dinner meal at the elegant Richmond Station, with their voices blending in animated conversation as they delved into their brief experience of life in Canada. Over the course of the evening, they confabulated about their aspirations and the possibilities that awaited them, discussing their prospective studies and the exciting opportunities that lay ahead.

Angelo returned to his house in a jovial mood and

lay beside Hintocha on his bed. "What do you think?"

"She is stunning and smart. I like her golden blonde hair and blue eyes."

In her cluttered and modest bedroom, Caitlyn retrieved her weathered notebook, its pages filled with the traces of her introspections and dreams. With a pen in hand, she jotted down words that danced across her mind, ink flowing from her thoughts onto the pristine paper. "He said pleasant things to me and paid for my lunch and dinner."

Over the course of the next two days, she became his guide, leading him through the vibrant streets of Toronto, exploring the city's hidden gems and iconic landmarks. Together, they strolled along the scenic waterfront, where the cool breeze off Lake Ontario caressed their faces, and the city's skyline shimmered in the distance. They explored the neighborhoods, where diverse communities thrived, and indulged in the tantalizing flavors of the cuisine, savoring the fusion of cultures that made Toronto a culinary haven. On the fourth day, as the sun began its descent, she invited him to dinner in her apartment. Before sitting, he opened a book. "You have an impressive library. Your books are all over the place."

"Books are an absolute delight for me, and I love buying and reading them. They are my passion."

They moved to a small dining room and settled into their seats. Flickering candles decorated the table, casting a soft glow that danced upon their faces. With every passing minute, the connection between them had deepened. They shared aspirations, fears, and susceptibilities, creating a bond that transcended the mere act of sharing a meal. After dinner, Caitlyn touched his face. "You differ from all the Italian guys in New York."

"Is this a compliment?"

"I think so. Your tone of voice, face, hairstyle, hands, and courtesy are very different. I wish to do something special with you. Do you like to travel with me to Vancouver for five days?"

"Yes, I would love to go with you. When do you want to go?"

"Tomorrow morning. Get a bag of toiletries and clothes and sleep here tonight."

Angelo got a suitcase and slept on a couch in her living room. At dawn, they took a flight. He beamed when she reclined next to him and rested her head on his right shoulder. In the afternoon, a van took them to Third Beach on the west side of Stanley Park. After arriving at the sandy beach, a blonde fashion director removed her sunglasses and welcomed Caitlyn with a quick hug and a cursory kiss. "Thanks for coming. Are you ready?"

"Yes. What can I do?"

The director ordered a female cosmetic artist to work on Caitlyn's face and hair. After the makeup, she asked Caitlyn to wear bikinis, skirts, and short pants. Two photographers held their cameras and took a series of photographs from different angles.

Angelo and Hintocha sat on a log, ogling Caitlyn's bare legs, arms, midriff, back, and half-naked breasts. "I hear your fast heartbeats and desire for her. She is gorgeous and smart as a whip.”

“I have never seen a glamor model like her. Do you know now why I want to get rid of the boy and be only a woman?”

“I know. What about Nina and Dinah?”

“I love them. Nina loves my mom, and Dinah is bodacious and outgoing. But Caitlyn is tender and more feminine than them. I feel Caitlyn’s love would fulfill my lesbian desires.”

“I hope she becomes your girlfriend.”

“But you are my girlfriend. Won’t you feel jealous of us?”

“Jealous of what? I am an immortal goddess, not a desperate streetwalker looking for sex and money. Enjoy your human life. I am with you, and nobody can take you away from me.”

“I did not realize she is a model.”

“She needs money to pay her expenses.”

In the evening, Angelo and Caitlyn dined in a Syrian restaurant on Denman Street and relaxed at an outdoor swimming pool in the Westin Bayshore hotel. “Tell me, why did you leave New York? Why didn’t you stay with your rich family?”

“For personal reasons. I love my mom and dad, but I couldn’t cope with the Italian men’s violence, misogyny, and homophobia. My grandpa treated women as housemaids for cleaning and cooking and bragged all the time about real men. All his friends were men, and all his business meetings were with men. He was the big boss of the five Italian families who ran the Mafia’s racketeering and enterprise. When he was alive, New York was the den of the Mafia. Churchmen, politicians, businessmen, judges, bankers, journalists, and even mobsters had feared him. He taught his hitmen how to threaten, kill, or maim his foes."

"Yeah, I heard he was a ruthless man. Were you afraid of him?"

"No. He loved me, and I inherited a lot of money from him, though my girlish behavior had embarrassed him."

"What is your girlish behavior?"

"It is about my physical looks and love for girls. I spent my life with my mom and her best woman friend. They showed me care and love. I wore skirts and lipstick when my dad was away."

"Why did you do that?"

"Because I feel I am a girl."

"How do you feel you are a girl?"

"I don't want to be a man. See how women touch and speak to each other and see what men do in our world. Men make wars, abuse women, deceive their citizens, pollute the air, and run the sex and drug trafficking business. History, or his story, is about men. Men committed all the massacres in history and ranted about crushing their enemies and building great civilizations. They founded empires and states on plunder and murder. Their industries damage our bodies, the environment, the animals, and the planet. I can't have an affinity with men...."

"So, do you hate men?"

"No. I don't hate anyone. Some men are humble and thoughtful, like the Tibetan Buddhist monks, but the majority are insolent and violent."

"You know so much about the world. Why do you wear colored overshirts and pink chinos? Are you nonbinary or a genderqueer?"

"No. I love women and feel like a woman."

"Do you support women's right to choose?"

"Of course. I support women's equality, freedom, and human rights, but I don't like labels and isms. I aspire to be a fantastic person."

She seized his hand. "Come with me."

They retired to their room. Caitlyn asked him to sit on the bed's edge and took off her white pleated top and black, high-waist skirt. His saliva slid down his throat, and his eyes gazed at her fair body and lace underwear. She pushed him backward and removed his loafers, socks, and pants. She trilled, staring at his legs. "Oh, my God. What are these feet and legs? Are you a trans girl?"

"No. I am half a boy."

"And half a girl? You don't look like the Italian guys in New York. Are you adopted?"

"No."

"How do you have a girl's legs? Do you shave?" She touched his leg.

"No. I am seventeen."

She licked her wide lips. "Gosh. Seventeen? Can I make love to you?"

"Yes, you can. Do what you like and enjoy. My body is yours."

Feeling oversexed, she pulled off his shirt and bra, sucked his pink nipples, and made love to him.

"Thank you."

"Why do you thank me?"

"For making me bubbly."

"Don't be silly. You need not thank me for sex. I enjoyed making love to you, and you have a damn sexy body. How did you get it? Do you practice yoga?"

"No. I don't know. Ask God."

The next day, they made love in the shower room. "I am sorry."

"Why are you sorry?"

"I felt I was aggressive."

"No, you are not aggressive." She touched his face. "You are tender and sublime. Your voice is soothing, and your softness is erotic."

"I hate the penis. It is fugly and a symbol of men's violence. In body politics, the penis is the army."

She tittered and played with his lips. "Come on, love. Do not be oversensitive and overanalytical. No need for politics when you are with a naked girl. Girls have vaginas and love the penis, and guys have penises for our survival and pleasure. The vagina is also ugly, but what can we do? There would be no life without our genitals. I saw a napkin attached to your underpants. Why?"

"I told you I am half a boy, half a girl."

"Do you get a period?"

"Yes. I get a period every month."

"How is that?"

"I have a vagina and other woman's things."

"Where?"

"Put your finger here."

He raised his leg, and she inserted two fingers into

his vagina. "Exciting. I love the female side of you. You should become a girl so we can be lesbians. I won't mind you wear women's clothes and have a girl's name."

"I wear women's clothes and lipstick in the house, but I cannot change my name and have a girl's name. The Luccianos would kill me."

On the third day, Caitlyn wore a black micromini, flared skirt, and a white sleeveless chiffon blouse. She and Angelo sat at the hotel swimming pool and had a light breakfast with a drink. A topless, strapping man leered at her racy legs. "Hello, sexy."

"Feck off."

"Calm down, gorgeous. I said hello. Would you like to chat and have a brew with me?"

"Piss off, English langer."

"This is racism."

"I don't give a damn. Bug off."

The Englishman moved his hand over her shoulder. Angelo grabbed his fingers. "Please, go away. She is my girlfriend. Do not make me angry."

He cackled and glanced at Angelo's body. "You?" He stretched the muscles of his arms and chest. "You challenge me, skinny boy?"

Angelo snuffled and pointed his forefinger at the Englishman's throat. The Englishman wrapped his hands around his neck and felt suffocated. Angelo placed his right hand on his back, and an invisible force shoved the Englishman up against a tree trunk. He crumpled to the tiled floor like a block of cement and could not move. His nose bled. "Help, help," Angelo shouted, staring at his hand. Waiters and assistants dragged the Englishman inside the hotel.

Caitlyn peered at Angelo. "How did you do that? How did you get that power? Are you a magician?"

"You can say that."

"Amazing. Thanks for standing up for me. Why did you say I am your girlfriend?"

He caressed her knee. "Because I love you. Do you like to be my girlfriend?"

"Of course. Your eyes are impressive. I love you too." She kissed him. "Can you teach me magic?"

"I cannot teach you magic, but I can do this." He carried her in his arms.

"How are you strong?"

"You need to be an Italian wizard. You are safe with me, and that is the main thing."

Back in Toronto, Caitlyn became anxious, sick, and frail. One day, Angelo sat next to her and placed his palm on her sweaty forehead to offer comfort and check her temperature. "Awehitecha, please heal her."

"Who is that?"

"She is a Supreme Goddess."

"I thought you were a Catholic."

"I am everything."

"It is not my head. My tummy is in pain. I need the goddess of drugs."

"I will take you to the hospital."

A taxi took them to Toronto Western Hospital at Bathurst Street. A nurse examined Caitlyn's blood pressure and took a sample of her blood and urine. Later, a physician informed her she was pregnant.

When he moved out of her room, she turned her scarlet face to Angelo. "I didn't expect that so soon. What should we do?"

"What do you say?"

"Should we keep the baby? We will begin our studies in two weeks."

"Let us be parents. It will be fun and joyful. I don't feel comfortable with abortion."

"Me too. I am shocked. Our families won't let us abort the baby if we tell them about the pregnancy. I am also not sure what to tell my family about you. How will we go to college?"

"Do not worry about all that. I will say nothing to my family before you give birth. Once we are parents, we will adjust our schedule. Our relatives and friends will help us when we need them, and I will hire a nanny. You should move to my house and live with me. This will save you money and make it easier for me to look after you."

Angelo removed Caitlyn's clothes and books from her apartment to his house and organized them in stylish wardrobes and bookcases with a sense of aesthetics. He enjoyed the unconditional love of an intelligent, charming lover. They shopped, cooked, cleaned, made love, hiked, studied, and went to college together. However, in the middle of her pregnancy, an enigmatic darkness had shrouded her existence. Emotional anxiety and depression cast their grim shadows upon her, their origins and purpose concealed within the impenetrable recesses of her troubled psyche. Night after night, as the moon's glow bathed the world outside, her restless slumber became a precarious realm where reality intertwined with the macabre. One late night, she picked up a chef's knife from the kitchen and moved its smooth spine on her bare, expanded abdomen. An unexpected presence materialized, shrouded in the cloak of a hooded female warrior. Mysterious and calm, the warrior appeared from the shadows, a phantom in the night. She moved; her footsteps made no sound. "Don't kill the girl."

Caitlyn panicked and switched on the light. "Who is that?" A palpable tension filled the air as her trembling hands closed around the hilt of the knife. A storm brewed within her, eclipsing the fragility of her condition, as she ascended the staircase. The upper floor revealed a bedroom bathed in shadow; its stillness interrupted by her arrival. In this dim room, her eyes locked onto Angelo with an intensity that shivered her spine. The burden of her state bore witness to a smoldering anger, her features contorted by a darkness that threatened to consume all reason. As she drew closer, a peculiar phenomenon unfolded within the room. Whispers, low and hoarse, came out from the walls. A chorus of spectral voices, haunting and foreboding, filled the space, their words laden with caution and an eerie sense of consequences.

"Do not dare harm the sacred body, or you will die," they warned, their voices carrying the weight of ancient wisdom. Now, Caitlyn stood alone at the crossroads of her untold destiny. Would she heed the spectral voices, allowing caution to guide her steps? Or would she plunge into the unknown depth of her chosen path? She tightened her grip on the knife and moved forward. Long-haired female figures, draped in dark hoods and skimpy animal skins, encircled the bed with an air of primal authority. Their hands clutched rusty spears and weathered swords, remnants of long past battles. Their presence was an impressive fusion of elegance and power. The mysterious warriors stood as Angelo's guardians. Each carried a mantle of mystery, veiled beneath the layers of their wild and tamed beauty.

Seeking refuge from the occult warriors, Caitlyn retreated to a guest room and covered herself with a heavy bed sheet.

Four months later, she celebrated the success of the first academic year and gave birth to a girl at Mount Sinai Hospital. Angelo carried the baby. "She is pretty like you, and she has blonde hair and blue eyes." When Caitlyn held the baby, he picked up his cell phone and called his mother. "Mom, I have become a father."

"Oh, my God. How?"

"My girlfriend delivered a daughter. You should take a trip and see her."

"Congratulations. Who is your girlfriend?"

"An Irish American from New York."

"Good, love. I am so happy for you. After six or seven days, your dad and I will come to see you and your family."

Bella called Nina. "Angelo is a father."

"Great, grandmother. A boy or a girl?"

"A girl for our girl."

"Wonderful. Colestah made a mistake when she said Angelo would have a boy."

"She is not a goddess to know everything in the world. She mixes predictions with ancient legends, though she is a remarkable woman. Did Angelo tell you about his Irish American girlfriend?"

"No. He loved a Swedish girl."

Later, a nurse brought a Notice of Live Birth form to register the baby's name. Angelo and Caitlyn had agreed to name her Elisha. The nurse asked Angelo about his surname. "Elisha should have her mom's family name. I don't believe in patriarchy."

"OK. The family name is McManus."

Angelo squeezed his chin and remained reticent. Caitlyn stroked his hand. "Where are you now? Why are you silent?"

"I have realized I had never looked at your official documents or asked about your family lineage. My memories swirled in my mind and remembered my family's outlaws who gunned down members of your family in their homes and bars."

The mention of the past had evoked emotions and memories. But with a loving gaze at the baby, Caitlyn redirected the focus of their conversation and recognized the importance of prioritizing the present and the future. "That was the past. We need to look after this baby."

He agreed, understanding the significance of her statement. Their child had brought a new chapter into their lives, an episode needed their full attention and dedication. "I am happy to be a dad. It is a tremendous step in my life. My parents will come next week. What about your family?"

"I am an orphan. My parents are dead, and I don't have brothers or sisters."

Bella and Leonardo flew to Toronto and met Angelo at the airport. Bella touched his face and shoulder-length hair. "Honey, what happened to you? You look more like a girl."

"My hormones are raging, but I am fine. We will take a cab."

As Leonardo entered the house, his face lit up with a warm and cheery smile. His eyes sparkled with joy and excitement as he approached Caitlyn and Elisha. He leaned in and planted tender kisses on Caitlyn's cheeks, expressing his care and affection for her. He kissed Elisha's head, with his heart brimming with happiness and gratitude. "Thanks for making me a grandpa."

Bella kissed Caitlyn and held Elisha. "She is very gorgeous."

"Thank you so much. I am very honored to meet you. Angelo told me interesting things about you. Do you like a cup of tea?"

"Yes, please." Leonardo gazed at Caitlyn's face when she stood in the kitchen and contemplated for a while. "Angelo, where is the toilet?"

"It is there."

"Come and show me how to use the hot tap." Angelo took his father into the bathroom. Leonardo closed the door behind him. "Listen, son. Your girlfriend has surprised me. What brought you two together?"

"She is in my college."

"Do you know her family?"

"No. She told me she was an orphan and her parents

died in New York when she was fourteen."

"Is she from New York?"

"Yes. She is from Hell's Kitchen."

"Good. Good. New York girls are attractive and bold. Do you love her?"

"Yeah. She lives with me."

"Are you thinking of marrying her?"

"Not now. I am not in a hurry. What's wrong, dad? You look nervous."

"Nothing is wrong. I remembered the stupid Irish-Italian wars in New York and Chicago. I am proud of you. How is the business?"

"Fine. I invested in magazines and newspapers and have a publishing company."

"Good. You are a big man now. Be a caring and generous dad and take care of your beautiful girlfriend and daughter."

After leaving the restroom, Leonardo held the baby and kissed her pink cheeks when Caitlyn went upstairs. "What is her name?"

"Elisha."

"Nice name. Elisha Lucciano."

"No, dad. She is Elisha McManus."

"McManus? What is this nonsense? Listen to me. The McManus...." Angelo placed his hand on his mouth. "Dad, I love Caitlyn, and I don't care about what happened between the Irish and us. We live in peace now."

"Don't close my mouth again. I am your father. Remember that. What? Your daughter should have our family name. Everybody gets their father's family name. That is the tradition."

"Dad, please, Caitlyn suffered from pregnancy and grief, not me. By the way, she is a model, and her photos appear in famous fashion magazines."

Bella crossed her legs. "Names are names. The main thing is love and the person's character."

"Mom, give her the incentive to enhance her love for modeling and fashion."

"Of course, my dear. I will do everything I can to support and encourage her. Her love for modeling and fashion is an accurate expression of who she is, and I want to see her thrive in something that brings her joy. But, what about the university? How will you study and look after your daughter and house?"

"I suppose we will need help and a nanny."

"Yes, you need a nanny. From time to time, I will take on the role of a babysitter for a brief period."

The next day, Leonardo and Bella surprised Angelo with a brand-new Honda car and gave Caitlyn money to furnish and decorate Elisha's room.

Caitlyn excelled in her studies, and Angelo got the highest marks in the university. They graduated with honors when Elisha was three years of age. After a celebration party with friends in their home, Caitlyn briefed Angelo about her academic ambition to pursue a postgraduate study on an indigenous community in Manitoba. "I got a full scholarship for my master's degree in anthropology. My research is on a Cree Nation at Split Lake in Manitoba. So, I need to go away for three months. I trust you won't mind."

"I won't mind at all. Do what you love, and I will look

after Elisha and write a book."

After Caitlyn's departure to Thompson city, a feeling of secrecy hung in the air like a whispering phantom. Angelo took feminizing pills and recorded his physical changes and emotional experience in a journal. He found himself drawn to the charm of nostalgia, a yearning to delve into the memories of Nina, who captured his thoughts. A photo album beckoned him like a forgotten treasure trove. With a delicate touch, he riffled through the photo album, his eyes skimming over the captured fragments of Nina's social life. Each photo held the power to transform him into the depth of his romance with her. He kissed a photo and called. "How are you doing?"

"Thanks, honey. I am well. What about you?"

"I am alone with Elisha. Caitlyn went to Northern Canada to do college work. She will be there for three months. Do you like to spend two months with me? I miss you. Please, come. I will pay your expenses and show you amazing places."

"I don't need money. OK, love. I will see you after two or three days."

With Elisha on his shoulders, Angelo greeted Nina at Toronto Pearson International Airport. After dinner, Elisha slept in her bedroom, and Angelo and Nina went downstairs to the kitchen to make tea. He surprised her with a warm kiss on her lips. "I missed these rosy lips." She blenched and turned her face to the right. When he embraced her and tried to kiss her again, she covered her mouth. "Stop it. I want a cup of tea."

"A cup of tea and a kiss."

"No. Just a cup of tea."

"You are still the same. You still look young and attractive. Come on, love. Let me kiss you. I missed you so much." His deft fingers unbuttoned her fitted shirt, and he tried to lick her breast cleavage.

She pushed his head away. "Honey, no. No. What are you doing?"

"I need physical affection from my first love."

"But you have a wonderful partner. I will not let you cheat on her."

"What cheat on her? How do you say that, and you have an affair with my married mom?"

"That's a different matter. I told you a thousand times I am a strict lesbian and will never have sex with a man."

"What happened to you? There is no man in the house." He opened his shirt, unhooked his bra, and mumbled a word, turning himself into a half-naked woman. "Look at me. Touch my breasts. Look at my bikini thong. Do you still think I am a man?"

Her fingertips grazed the bridge of his nose, a fleeting caress laden with unspoken emotions. A solitary tear, glistening like a precious gem, escaped from the corner of her eye, tracing a path down her cheek. "You are gorgeous, but I can't."

"Why? You kissed me every day when I was in New York. Caitlyn knows I love you, and she knows you are here." He loosened her white bra.

Her hands covered her breasts. "Honey, please, don't touch me. Give me the bra. I cannot make love to you."

"Why? Don't you remember our romance in your house? You know I love you."

"I love you too. But no to sex with you."

"Come on. I wish to massage your body. Did you forget those days when you bathed me? The images of your body and kisses are still in my head." He played with her long hair. "What's going on? You have sex with my mom. Don't you want to have a romance with your best friend's child? Do you still think of the man who had the penis? I am a true woman. I want you, and my body pulls me to you. Caress me like in the old days. You agreed to live with me for two months. Are you becoming religious or what?"

"Honey, I love you so much. I can't...."

After getting her bra, Nina wept and darted to the living room. A swell of frustration moved through Angelo's veins, a tempestuous storm within his being that demanded release. In a sudden act of impulsive fury, he turned his face back and thwacked a wall cabinet, damaging its door and shelves. "Oh, dear! What happened to me?" He stared at his hand. "How do I have this power? Why don't I feel pain when I hit something? What can I do?" He closed his shirt.

Hintocha appeared beside him. "Do not be hasty and insistent. Apologize to Nina and be kind to her. We love her. Did you forget her love and care for you? She is a sensitive lesbian."

"But she thinks I am not a woman."

"That is not the issue. Nina is a woman full of deep emotions. It is hard for her to have an affair with your mother and give her full love to you. I feel something else is bothering her. Please, say sorry and tell her about your gender transition."

He lumbered into the living room and massaged Nina's shoulder. "Honey, please forgive me. Come with me to the bedroom. I am sorry. My love for you is so great that it surpasses all the thoughts in my head, and I would do nothing to hurt you. My genes want to meld with you. I don't know why. You are the only friend who understands the depth of my soul."

They moved to a bedroom on the first floor and lay on the bed without taking off their clothes and shoes. He rested his head on a pillow and stared at the ceiling, and she put her left arm on his chest. "Honey, you are my true love, not your mother or any other person. I love you for tons of reasons, but please understand, I cannot make love to you. My love for you has nothing to do with gender, morality, or religion. I do not follow any holy book or religion. But for emotional reasons, I cannot have sex with you and your mom. What is going on in your head? Why did you ask me to spend two months with you? Did you have an argument with Caitlyn?"

"No. Caitlyn adores me, though she doesn't want us to get married. I don't know why."

"But you are in love with Dinah. Why didn't you ask her to come here? You saw her every month and made love to her in my house. Does Caitlyn know about your affair?"

"No. I told her nothing about Dinah."

"Does Dinah know about Caitlyn and Elisha?"

"No. She knows nothing about my life here."

"What happened to you? Don't you think your sex is a problem?"

"What do you mean?"

"You make love to Caitlyn and Dinah and then you want to have sex with me."

"What can I do? I have an abnormal body and an insatiable desire for love. The masculine side loves Dinah, and the feminine side loves Caitlyn and wants to be a lesbian. And my whole body loves you. The boy and the girl in me are vying with each other. To clear the air, I asked you to come here because I have a medical appointment for a penectomy."

"What is that?"

"It is about the surgical removal of my penis."

"Where is your penis? You are a woman now. So, why do you want to remove the penis? Your tiny manhood is lifeless."

"I wish to be one person. I wish to be a woman and a lesbian like you."

Her fingers tickled his face. "When you are a boy, you look like a trans woman. Do you take pills?"

"Yes. I take pills every day."

"How long have you been taking them?"

"Four years."

"Why didn't you tell me? Does Caitlyn know about them?"

"No. You are the only one who knows about the pills. I mean, you and Hintocha."

"What does Caitlyn say about your body?"

"She enjoys every part and has never asked me to fix my pecker. I don't know why she is not interested in intercourse. She even asked me to be a woman and have a woman's name."

"Weird. It seems she has lesbian feelings or an affair with a girl."

"Maybe. All our close friends are women, and a half of them are lesbians. Caitlyn asked me many times to wear women's clothes when I was with her or when our women friends visited us. I think she is not interested in intercourse because she reads as we breathe air. She loves books and writes every day."

"So, I do not understand why you need to get rid of the dysfunctional penis if Caitlyn loves you and doesn't like intercourse. Look at yourself. You have a woman's face, a vagina, breasts, and a hairless body. You can go out with lesbian friends, and your hidden dick won't bother them."

"I can be a woman only for two hours a day. That is why I want to be a real woman like you. It is my body and choice."

"Does Caitlyn know about the operation?"

"No. What would she say in my house?"

"Honey, you can't have a serious operation like that without her consent. She is your partner and the mother of your daughter. Please, wait. You should talk to Colestah because she knows about people's spirits."

"With due respect, what does she know about gender dysphoria and transitioning?"

She patted his hand. "Behave. Do not believe the media's gender stereotypes. Although Colestah is a traditional woman, she understands people's hidden souls and emotions. She told you about Hintocha, the eagle's eye, and your internal power. I will ask her to come here."

"But she doesn't like to fly."

"Her daughter will bring her here. I will call her before she sleeps." She left the bedroom and called Colestah. After the call, she rested beside Angelo. "Your daughter is gorgeous. Do you wish to have another child if you can?"

"I don't know. An old incident had put me off. Do you remember the Irish moron who chased us and wanted to kill me? He was Caitlyn's dad."

"My God! Did you tell Caitlyn what happened to him and how he died?"

"No. I wish to tell her the truth, but I think she would hate me or kill me. One night, I made love to her and imagined her dad watching us and holding a knife. Sometimes I feel scared."

"Fear nobody. No one can defeat a heart full of love. You are strong, and there is a goddess with you. Tell me, how does Hintocha feel when you make love to Caitlyn and Dinah?"

"To her, it is like watching an erotic movie. Can I tell you a secret?"

"Yeah. Say anything."

"Hintocha and I make love to each other."

"How?"

"I turn myself into a woman, and she appears and does what lesbians do. It is an ecstatic and sensual feeling. It is hard for me to describe it."

"You are lucky to have three lovers. I feel jealous. I wish to have sex with a goddess." She laughed. "What happens to your penis when you make yourself a woman?"

"It hides inside my vagina, and I can't use a dildo. That is why I am frustrated."

"Think of the good things you have. You are rich and have a gorgeous girlfriend and a daughter. Talk to Colestah when she comes. I am sure she will find a solution for you. But now, why do you want to make love to me if your secret lover is the goddess of love and seduction?"

"I like the real human thing." He felt aroused and gave her a deep kiss.

"Stop it. Touch yourself if you want to have an orgasm. I will keep my eyes shut."

They slept in the bed. Two days later, Colestah and Talisa arrived in the mid-afternoon. After eating wild rice with sweet potato, Nina and Talisa went out for a ramble, and Angelo sat beside Colestah in the kitchen.

"I am happy to see you again and don't know how to start this conversation. As I look like a girl and feel and think like a woman, I wish to be a real woman. This body is not mine."

Colestah urged him to have a shift in perspective from the surface to the depth and from the obvious to the subtle. When she said, "Feel with your heart and do not think with your eyes," she wanted him to move beyond superficial judgments and engage with reality in a more profound and empathetic manner. "The world is full of illusions." She aimed to remind him that perception may not always reflect the underlying facts of reality. "You have the spirit of a woman."

"I know that, but I want to change my male genitalia and be a woman with a full vagina."

With an artificial smile, she stroked the back of his hand. "Oh, no. That will offend the Great Spirit. You have two divine spirits. One spirit is for the girl, your real you, and one is for the male elements in you. I told you there is a holy goddess in and with you for a sacred purpose. You are an exceptional person, and your delicate human body cannot bear two or three souls. A Supreme Goddess will make you a flawless woman at the right time."

"What a Supreme Goddess? Do you want me to wait for a goddess to change me? There is no boy in me, and Hintocha is not a typical woman. She is like a ghost. Besides, I crave to be free from the shackles of men. This is my freedom. My body, my choice."

Colestah grimaced and banged on the wooden table. "Choice? What choice? Tell me. You came to this world without a choice. Did you choose to have two eyes and two ears? Did you choose to have two lungs, two kidneys, and a heart? Did you choose to have two arms and two legs? Can you choose to live without air and food? To enjoy the essence of your existence, you must learn how to live in harmonious symbiosis with Mother Nature. She, with her infinite wisdom and boundless beauty, holds the key to unlocking the secrets of a fulfilled life. You will lose your divine power and bright future if you let humans remove your genitals in a hospital. Surgery will never make you a true woman."

"How do you say that? That is transphobia?"

"Listen to me. The noble woman is a divine soul, not

a gender choice or an abstract idea in a feminist's head. The Great Spirit or God creates the human life in women's wombs, not in men's bellies. No man can get this divine honor even if he chops off his penis. As no trans man can produce sperm, no man can get a womb and become pregnant through surgery and drugs. An apple cannot be an orange because it feels it is an orange. Menstruation, pregnancy, breastfeeding, and menopause affect the woman's thinking, emotions, body, hormones, and mental health. So, the woman is not a feeling in someone's head or an imaginary social concept in a patriarchal society, as radical feminists and gender folks say."

"So, what do you think of the trans people?"

"They can say anything about themselves, and we must do no harm to them. I do not hate them and do not wish to discourage you. But you are special. You are not like anyone else in this world. You are a splendid girl in body and spirit, and there is a majestic goddess with you, but you need to feel your deep feminine essence. Your heroic spirit will grow in your heart. According to our legends, you are the chosen sign of the Eagle Goddess and the bearer of the Merciful God of humanity that we wish to see. You will be a woman soon, very soon, and a Supreme Goddess will make you a superb goddess when the Goddess Hintocha leaves you and meets her divine lover. Please, do not lose your divine power for desires and material gratification. Believe me. You are more powerful than those bogus action heroes you see in movies. Our people will long for your power. The persecuted people of the world will need your might to protect them. Take diligent care of Elisha. I checked her eyes. She will be a remarkable celebrity and love you more than anybody else. I also saw danger in her eyes. Guard her and stop wasting your precious time on a tiny piece of droopy flesh between your thighs. Hintocha and other goddesses love you and will always protect you. Do not let desires control your life. Your body is sacred. It is the body of our ancestors. May the Great Spirit bless you forever."

"I appreciate what you say, but why me? Why did Hintocha and the Eagle Goddess choose me? What have I to do with your people? I am half-Italian, half-English."

She rapped the table. "What is this total hogwash? Didn't Bella tell you the truth? Look at yourself and look at me. You are one of us."

He lifted his head and held his tongue for a moment. "What do you mean?"

Shiny tears filled her deep-set eyes. She tickled and kissed his hand. "I want to disclose a secret, but you must not tell the Lucciano family about it. Do you promise me that?"

"Yeah, I promise."

"Bella cannot have babies because she is sterile. Nina got her an egg to save her marriage and make Leonardo and his family happy. You belong to Nina's family." Colestah burst into tears.

He cuddled her and cried. "How do you know that?"

"Bella visited me when you were eight to let me heal her sickness and menstruation problems. When I told her you don't look like her, she said Nina denoted an egg that became you. She didn't tell her husband about it to avoid his anger."

"I see. Bella had never been sick in the last twelve years. But why did Awehitecha choose me?"

"Because of her love for you. She placed her eagle's eye on your leg to hide a divine mystery and protect you. A world event will take place when Winona forgives her daughter Hintocha."

"Who is Winona?"

"She is the Supreme Goddess who created the Americas and the First Nations."

"Oh, my God."

"So, do you think the Supreme Eagle Goddess would put her sacred eye on an ordinary leg? Do you think the Supreme Goddess Winona would ask her daughter to be with a normal human? They touched your body because it is holy. Nina and others will tell you the truth."

"Is Hintocha Winona's daughter?"

"Yes, Hintocha is her daughter. Winona detained her with you to protect you from the archdemon Tawiscara, who does not want the First Nations to unite and be free. Our gods accepted the arbitrary foundation of the United States and the status quo, but Awehitecha, Winona, and the Goddess of the Oceans and Seas Achiqueta want to restore this land to us. Awehitecha will appear to liberate our nations when you become forty."

"What will happen when I am forty?"

"The world will totter, and the Divine Being will transform you into an impeccable goddess. When that happens, the superpowers of the world will tremble in fear."

"Wow! You are marvelous. Thank you." He kissed her forehead and stormed out of his house. "How was that, Hintocha? Are you surprised? Why didn't you tell me you are Winona's daughter?"

"There are things I can't do and say. My mom asked me not to tell you about her. I knew nothing about Nina's egg and Bella's pregnancy. I wouldn't have asked you to have sex with Nina if I knew she was your mother. Talk to her. I hope she will tell you everything. I love you."

Angelo sauntered around the house and gazed at Nina. The sight had ignited an immediate, powerful response, as he sprinted toward her with an urgency that conveyed his eagerness to be with her. He kneeled before her, wrapping his arms around her legs in a tight hug. The gesture had shown his profound affection, as if it cast aside all barriers and pretenses in favor of a raw and genuine expression of attachment and love. "Mom, mom."

"Talisa, please go to your mother. Thanks for walking with me. I will see you after an hour." Talisa entered the house and took a seat next to her mother. Nina rubbed Angelo's head. "Why did you call me mom?"

He looked up at her with innocent eyes. "Colestah told me about your donated egg."

"My goodness, how does she know so much? I promised Bella not to tell anyone about it."

"Bella visited her and told her about your egg. Now I

understand your love affair with her."

"Get up, my precious child." He stood, and she kissed him with all the tender passion she had for him. They sat on a garden bench, cuddling and fondling. "Yes, my love. Do you realize my emotional adventure with you? Do you understand why I cannot have sex with you? I am your mom and will always care for you. It was so hard for me to be patient when the Luccianos called you their boy. You belong to our divine family."

"What? Which divine family?"

"I am Achiqueta, the Supreme Goddess of the Oceans and Seas. Anna Awehitecha is my daughter, and you are her sister."

Angelo and Hintocha shivered and swooned for twenty seconds. "My Goddess, my Holy Goddess. What have I done? I am so ignorant and stupid." Hintocha wept and slapped the sides of her face.

Angelo shook his head. "Oh, my God. Oh, gosh. How am I Awehitecha's sister?"

"You are the Goddess Anohitecha."

"Oh no. Oh no. Oh, my Goddess. What a fool I am." Hintocha banged her head on a stone pillar.

"Hintocha, be quiet." He touched Nina's arm and hand. "Am I a goddess? How are we goddesses?"

"We are the goddesses whose names start with the letter A because our family was the first to exist. Get up and turn your back. I want to take you to a place. Don't be afraid. Hintocha, please stay here to look after Elisha. I want to have a private conversation with my daughter." She embraced his back and soared with him to the north. They landed on a stony beach surrounded by trees. "Wow! I don't need an airplane if you can fly."

She closed his mouth with a kiss and hugged him, with floods of tears streaming down her cheeks. "Oh, Anohitecha, my beloved daughter. I miss the old days with you."

"Daughter? What daughter? What did you say my name?"

"You are Anohitecha. You and Awehitecha are twin sisters."

He opened his mouth wide. "Twin sisters? How?"

"You and Awehitecha were born together. We were with my mother, the Goddess Kotyanga, in the lower sky over the Milky Way galaxy. One day, equal to one thousand years on earth, our best friend Winona and ourselves descended on this planet when it was a ball shrouded in a blazing inferno. Winona created the Americas, and I made the oceans and the seas to cool the earth. My mother made the galaxies, the stars, and the planets, and Awehitecha created the moon, the air, the animals, and the fish. You decorated the galaxies with colors and lights."

"You? Wait a minute. What do you mean?"

She wept, and he rested his arm on her shoulders. "You are the goddess of cosmic beauty. You were the most beautiful warrior goddess."

"How I was born in New York, and you say I was a warrior goddess?"

"You were born a girl in the third sky and reborn a half-human in New York. That is why you have this unusual body."

"I still cannot fathom how Bella became pregnant

with me. Can you explain that?"

"OK. I met Bella at New York School of Design when she was nineteen. We became best friends after she showed me her sincere compassion and love for the indigenous people. I thought we would be lovers until I find Awehitecha. But Leonardo saw her in a hotel and asked her to marry him. She was afraid to refuse his proposal when Sandro and his Mafia were powerful and vicious. One night, she surprised me when she told me about her uterus and ovarian problems and the desire to be a mother to save her marriage and to please Leonardo and his family. She begged me to donate an egg. I couldn't tell her I am a goddess and don't get menstruation. So, I turned you into an ovum to let you experience the human life before you become the leader of the world. I erased your memory and reset you into the default state of light."

"Which light?"

"We are transcendental, divine lights. We don't have organs inside our body." Her hand delved into her body and extracted a luminous sphere.

He held the ball of light. "What happened? How did you put me in Bella's womb?"

"I didn't. Because Bella is an earthly woman, I asked Jodasiya to give you a human spirit and install you in Bella's womb."

"Who is Jodasiya?"

"She was the female chief of the Seneca Nation and a plucky warrior of wisdom. She protected her people and healed their sickness with herbs and plants. Men drowned her in a river, but Awehitecha saved her spirit and kept her body in Chautauqua Lake.”

“Fascinating. How did Jodasiya make me a human?”

“I asked her to whiff her human spirit on you before putting you in Bella’s womb. After that, she pretended to be a doctor. I caused Bella to sleep in my home, and Jodasiya placed you in her womb. You were supposed to be a girl, but you became who you are now because of Leonardo’s sperm and Bella’s hormones and blood. So, you have a tad of human genes.”

“Why don’t I feel I am a goddess?”

“Do you remember how your small hands stopped the bus at Times Square? You are a goddess, but you don’t remember that because I erased your memory. Squeeze this rock.”

He compressed a gabbro rock and ground it into a powder. “Unbelievable.”

“You look human and have human feelings and emotions because you lived in Bella’s womb and got her characteristics and earth’s food.” She pulled the waist of his pants and underpants and exhaled. “Look now.”

“Oh, my God. Where is the penis?”

“Was that what you wanted to remove? That’s better than surgery. I will change your face and neck after we find your sister.”

“What about Colestah? How do you know her?”

“She is the most respected woman in the Seneca Nation. I altered my looks and joined her tribe because I didn’t want her to suspect me.”

“I can’t remember your original face. How did you look before you came down to earth?”

She gave him thick sunglasses. “Go back.”

He moved thirty yards away from her. She ascended into the boundless sky, pirouetting above the tranquil lake. Adorned in a billowing white cloak, her body stirred ripples of luminescence on the water's surface, casting an entrancing glow akin to the brilliance of the moon in its fullest splendor. Angelo's gaze transfixed on the heavens above. He stood rooted in awe, his hands finding comfort on his trembling thighs. An involuntary spasm moved through his body, causing him to falter, ceding control as he kneeled on the harsh, unforgiving terrain of the rugged shore. "Glory be to you, my holy mother, the majestic illuminator of darkness." Nina darted across the serene surface of the lake, her footsteps defying the natural order. As she drew nearer to him, a strange transmutation occurred, her figure shrinking in a surreal display of proximity, as if the essence of her being had adapted to match his presence.

"I loved your platinum, golden hair and long white dress. How tall were you?"

"Three hundred feet in the sky and fifty feet on earth, though my spirit covers my universe."

"What is this place?"

"This is Georgina Island, and this water is Lake Simcoe."

"Why did you bring me here?"

"The devils cannot come to this part of the island and hear what I tell you."

"Who are those devils?"

"Gods made them from fire and energy to praise and serve them. But when Winona made the First People, they became envious and tried to eradicate them. Because they failed to do that, they seduced them and made them fight each other.”

“Why do the devils want to listen to you?”

“Because of Awehitecha.”

“What is the problem with her?”

“The devils know Awehitecha wants to kill them, unite our goddesses, and liberate the indigenous peoples worldwide. The devils want more troubles in the sky and on earth.”

“What happened to grandma?”

“No idea. Four centuries ago, she descended to the earth to teach our people how to harvest, tame wild animals, cook, heal, and make homes. But later, she disappeared when the wars started between our people and the white settlers in the seventeenth century. People said she healed the injured and protected women and kids, but we don’t know what happened to her. Iroquois legends say Tawiscara poisoned her food and killed her, and people buried her in Ogoki in the middle of Ontario. A Christian relic hunter discovered her grave and stole her remnants in the night. Two days later, our people killed him and buried my mom’s body in a secret place. Some said the secret place was in Attawapiskat near Akimiski Island in James Bay. Of course, this is not true because the Great Spirit made my mom of light. Our simple people mean my mom’s clothes and ornaments.”

“I thought goddesses do not die.”

“That’s true, but one intangible substance called Ahseciwa can kill a goddess.”

"Why did you leave the sky?"

"Because of your sister. One day, Hintocha came to me with a nervous face and said Awehitecha fell in a black hole connected to the earth. I wondered why she couldn't save herself and come back. So, I lost my temper and didn't know what to do. I came down and combed forests, oceans, deserts, and mountains to find her. Goddesses said she fell in Canada because the bald eagles were her warriors. Others said she descended in the Amazon jungle because the jaguars were her friends."

"Did you ask Winona to find her?"

"Unlike you, Awehitecha is an independent and obstinate person. No goddess knows her plans except the Supreme Mother of the Goddesses, who began the creation of our goddesses and wrote Gayadosha."

"Who is the Supreme Mother of the Goddesses?"

"Our limited sights cannot perceive Her, but She perceives all sights. She is the only goddess who had no beginning. All the other goddesses came into being after her."

"What is Gayadosha?"

"It is a sacred book written before the creation of the universe by the Supreme Mother in an arcane language full of cryptic letters and symbols. Only your sister knows how to decipher it."

"Why didn't my sister communicate with us?"

"I don't know. I believe she is alive because of her eagle eye mark on your leg. Our sacred epics say your sister and you will liberate the First Nations from white colonialism. But now, live a normal life and do not interfere in politics until we find your sister. I do not know why she placed the sacred code on your leg and do not know what will happen before you become the world's leader."

"Why don't I remember my past?"

"Because I blotted out your memory."

"Please, restore my memory."

"OK. Rest your head on my thigh."

He rested the back of his head on her thigh. "Close your eyes and hold your breath." In her palm, an orb of luminosity materialized, its radiance emanated a glow upon her delicate body. She pressed the incandescent sphere against his forehead, and his body teetered like a mirage on a distant horizon. "Open your eyes."

He opened his eyes. "Oh, no, I remember you now."

She touched his face. "Good. Do you know now why you are a special goddess and why Winona asked her daughter to be with you?"

"You don't understand. Why didn't you restore my memory when I was with you in New York? I don't believe what we did together. Why? Why?" He got up and pottered to a protruding rock, crying. "Oh, love, I am so sorry to put you in this situation. I will always be there for you." Clasping the weighty rock within his grasp, he poised at the water's edge, contemplating the impending act. With a resolute motion, he propelled the rock forth, its arc tracing through the air before succumbing to the lake's placid depths. The ripples diffused across the water's surface, marking the passage of its trajectory. "Damn it. Please, forgive me."

The ginger-orange-haired warrior appeared and

hugged him, scowling at Nina. "Hello, mom. You are a disgrace."

"Anohitecha. Anohitecha. What did you do?"

"You are despicable." She kissed Angelo's face and looked into his eyes. "Do you know me now?"

"Yes, you are my mother."

A red-haired warrior with a short sword sprang up beside Angelo. "Hello, Angela."

"Hello, Amitola. I missed you, sister."

Nina frowned. "Why did you do that to me? Why did you deceive me all these years? When did you have two daughters? I thought Angelo was you?"

"Angelo is my daughter, Angela. She made herself look like me, and you erased her memory and abducted her without her consent to please your shameful adultery with an unfaithful wife from this planet. How dare you do that? I can't believe my daughter wanted to have sex with her wicked grandmother."

"How do you say that about me? Why didn't you tell me Angelo was your daughter?"

"Why? You abandoned me and our shared path, betraying our moral code that once bound us together. Aren't you ashamed of yourself and of your disgusting behavior? You have an abominable affair with a mortal married woman from this corrupt planet. Shame on you. You are the supreme goddess who created the seas and the oceans. Did you forget that? You lied and pretended to be a member of the Seneca Nation. You forsook our divine kingdom and came down to this decadent earth. Tell me, do you know any supreme goddess who betrayed her divine family and humiliated herself like you? Is the perishable woman Bella more important than us?"

"No. That's not possible. I love all of you. I am in shock to know you have two daughters."

Angelo caressed Anohitecha's left hand. "Mom, my grandma loved me and cared for me more than anyone else. Whatever happened between her and us, we need to protect our family and find your sister. Forgive her for my sake. We need to have a plan for Caitlyn, Elisha, Leonardo, and Bella. It is not good we leave them and go up to the sky."

"I know, honey. But my mother and sister had made our operation more complicated."

Nina shed a tear. "Please forgive me. I promise to be with you all the time. But I cannot leave the earth because of Anna. What do you want me to do?"

Anohitecha touched Angelo's shoulder. "First, stop your stupid affair with Bella. Second, we need to fix Angela's abnormal body."

"Only the Mother of the Goddesses and Winona can do that. Angela needs to pray to them."

Angelo kissed his mother's face. "Can you take me to Jodasiya?"

"Yes. I will take you to her lake."

"Grandma told me about the liberation of the First Nations. Are we supposed to revolt?"

"No. We don't encourage military actions and homicide. When our people used guns, the white occupiers defeated them. My heart tells me my sister will come back to reinstate justice and the human rights of our peoples. We will not rest until they become free."

"What about the other people? Do you want them to leave America?"

"No. We are not like the Nazis. We need peace with everybody, and our people want their country back. Do not perform public miracles and do not tell anybody else you are a goddess. Let us go home and see your guests." She paused. "Wait. I smell my sister's scent."

A bald eagle came down and dropped a rolled letter on the ground. "It is from Awehitecha." She stared up. "Awehitecha. Awehitecha."

"What does the letter say?"

"Dear mother, sister, Angela, and Amitola. I am happy to see you all together. The eagle's eyes are my cameras. I am fighting the last evil gods and their devils in the boreal forest. Do not come to help me. I do not want Tawiscara to kill the First Nations. I will see you when the war is over because our sacred Gayadosha says the Eagle Goddess will bring glory to the poor nations when the goddess of love becomes free. My love for you is eternal. Anna Awehitecha."

Nina wept, and Anohitecha placed a hand on her shoulder. "Do not worry about my sister. I am sure she will defeat all the evil spirits."

"It is hard for me not to see her. I miss her."

"Mom, what should I tell Caitlyn?"

"Don't tell her anything about us, though I want you to love her as much as possible. I have deep feelings for her because I killed her father."

"Oh, my God. What did you do?"

"I dropped the plant pot on his head. He was an evil man. Forget this matter. Let us go back." They flew back to Toronto.

Angelo stepped into his bedroom and saw Hintocha reading a magazine on the bed. "What can you tell me about your reactions and screams?"

"Your mom has shocked and surprised me. I am sorry for treating you like a child. I never expected you to be Anohitecha, though I am so eager to reconnect with you."

"Wrong. I am Angela and Nina's granddaughter. The goddess with the orange hair is Anohitecha and my mother. My aunt Anna Awehitecha is alive."

"My Goddess. How is that?"

"It is a long story. I am happy to get my memory back."

"My love for you has increased, though I miss Anna. I am pleased to know she is alive. You were not born when Anna and I threw comets at planets and our mothers grounded us inside a black hole."

Colestah and her daughter returned to their home in Salamanca. Nina's family crossed the border by car and visited Lakeside Park in Mayville, Chautauqua County. With Elisha on her shoulders, Nina walked with Angelo to the shore. She rested on a rock, praying in a Seneca dialect. A wavy image of a woman's face showed up on the water surface. "*Awe det hato kha gade.*"

Angelo widened his eyes. "What did she say?"

"She said she is happy to see me alive."

Nina put her hand on Angelo's shoulder. "*Hak kheja de* Angela [My granddaughter Angela]."

The woman in the water grinned and poked her lips out. "*Hoda swi yoh.*"

"She says you are lucky."

"Can she get out of the water?"

Jodasiya emerged from the water and kissed all of them. "*Sadog weta, hak ha wak*? [Are you well, my daughter?]"

Angelo gaped at her dry hair, crisp dress, and bare feet. "Yes, I am *ga dog weta* [I am well]."

She chuckled and kissed his nose. "I love you."

"You speak English?"

"I speak anything I want." She patted his head. "Take care of yourself and love your mom, sister, and grandma, my little girl. *Geniyewoh* [See you again]." She turned her back and dived into the water.

"I wish to see her more. She looks fabulous."

"You know now where she lives. You can come back and talk to her."

From Mayville, Angelo drove to New York. Nina, Anohitecha, and Amitola went to their homes. Angelo entered Leonardo's house, and Elisha slept on a couch. Bella stood in the kitchen to wash a frying pan, plates, and cutlery. Angelo whistled behind her. Her outer clothes disappeared, and she dropped a plate in the sink and shivered. He put his arms around her waist and kissed the top of her shoulder. "I like your floral underwear."

"Your hands are icy. What happened to your voice? Stop your nutty magic. Your dad will kill us if he sees you kissing me."

"Don't be afraid of anyone when I am with you. I locked the doors." He licked the back of her neck.

She smiled. "That is sweet and romantic." After

wiping her hands, she turned her face. "What are you doing?"

He held her up and kissed her pink lips. "I love you."

"I love you too. Where are my clothes?"

"Here they are." He put her on the breakfast bar and buried his fingers in her caramel hair. "I love you so much. Thanks, Bella, for everything you have done for me." He kissed her lips.

"You have never mentioned my name. You always called me mom. Why did you kiss me and touch me? Is there something wrong between you and Caitlyn?"

"No. I love you and want to thank you for the many wonderful things you have done for me."

"No need to thank me."

"How could you cope with the most dangerous Italian family?"

"Things have changed now. I love your dad. He is a decent man, and I am his true love. He had never cheated on me, despite his wealth and influence. But tell me. You have been bawdy with me this morning. Why?"

"Colestah told me the truth about you and me. You are not my biological mom."

She fingered his face and lips. "That's true, but please, don't say I am not your mom. I cared for you more than anyone else. I am your mother because you were in my womb for nine months, and I suckled you for over a year. Remember these facts. It will hurt me if you stop calling me mom. You are my child, even if Nina had donated her egg."

He kissed her hand. "Come and sit at the table. I

want you to tell me your story with Nina."

They sat at the dining table. Bella told him about her pregnancy and love affair with Nina. "Please, don't tell your dad what I have told you. He doesn't know about the affair, and he believes I am your biological mom."

"Let us have a cup of tea with Nina."

"OK. I will get my jacket."

Angelo called. "We want to see you now."

"That's great. I am ready to welcome you."

Bella, Angelo, and Elisha visited Nina in her house. Angelo kissed her, and Emma rested her head on her left shoulder. "Come on. Kiss her on the lips. No more secrets between us."

"You are naughty." Bella kissed Nina's lips.

Angelo embraced them. "I am the luckiest guy in the world."

Bella held Nina's hands. "Are you going to tell me the truth about our son, daughter?"

"What do you want to know?"

"How is Angelo so powerful?"

"Well, as Colestah said, there is a goddess with him. She grants him wisdom and gives him supernatural powers. Some people are tall and fat, and some are short and slim. Mother Nature has her own mind. She made Angelo who he is today. The main thing is the love we have for each other. I love you, though we need to talk about our affair."

Angelo heard a female voice in his ear asking him to go to the bathroom. "Excuse me. I need the toilet." He entered the bathroom and locked its door. "Our Holy Supreme Mother, please fix my body. I cannot live like this. I want to be me."

He heard a celestial voice asking him to roll down his pants and remove the adhesive tape and the eagle's eye. After removing them, his eyes stared at the eagle's eye. "I love you, aunt. But no more spying on me. I want to be free and do what I want without your surveillance. I am not a little girl." She threw it in the toilet bowl and flushed it. A sudden trembling reverberated through the bathroom, causing the floor beneath him to shake. The ceramic tiles rattled and cracked, filling the air with a horrific cacophony. The flickering lights overhead dimmed, casting eerie shadows that danced across the walls.

His heart raced, thumping in his chest like a trapped animal desperate for escape. Fear tightened its grip around him, weakening his muscles and nerves. He stumbled back, clutching the edge of the basin for support, as the walls seemed to close in on him. The darkness descended, consuming the room in an abyss of murky shadows. The only source of illumination came from the faint sunlight streaming through a small window.

As he stood there, bewildered and disoriented, a low, guttural moan pierced the silence. It emanated from somewhere in the bathroom, growing louder and more menacing with each passing second.

After taking a deep breath to suppress the tremors that wracked his body, he stepped inside the shower room, his hand shaking as he reached for the tap. The moment his fingers touched the tap, a chilling wind swept through the bathroom, extinguishing the feeble sunlight, and plunging the shaking room into profound darkness. The moaning grew louder, reverberating through his skull, as if the sound sought to shatter his sanity. Gritting his teeth, he turned the tap on. The shower door creaked closed, and total silence prevailed. Three minutes later, the lights came back on, and a tangerine-haired woman sat naked in the shower room.

Nina's concern grew as she placed her cup of tea on the dining table. The passage of time had become unnerving, and the bathroom door remained closed for over thirty minutes. She stood up from the dining chair and walked, her footsteps echoing in the otherwise quiet house. With each step toward the bathroom, her soul pounded with solicitude and growing anxiety. What could cause such a delay? Was Angelo in distress, or was there something more sinister lurking behind the closed door?

She knocked on the bathroom door. "Angelo, are you all right?"

"I am not Angelo."

"That's not your voice. Who are you?"

"I am nobody."

"What happened?"

"Leave me alone?"

"Open the door."

"Stay away from me."

"Please, open the door."

"Go away."

Nina rushed back to the kitchen and got a slotted screwdriver from a low drawer. Bella gazed at her. "What's wrong?"

"Angelo doesn't want to leave the bathroom."

Nina used the screwdriver and opened the door. She and Bella dashed into the bathroom and saw a naked woman sitting in the corner of the shower room, with her face between her knees. Nina turned off the showerhead, and Bella fetched a towel. "Oh, my God. Who are you? What did you do?"

"I am Angela. I did nothing."

"Who damaged the walls? Did you fall?"

"I don't know."

"What happened to your body and voice? How did you get this hair color?"

"This is the real me."

"Where are your clothes?"

"Gone. I feel cold. Cover me."

Bella covered Angela with the towel and took her out of the steamy bathroom. "I want to go out. Get me clothes."

Nina got her underwear, pants, and a floral blouse. "Where do you want to go?"

"I want to tell the world the truth. Why did you do this to me? Why?"

"Angelo, wait."

"I am not Angelo. I am not a boy. Don't you see? I am Angela." She put shoes on and held Elisha.

"Where are you taking the girl?"

"She is my daughter." She left the house.

Bella shed tears. "That was not our son. Who was that woman? When will you tell me the truth?"

"Angela is my granddaughter and your child, but with a new body. Don't worry. She will come back."

"I don't understand. Didn't you donate your own egg?"

"No. The egg was my granddaughter's. Three days ago, I met my daughter and her two girls. I want to be with them. So, our affair is over, as we knew it would be. You are my best friend, and I will always love you. Love Leonardo. He is a good man."

"Are you leaving me and your house?"

"No. My family lives here in Manhattan."

"That is good. Oh, my God! I recall Colestah, who said Angelo will become a woman at twenty-one. How did she know that?"

"She is a telepath."

Angela took a taxi and went to Leonardo's office on Wall Street. A secretary and a bodyguard stopped her.

"Get away from me. I want to see my dad."

"Please, wait here," the secretary said.

Angela waved her hand, and an invisible force tossed the secretary on a couch. The bodyguard pulled his gun and tried to interfere, but Angela warned him. "Stay where you are, or I will kick you out of the building."

She moved into Leonardo's office and closed the door. "Hi, dad. Surprise."

He gazed at her. "Who are you?"

"Don't you want to kiss your granddaughter?"

He kissed Elisha. "Answer me. Who are you?"

"Do you remember my intersexual body? A miracle happened an hour ago and made me a real woman. I am now your daughter, Angela."

"How do you want me to believe you?"

She gave him a passport and a driving license. "Do

you believe me now?"

"Gosh! I believe you. Who changed your body?"

"I am a divine person of miracles. You remember how I defended grandpa in the restaurant and stopped a bus. My goddess has changed my body."

"What do you want me to tell the family?"

"Nothing much. Throw a party in the house and tell the family I have become a woman, and, so, you have a daughter." She looked around. "I don't like this design. What about this new one?" She waved her hands, and Leonardo found himself in an elegant office.

He rested his face on his hands. "I don't know what to say."

"Remember, your dad asked you not to defy me, and you said you won't prevent me from doing the things I love. You will lose nothing, and we won't tell the media about our family affairs. What happens between us will remain in the family. Don't say a word about me before I see you in the morning."

In the morning, she visited him and gave him two air tickets. "These are for you and mom. I will see you in St. Lucia. Don't tell the family about it."

Forty days later, Caitlyn arrived at the airport and saw Angela holding her daughter. "Excuse me. Who are you?"

"Hello, Cat Hen. I am your sweetheart. I am a real woman now. You wished me to be a woman. Do you like my new body and hair?"

"You are stunning. How could you do all that in three months?"

"I used my magic."

"What should I call you?"

"Call me Angela. It is now my official name. Here is my new passport."

"What about your parents?"

"I told them about my transitioning, and we have reached a deal. My parents are empathetic."

"That's good."

Angela played romantic music and made love to her every day. "Did you miss me so much? What is going on? You have been horny in the last week."

"I love you and want you to be with me forever. I am the happiest woman in the world."

"Great. Have fun."

Later, Caitlyn entered the study room on the first floor and noticed a printed manuscript entitled "The Lesbian." She sank into a cushioned chair and read sections of the script. Angela came into the room. "What is this document?"

"It is the manuscript of my new book."

"What about the title?"

"I want to tell people about my lesbian feelings and desires."

"Ha-ha! I have been happy and silent about the transformation of your body because I enjoy it. What happened to your penis?"

"I got rid of it."

"Do you know what this script means?"

"Yeah, I know. I am not afraid of anything."

"Be mindful. Your dad is a famous magnate and the godfather of your family. Are you going to publish it?"

"Yes. It will be out next month."

“I want a signed copy. Make it a movie.”
“I will.”

Chapter 3

Elisha had a unique upbringing, with a significant part of her childhood and adolescence spent with Angela. During that time, her active mother occupied herself with pursuing her doctorate and engaging in research work, as well as acting in films in remote regions. To her, Angela was the sole confidante, the teacher, the entertainer, the mentor, the banker, the chef, the guardian. At sixteen, she took her to Byblos Downtown restaurant after winning a teen modeling competition. "Mom, I want to devote my heart and energy to modeling, fashion, and beauty business. I don't have a sophisticated mind like yours. It's no good that I spend four years studying something I do not love. It would be a waste of time."

"OK, honey. Do what you like. The best life is the one

you love. Your future comes first from you. Do not feel shy to tell me anything. I will sponsor what you do and attend your shows."

Thanks to her elegance and Angela's support, Elisha became the youngest successful model in Canada. One sweltering day, she wore a short skirt and a cropped T-shirt and went out with Angela for a perky walk in High Park. After a while, they sat on a bench and drank orange juice. Elisha gave her a quick kiss on the face and held her hand. "Mom, I want to tell you a big secret?"

"What is it, sweetheart?"

"I am a lesbian like you. What do you think?"

"Wonderful. That is so great, love. You have my full support."

"How can I tell friends and the media about my lesbian sexuality?"

"Confidence and positiveness are powerful tools for living a fulfilling and authentic life. It is important to embrace who you are and do what you love and not let the fear of judgment or what others might say hold you back. This is your life. Enjoy it to the full. Do you have a girlfriend?"

"No. Can I sit on your lap and give you a kiss?"

"Of course. I am the one who loves you."

She sat on her knees and flung her arms around her neck, resting her lips on her mouth. "I love you. You are the most awesome mom in the world. Please, do not tell the quirky mom about what I say to you. Keep the lesbian thing a secret between you and me."

"OK, honey."

She embraced her and closed her eyes, and Angela's hands rested on her thighs. Two days later, they and Caitlyn spent five hours on Woodbine Beach, snacking, drinking, and playing volleyball and badminton. Before sunset, Elisha vaulted on Angela's upper back, hurting her neck. "Sorry, mom. I didn't mean it."

"No problem. That is why daughters have moms. Do you feel hungry?"

"Yeah."

"OK. Let's go home and have dinner. I feel tired."

On the way home, Caitlyn stopped the car at a supermarket to get food and magazines. After dinner, Elisha got a lotion bottle to relieve muscular spasms. "Go to bed. I want to massage your neck after I change my clothes."

Angela lay topless on a bed. Elisha, sporting French panties and a strapless bra, squatted on her buttocks and rubbed her back and neck with the medical ointment. She tickled her inverted waist and armpits with a frivolous spirit and caressed her. When she chuckled, she hugged her and kissed her ear.

Angela put on a loose shirt and entered the family room, seeking a kiss from Caitlyn, but she swung her face away.

"Are you OK? You ate a little."

"I do not feel well."

"Your nose and eyes are red." Her fingers touched her forehead. "You are hot. Maybe you got flu or a bug from the beach. Go up to the bedroom and have some rest. I will tidy up the kitchen and watch a movie." After cleaning the kitchen, she and Elisha made popcorn and sat beside each other in the home cinema to watch a lesbian movie.

The next day, Angela stretched her arms to embrace Caitlyn in the bathroom, but she urged her to stay away from her. "Don't touch me. I do not want you to get an infection."

"Are you infected with a virus? Do you need lemon juice with raw honey or medicine?"

"No. I want to be alone."

Angela wished to slumber with her in their bedroom, but Caitlyn asked her to sleep in another room. She pulled a coverlet out of a storage room and dozed on a couch bed in the living room. At the stroke of three o'clock, silence draped the house, broken only by the soft sound of Elisha's footsteps as she tiptoed out of her room. She reached the kitchen and filled a glass with water from the faucet. As she turned back, her ears caught a peculiar mumbling sound drifting from the direction of the living room. She entered the room with cautious steps, mindful of the creaking floorboards that threatened to betray her presence. She saw Angela sleeping topless with her left hand on the right breast. Angela opened her eyes when she sensed her presence. "Hi, darling. What is the time?"

"Three o'clock. Why are you here?"

"Your mom is not feeling well."

"What's wrong with her? She talked a little in the last couple of days."

"I do not know. She said she caught a virus."

"Can I sleep with you?"

"Yeah. Come in." She shifted her body backward,

and Elisha glided under the cover and hugged her.

Caitlyn woke up at seven and saw her daughter's left arm on Angela's bare breasts and left leg on her naked belly and thighs. She shambled to the kitchen and made a cup of green tea. Angela came in fifteen minutes later and wanted to kiss her, but she moved away from her. "Darling, what is going on? Why don't you want me to kiss you or talk to you? Did I do something wrong?"

She frowned as she tried to sip her tea. "She is sixteen, for God's sake."

"Who? Elisha?"

"Yeah, who else? What is going on between her and you? Why was she with you in bed?"

"She is our girl. I do not understand what you mean."

She opened a drawer and picked up a magazine. "What did you do with Elisha?"

"Can you explain?"

She opened the magazine. "Look at these photos. Why did Elisha sit on your knees in High Park and kiss your lips? Your hands were under her skirt? Did you touch her underwear?"

"Who took these photos? I will sue the magazine."

"Forget that. What happened between Elisha and you?"

"I don't remember."

"How don't you remember? Elisha is a celebrity, and the paparazzi follow her. Why did you allow her to sit on your lap and kiss your lips in public?"

"She is my daughter. Do you spy on me?"

"I became suspicious of your behavior after you bathed her last week."

"What's wrong with that?"

"Do you think it is acceptable to touch and see your daughter's naked body?"

"We are women. I bathed her all her life. I am not a stranger."

"What about the other day when she rubbed her nipples on your back and kissed your neck?"

"I am flummoxed by what you say." She twiddled with her hair. "Oh, my God. Do you think I had sex with our daughter?"

"Why does she grope and kiss you? Why?"

"Ask her. I am not a psychologist."

"But you are the father, the mother. I don't know what to call you."

"There is nothing erotic between us. Elisha told me a secret five days ago and became jolly after I said I would give her my support. I think she is perky with me because I do many good things with her. Her behavior is natural."

"What is the secret? I want to know."

"I promised not to talk about it."

"OK. I will ask her."

"Come here. She told me she is a lesbian like us."

"Huh, like mother like daughter. Why didn't she tell me? How is she a lesbian?"

"I am not an expert in her sex and sexuality. We are lesbians, and maybe she loves a girlfriend. Why don't you talk to her? When was the last time you asked her about her personal life?"

"I have been busy looking for a better job."

"Don't worry about finding a job. You can work with

my mom, and I can give you as much money as you want. I hope you spend more time with Elisha. Give her hugs and kisses and take her out so she can feel you love her."

"Yeah, I am sorry. You are right. I feel guilty for not spending enough time with her."

Elisha left the living room and had breakfast. Caitlyn came to her. "We want to go to Vancouver for six days. We need private time for ourselves. Can you stay alone?"

"Yeah, no problem."

In search of a fresh start, Angela and Caitlyn boarded a plane bound for Vancouver Island, a picturesque haven for breathtaking landscapes and tranquil seclusion. The journey reflected their shared resolve to rejuvenate their relationship. A day later, Elisha entered the home office and checked out books on a shelf. Angela's book, *The Lesbian*, had captured her eyes. She opened it, glanced at the dedication page, and read, "For Caitlyn, with immense love and respect." After taking the book to her bedroom, she flumped down on the bed and pored over Angela's passion for lesbian romance and sexuality. She massaged her body after picking up steamy photos of Angela. She pondered over Angela's thought of lesbian love and wondered how she grew up in a lesbian household. Her curiosity moved her back to the office to go through the private files and albums of her mothers.

Angela and Caitlyn came back with joyful faces. Elisha wanted to explore her sexual attraction to Angela and her lesbian fantasies. So, under the guise of fashion and modeling, she sat on her knees, asking her to comment on her sexy clothes. "What about this black lingerie?" "Do you like this sequin miniskirt?" "Should I wear this shelf bra?" "Do you want me to try on this string bikini?" Angela responded with playful humor and loved to run her fingers over Elisha's body.

One night, Elisha painted her lips pink berry and wore a black bodycon crisscross dress. After getting a glass of red wine, she entered the home office and found Angela focusing on a computer monitor. "Are you OK?"

"Yes, I am fine. I have been thinking of a new chapter for my book."

"What is it about?"

"It chronicles the story of an unwed professor desiring to teach her adolescent daughter about love and relationships."

She grinned with her white teeth. "Nice. I think I have an idea. What about we pretend you are a single professor, and I am your stupid daughter? What do you think?"

She laughed. "That's a fantastic idea, though you are not stupid."

"OK, sexy genius professor, tell me about love and romance."

"Not like that."

She waggled on her bare knees and played with her lips. "Oh, not like that, *signorina*." She tittered with a voluptuous smile. "OK. Suppose I am a foolish girl, and you, Professor of Romance, want to teach me about love. Put your hand under my armpit and say love is a sexy bond between two turned-on babes. I read your book, *The Lesbian*, when you were in Vancouver. Why did you write it?"

"Because of personal circumstances. I love being a lesbian for emotional and psychological reasons?"

"What do you mean by that?"

"I mean, my lesbianism is a choice, not genetic."

"What about that thing between your legs?" She moved her hand down to her crotch. "You have a beautiful, shaved vagina."

"I don't shave."

She put a hand on her mouth. "How?" Her arms encircled her neck.

"There is no hair on my body except my head."

"Can I touch your vagina?"

"Behave. Not now."

"So, how did you make my mom pregnant?"

"I had a penis before I became a woman."

"Amazing."

"What do you think of my book?"

"Lovely. Lesbians and trans folks should read it. You understand how lesbians feel about their sex and emotions."

"There is a pretty woman in me."

Elisha cackled. "Where? Here? Here? Here?" She tickled her waist and made her chuckle.

"Stop it. Be serious."

The tip of her tongue licked her lips. "Be serious, be serious. Are you talking to me? Look at me. We crazy Italians can shoot you in the head. What are ya gonna do?" After putting her forefinger in the wine, she sucked it deep in her mouth and kissed Angela's painted lips with her hand squeezing her left breast. Caitlyn came in and saw the sensual kiss. "For God's sake. What are you both doing here? Enough." She grabbed Elisha's forearm. "When will you ever stop behaving like a spoiled brat?"

"Why do you hate me? Can't I have fun with my mom?"

"This is not fun, and you know it. Why are you wearing this dress in the house?"

"Do you want me to be naked?"

"Gosh! I didn't mean that. Why don't you get a girlfriend if you want sex?"

"She has distracted me. Take her away and put her in a cage."

Elisha stuck out her tongue at Caitlyn and kicked a willow basket before leaving the office and slamming the door.

"Darling, be kind and patient with her. We are her only family in Canada. She is a model and likes to show off her stunning body and clothes. You need to tell her she is gorgeous, and her clothes are super cool."

"Why do you allow her to kiss you and touch you? What happened to you? You promised me to stop seducing her."

"I didn't seduce her. She came in and sat on my knees. I will do nothing to hurt her, and I will never break her heart. She has no brother or sister, and we need to educate her about sex."

"I know what she wants. She wants sex with you."

"And do you think I want sex with her? Come on,

honey. Do not be harsh on her. We love her, don't we?"

"Whatever. I had enough of her lewd behavior. And what about you? Do you think incest with a sixteen-year-old girl is OK?"

"What incest? Calm down. You are my love. Our daughter behaves in a certain way, maybe because she has bipolar disorder or autism. Do you remember when she said she is the sexiest model in Canada? It is natural for someone who loves fashion and follows glamorous lifestyles to feel jealous when seeing models at celebrity parties or traveling to attractive tropical places. We shower together and walk naked in the house, and Elisha may want to imitate us or prove she is stunning. She needs attention and entertainment. When was the last time we traveled together as a family? So, what about we stop working on the weekend? We should travel or go out to cinemas and concerts."

Caitlyn subdued her ire when Elisha cuddled and kissed Angela's lips. "I don't know how to stop her erotic behavior with Angela, who can't restrain herself. We need to sort out her loneliness and social isolation. I wish to know why she doesn't use her beauty and promising career to attract friends," she wrote in her journal. However, after celebrating Elisha's eighteenth birthday, she took her to Alaska, hoping that a change of environment and dedicated time together would provide a space for bonding, open communication, and resolving problems. Four days later, Elisha abandoned her and returned to Toronto. When Angela opened the house door for her, she pushed her back against a wall and kissed her lips and face with her hand between her thighs. Angela did not chide her.

"Honey, stop it. Wait a minute. Why are you back? You planned to spend two weeks in Alaska."

"I missed you so much. There is nothing in Alaska but freaking mountains and boring lakes."

"OK. Let us have dinner. I made spaghetti with spinach and sundried tomatoes."

Elisha sat on a chair, touching Angela's feet with her toes, and flirting with her, saying nothing. After eating and cleaning the kitchen, Angela stood under the shower singing Tracy Chapman's "Baby Can I Hold You." When she put shampoo on her hair, and clouds of steam filled the bathroom, two hands caressed her breasts, and a kiss descended on the middle of her back. "Love, are you also back?" There was no answer. After rinsing the shampoo out of her hair, she turned his face and wavered when she saw Elisha standing naked. "Honey, why are you here?" She covered herself with a bathrobe and left the shower room. Her body shivered when she sat on a kitchen chair.

Elisha wrapped herself with a towel and rested on her knees, despite her obvious uneasiness.

"Sweetheart, what happened to you?"

"I love you." She opened her robe and put her right hand on her breast. "Is this a taboo or a problem?"

"I love you too. I am your mother, and my love for you is not about sex. You told me you are a lesbian. There are sexy lesbians and models like you. Why don't you get a girlfriend?"

"I don't need to look for a girlfriend because you are my only girlfriend." She uncovered Angela's shoulder and licked the side of her neck.

"Honey, you cannot do that."

"Do what?"

"You know what I mean."

"Who are you, Angela? Who are you?"

Angela gazed at her with sparkly eyes. "What is this silly question? I am your mom."

"I don't believe your claptrap, and I have never believed your stupid lies."

"Am I a liar? I swear I have never lied to you."

"I had a fight with my lunatic mom. I hate her."

"Why?"

"Because of you."

"What did I do this time?"

"Is it true?"

"What is it?"

She buried her fingers in her dripping hair and cried. Angela glanced at her eyes and wept. "Honey, your tears break my heart. I love you. What do you want to tell me?"

"Who is my dad? Tell me the truth. Who is my dad? Did you adopt me when I was a baby?"

Her fingers wiped her face. "I was your dad."

"Stop lying. I am not a jerk. You said you became a woman and your penis disappeared. Who believes this crap?"

"That's what happened. I do not lie."

"I wanted to have sex with you in the last two or three years because I had never believed you were my father. Only a stupid fool would say you were my dad. You look like a fantasy woman, and I have fair skin, blonde hair, and blue eyes. When I confronted my mom in Alaska, she said you were not my dad."

"What? This is untrue. Your mom and I made love for a couple of weeks in Vancouver and here, and she became pregnant."

"How did she become pregnant without your dick?"

"I had a penis when we made love."

"Oh yeah, and your penis became a vagina, and your dark hair became orange, just like that. How did you make my mom pregnant when you didn't have male testicles?"

Angela turned her face to the left. "Testicles? What testicles?"

"Normal men have testicles. Don't you know that? My mom touched all your body, and she didn't see any testicles. Have you ever gotten an erection and seen your semen? Have you ever masturbated?"

Angela lowered her lips. "My vagina gets orgasm. I touch my vagina."

"Your vagina? Your vagina won't make a woman pregnant. How did your penis disappear? How did you make love to my mom without the testicles?"

"I don't know. A supernatural event happened to me and removed my penis."

"Are you an alien now? Why do I have blue eyes and blonde hair? You have orange hair and honey eyes, and you don't look like your dad or mom. Why am I called Elisha McManus if I am your daughter? My mom told me how you met her for the first time when she sat crying in High Park. Did she tell you why she cried?"

"No. I thought she cried because she missed her Irish

family. You have your mom's family name because I oppose social patriarchy and men's control. Your mom suffered from pregnancy, not me. I am surprised. Your mom had never said I was not your dad. What you have said has bewildered me. Did she have sex with another man?"

"I don't care." She dropped her towel on the floor and rested her arms on her shoulders. Angela closed her eyes and turned her face to the right. "Look at me. Tell me the truth and nothing but the truth. I touched you and kissed your lips a hundred times in the last two years, and you said nothing. Why didn't you stop me? Why didn't you scold me for caressing you?"

"Because my feelings and sensuality are not like your mom's and yours, and I foresee the future."

"What future?"

"I expected what happened between you and me, and my spirit told me about your love for me."

"Which spirit?"

"It is like an intuition. What happened between you and your mom has not surprised me. I am aware of your mother's miserable background and mental problems. My love for you is real."

"I will not let my mom stop me from loving you. You are a lesbian, and I am a lesbian. Please, don't break my heart, or I will kill myself. I need you. Come to my bed. I want you to touch every cell in my body and make me happy."

Angela and Elisha made love that day. Four days later, Caitlyn slinked into the house at six o'clock in the morning. After taking off her shoes, she peeked into her bedroom door and saw Elisha half-naked and sleeping next to Angela. She sighed and went downstairs to the kitchen.

Angela woke up an hour later and greeted her. "Hi, darling. When did you come back?"

She slapped her face. "You are a bitch and a piece of shit." A gust of frigid wind clattered the windows, causing her to shiver. Her natural instincts screamed at her to flee, to find safety before it was too late. She darted toward the back door, her heart pounding. The floor creaked beneath her hurried footsteps, amplifying the fear that gripped her. As she reached the door, her trembling hands fumbled with the lock, and before she could run outside, a powerful hand clamped around her upper neck, cutting off her breath and lifting her off the ground. The grip was strong and merciless. Her eyes widened with terror as she looked up, desperate to see the face of her assailant. A hooded woman stood before her; her features hidden in the shadows.

Caitlyn's body tensed, the acute pain in her neck intensifying. She tried to scream, but only choking gasps escaped her constricted throat. "Angela, help me. Please, help me. I am sorry."

"Ami, leave her. I am fine." She dropped Caitlyn on the floor and vanished.

Angela rubbed her tingling cheek with sad eyes. "That hurt. Why did you hit me?"

"Who was that creepy woman? How do you know her name?"

"That is not important. Why did you abuse me? What did I do?"

"How did that woman enter our house? Who is she?"

"She is my invisible bodyguard. Don't hit me again."

"You have made me angry. Did you have sex with my daughter?"

"Let us sit and talk." She tried to hold her hand.

She winced away. "Are you a stupid jerk? I am your girlfriend, and you have sex with my girl? Are you a psychopath? You can't sleep naked with my daughter. Moron."

"Why not?" Elisha interrupted.

Caitlyn stared at her seamless panties and demi bra. "Shut your mouth."

"Go to hell."

"Shut up, whore." Caitlyn threw a water glass at her. Elisha lowered her head, and the glass hit the edge of a door and smashed. "I will kill you."

"Kill yourself, stupid woman."

"Caitlyn, for God's sake, you could have killed her. What is going on between you and her? Calm down. Stay here. I will talk to her."

"Idiot. It is about you and her. Make love to any woman you like, but not my daughter. I am your girlfriend, dope."

With a loose garment on her shoulders, Elisha came back and threw photos on the breakfast bar. "What is this, mom? Your deception and lies are over. Don't you ever lecture me about sex and adultery. I know you have an affair with Danielle."

Caitlyn's face reddened. Angela peeped at the erotic photos, and Caitlyn tried to cover them with her hands. "Dammit. Yes, I have a casual affair with Danielle. She is a model like me. Who took these private photos? How did you get them? Were you spying on me?"

Elisha rested her fingers on her waist. "Do you want to give us a sermon on infidelity? Why didn't you tell us about the affair? I have been watching you for the last five years. You lied about your research work and acting to travel with Danielle and have sex with her. That's why I love Angela. At least I have sex with the woman both of us know and love. Why didn't you tell us about Danielle?"

"Did Danielle give you the photos?"

"No. Leah installed cameras in her mom's house and followed you. She told me about the affair. Shame on you."

She inclined her head and settled in a chair. "Please, please, listen and try to understand what I want to say. A perp murdered my dad, and my mom died of cancer when I was a girl. A rapist raped me in a store in New York. So, I hated men. Yes, men are Satan's fecking bastards and a bunch of sociopaths. I came to Canada after the rape to forget the distress and needed a woman to love and comfort me. Danielle's uncle and brother raped her when she was a girl. We spend time together to ease the trauma of abuse and sexual assault. Yes, I have a love affair with her. But I do not love anybody more than this lousy woman, though her family killed my brothers, uncles, and grandparents. Yes, in the beginning, I wheedled Angela because she is a tycoon's daughter. But I loved her after you were born. I also wanted the Italians and the Irish to stop their stupid Mafia war. I am a lesbian, and Angela has a feminine heart and a seductive body. Have sex with any girl you like, but not with Angela. Angela is mine and will always be mine. She is a true caring woman.”

“So, who is my dad?”

“The rapist. He was a white man.”

“Where is he?”

“He is dead. A hefty man killed him in the store and rescued me.”

“Who is this man?”

“I do not know him. He covered his face before he shot the rapist in the head and smashed his face on a glass counter. I was too upset to look at his face. He uses a fake name, and I think he is a rich man from England. When I told him my name, and I am a poor Irish girl, he gave me twenty thousand dollars and asked me to live in Toronto. He sent me printed letters, and I sent him a card every two or three months to thank him for paying for my studies. I wish to know him.”

Angela coiled her hair up in a knot and fastened it with a claw clip. “Where did you send the cards?”

“To England.”

“Oh, dear. Why didn’t you tell me about the rape and the money you got from this man? I thought you earned extra money from films, modeling, and magazines.”

Caitlyn gazed at her daughter. “Listen to me. You cannot have a sexual relationship with Angela. Our families and the world know she is your mom. Suppose a guy blabbed your affair. People will vilify both of you and investigate your identity, and the Luccianos will bury you alive. Angela’s dad is the godfather of the Italians in New York, and his crazy people will crucify you on a tree to protect their family's reputation. Can you have a decent future if people know you are a rapist's daughter?"

Elisha grabbed Angela's arm. "It is too late now, and I don't care. I love Angela and want to be with her."

"Angela, say something. Sorry for hitting you, but I have been your partner for nineteen years. Even if Elisha is not your child, you cannot cheat on me. Or do you love Elisha more than me? Let us sort out this mess and start a new beginning."

"I do not know what to say. I love both of you."

"What happened to you? Don't you know what to say to the girlfriend who loves you? Yeah, Elisha is younger and sexier than her mom."

"Not that."

"Shut up. I will never forgive you for having sex with my daughter. You are lucky you are still alive." She seethed, her voice dripping with rage. "I wanted to kill you because your psycho family killed my brother before my eyes and threw his body in a river. I was too frightened to tell the FBI about your cousins who gave me money and asked me to keep my mouth shut. You had not taken part in killing, but you carry the blood of your evil family that stained my life." Her memories of her family, fraught with darkness and secrets, flooded her thoughts. She had tried to escape her painful past, to start anew, but the affair between Angela and Elisha had demolished her dreams.

"What can I do for you?"

"Nothing. I am not even sure you are a human. How did you become a woman without surgery? How did you get orange hair? Who are those scary fighters who stand around the bed when you sleep?" She tried to touch Elisha. "You are my daughter, though you remind me of the rapist. I am leaving Canada. I got an excellent job in New York. Come and live with me. I know models there."

"No. I am staying with Angela."

Chapter 4

Caitlyn left Canada, and Elisha enjoyed her free love with Angela, but not for long. She departed from Toronto after signing a permanent, full-time contract with a modeling agency in New York City. Thanks to Bella and her associates who provided the job.

One day, Angela traveled to Chautauqua Lake to see Jodasiya and learn from her wisdom. She parked the car at the end of Elmwood Road in Mayville and descended eight steps to the lake water. "Mom, Mom."

Jodasiya came out of the water and kissed her on the lips. "Yes, love. How are you doing?"

"I miss you and wish to know you better. My family didn't tell me much about you."

She sat on a dry lawn under a tree overlooking Hartfield Bay. "Sit, my love." She sat beside her like a humble disciple, and Jodasiya held her hand. "I was a formidable woman and the Iroquois people's leader before they split into six tribes. I built the first bridge over the Niagara River and adopted a white dog. The people on the north side of the river asked me to kill and cook the dog. I refused. So, they destroyed the bridge. I felt sad and moved south. The people in this land built a reed boat for me. I traveled by their boat to the north until I reached Lake Ontario. There were cocksure and hairy men on canoes following my boat. Some wanted me to travel to the Sacred Stream, now called the St. Lawrence River. Others wanted me to return to my people. So, the two groups fought each other and sank the boat. My dog and I drowned, and the fighting men searched for us and found nothing but fish and pipeworts. Your sister was with her mammal animals in a place near what now you call Quebec City. She saved me and made me an eternal spirit. She was like my mother or big sister. The indigenous tribes in this land are my direct offspring. I live in a mansion at the bottom of this lake."

"How do you breathe in the water? What do you eat and drink?"

"I said I am a spirit, and I do not eat your food and breathe your air to live."

"What happened to your dog?"

"He is alive and well." She cast a pebble in the water. "Chikasota." A white wolf dog appeared out of the water and licked Angela's hands.

Angela's hands rubbed the dog's furry back. "He is adorable and lovable."

"Now, tell me. What happened between you and your girlfriend? Why did she leave you?"

Angela gazed at her broad face and square jaw. "How do you know that?"

"A fragment of my spirit lives in you. Did you love your girlfriend?"

"Yes. Caitlyn was my love and soul."

"No human woman would love you more than her. Someday, she will be back with you. But now, education is your way to the future. It will train your mind to think and appreciate what you have. Be free from the shackles of men's world, and the universe will talk to you. Live with your wishes, but, please, love, a sexual relationship with Elisha is not good for you or her. One day, the Mother of the Goddesses will purify you from the human elements and make you a full goddess, as you were in the sky, but we do not know when she will do that. May the kind blessings of our supreme goddesses be with you. Go back to your home. I love you." She kissed her and dived with her dog into the lake.

Following Jodasiya's advice, Angela signed up for a course on ancient Egypt in the Department of Near and Middle Eastern Civilizations at the University of Toronto. When the first evening lecture ended, a slim, brunette woman with upturned eyes came to her and shook her hand. "*Bonjour*. How are you? I guess we are the oldest *peuple* in *la classe*."

"Maybe, mademoiselle. You are perceptive."

"My name is Camille Labonte."

"I am Angela."

"Angela? Nice name. Are you *Espagnol*?"

"No way. I am *un misterioso Italoamericano*." She chuckled. "I am an Italian American from New York City."

"You like Egypt?"

"Who doesn't like Egypt and the pyramids?"

"Your long ginger hair is beautiful."

"Thank you. My hair color is natural."

"Nice meeting you. *Au revoir*."

"*Au* so long, Jane." She grinned with a sly smile and flapped her hand.

Hintocha appeared. "Who was that?"

"One of God's bewitching nymphs."

When the second lecture finished the following week, Camille stood beside her. "*Bonsoir*. Do you like a *tasse* of tea?"

"A taste of tea? Yup, I do."

As they strolled to a coffee shop on College Street, a feeling of familiarity lingered between them. Their lips were half-closed, creating an atmosphere of comfort and mystery, as if they shared a silent understanding with no words. In the shop's warm ambiance, Camille asked for herbal tea, and Angela ordered a cappuccino. They settled into a cozy corner near a window.

"I am from France, from Bordeaux."

"I recognized that because of your accent."

"Do you speak *Français*?"

"No. I am not lucky."

"What do you do in Canada?"

"I live here and write books. What about you?"

"I came a month ago, and I like *photographie* and

traveling. Do you have a *famille* here?"

"No. I am alone. Freedom."

She smiled. "Where do you live?"

"In a house in a neighborhood called Roncesvalles. Where do you stay?"

"I stay in a hostel in Kensington Market."

"Do you have a car?"

"No. I use the bus."

"I have a car. I will pick you up next time." Angela opened her wallet and gave her a business card. "Send me a text about your address."

"Oh, *merci.* You are perfect."

After leaving the coffee shop, Angela asked for a taxi to take Camille to her place and gave the driver thirty dollars.

Hintocha appeared. "Are you thinking of a new romance? I saw your eyes staring at her hair and hands. Do you like her?"

"It is too early to tell. I think Camille is a lovely girl. I like her shag hair, and her green eyes are magical."

"What about Elisha?"

"She makes things more complicated. The world thinks she is my daughter."

After the third lecture, Angela took Camille to her house and made spaghetti carbonara and frittata with pesto and red peppers. After eating, drinking wine, and tattling, she touched Camille's hand. "I have an empty guest room. Stay with me for free."

"Oh, you are *généreuse.* When can I come?"

"What about tomorrow afternoon?"

"That is super. I am happy. *Merci beaucoup.*" She

gave her two kisses.

Camille moved to a room on the second floor, and Angela treated her as a nonchalant friend. Sex was not their precedence, and Camille expressed no interest in physical intimacy, preferring to improve her spoken English.

One midnight, Angela lay in her bed. Hintocha held her hand. "I am not sure about her. She brags about France and French things. It will be difficult for you to please her."

"Why do you say that? Are you jealous of her?"

"Shut up. How do you think a goddess envies a woman? She prattles like the kooky psychologists who speak jargon, and her jokes are irritating. What did she mean by the psychic self and the ego of consciousness? What is this mumbo jumbo?"

"She went to school, not like you."

"Do you mean I am a bonehead?"

"No. I mean, you did not go to school."

"Goddesses do not need schools and books. Schools make people's shallow minds like robotic machines. I am a free spirit."

"How are you free, and you are like a genie?"

"I am free because nothing controls my spirit, and nobody tells me what to wear and what to do."

"I like your pink lipstick and Abenaki dress. Did you like my pasta carbonara?"

"I do not eat your yucky worms. Ugh."

"I do not eat worms, crazy girl."

"Crazy girl? I can blow up your ass. Oh, honey, I wish you know how much I love you."

"I love you, sweetheart. You are my best friend. You know my life in this insane world. I should have stayed in the sky and enjoyed the peace. If the people know the earth's insignificant size in the universe, they won't hate and fight each other. But what can I say about myself and my life? Sometimes, I feel alone and frustrated."

"Why, love? I am with you."

"When will your mom make you free?"

"I do not know. She is unpredictable."

"Why did she make you a child and locked you up inside me?"

"I caused a Great Lakes blizzard because of the high rate of rape and crimes against women. That was five months after you were born. I thought it would be fair to freeze the criminals. But my mom got angry because twenty-nine people died."

"How did your mom put you inside me?"

"She deprived me of my powers and pushed me through your chest when you slept in your dad's house. That is when you started talking. After that, I taught you ten words every day."

"I wish to do wild things with you."

"We will do that when my mom forgives me or when you are in extreme danger. If people hurt you, horrible things will happen."

"Like what?"

"Like chopping off men's heads and blowing up towns and cities. So, stay out of trouble. Enough talking. Take off your clothes and close your eyes. I want to make love to you."

After getting naked and closing her sleepy eyes, Hintocha made love to her. Angela grasped the white linen bedsheet and blared after achieving an orgasm. "Breathe deep and sleep. I love you."

"I love you too. Good night."

At five, Angela jumped off her bed. Hintocha opened her eyes. "What happened?"

"I had a dreadful dream. I need to breathe fresh air and think." She padded naked into the bathroom and washed her face. Serenity overwhelmed the house for an hour before she got dressed and called Bella. "Mom, don't go out today. Please."

"Good morning. What is the time now?"

"It is six o'clock."

"What's the matter with you?"

"I had a terrible dream about you. Please, mom, stay at home."

"Today is our anniversary. Your dad and I will go out in the evening for a memorable party."

"Please, mom, listen to me. Have the party at home. Don't go out."

"Why are you worried? Do not overreact. Your dad's family will be with us. We will be OK."

"I beg you, mom. Please, trust me. There will be a crime against you. You know I see the future."

"Honey, calm down. Your father and I want to have fun and enjoy our day. Manhattan is safe. Do not brood over your fears and concerns. I will ask your dad to get his bodyguards."

"Where is my dad?"

"In New Jersey. He will be back after two or three

hours. Again, don't panic. We will be fine. Have a lovely day and take care."

Angela switched on the TV and sat in the living room watching the news. In the evening, Camille asked her to dine with her at a restaurant. "I can't go out. I want to stay here."

"You spent the day watching the *télévision*, and you ate a little food. Why?"

"My heart is pounding fast like a car engine, and my inner eyes see what others cannot see. It is like the spirit that feels every soul that floats in the world."

"You are very *mystérieux*. I hear you speak to a girlfriend and laugh in the middle of the night. You always say, 'Good night. I love you too' before you sleep. What better can I say now? I will go to the kitchen and cook dinner."

"Thanks, honey, and sorry for not helping you. I am upset today." Eleven minutes later, she leaped off the couch like a wildcat and embraced the wide wall mounted TV, sniveling and whimpering like a hungry baby. "Mamma, papa. Mom, dad."

Camille heard her cries and jogged into the room with a kitchen towel in her hand. She placed her hand on her shoulder. "Why are you sad and crying? What happened?"

"Criminals have killed my mom and dad."

"Oh no, I am sorry. How?"

"I do not know. Please, I want to listen to the news."

Dressed in a suit and clutching a microphone, a female reporter stood amid a throng of onlookers, her gaze fixed upon a cordoned-off Italian restaurant on

Fifth Avenue. Police officers, their expressions tight-lipped, formed a barrier around the restaurant, keeping the crowd at bay.

The reporter adjusted her microphone, preparing to go live. As her camera operator gave her the signal, she took a deep breath. "Good evening, everyone. This is Liz Thompson reporting live from Fifth Avenue. New York City is bemoaning the tragic loss of Leonardo and Bella Lucciano. This is a somber day for their families and the Italian community. Leonardo was an outstanding and prosperous Italian leader in the city and New Jersey. He was the eldest son of Sandro Lucciano, who unified the southern Italian clans and vanquished the Irish mob in Hell's Kitchen. We do not know if the gruesome atrocity relates to a Mafia-style crime."

Angela stood. "I am going to the airport. I must go to New York to see the family. Stay in the house and look after yourself."

"I will come with you to the airport."

"Thanks." Angela entered her bedroom and got clothes, a passport, and a wallet. "Hintocha, why didn't your mom stop the killing?"

"Sorry, love, but Leonardo and Bella are not of our creation. Their God should have done something for them, but He doesn't care."

"And what about our chicken goddesses? Why didn't they defend our people when the Europeans massacred them and looted their lands?"

"Our goddesses do not control the gods who didn't want to fight God and His evil warriors and obedient angels. My mom has a plan for all of us. I wonder why your grandma didn't protect her best friends. Please, be patient for a while."

"OK. Stay here to protect Camille." Angela locked her office and called her cousins. She gave Camille five hundred dollars at the airport, and she gave her a hug and two kisses. Two dozen Italian relatives welcomed her at JFK International Airport and exchanged tearful condolences. They moved to their house in Brooklyn.

Marco puffed on a cigar. "We must take revenge and shoot the dogs. The stupid American government must know that no one can demean the Italians in this hateful country."

"Who murdered my mom and dad?"

"The FBI pigs."

"The FBI? Why?"

"Two fugitive guys from the Bonanno family holed up in our restaurant, and the FBI morons shot like crazy and killed your mom and dad. They are dirty animals," Franco said.

"Why didn't our bodyguards kill them?"

"Your dad asked us not to shoot back."

"What should we do?" Riccardo asked.

Marco tapped the end of his cigar. "We must kill them. This crime is against all of us."

"Yes, it is a crime, but please, uncle, be patient for a while. I have a plan. I know how to avenge the murder in my way. You stay away from this crime. I don't want to see anyone of you in jail."

"You are the boss," Nicolo said.

"Thanks, cousin. I am a servant of the family and one of you. I will stand by the Lucciano family and the good

Italians in New York and America. Tell the journalists outside the house we are mourning the good old days and asking God for forgiveness and peace. We are not looking for revenge."

"What do you want to do?" Riccardo asked.

"I know how to get things done without fuss. I mean the Sicilian way of doing things. But before that, we need to be together as one family and offer love and practical support to our community. Be calm for a while until we bury my parents. Let us arrange a fantastic funeral and tell everybody that the Lucciano family and the Italians in America are one people. Invite all the heads of the Italian families to our funeral and dinner."

"*Grazie, Madrina.*"

Ten minutes later, Nicolo bowed and muttered into Angela's ear. "A Native American woman wants to see you."

"Let her come."

Nina came in, and Angela folded her in her arms for a minute, sobbing. She held her hand, turning her face toward her loquacious relatives. "Listen, everybody. This beautiful woman is Nina Seneca. Some of you know she was my mother's best buddy and my nanny for seventeen years. Yes, I was still a baby when I was seventeen. Nina is one of us. Protect her and do good things for her."

"Can I talk to you?"

"Yes, of course."

Nina took her to a quiet corner. "Sorry for Bella. We shared unforgettable laughs and tears. I will miss her."

"This is life. Death is what dies inside us."

"Did you foresee anything?"

"Yeah. I saw the crime in my dream."

"Why didn't you tell me? I could have saved them."

"I thought they invited you to the party. Why didn't Bella invite you?"

"She told me nothing. I guess Leonardo wanted only the Italians to be there."

At midnight, Elisha entered the house with a sullen face and weary red eyes. Angela embraced her, kissing her forehead. "Listen, ladies and gentlemen. This is my beloved daughter, Elisha. My dad and mom loved her so much." Her relatives hugged and kissed her.

Angela opened a curtain and saw nine reporters standing outside the house. "Tell the press guys I will make a statement after the funeral."

Three days later, Bella's parents and sister and hundreds of dignitaries, including the Governor and the Mayor, had attended the funeral service at the Basilica of Regina Pacis in Brooklyn. Nina and Elisha sat on Angela's right side, and an olive-skinned blonde woman in a black gown sat on her left side.

After the broadcast funeral service, journalists surrounded Angela on the church's top step.

"What is your family going to do?"

"My family and the good Italians believe in mercy and reconciliation."

"Do you mean there will be no retribution?"

"We live in the twenty-first century. The former, dreadful days of the Mafia are over. I advocate love, not retaliation. However, if certain guys think they can play dirty with the Italians, they will die."

"The Governor and the Mayor say the court must charge the FBI officers who shot your parents with first-degree homicide. What do you say about that?"

"They can say what they like. I have faith in the justice system of this country."

"Are you going to attend the court hearings?"

"No. The court will not bring my parents back. Life moves on like the sun in the sky."

"We heard you are the first godmother of the Sicilian Commission. Is this true?"

"I have been in Canada for twenty years and have no relation to the Italian businesses in America. I own nothing here except the profound love for my family and community. The Mafia's parenthood, like feudal patriarchy, is oppressive and anti-women."

"What are you going to do?"

"I am eager to spend time with my relatives. It has been a while since I have seen a lot of them."

"Are you going to stay in America?"

"No. I will go back to Canada, where I can keep a grip on my sanity."

"What do you do in Canada?"

"I am an author and entrepreneur. Excuse me. I must leave. We have a burial service. Remember us in your thoughts and prayers. Thank you."

Angela stood at Leonardo's grave in the Holy Cross Cemetery. The olive-skinned woman placed a red rose on the coffin. "Bye. I will miss you." After the formal interment, the Lucciano family prepared a communal feast in ACE Hotel. When Angela held a glass of red wine, Nicolo whispered into her ear. "Martina wants to talk to you about private matters."

"Who is she?"

"She will tell you."

"Where is she?"

"Come with me."

Nicolo took her to a quiet room. "Hi, Angela. I am Martina Lucciano. This is my mom, Lara Russo." Lara stood and shook her hand.

Nicolo left the room. "Yes, what can I do for you?"

"Nothing. I want to tell you the truth."

"Which truth?"

"I am your half-sister."

"How?"

"My mom was our dad's chief secretary in New Jersey. He had a long relationship with her."

"My dad had never mentioned you or your mom. What is the story?"

"Our dad had an affair with my mom because he knew about your mom's love affair with Nina. He didn't want to tell you that and hurt your feelings."

"I see. Do you live together?"

"No. My mom is in Newark, and I am in Hudson Yards."

"Do you have a family?"

"No. I am single."

"What do you do?"

"I am the CEO of our dad's company. A fifth of our dad's wealth and the house will be for you. How do you want me to pay you?"

"I, I don't know. We will talk about it later." Her eyes became tearful. "I am pleased to meet both of you and so happy to know I have a sister." She gave them warm hugs. "Does the family know who you are?"

"Everybody knows me and my mom. You are the last person to know." She gave her a business card. "I hope to see you again soon."

Martina and her mother left the room. Bella's sister, Emma Clark, met Angela and gave her a thick envelope. "There are cards and personal letters for your dad. Don't show them to anyone else. I promised your father not to tell anyone about his private correspondence with your ex-partner."

"Thanks." Angela met heads of Italian families and told her relatives she wanted to spend the night with her daughter.

Angela and Elisha moved to 1 Hotel Brooklyn Bridge at Furman Street and got a room on the ninth floor overlooking the East River. After closing the curtains, Elisha pulled her to her body and kissed her lips. "How do you feel now? Come to bed." She took off her clothes and rested her head on her breast. "You have been silent. What is going on?"

"I have been thinking of Martina and of what she said to me. She is my half-sister."

"How is that?"

"My dad had an affair with her Italian mom, who was his New Jersey secretary. The whole family knew about the affair except me. My mom told me my dad had never cheated on her. Poor woman."

"Gee. How do you feel about that?"

"I can't change the past. Martina is the CEO of my dad's company. So, be happy. Your aunt is one of the richest and most influential women in New York."

"Aunt? I remained silent when you kept saying I am your daughter."

She buried her right fingers in her hair. "Honey, I cannot say you are my lover and girlfriend. I do not need a war with the Italians and the crazy Irish."

"My official name now is Elisha Lucciano. I feel closer to you than to my mom."

"Where is your mom?"

"In Dublin, attending a conference." She opened a tote bag and gave her an envelope containing three photographs.

"Who are those guys?"

"They who killed your mom and dad. Haven't you read the papers?"

"No. How did you get them?"

"I got them from my mom's cousin, Niamh. You should do something before they go to the court."

"Do what?"

"Use your magical power."

"Which magical power?"

She caressed her breasts. "Come on, love. Please stop playing games with me. My mom told me about your power and said you can be a superwoman. Why didn't you tell me about it?"

"I didn't need it when you were with me. We had no troubles with other people."

"You should use it now. Your furious family is on the warpath and going to massacre many FBI officers. So, do something before we see a bloodbath."

"I will, but I am tired now. Let us sleep."

She slumbered beside her. Her uncle and cousins assembled in the Carroll Gardens home and agreed to use sniper rifles to assassinate the two FBI agents at the Criminal Court in Manhattan.

At nine o'clock in the morning, Elisha switched on the TV. "Look. The police cars are heading toward the Manhattan Bridge. The convicts are in this van."

Angela wore a robe and slumped in a gray balcony chair, and Elisha stood at the open door with her arms crossed. With her hands resting on the sides of her head, Angela's eyes concentrated on the Manhattan Bridge. The intensity in her gaze was palpable, and it showed that she immersed herself in the sight before her. "*Niyeohsa, niga nahgwahs. Gane gohso geh. Sgeno* [My mother, I am angry. Do your best. Amen]." A moment later, the driver of the security vehicle yelled. "I can't control and stop the damn van. It is speeding up like a rocket. Jesus! The stupid brakes have stopped working. My God...." The whooshing van flew over another car and plunged into the East River. Angela jumped off her chair after watching the huge splash. "Rescue the driver."

Elisha gaped at Angela and retired to the room to watch the news. "Oh, my God. The van fell into the river. How did you do that?"

"I am with you. I did nothing."

An anchor swiveled his chair and rested his arms on the news desk. "We do not know what happened. There was a sudden accident on the Manhattan Bridge, and the police van plummeted into the river. We see three rescue boats making their way toward the Bridge....

Here are four or five divers carrying their scuba equipment. We hope they will rescue the men in the ill-fated van as soon as possible."

The divers saved the driver and three police officers and found the two FBI agents, who killed Leonardo and Bella, hanged with steel chains around their necks. Angela kneeled at the bed, and a tear rolled down her cheek. "Thank you, my love. I will be a positive person and serve the people who need care and love. *Yaweh* [Thank you]." She picked up her cell phone and made a call. "*Zio, la festa è finita* [Uncle, the party is over]." She glanced at Elisha. "Let us go."

"Where? Don't you want to eat something?"

"We will eat delicious food later. Come with me. We have wonderful things to do."

A taxicab took them to Leonardo's house. Angela made a call to a cousin. "Good morning, Gabriele. Do you like to get papa's home?"

"For how much?"

"What about ten million bucks?"

"Eight million bucks."

"OK, *mascalzone*. But I need cash today."

"No problem. I will get cash and give you a check before lunch."

"Thanks. I will wait for you in papa's home." She called Nina. "Grandma, where are you?"

"At Leslie-Lohman Museum."

"Elisha and I want to have dinner with you."

"That's great."

"See you at six at St. Patrick's Cathedral."

"Do you have a grandma? Who is she?" Elisha asked

when Angela finished the call.

"Yes. She is Nina."

"Why did you call her grandma?"

"Because she is my grandma."

"You are full of secrets. Did your granddad have an affair with her?"

"Who knows?"

They went to a restaurant and had breakfast. Later, Gabriele handed Angela a check of six million dollars and a duffel bag of two million dollars in cash. "Thanks, cousin. It is all yours. Here are the house keys and papers. Please, donate the unnecessary furniture and clothes to a charity."

At noontime, Angela and Elisha took a taxi to Brooklyn and sat at a dining table in Marco's house. Angela stood with a glass of red wine, gazing at her uncle, aunts, and cousins. "God, in His way, has avenged the murder of my dad and mom. Do not ask me how I did it. Wait. I am not saying I am God. The main thing is that none of you would go to jail. You don't need snipers and rifles when I am here." She smiled. "I want to thank every one of you for your enormous love and support. You taught me how to forgive and love. I am not your godmother, but I am your daughter and sister. My heart will never forget the love you gave me. I love you. Amen."

She and Elisha returned to their hotel after lunch and made love. In the evening, they and Nina dined at La Grenouille. "I know you are sad because you lost your best friend. But, please, I want to see Colestah as soon as possible. Can we visit her tomorrow?"

"OK. I will make two or three calls."

Nina called Colestah and two friends. "Good news. We will fly tomorrow on a private jet at ten o'clock in the morning."

In the hotel room, Elisha wore a dark-blue baby doll nightdress and stroked Angela's hand. "You called Nina grandma ten times. Why?"

"Honey, I told you she is my grandmother."

"Are you kidding me?"

"No. Believe me. I am telling you the full truth. Nina is my biological grandmother."

"But she doesn't have children, and she doesn't look like you."

"She has two daughters. One of them is my mom."

"Who is she?"

"You don't need to know. What I can tell you is that Nina had donated an egg to Bella."

"So, what do you think of yourself?"

"A half of me is a mystery, and the other half is an alien woman."

"Do the Luccianos know about your relationship with Nina?"

"No. They don't know, and I will tell nobody else about it."

"Does my mom know?"

"No. Keep this private matter between you and me. We will tell your mom the truth at the right time."

In the morning, Angela and Nina took off to Olean Airport in Cattaraugus County. Talisa drove them to her mother's house. Angela met Colestah and kissed her wrinkled hands. "Who is the main chief here?"

“What do you mean?”

“I mean, who is the top leader of the Seneca Nation?”

“He is Nakamo Bigfire.”

“Where does he live?”

“In a house at Old Route Seventeen.”

“Can I meet him?”

“Yes, you can. Nina knows where he lives.”

Angela held her hand and took her to the guest room. “I love you so much.”

She placed her cashmere fringed shawl around her shoulders and kissed her forehead. “I love you too.”

“Please, accept this little gift from me. It is for you and your people.” Angela gave her a sports bag.

She opened the bag. “This is a lot of money.”

“The tremendous honor I receive from the Great Spirit is worth more than all the money. If I had not met you, I would not have recognized my divine power. I aspire to be a valuable individual and assist those who need help.”

“May the Great Spirit bless you. You are a noble woman. Love is beneficial and wise, and the rain falls on the good and the bad. Live in peace with Mother Nature and all her people. Do not let the delusions of the world deviate you from the right, humble path. Take Talisa’s truck.”

Angela and Nina moved southwest and parked the Ram truck at a house engulfed by a forest. Nina talked to a Seneca man, who took her and Angela to a stone cabin. They met Nakamo Bigfire, who sat crossed-legged on a wool rug. Angela sat before him, glancing at his amber headband, bone choker, and breastplate.

"Sir, I am honored to meet you and know your gallant nation. Please, this is a check of six million dollars for your people on this remarkable reservation. Pray for me." Tears flooded Nina's eyes. Nakamo put his right hand on Angela's head. "The light of the divine is in you. May Hawennio fill your kind heart with beauty, and the Great Spirit makes you strong. May the gentle winds of Heaven take your sadness away. Walk with love through the world to wipe out people's suffering and worries." He gave her a blue beaded pendant. "Wear this necklace all the time. I inherited it from our divine warriors. Stay with us for a meal."

"Thanks. I must go."

"The ground under your feet is holy. Go in peace." Nakamo's three male companions hugged her and shook hands with Nina.

After leaving Nakamo's cabin, Nina cuddled her. "I love you so much. Thanks for supporting Colestah's community."

"I consider myself one of them."

"Ah, I wish your mom and aunt were with us. I miss them so much."

Angela returned to Manhattan and met Martina in her office on Park Avenue. After a moment of silence, Martina set the tone for the conversation. "So, sis, what are you going to do?"

"I want to go back to Canada."

"How is life there?"

"Canada is a fascinating country and quieter than here. I am an avid writer and entrepreneur."

"That's good. OK. Let us talk business. Do you want

cash, or do you like to invest and have shares in our dad's company? Or do you want a combination of shares and cash?"

"I know nothing about our dad's business. So, I prefer money. How much am I supposed to get?"

"Two hundred million dollars."

"Wha-What?" She swallowed her saliva and wiped her lips. "That's too much."

"Our dad was a billionaire, and he loved you so much for being honest with him. Two hundred for you, two hundred for me, fifty for my mom, one hundred for Uncle Marco, one hundred for Aunt Viola, eighty for the cousins, and five for Elisha."

"What do you want me to do?"

"Send me your bank account details. Open six or seven accounts in different banks. As they say, don't put all your eggs in one basket."

In the morning, Angela returned to Toronto, and Camille welcomed her with warm affection. "Let us go out for dinner. I want to know more things about your Italian family." They dined at a Thai restaurant on Roncesvalles Avenue, and Angela spoke of her happy childhood in New York and immense love for Bella and Leonardo. Camille touched her hand and shed a tear when she saw her teardrop.

At home, Camille fetched a small book of photos from her room and sat next to her. "Let me show you my family. This is my mom. My dad. My sister. Me in Paris...." She scanned Angela's eyes and lips. "I am single and feel attracted to you. You are a wonderful person. Do you like to be my *compagnon*? I do not mean I want a marriage relationship."

"Anything you say." They kissed, caressed, and made love on a loop carpet. "What about we sleep here tonight?"

"As you like."

A week later, Elisha traveled to Toronto to attend an evening fashion show. After the show, she got a taxi to West End. When the cab approached Indian Road, she saw Angela and Camille leaning on a tree and kissing each other's lips. Two tears popped out. She wiped the tears and glanced at the taxi driver. "Oh, I forgot something. Please, take me back to the city center."

In the morning, Angela called her. "Where are you? I waited for you last night. Doing Okay?"

"Yeah. Sorry. I had to come back for urgent work."

Angela authored books and recorded her sexual and emotional behavior. One afternoon, she visited The 519 LGBTQ center on Church Street. The center director entered a hall, delighting the audience with her tight dress and tumbled hair. "Hello, everyone. Today, I have a special surprise for you. An amazing person will tell us about her unique experience of sexuality and gender identity. Few people dare to talk about such a controversial topic, but this special person knows no fear of the state and conservative media propaganda. So, without further ado, let me introduce our most interesting patron and guest, Angela Lucciano."

Angela walked into the packed hall and saw Camille with a pride scarf around her neck. She waved to her and started her lecture. Camille wiped her snub nose and left the brown building. After her speech, Angela donated two million dollars and sought Camille in and around the building, but could not find her. She came back to her house, searching every room. She realized Camille had collected her books and clothes and left the house in a hurry. Her first reaction was to call her on the cell phone, but there was no answer. The next day, she drove to the university campus and asked students about her. She sent flirty texts to allure her, but she did not reply. In the morning, she steered through the city center and parked the car near T & T Supermarket at College Street in Chinatown. With her lithe arms resting on the steering wheel, she prayed. "Mom, help me find Camille for the sake of love."

A minute later, Camille left the supermarket with a bag in her hand. Angela got out of the car and bustled toward her. "Camille, Camille, what happened? Why didn't you answer my calls and texts? Your absence has worried me. Why did you leave me?"

"I needed some time for myself."

"Oh, dear. What is the problem? Do you want me to take you to a specialist?"

"I do not need anyone. I know how to take care of myself."

"So, what's wrong? Can we talk? I am sorry if I offended you. Please, come and sit in the car. There is always a solution."

With her head down, Camille lumbered and sat in the car with a forlorn face. Angela held her hand. "I massaged your body four days ago. We have been in love and friends for months. Even if you stopped loving me, there is a way to say goodbye. So, why are you upset? Why did you leave me?"

"Why didn't you tell me you are bisexual?"

She laughed. "I am not bisexual."

"But I saw you in the LGBT center."

"The place is called The 519, not the bisexual nightclub. I went there to talk about my personal experience."

"What is personal experience?"

"About my lesbianism."

She glowered and twisted her thin lips. "Excuse me. French people are not stupid."

"I didn't say the French people are stupid. Be honest with me. Why were you there?"

"I was a lesbian before I met you and had a girlfriend in France."

"Like you, I am a lesbian, not bisexual or pansexual. I have a strong sexual desire only for women. The LGBTQ center invited me, not only because I fund it but also to let me talk about my book and why my lesbianism is a choice. Come to the house, and I will show you the book."

They went to the house, and Angela showed her the cover of her book, *The Lesbian*. "Do you believe me now?"

With fixed, curious eyes, she flipped through the book. "Pardon me. I am very sorry. I thought you were bisexual. Can I come back here? I love you and enjoy life with you."

"You can. I love your sweet company, and no more running away."

Chapter 5

On a sizzling summer day, Camille went to the Toronto Zoo to take photos, and Angela declined to go out with her. "I don't like to see caged animals." Instead, she ambled to Toronto Eaton Centre to get clothes and magazines. While sauntering alone in the bustling shopping mall, she spotted the *New York Times* headline "MODELS MISSING." As she delved into the article, she discovered the disturbing news. Elisha and three prominent models had vanished without a trace, their disappearance shrouded in mystery, leaving the fashion world in a state of shock. These models had been at the height of their career, gracing runways and magazine covers with their charming beauty, but now they were gone, leaving behind a void that seemed impossible to fill.

The article provided sketchy details of their last known whereabouts, capturing the aspects of their lives before their sudden absence. Interviews with friends, colleagues, and family members revealed a haunting narrative, painting a grim picture of the uncanny circumstances of their disappearance. FBI agents and NYPD detectives thought sex-trafficking brigands had abducted them after luring them to a posh photo party in Midtown Manhattan. They did not reveal the identity of the abductors, assuming they would demand a large ransom.

Angela dropped the newspaper on a table and called Camille. "I want to go to New York to see the family for an urgent matter. I will leave a key for you under the blue pot beside the fountain. Take care of yourself. I love you."

She picked up her passport from the house office and flew to New York. When she hugged her mother in her East Village house, her shoulders shook, and her tears soaked the top of her dress. "I love you so much that I think of you every moment. I am sad and angry because the beasts abducted Elisha. She is my true love. I would destroy the world if something bad happened to her. She has been my lover since her mom left me."

"I know, sweetheart. I have come back to my house after I heard the sad news."

Angela gazed at her shimmering eyes and kissed her face. "I need your love. Can you help me find Elisha?" She leaned her head on her mother's chest, and she embraced her, her hands moving in soothing circles on her back. "I am with you, my love."

"Can you give me your car?"

"Why do you need the car? Where do you want to go? The FBI is looking for Elisha and her friends."

"I do not know what to do. I should drive and use my inner vision."

"Wait a minute. It is a rainy day. I will get clothes and come with you."

Angela drove her mother's car to the Viceroy Central Park Hotel. "Why did you stop here?"

"Elisha and her chums were here. I want to feel their spirits." She rested her temple on the steering wheel and closed her eyes for a minute. "How can I use the satnav?"

"Press this button and type an address here."

Angela switched on the satnav and stared at its screen. "Where is my girl?"

"Your girl is in Chester. Drive the car. I will take you there."

Anohitecha gaped. "How could you do that? That is not the original voice."

"That's the voice of my soul." She pointed at her chest and steered the car to Orange County. On the way, she stopped in Hackensack for a quick meal in a restaurant. Later, they stayed in a room in Holiday Inn Express at Bryle Place, Chester.

At five o'clock, Angela woke up and kissed her mother. "Mom, stay here and keep your phone with you. Stay safe. I love you."

"What safe? I am a supreme warrior goddess, and no one can hurt me. I must come to protect you."

"Bloody earth. I forgot we are goddesses." They sat

in the car and turned on the satnav. "Where should I go?"

"Turn left and then turn left. Take West Avenue.... Slow down.... Turn right." She drove in low gear on Conklingtown Road for ten minutes. "Your destination is on the right."

The car came to a halt, its engine purring into silence as they reached a desolate stretch of land near a clump of low shrubs. The air hung heavy with a haunting stillness, broken by the distant rustling of leaves. They stepped out of the car, their eyes fixated on a path that led, through the untrimmed, dense bushes, to an isolated, shabby farmhouse, weathered by time and neglect.

At a forsaken corner, a solitary tree stood sentinel, its gnarled branches reaching out like grasping fingers. With feline agility, Angela scaled the tree's trunk and crawled on the shoddy roof of the first floor. She snuck a peek through a tinted window, revealing a shocking scene. Elisha and her friends, once vibrant and full of life, now lay on thin, grimy druggets with their cuffed hands behind their backs and gray adhesive tape sealing their mouths. After sneaking into the room, she placed her hand on Elisha's mouth. "Honey, it is me." She removed the tape from across her mouth. "How many guys are they?"

"Four or five."

She broke her fetter. "Stay here and do not make a noise. I love you." She kissed her head and Nakamo's necklace and opened the room door. A burly man ascended the stairs with a beer bottle in his hand. As he reached the top, a scowl etched across his face, and his eyes pierced through the dimness. He took a deliberate step forward, the floor creaking beneath his weight. A sinister smile twisted his lips, revealing a glimmer of sadistic satisfaction in his eyes. "Who are you? What are you doing here?"

"I am your hell, fathead."

The man raced toward her, and a door on the left side swung open, hurtling outward with force, and collided with the man's face and knees, halting his menacing advance. A resounding thud filled the air as the impact reverberated throughout the hallway, immobilizing him. Pain engraved across his body, making him baffled and dazed by the unexpected blow. After falling on his back, Angela pressed her grip on his ribs. The pressure of her hand had disabled his stubby limbs, and a membrane zipper sealed his lips. She crept downstairs and found two bearded, blue-eyed men mumbling in the kitchen. "What are we getting for breakfast?"

"*Gówno*," one said.

Angela and Anohitecha dashed into the kitchen and drubbed their chests with their palms, contusing their ribcages. One of them seized a carbine bayonet and attacked, but Anohitecha's fingers clutched and wrung his thick wrist hard as if they were steel clamps. "*Pieprzyć cię.*" The man cursed and fell to his knees.

Angela snatched a claw hammer off a counter and hurled it at the other man's forehead. He bellowed, and she kicked his genitalia. "Who are you? What is your language?"

"*Polski*. You made a big mistake. The Mafia will kill you and your family."

"Shut your mouth." Angela dragged them outside the house and tied their bodies to a rotten wood pillar with a metal chain. "Watch your back. A guy is holding a gun." Angela whirled on the doorstep, and her mother threw an antique cleaver at the gunman's temple. He fell on his back, and Angela dipped her head and vomited on the ground after seeing the gunman's split skull.

"Yuck. Thanks, mom." She rinsed her mouth with tap water and covered the dead gunman with a stained floorcloth. In the living room, she found a DSLR camera on a table. She checked it and saw half-naked photos of Elisha and her friends. With the camera on her shoulder, she trotted upstairs and freed Elisha and her friends. "It is over. Let us go home. I love you."

Elisha kissed her. "My hero, I love you. How can we thank you?" The feeble, grubby models wept with dark tears running down their dirty cheeks and hugged her. "Thank you. You are a superstar." They jumped over the incapacitated kidnapper and stepped outside the main door. Elisha frowned at the shackled abductors. "Wait." She booted their chests and faces and swore at them. The other models used foul language and spat on them. After leaping on the grass, Anohitecha blew a gust. The dilapidated house collapsed and buried the abductors in a sinkhole.

"Gosh. Who did that?" a model said.

Angela smiled. "The hybrid vampires."

Elisha and the models gazed at Anohitecha's brawny

body and revealing costume. Unaccustomed to such a formidable presence, they couldn't help but shiver. Their frailness laid bare in the face of her physical power. "Don't be afraid. She is my mother," Angela said.

"Nice to see you. Thanks for coming," a model said.

Anohitecha opened the car trunk and covered their upper bodies with Native American shawls. They went back to the Holiday Inn. "I need a shower," Elisha said.

"All of you need a wash and a decent breakfast. But no phone calls. Stay in the hotel. I will get you clothes." Angela fetched clothes from her mother's car. After breakfast, she drove Elisha's friends to their homes in New York. Elisha's arms enfolded her neck from behind and stayed in the car. "Come with me and give me a big hug. I had an awful time with the Polish rats."

"You need to rest, and I want to spend the night with my mom. Come to Toronto after you recover. We need to discuss many private matters. Do you remember your mom's phone number?"

"Why? What do you want from her?"

"I want to send her a text."

"Do you love her?"

"I love everybody."

"What about that girl?"

"Which girl?"

"I heard you have a girlfriend in Canada."

"She is not my girlfriend. She is a French tourist. We are just buddies."

Anohitecha got a pen and a piece of paper, and Elisha told her Caitlyn's phone number. Angela sent a text. "I have brought you the finest gift in the world. You will get her after ten minutes." She drove for five minutes and stopped the car in front of Caitlyn's house. "Honey, you need your mom after this ordeal. Don't tell her anything about my mom. I will be in Canada tomorrow."

Elisha left the car and gave Angela a fervent kiss on her lips. "I love you so much. Thanks for saving my life. Bye, love."

"Be well, my love. See me in Toronto."

Caitlyn welcomed her daughter with tears and kisses. "Happy to see you, sweetheart."

"Thanks, mom."

"Where is Angela?"

"She is going back to Canada. I want to eat and sleep. It was like hell, but Angela," she paused and cried. "She is my everything. We are so lucky to know her. Please forgive me. I am sorry."

"Honey, don't be sorry. Thank God you are alive. I couldn't sleep and work when you were away, and I don't know how to thank Angela for bringing you home."

"She loves you, and I feel guilty for damaging your relationship with her. But what can I do? I love her so much."

"Angela has an angel's heart. Don't feel guilty and sad. It is wonderful that both of us love her. We will find a solution. But now, you need to relax. What do you like to eat?"

"Anything."

Angela parked the car at her mother's house on

Second Avenue. When she stood on the sidewalk, Anohitecha clenched her hand. "Wait."

"What do you want?"

"I see an eagle. I feel my sister is here." She looked at the sky, and an eagle swooped down and gave her a small piece of paper. "Sis, the Mafia has abducted Martina. Follow the Eagle and save her. Anna."

"Oh, my God. Who abducted her?"

"I don't know. Take my key and stay home." She gave her the house key and disappeared.

The eagle flew to an underground parking garage at Exchange Place. Anohitecha appeared, looking around. "*Dagoh neyuk*? [Where is she?]"

The eagle shrieked. "*Oyono* [Four]."

She and the eagle vanished, and in the blink of an eye, they materialized on the fourth floor. "*Dagoh noneyodo*? [Which door?]"

The eagle whispered. "*Yowane* [Six]."

Anohitecha walked to the sixth room. "*Wahyeh* [Go]." The eagle flew out, and Anohitecha harnessed the depth of her extraordinary abilities and focused on her sight, piercing through the concrete wall. Her eyes saw Martina manacled and confined to a chair in a desolate corner. As her gaze surveyed the room, it fell upon four men engaged in tense bickering, with their hands clutching assault rifles. With steadfast determination violating the laws of physics, she strode forward, passing through the solid wall as if it was a wispy veil. She erected a bullet-proof glass box around Martina, shielding her from harm and her abductors. Her stare turned toward the abductors. "Leave the building, or I will kill you and send you to hell."

An armed man sniggered and fired two bullets at her. She smiled. "Your stupid bullets can't kill me, but my hands can make you hashed meat." In a display of her formidable powers, she swirled her hands with fluid grace, conjuring a swirling vortex of wind that grew in strength and intensity. The powerful whirlwind seized hold of the four gunmen, lifting them from the ground, their startled faces contorted with disbelief. Like discarded leaves caught in a tempest, the gust carried them toward the windows, their desperate cries lost amidst the roaring wind. With a forceful release, the whirlwind flung them through the shattered glass, their bodies hurtling through the air before falling on Exchange Place. Eight eagles tore off their clothes, lacerating their bodies.

The whirlwind subsided, and Anohitecha grinned at Martina and removed the glass box and the handcuffs with a click of her fingers. "Come with me."

Martina quivered. "Who are you?"

"I am a warrior."

"I saw your action. Are you a human?"

"No. I want to take you to your sister Angela. She is in my house. Please, hold my hand."

Martina's shaking fingers touched her hand and disappeared. Four seconds later, she found herself in Anohitecha's house. "Hi. How are you doing, sis?" Angela hugged her.

"I am good. Thanks to the warrior. Who is she? She is incredible."

"She is my mom."

"Your mom? How is that?"

"She created me."

Anohitecha appeared. "You will stay here. Call your family and tell them you are with your sister."

"Thanks for saving my life. We need to call the cops. The abductors killed my driver."

"Leave this matter to me. I will make some food."

When Anohitecha went to the kitchen, Martina sat next to Angela, putting her hand on her knee. "Who is she? She walked through a wall. One abductor shot at her, but nothing happened to her body. She threw the four abductors out of windows without touching them. She made a bulletproof glass barrier to protect me. How did she bring me here? How did she get me inside this house?"

She cuddled her. "My mom is a goddess."

"What kind of goddess is she?"

"She decorated the galaxies and fought the evil gods and their devils."

"And you believe that?"

"Yes, I believe many things. My mom doesn't lie. She will show you what supreme goddesses can do. Who abducted you?"

"Russian and Ukrainian Mafiosi. They wanted a huge ransom."

"I see. How do you know they are Russians and Ukrainians?"

"I learned Russian, and I recognized the Ukrainians from their finger tattoos."

"Interesting. They fight each other in Ukraine, and here they are comrades in crime."

After dinner, Martina touched Anohitecha's hand. "You are a real woman. Angela told me you are a goddess. How can you be a goddess?"

"It is not my choice. Come with me." She patted Martina's and Angela's shoulders. A moment later, they found themselves huddled in a flying fishing canoe. "Oh, my God. Oh, my God." Martina caught Angela's hands and trembled.

The canoe moved south and landed on an island shore. Martina stretched her legs and removed her jacket. "What is this place?"

"This is Governors Island." A wine bottle and three glasses appeared in Anohitecha's hands. "Let us have some wine."

"Incredible."

"Please, don't tell anybody about me or what you have seen. One day, your sister will be the leader of the world."

They sipped wine before returning home. Angela kissed Martina's face. "Stay the night with my mom. I have something to do."

"Where are you going?"

"I am the godmother. I will never allow punks to play dirty games with our women."

"Be careful."

Angela met her cousins Franco, Nicolo, and Viola's son, Salvatore, in the Carroll Gardens house. "I have saved Elisha and Martina from the Polish, Russian, and Ukrainian dweebs. Do you know where their bosses live?"

"The Polish guy, Jacub Janeczek, owns the biggest

building on Hubert Street in Tribeca. His bodyguards are on the first floor," Salvatore said.

"The Nazi Ukrainian boss, Borysko Koval, and the Russian don, Ivan Tsvetkov, are in Brighton Beach," Franco said.

"What do you want us to do?" Nicolo asked.

"Take me to their homes."

"Do you need a gun?" Nicolo said.

"No. Get guns for yourselves."

An hour later, the three cousins took Angela to Brighton Third Street. "The Ukrainian guy is in this house."

"OK. Stay in the car and keep your hands on your guns."

She went up seven stairs and knocked on the white door of a two-floor building. A man opened the door. "Yes."

"Hi. I am Angela Lucciano. I want a word with Borysko."

The man lighted his cigarette with a match and sneered. "Borysko Koval doesn't live here."

"Amazing how you know the full name well. Don't be a fool and don't make me angry."

"Wait a minute." The man closed the door.

Angela pushed the door, dropping it on the floor. She moved into the living room and saw Borysko frivoling with two blonde women. A man pointed a gun at the back of her head. "I don't hold a gun. I am Angela, the leader of the Lucciano family."

Borysko laughed and smoked his cigarette. "Foolish Italians. They send hookers to talk to me. You idiots never learn. How dare you come to my house!"

"Your guys abducted my sister. They are dead. One of them was your son, Fedir. Tell your man to put his gun down if you want to see your dead son."

Borysko asked the women to leave the room and stood to beat Angela, but a tomahawk hit his head and killed him. Angela turned her back and found the gunman dead with a knife in his neck. "Thanks, Ami, for coming." She gave her a kiss.

"I will follow you."

Angelo sat in the car. "Borysko is dead. Let us get Ivan."

They moved to Brighton Twelfth Street. "Ivan lives up there on the fourth floor." Franco pointed his finger up.

After leaving the car, Angela's eyes shot upward. In a split second, she leaped into the air and landed on a steel balcony. She entered a room through an open window and saw Ivan and three men smoking and playing cards. "Hello, Ivan. Long time no see."

Ivan's friends pulled their guns. "Put your guns down if you want to live. I want to talk to the boss."

Ivan placed his cards on the table. "What do you want?"

"Why did you ask your stupid brother to abduct my sister?"

"I haven't seen Alexei for two months."

"You will never see him again, and I will never see you again. Goodbye, loser." Angela vanished, and with the speed of light, Amitola threw spears and arrows at Ivan's and his men's faces. Their blood covered the table and ran to the floor.

Angela rested in the car. "Gosh! How did you jump fifty feet in the air?" Nicolo asked.

"I am the real godmother. Did you forget that?"

"What happened?"

"They are dead."

"What about Jacub Janeczek?"

"I will get him later. Go home."

Angela hugged and thanked her cousins and moved to her mother's house. "Where is Martina?"

"She is sleeping in my bedroom. She had a rough day. What do you want to do?"

"We need to get Jacub Janeczek and finish him. He planned Elisha's abduction."

"Where does he live?"

"In Tribeca. Ask Ami and the sword warriors to protect Martina and come with me."

Amitola and ten female warriors appeared in the house, and Angela and her mother flew to Hubert Street. They snapped the locks of a building gate and went up to the fifth floor. "Wait here. I am going to look and see how many people are in the house." Anohitecha walked through a wall and came back after ten seconds. "He and his wife are sleeping, and their daughter is in her bedroom."

"Let us take him to the river."

"I will do it. Wait for me there."

Angela flew and landed on a wooden bench at the Hudson River. Anohitecha entered the apartment and seized Jacub after hypnotizing him with her sight. A minute later, they showed up at the river. Jacub woke up with wondering eyes and moved his hands on his tattersall pajamas. "Who are you, people? How did you get me here?"

"I am Angela Lucciano. What happened to you?"

"What do you want?"

"Your father and my dad were friends. Why did you ask your muppets to abduct my daughter?"

"Who is she?"

"Elisha."

"That was a mistake."

"That was a crime. We killed your two brothers. I think you should join them."

"Please, can we talk?"

"I will send a birthday card to your wife. But for you, it is a judgment day because you ordered your bandits to abduct Elisha. Can you swim?"

"No. What do you want to do?"

"I will teach you how to swim." Angela grabbed his waist and collar and threw him in the middle of the Hudson River. "Oof! Mom, I am tired. I need to sleep."

As the morning sun cast its gentle rays upon the city, shocking headlines appeared, sending tremors through the fabric of its existence. The news raced through the streets, murmured in low voices by startled citizens and underscored by the wailing sirens of law enforcement vehicles.

The murder of the Mafia bosses had gripped the city in an unprecedented state of uncertainty. Their murder had shattered the web of their conglomerate, leaving behind a rage that threatened to plunge the city into uncharted territory.

Rumors floated through the city's alleys and cafes, speculating on the identity of the assailants responsible for these audacious acts. The ominous nature of the murders had deepened the mystery, leaving the city's inhabitants to grapple with a sense of skepticism and vulnerability.

The Luccianos knew the truth. At noon, they threw a barbecue party for Martina and celebrated the death of her abductors.

In the afternoon, the story about the abducted models had unraveled, sweeping across the country. The striking end of the abduction had seized the consciousness of the nation. News networks buzzed with breaking stories that painted a harrowing picture. Shocked citizens spread words, and the media churned out stories. From bustling city streets to quiet suburban neighborhoods, people's eyes had glued to screens broadcasting the unsettling details of the abduction.

The next day, Angela flew to Canada, and Nadia Andino, a TV host, interviewed the classy models in New York.

"As usual, you look stunning. Thank God you are back with us. Tell us what happened?"

Kristin Jenner rubbed her knees. "A handsome guy came to our studio and conned us to Viceroy Central Park Hotel. We thought he worked for women's fashion magazines, but that was nothing more than a scam."

"Another man welcomed us in the hotel and said he works for an entertainment company that films luxury parties and events for celebrities. He looked gentle and friendly," Meghan Graham said.

"How could they abduct the four of you? Why didn't anyone of the hotel workers see you?"

"We went up to a suite on the third floor and drank wine. We think there was something in the wine that caused us to lose consciousness. As far as how the captors transported us from the hotel to Orange County, we still do not know. They lure girls into prostitution or pornography," Emily Singer said.

"How do you know that?"

"They didn't beat us ... or do that thing. They took many photos."

"What sort of photos?"

"They asked us to take off our clothes."

"Oh, dear. That's awful. However, who rescued you? People want to know."

"A stunning woman. Her name is Angela."

"Who is this brave woman?"

"We don't know her. She has long, amber hair. She popped out of nowhere and whacked the Polish guys."

"How did she know your place?"

"We do not know."

"Elisha, you are silent. What about you?"

Elisha rested her hand on her bare knee. "It was a hellish nightmare. We slept on a dirty floor and ate eggs and beans and bread for a week. The procurers are sex traffickers. They run underground brothels and sex escorts outside the country. Thank God we are here."

"The cops say they pulled four bodies from the rubble of the house. Who destroyed the house, and who is the woman who saved you?"

"The house fell in a sinkhole. The woman who saved

us is an angel from heaven and my new hero.”

“Where does she live?”

“We do not know. She dropped us off at our homes. She knows New York very well,” Kristin said.

“A tall woman warrior with orange hair was with her. She called her mom,” Meghan said.

“What do you mean woman warrior?”

“She has muscular arms and legs and stunning abs. She wears a fantasy war costume.”

Two days later, Angela snuggled with Camille in the living room. Elisha texted her. “Watch me. I have an interview on CBS in seven minutes. See you tomorrow.”

Angela changed the TV channel. Camille gave her knee a light slap. “We didn’t finish the film.”

“This is important. I have recorded the film.”

An anchor interviewed Elisha and asked about her torment and the sex traffickers. “Who saved you from the Polish villains? You should have an idea about her.”

“Yes, I know her.”

“Who is she?”

“She is Angela Lucciano.”

The interviewer put her pen down and paused for a moment. “Is she related to you?”

“She is my mother and Leonardo Lucciano’s eldest daughter. She lives in Canada.”

“Interesting. How did she know the place where the Polish guys held you as a hostage?”

“She has a sixth sense, like a hypnotist.”

“How?”

“She sees invisible things and predicts things, and her imagination or intuition is incredible. I appeal to the cops and the FBI to forgive her for taking the law into her hands. What would you do if depraved psychopaths abducted and raped your daughter?"

Camille goggled at Angela. "Why didn't you tell me you have a daughter?"

"She is not my daughter."

"Are you telling me the truth?"

"Yes. I have never had sex with a man and have never been pregnant. So, how would I be a mother? Elisha talked in a metaphorical sense. Her mom was my first girlfriend, and Elisha is not my biological daughter. I swear."

"How did you save her? Are you a secret agent or a commando? What is the story? I thought you went to New York to see your Italian family."

"I picked Elisha up after her release."

The next day, Elisha arrived in Toronto. Angela locked her bedroom door and caressed her every day. Camille roamed in the city and kept herself engaged with people and landscape photography. She thought Elisha needed Angela to comfort her.

There had been a meaningful change in Angela's online social life. She had eighty-three online female friends, but after Elisha uploaded personal photos, Angela gained significant attention from hundreds of models and socialites who followed her and posted romantic texts and comments on her social media pages.

One day, Camille placed her laptop on Angela's thighs. "Who are those half-naked *femmes* who send you bikini photos and say they love you? Who is

Caroline, who says she wants to suck your lips and nipples? Why do you hide things from me?"

"Please, don't be jealous and huffy. These women live far away from here. I didn't force them to follow me on social media, and I do not hide things from you. You live in my house, and you can check my rooms, papers, bags, and phones."

Later, Elisha and fourteen US models traveled to Toronto to thank Angela for her heroic action. They invited her and Camille to a boisterous party in a nightclub in the Entertainment District. Dressed in a funky Hawaiian short-sleeve shirt and tapered linen pants, Angela got sensual hugs and kisses while dancing with the stylish models. When she moved to their hotel suite after midnight, Camille held her hand. "Come on. It is too late. Let us go home."

A model took off her shirt and gave Angela a kiss and a glass of wine. "She will stay with us tonight and tomorrow." She nuzzled and licked Angela's bare shoulder. Another model walked her fingers down Camille's uncovered arm. "Stay and have fun with us. You won't regret it."

"I am not staying here. I am going home."

Angela gave her two hundred dollars before the models dragged her to a bedroom, persuading her to fondle and sleep with them. Other models slept in sleeping bags and on couches.

At ten, Angela woke up half-naked, gazing at two topless models sleeping beside her. After picking up her phone, she went to the bathroom and rested on the toilet seat. She called Camille, and a model entered the bathroom. "Have you finished?"

"Yeah." The model sat, and Angela washed her face. When she wiped her face with a towel, the model took off her underwear and entered the shower room. "Have a shower with me."

"Thanks." She left the bathroom and met Elisha. "I want to go home."

"After breakfast. Why the hurry? Come with me."

They descended to the hotel restaurant, and Angela called Camille six times. "I am worried about Camille. She didn't answer my calls."

"Drink your coffee and don't worry about her. She would call you if something happened. She is still sleeping."

Two models joined their table. One of them rubbed her fingers on Angela's face. "I wish I have your smooth skin."

"Thanks." She sipped her coffee. "I must go. I feel something happened to Camille."

"Come on. Nothing happened to her. I guess she didn't like what we have done with you. Women are jealous. You know."

"I must go. I will see you later."

A taxi took her home. After entering the house, she heard a clang in the kitchen. "Hi, Camille. Why didn't you answer my calls?"

She kissed Angela's lips. "I woke up five minutes ago. Did you sleep well?"

"Yeah. My head is heavy. I had too much alcohol." She stared at her dark red bikini. "Do you feel hot?"

"Yes. I feel hot and horny after seeing the sexy girls.

I want to have sex with you right now. Sit on the bar.”

“I am tired. Can we have sex later?”

“It won’t take long. I will do the action.” Angela lay on the breakfast bar, and she took off her shoes and pants and climbed on the countertop. “Close your eyes. I want my tongue to wipe your body.” Angela closed her eyes, and she licked her legs and opened a drawer to get a spike dagger. Sensing danger, Angela opened her eyes and kicked her in the face, throwing her on the dining table. She scowled and rubbed her face. “Do you hit your girlfriend? I thought you loved me.”

“Why are you holding the knife?”

“To cut the pineapple.”

“You are fake.”

“I am not fake. I know you are a fraud. Why do you pretend to be a normal woman, Goddess Angela?”

“How do you know me?”

With a wave of her hand, the woman cast an enchanting spell upon herself. In a shocking display of dark colors, her appearance changed. Her skin turned into a deep shade of crimson, and her eyes sparkled with fire. Her hair transformed into long tresses of tangerine, cascading down her back like a river of molten lava. “Does it matter? Your mom and her witchy sister are bad, bad girls. Where is the eagle’s damn eye? Where is the secret code?” She jumped off the floor and choked Angela’s neck with a string. Angela punched her breasts, and her body hit the ceiling. She fell to her feet and threw the marble countertop at her, but Angela’s fists crushed it. “Did your mom teach you how to fight? I don’t like to kill you because you are the only good one. Give me the code. I don't want to waste my time with you."

"You will never get it."

"You left me with no choice but to kill you." She jumped, and a steel fireplace poker penetrated her throat. A liquid tar came out of her mouth and eyes.

"Mom." Angela gawked at Anohitecha.

"She is Tawiscara's last wife, Quoiayica." She cuffed Quoiayica's head, and her body turned into ashes. "Go to Camille. She is in her bedroom. I will clean the mess and see you later."

Angela sped upstairs and saw Camille chained and crouched in a corner. She removed the duct tape from her mouth and cut the chains around her hands and ankles. Camille hugged her and cried. "Who was that witch? How could she make herself like me?"

"That was a devil. You are safe with me."

"I am scared and want to go home."

"I understand. Have a shower to calm yourself down, and I will prepare food for you."

"Please, don't leave me. I am afraid."

"OK. I will sit in the bathroom."

"How are you so powerful? How did you break the chains with your hands?"

"Who knows? I am an angel." She carried her and took her to the bathroom.

Four days later, Camille addressed Angela with a friendly spirit. "I told you I was a lesbian before I met you. My ex-girlfriend wants me to be with her again. So, I want to go back to my country. What happened to me last week had frightened the hell out of me." She kissed her. "Many beautiful women love you, and that will not make me worry about you. *Merci* very much for the marvelous things you did for me. If you come to France one day, I will do my best for you. I will text you and send you photos."

"Doing what you love should be your priority. I will be fine on my own. Thanks for your amazing company and for letting me know fascinating things about France and French food and culture."

She entered her bedroom to collect her baggage, and Hintocha appeared in Angela's bedroom. "Poor girl. Though I am not too fond of her narcissistic ego, I feel sad for her. The white French think they are superior to other nations. I respect the down-to-earth people."

"Thus spoke the Goddess Athena. What about the down-to-my-gut woman?"

"Shut up. Take this."

Angela pressed a hand on her abdomen and bent forward. "Why did you kick me?"

"To remind you of the boss here. I am a goddess, not a street girl."

"And I am the Goddess Angela." She raised her fists. "Come and fight like a real goddess."

"Are you making a drama now? I haven't kicked you hard."

"Honey, I am kidding. You will always have my deepest affection."

"I know that, though your erotic promiscuity with the models had amazed me."

"My heart goes out to the women of the earth. I had an exciting time with the models because I don't like to see people in a sad mood."

"Yeah, but you don't need to sleep with every woman on earth."

"I can't control my emotions. My human traits desire women all the time."

"I wish to make love to you away from this screwy planet. I feel I am losing my patience."

Camille packed up her belongings and left. Elisha heard about her departure and flew to Toronto to retell Angela about her love for her. One night, she wore a black bikini and asked her to sit with her in the warm bathtub. When she rested opposite her, she massaged her feet. "I have never loved a woman as much as you. You are so special. When can I be your girlfriend?"

Angela pulled her to her thighs and embraced her narrow shoulders. "Honey, my deep love for you is infinite, and the intimate bond between you and me is timeless."

"What does that mean?"

"You are my love, but I told everybody you are my daughter. You told your friends and the world I am your mother. Your birth certificate says I am your mom. My family and your mother's family believe I am your second mother. Your modeling agencies will end your work with them if you say you are my girlfriend. Do you want to say you lied about your relationship with me?" She paused and kissed her neck. "This is your house. You can come here and spend more time with me, but I can't make our love public. You are smart and understand how things work in this world."

"I know. I guess I am a dimwit."

"No, darling, you are not. Forget the irretrievable past and appreciate the moment. Fill your heart with love because it is our life."

"There is one more thing. I apologized to my mom for ruining her relationship with you. I feel guilty because of her love for you and her wish to be with you again. But she does not know how to stop my affair and reconnect with you because you live here. Do you still love her?"

"Do you want to know the truth?"

"Of course."

Angela covered her with a robe and carried her to the bed. "Do you promise to keep this conversation a secret?"

"I promise, Madam Secrets."

"Let me tell you something about your mom. Your mom was my greatest love. It is difficult for me to forget her."

"Despite what she did to you?"

She rubbed her hand. "I witnessed the death of your mom's father in New York."

"Oh, my God. Did you kill him?"

"No. I was a kid. He was a smug member of the Irish Mafia. One day, he tried to hurt me when I was thirteen because I threw a knife at him when he wanted to kill my granddad in a restaurant, but a flowerpot fell on his head and killed him in front of me. My grandpa and great grandpa Stefano killed his dad Cian beside his Irish bar on Eleventh Avenue and dumped his body in the Hudson."

"Why did they do that?"

"Because of alcohol, fish, and prostitution. Cian prevented the Italians from selling wine, cheese, and fish in his neighborhood and called Italian women whores. Stefano died in Italy, and the FBI could not arrest Sandro because of the lack of evidence and fear. I care for your mom because she grew up as a poor orphan with little love. Not to mention the swine who raped her."

"Who was he?"

"A scummy nerd. His name was Evan Sullivan."

"How do you know that?"

"My dad killed him."

"Gee! Leonardo was a nice man. How?"

"One night, he and Bella attended an evening concert and strolled in the Theater District. They heard your mom screaming in a dingy store. My dad fixed his hat, covered his face with Bella's scarf, and broke into the store. He found Evan raping and spanking your mom on the floor. The rape had enraged him, forcing him to shoot Evan dead."

"What happened after that?"

"My dad supported your mom with affection and money after she told him about her tragic life. He asked her to contact a Scottish Catholic family in this city and paid for her travel and education without revealing his identity and home address. Bella's sister in London received your mom's cards and letters and sent them to my dad."

"Why didn't you tell my mom the entire story?"

"I knew nothing about the rapist or about my dad's

involvement. But after burying my parents, Bella's sister, Emma, gave me your mom's cards and letters, which she sent to my dad. So, when I asked her why Caitlyn sent cards and letters to her, she told me the truth about your mom's rape."

"I loved Leonardo. He was very kind."

"I owe him a lot. I am rich because of him. After your birth, he wanted you to have our family name, but when I told him about my love for your mom and the unfortunate death of her father, uncles, brothers, and grandpa, he changed his mind. I had never said an offensive word to your mom, and I do not know how I will tell her Leonardo had rescued her and killed her rapist. It is interesting how God or the Great Spirit had arranged my first meeting with her. We had never organized our life. Our spirits were free."

"Thank God she did not abort me. You should write a book about her life."

"I will."

Chapter 6

In September, Elisha invited Angela to New York Fashion Week. Angela accepted her invitation and flew to Manhattan in the morning.

In the early afternoon, two FBI officers knocked on Anohitecha's house door. She opened the door, and they peeked at her body. "The FBI." They showed her their official identity cards.

"Yes, how can I help you?"

"We need a word with Angela Lucciano?"

"Yes, sure. Please, come in." She guided the officers to the living room.

"How do you know Angela?"

"I am her mother."

"How are you her mother?"

"I don't need to prove that to you, and I think you

are not here to know about my personal life.”

Angela wiped her face with a hand towel and entered the room. “Yes, what is going on here?”

“We are FBI officers. I am Byron Douglas, and my colleague is David Tilson. We need to talk.”

“No problem.” Angela sat in a chair.

“Do you know Jacub Janeczek?”

“Yes. Jacub’s father and my dad were friends.”

“We found Jacub’s body in the Hudson River.”

“Oh, my God. That’s horrible. Who killed him?”

“We don’t know, but we know you killed his two brothers.”

“This is not true. I killed nobody.”

“Your daughter Elisha and other models told the press you killed their abductors, including Jacub’s brothers.”

“They credited me with rescuing them when the captors were not around. After that, the crappy house fell into a sinkhole and killed them.”

“How did you rescue them?”

“I skulked into the house from the back door.”

“How did you know the place?”

“I see what you can’t see.”

“What do you mean?”

“I mean, I see your two tall sons, and I see your two brunette daughters and son.”

The officers gazed at each other. “But we found a body with a cleaver stuck in the head and two bodies wrapped with chains.”

“And you think this woman did all that?”

“But you were there.”

"Yes, I was there to save my daughter and her friends. Do you think I made a deep crater with these hands? You know my dad's family used guns to kill gangsters, not sinkholes. I think the captors killed each other for money."

"What about Jacub?"

"Maybe a model's father killed him and threw his body in the river after knowing about his gang."

"We found no shots in his body."

"So, do you assume I carried an obese man and threw him at a place full of people? Did anybody or any surveillance camera see anything?"

"No. What about Martina?"

"What about her?"

"We know the Ukrainian and Russian Mafia had abducted her. A gang killed four of her abductors and their bosses."

"Is it an Italian gang? I know nothing about the Ukrainian and Russian Mafias. I live in Canada."

"But local witnesses saw you and your cousins in Brighton Beach on the same day when hitmen killed them."

"We had a quick snack in an Italian restaurant. My cousins didn't hurt anybody."

David stood and inspected a wall decorated with Native American traditional weapons. "What do you do for a living?"

"I am an artist."

"Who would use such weapons to kill the Ukrainian-Russian gangsters?"

"You are the forensic experts." Angela smiled. "Do

you think the Italians would use tomahawks, spears, and war clubs to fight Mafia mobsters armed with machine guns?"

"You tell me."

"Yes, I will tell you one logical thing. Italians can forgive everybody, but they will never ever forgive the villains who play dirty games with their women. That's all I can say now. Please, leave. My daughter has a fashion show, and I need to be there. Wait. A fat guy is holding a machine gun and heading to the subway in Brooklyn. He is wearing a blue T-shirt and a black cap. Get him."

The officers ran out of the house, and Anohitecha embraced her daughter. "Don't worry, my love. No one can hurt you when I am here. I always watch you."

"Thank you, mom. When will we leave this mad planet?"

"When my sister defeats our enemies."

After putting on a burgundy off-shoulder, frill trim bodycon dress and brushing her hair, Angela called Elisha. "Where is the fashion show?"

"In Spring Studios, at St. Johns Lane, on the sixth floor. I got you a VIP front-row seat."

"Great. See you soon."

Hintocha entered Angela's body. "Let us see the sexy girls."

Angela took a cab and turned up at the Studios. On the sixth floor, she walked to a dim, festooned ballroom. Not knowing where to go and what to do, she peeped behind hanging drapes to see Elisha. An African American model patted her right shoulder. "Excuse me, ma'am. May I help?"

"Yes. I am Elisha Lucciano's mom. May I see her for a moment?"

"Do you have any proof?"

"Yes. Here is my driving license."

"Just a minute."

"Hi, mom." Elisha kissed her. "Nice dress. Here is the ticket. Go here. A woman will take you to your seat."

Angela glimpsed her black, strapless gown. "You look stunning. Is your mom here?"

"I don't know. I have not seen her. Go now. The show will start after twelve minutes."

A woman inspected her ticket and directed her to a seat. A guest, wearing a white jacket, glanced at her face and bare shoulders and shook her hand. "Are you a fashion designer?"

Hintocha laughed. "No. She is a goddess who can destroy your planet. This guy thinks you have a fashion company."

"I wish. No. I am a model's mother."

"Who is your daughter?"

"Elisha."

"Elisha Lucciano? Her charm is unquestionable, and her success as a model has been remarkable."

"Thank you. You are kind."

Anticipation charged the atmosphere as the show began, with the air filled with glamor and excitement. When elegant and slim models entered the long hall, their presence had commanded attention, and their strides had captured the pith of the event. The runway became a stage where extravaganza and fashion had merged into a visual show.

Amid the parade of models, a moment of personal connection had unfolded. When Elisha saw Angela, a warm smile graced her lips, and her gesture, waving her red nail-polished fingers, was an affectionate way of recognizing Angela's presence amidst the glamor and spectacle. Angela waved back and turned her face around to see if Caitlyn was there. Eleven minutes later, Elisha appeared on the runway holding a Christian Dior handbag. When she got close to Angela, she tossed an iPhone on her thighs.

Angela stared at the phone. "She wants you to check the last messages," Hintocha said. Angela pressed the Messages app and read the following text from Caitlyn. "Hiding in the restroom in Chase Bank, Cooper Square. Guys are shooting. Love you. Take care."

Panic raced through Angela's veins, causing her to quiver. "Come on. Let us go," Hintocha pleaded, her voice trembling with urgency.

Angela left the venue and met Elisha. "Here is your phone. Stay here and enjoy the show. I will do my best for your mom."

As she stepped out of the building, she approached a waiting taxi. Leaning toward the open window, she informed the driver of her destination. "Please, could you take me to Chase Bank at Astor Place?" The driver nodded, and the car merged into the flow of traffic.

Minutes later, the Sikh cabbie slowed the car, his brow furrowing in concern. "Oh, no," he muttered, his voice tinged with dismay. "What is going on here? Sorry, ma'am. The police barriers have blocked the road." The flashing lights of the police vehicle and the armed officers had created an imposing roadblock, preventing any further passage.

She turned to the taxi driver. "Is there another route we can take?"

The cabbie shook his head, a hint of regret in his eyes. "I am afraid all the nearby streets are affected. Looks like something significant is happening. It might take a while for the road to clear."

"Can you drop me off at the nearest point of pedestrian access? I will walk from there."

The bearded driver wiggled his turbaned head and navigated through a series of side streets until finding a suitable spot to stop. Angela paid the fare and thanked him for his help before stepping out onto the sidewalk.

Approaching the scene with caution, she saw law enforcement cars and officers positioned with steady focus. Bullet-proof helmets and vests had adorned their firm figures, and their stern expressions mirrored the gravity of the situation. Their guns pointed at the bank, suggesting a heightened state of alertness.

Seeking answers, Angela talked to a tall bystander, hoping to gain insights into the unfolding events. With a sense of urgency in her voice, she asked, "What is going on?"

The bystander glanced at her and took a moment to collect his thoughts, his gaze shifting toward the bank before returning to meet hers. "I am not sure," he replied with apprehension. "There seems to be a potential threat in the bank. The cops came to secure the area and ensure the safety of everyone involved.”

“Anything else?”

“I overheard people saying there might be a hostage situation inside.” His voice hushed with concern. “Please, be careful. It is a tense situation, and the authorities are working to resolve it.”

“Thank you.” Angela surveyed the scene, and her gaze fell upon a paunchy NYPD officer carrying a megaphone and standing in front of nine police and FBI cars. “Sir, let me go into the bank. I know how to deal with this problem.”

The agitated officer gave his attention to her, his stare meeting her gaze with surprise and doubt. The weight of the situation was clear in his eyes, though he kept his professional composure. “And who might you be?” His gruff voice carried a note of suspicion. “What makes you think you can manage this risky situation?”

“I possess unique abilities and have the power that can bring about a peaceful resolution. I want to help, to ensure the safety of the people inside the bank.”

“Well, ma’am. Can’t you see what is going on here? Please, stay away. This is a serious situation.”

“Please, let me help. I am Angela Lucciano.”

“Lucciano? Do you think this is an Italian Mafia war? Thanks, buddy. We do not need your help. Don’t you see the cops and the FBI officers?”

“I am sorry.” Angela abandoned the officers and moved toward a crowded Starbucks Coffee shop. Seconds later, she crossed Astor Place and Lafayette Street and hotfooted into the bank with her hands up.

An NYPD officer swore. “Who is that stupid girl?

They will shoot her."

Angela stood at a counter, her eyes scanning the hall. Squatted people, their faces etched with fear and helplessness, attached their bodies to glazed walls. Their eyes met hers, pleading for salvation or a glimmer of hope.

The presence of a bearded, frizzy-haired gunman had drawn her attention. He stood at the center of the hall, and she took a step forward. But before any dialog between them, the NYPD officer with the megaphone provided a reminder of the collective efforts to diffuse the situation. "We have negotiators on their way. We are here to ensure the safety of everyone. Please, let us resolve this situation without harm."

Angela added her own plea. "Listen to them. There is a chance for redemption, for a different way. Don't let fear and anger dictate your action. I am a woman of peace. Please, can we talk?"

The gunman smiled. "Good, woman. I also believe in peace." He stretched out his hand, and Angela wanted to shake his hand, but in a sudden act of aggression, he reacted with violence, striking her lower neck with the butt of his machine gun.

The impact sent a jolt of pain through her body, causing her to collapse to her hands and knees. When she tried to get up, the gunman hit her neck twice. "Stupid goop." Angela fell on her face and shut her eyes like a dead person. The gunman kicked her legs and abdomen and hauled her behind the counter. "What a bitch."

An armed accomplice appeared from behind a

teller's desk. "What happened?"

"This hooker wanted peace. Peace, my ass. Look at these sexy legs and boobies." They tittered.

Angela's body convulsed and vibrated up and down and left and right, and a guttural yawp came out of her slobbering mouth. The two gunmen and the cowered hostages gaped at her. They shivered in fear when Hintocha left her body without ripping off her clothes. With two braids on her covered chest and orange stripes prettifying her eyes and biceps, she shrieked like a ferocious brown bear. "I am angry. I will kill you, scumbags." Her fists clenched when she made herself seven feet tall and marched toward the gunmen. A brigade of female warriors holding iron-tipped spears and metal eagle shields appeared and guarded the hostages.

"Do not move." The first gunman fired shots at Hintocha and the warriors, but the bullets vanished in their bodies, as if they were invisible ghosts. He quivered, and his friend crouched behind a wall. Hintocha seized the man's gun and broke it on her knee into two halves, grabbed his arm, and threw him twenty feet away. Anohitecha showed up. "Get the other guys." She flashed to the gunman and grasped his ankles, swinging him up and down, hitting his head on the floor, and saying, "Don't you ever hit my girl." With his skull bleeding, she carried him and stopped behind the glass facade. "What the hell is happening? Who is that giant woman? What is she doing there?" an officer said.

Anohitecha flung the gunman through the front glass. The glass shattered into a thousand pieces, and the gunman's bloodstained body rolled like a log toward the standing law enforcement officers. "Holy crap! Wonder Woman is back," a policeman jested.

"She is the new Supergirl," another officer said.

The other criminal and two masked gunmen fired bullets at Anohitecha and Hintocha. "Suckers, put your guns down." Hintocha roared like a wild beast. They tottered, and their guns fell on the floor. She trod toward one of them and hurled him on a counter. Anohitecha dropped a heavy desk on his body when he cursed and crushed him. After that, she sat beside Angela, rubbing her head and back. Hintocha stared at the shooters. "Don't move your arms and legs, dum-dums." Her words had frozen them and paralyzed their limbs. She grabbed their belts and pitched their bodies outside the bank.

"We have crazy witches in the town. These gigantic hags are doing our job," a startled officer said.

To Hintocha's surprise, the gang's boss came out of an office with his left arm around Caitlyn's neck. "What did you do to my friends?" He stared at the warriors. "Who are these freaking zombies? Leave the place, or I will kill this woman."

Anohitecha stood and swung her arm as if she flung something at him. A hardwood tomahawk appeared and split his skull, splattering his green army coat with blood. Caitlyn shuddered and yelled, and Anohitecha hugged her. "Caitlyn, calm down. It is over. Do not worry." She looked at the warriors. "Let the people go out of the bank. They are out of danger." The warriors vanished, and the hostages ran out of the bank.

Caitlyn looked ashen and unsettled. "Who are you? How do you know my name?"

"I am Angela's real mother. Come with me. I love you and love Elisha." She caught the boss's pants flare, dragging him on the floor and plodding to Angela. When Caitlyn saw her stationary body, she hunched down and cried. "Angela, Angela."

"Your Highness, take Caitlyn to her home, and I will take Angela to Jodasiya to heal her," Hintocha said. Anohitecha took Caitlyn to her house, and Hintocha carried Angela on her shoulder and pulled the gang's boss out to the law enforcement officials. "It is over, guys." She made a funny face.

Reporters and onlookers took photos of her. An officer's irritated eyes scanned the brutal taking of life. "Did you kill him with an ax? Who are you?"

She ignored the questions, opened a car door, and put Angela in the rear seat.

Another officer pointed his pistol at her. "This is an FBI car. Don't move. You are under arrest."

"Shut up and go home, little man." She raised her lean arms, causing the law enforcement vehicles to hover in the air like alien spacecrafts. The officers and watchers became petrified. "Who are you? Are you a superwoman?" an officer said.

She dropped her arms down, and the vehicles landed on the street. In a second, she was behind the steering wheel. "I will kill you if you follow me." She gazed up at scattered clouds. "*Gehgeyo danohso gyiyohe* [Bring down abundant rain]." Bolts of lightning tore through the gray sky, and thunderous booms resonated through the atmosphere, shaking the surrounding buildings. The heavens seemed to roar in unison with the turmoil unfolding below. As the storm intensified, a torrential downpour ensued, drenching the streets and parks in the immediate vicinity. The relentless deluge served as a metaphorical cleansing, washing away the strains of discord and violence.

Hintocha drove a black Chevrolet Suburban for four hours until she reached the town of Owego in Tioga County. She parked the car at a vacant house near the Susquehanna River. Like a specter, she walked through a stone wall and opened the main door from the inside. She cradled Angela in her arms and laid her down on a bed before taking off her dress and shoes. She fetched a small wet towel and put it on her flushed forehead. Emotions were high. Her right hand held her left hand and rubbed it on her face. Two long tears rolled down her face. Angela turned her head to the left and cleared her distracted eyes. "What happened? Where am I?" She gazed at Hintocha's face.

She wiped her tears. "You are with me." She kissed her hand.

"I am happy to see you again. When did you leave my body?"

"Sit back and relax. I suppose you are hungry." She rubbed and kissed her belly. "I will take your purse and get food. Don't move and stay warm."

She brought back food from a nearby restaurant. After sitting next to Angela, she had two bites and sips. Angela stared at her shining teeth and brilliant lips. "Is this the first time you eat and drink?"

"It is delightful I eat and drink when I am with you."

"I forgot. What did we eat and drink in the sky?"

"We ate fruits and drank from rivers of water and wine." She kissed her lips. "I love you, honey."

"I love you too. Where are we?"

"In the town of Owego."

"What are we doing in this house? How did we come here?"

"We will stay here for one night. I got a car. We will go to Canada tomorrow."

"How did you learn to drive?"

"I can drive anything."

"I left my passport at my mom's house."

"Someone will get it after we go home. Do not talk and finish your food." She put her hand on her mouth and blew misty air on her face. "This will strengthen your body. I am free now and want to enhance my love for you." They cuddled and slept beside each other.

After a cheese sandwich breakfast with a cup of coffee, Angela rested in the car and noticed a pile of documents scattered on the floor mat. Intrigued by their presence, she picked them up, examining the contents with curious eyes. The bold words "Federal Bureau of Investigation" decorated the top of the documents, confirming her initial suspicion. "Is this an FBI car?"

"Yes. I borrowed it."

"How did you get it?"

"I will tell you the full story in Toronto."

Hintocha drove west to Chautauqua Lake and stopped the car on Manor Drive at Prendergast Point.

"Hold my hand and come with me."

They strolled to the Lake. Hintocha immersed her right hand in the water and made a rhythmic ripple. "Jodasiya, we are here."

"Yes, I hear you."

"Angela is here."

Jodasiya popped up from the lake and enfolded her arms around Angela, who groaned and massaged her neck.

"What happened?"

"A guy hit the back of my neck."

"Let me see." Jodasiya pulled up her hair and looked at purple bruises. She touched Hintocha's hand. "Your Highness, get me five leaves from that tree." Hintocha brought the green folioles to her. Jodasiya chewed the bitter leaves and spat them on Angela's neck. Seconds later, she wiped the spittle with her sleeve, and the bruises disappeared. "You are fine now."

"Thanks. I love you."

"I love you too. Take diligent care of yourself. Go home and do not forget me." She kissed them and plunged into the lake water.

"Why doesn't Jodasiya spend more time with us?"

"She can't leave the lake for over fifteen minutes in peaceful times. She does commendable works for the First Nations."

"I see. How will we cross the border? We do not have passports."

"Again. Why do you keep saying dummy things? Did you forget who we are? We are goddesses. No human can stop us." She drove north and halted the car on

Busti Avenue near Front Park in Buffalo city. "Get out." When Angela left the vehicle, Hintocha snapped her fingers, causing the car to disappear.

"Where is the car?"

"Be patient. We will get it in Canada."

"What about the crossing?"

"Think and stop asking questions. We will walk on the Peace Bridge. Come close to me." She clutched her head and ears and disappeared. After turning up at a tree at Concession Road, she pressed her back against a lamppost. Angela left her body. "What did you do? I felt cornered in a hutch."

She chuckled. "You were inside me. Let us get food and ice cream. The car is over there."

"Here is a McDonald's. Do you like burgers?"

"I don't eat slaughtered corpses. You should also stop eating meat."

After eating vegetarian Chinese food in Happy Jack's restaurant on Niagara Boulevard, Hintocha touched Angela's hand. "Honey, guess what? We will go to the Niagara River and the Falls. They are special places for my mom and me. The First Nation lived around the water."

She drove north and parked the car in the Fallsview Tourist Area. They wandered to the Falls with their hands together, fondling and kissing. "The people are staring at us. They think we are lesbians."

"What happened to your brain? We are lesbians. Did you forget our sex? Let them say what they want. Who cares?"

Hintocha moved west to Hamilton and north to the

downtown of Mississauga and stopped at Square One Shopping Centre. She took Angela to Sephora, a cosmetics store, and got red lipsticks, perfumes, and a nail polish set. Angela gazed at her face and grinned. "Why are you smiling? I love make-up. Use your credit card."

They sat in the car. "The girl didn't see the name on the credit card." Hintocha gave her a copy of *The New York Times*. "Wow. You are on the front page. The paper calls you Wonder Woman. Did you kill the bad guys in the bank?"

"I think so. Your mom got revenge on the person who struck you."

"What happened to Caitlyn?"

"She is safe with your mom. Elisha will look after her if necessary."

"Did you tell her who you are?"

"No. Caitlyn will know me at a later time."

Back in the comfort of her home, Angela couldn't shake the feeling of an overwhelming connection to her best soulmate. She touched Hintocha's face and kissed her lips. "Honey, please, do not disappear again. I want you to be with me all the time. I feel I live a double life as a goddess and a human."

She nuzzled her nose and lips. "You are my love. When you slept in Owego, my mom came over and set me free because I saved the hostages in the bank. Stay here."

She brought a chocolate chiffon cake with four candles on it. "Happy birthday, sweetheart."

"Is it my birthday today?"

"Yeah. Today is your fortieth birthday on earth."

A wave of fear washed over her, causing her heart to race and her thoughts to spin with uncertainty. Hintocha held her hand. "Honey, what's wrong? Why did you panic?" She tickled her face.

"Colestah said a significant event will happen to the world when I become forty. I feel scared."

"Be confident. You are a goddess, and I am with you. Don't believe in superstitious legends."

"The Seneca Nation says Colestah's predictions are inevitable. She doesn't lie."

"I don't say she lies. But stories are stories, and no one can harm you when I am with you. We are divine. So, open your sexy mouth and taste my delicious cake." She put a piece of cake in her mouth and licked her lips.

Angela remained silent for fifteen seconds. "What should I say? I wished I could remove all the human elements from my body and restore my full divine nature. You said nothing about this matter."

"Your mom and grandma are supreme goddess. I can't interfere without their permission. You should have asked them to purify you and restore your original being after the death of Leonardo and Bella. Anyway, I have good news for you. I will erase the human components and make you as you were in the sky."

"It is too late."

"No, love, it is not too late. I could not make you a full divine goddess because of the Lucciano family and because I was not free. But now, you can be as you were in the sky."

"How?"

"What about a surprise? Lie on the couch and close your eyes." She reclined on her back on a couch and shut her eyes. Hintocha stretched her fingers and lifted her hands over her body. "*Taoya Wagoha, ogagasado haho yeoh degenowa tah agonoh …* [Holder of the Sky, make her a virgin goddess and remove …]." A sudden and terrifying presence had materialized behind her. A colossal brown monster, with squinting red eyes filled with malignity, had struck without warning.

The monster's immense strength propelled her forward, her body colliding against a wall. The wall collapsed, and she fell on a table, dropping books and framed photos on the floor. Angela's eyes widened in terror as she gazed at the grotesque features of the monster who cornered her. His long, gnarled fingers curled in a menacing manner, and his broken teeth protruded from his snarling maw.

The monster put his hand on her face. "Give me the code, or I will cut off your body."

Hintocha got up and stepped over the fallen books and pictures. "Dagwano, stop it and don't move. I am coming to kill you."

Dagwano giggled. "You stupid girl cannot stop me. God made me of fire and more powerful than you." With a mighty heave, he seized a wide bookshelf and hurled it toward Hintocha, aiming to crush her beneath its weight. The air filled with the sound of splintering wood and the rustle of pages.

Before she could react, the bookshelf crashed down upon her. Books tumbled and cascaded around her, burying her beneath their weight. Yet, as if this assault was not enough, the monster conjured a ball of orange fire in his hand. The fiery sphere glowed with an intense heat, flickering and cracking with destructive energy. With a sinister grin, the monster unleashed the ball of fire, hurling it toward Hintocha.

The blazing projectile hit the bookshelf and books, igniting a roaring inferno. High flames engulfed the wooden structure, devouring the pages and their literature. The fire raged with a fierce intensity, dancing and leaping in a destructive ballet.

Angela twitched. "Mom."

"Your mom is not here. I will leave you if you give me the code."

"Go to hell."

"Not before you, stupid girl." With his left hand on Angela's belly, Dagwano pulled a double-bit axe and wanted to chop off her body. Angela yelled. "Mom." Her trembling body evaporated in a water whirl. A woman cropped up in a full suit of armor with a gunstock war club in her right hand and a bald eagle on her left arm. "But I can stop you, piece of shit. What did you do to her?"

"I sent her to hell."

She hit his forehead with the club, and the sharp spearhead spike stuck into his bulgy eye. Dagwano shrieked, with his fists smashing the surrounding furniture. "The Eagle Woman! How did you come back? You died in Great Bear Lake. I will kill you." He swung his right arm, but she twisted and dismembered it when a brown bear ripped off his back, and four eagles pulled apart his long ears. There was no blood, but smoke came out of his arm and head. She trilled at her eagles. "Get him." Their sharp talons ripped up Dagwano's wrinkled face and hairless head. A purple-haired warrior appeared and slit his flabby chest open with a tang machete. The eagles cut out his clammy heart. He collapsed on his knees and smoldered, turning into dark cinders. The Eagle Woman kissed the warrior. "Thanks, Xiola. You can go now." Xiola vanished.

Hintocha extinguished the fire with five spits and flounced to the Eagle Woman. "Where is Angela? Who are you, witch?" She yapped and struck with her right hand, but the Eagle Women grabbed her fist and slammed her down on her back. She sat on Hintocha's abdomen and slapped her face. "You fool. All the terrible things happened because of you."

"Watch your back," Hintocha cried out.

A gigantic horned fiend raised his stone club, and the Eagle Woman's left hand crushed the bones of his right wrist. Her right hand grabbed his neck, with her sharp nails growing like drilling screws penetrating his throat. She pulled out his mucous trachea, and with flaming eyes, she became so furious that she broke his horn and hurled him through three walls. Her eagles and bear ripped him apart.

Hintocha looked at the enormous holes in the walls. "My Goddess, who are you?"

The Eagle Woman turned her face and gave her a light slap. "You witch, have you forgotten me? I am Anna Awehitecha."

Hintocha gawked and bowed, with her shaky hands

resting on her knees. "My Glorious Goddess and Queen of Heaven, I am sorry. I beg your divine forgiveness."

Awehitecha pinched her nose. "We were happy in the sky. Why did you drop me on this stupid planet? Why did you push me?"

"I swear I didn't intend to chuck you out of the sky. I thought it would be fun to play games with the mad people of the earth. You are all-powerful and the Commander-in-Chief of our supreme goddesses. Why didn't you come back?"

"Did you forget? You put me in a void sphere and exposed me to militant gods and devils, who shut me off in forests."

"Please, forgive me. You are my true love. Where is your niece?"

"I don't know. She disappeared into the swirling water. Tawiscara swore to kill her and my sister."

"Why he wants to kill them?"

"Do the devils need any reason to corrupt and kill? What did you do to Angela?"

"Nothing. I asked the Holder of the Sky to make her a full goddess."

"The Holder of the Sky? You know that only my sister or I and the Mother Goddess can make her a full goddess. You were not supposed to play games with her fragile emotions."

"But my mom didn't let me talk to anyone else, and you disappeared. So, what did you expect me to do for your niece? Talk about the sun and the moon? I have feelings, and I have a true love for Angela. This love differs from our divine affection in the sky. What am I supposed to do now?"

"You will be under my command for twenty-seven days every month. You can go anywhere and do what you like for three days every month."

"Where did Angela go?"

"I said I don't know. I don't think she died in the raging water because Gayadosha says she will lead the nations of the earth. You seduced her and made love to her for twenty-two years, as if you were her mistress."

"What mistress? Did you expect me to be a nun? Yes, you are my superior, but why do you talk to me like that? Do you think I was happy when I lost you? Am I not your eternal love?"

"You are. I am not angry at you."

"Do you know why our mothers had chosen the most vicious Italian family?"

"Because my mom was Bella's lover. You know the rest of the story."

"What about my desires and emotional needs? I wanted to celebrate Angela's birthday and make love to her, but now you are here. What do you want me to do for you?"

"Forget my niece and follow the seventh chapter of Gayadosha, which we signed in Andromeda. I do not need more nonsense and tricks."

Hintocha touched Anna's hair. "Your white hair reaches your knees. You need a haircut."

"Yeah. I need to change my shape and disguise myself as a human. My new odyssey has started." She spun around and turned her primitive dress into a short sundress, exposing her sleek arms and legs. She buried her fingers in her hair, cutting and making it a maple-brown bob with curves. Hintocha's body joggled. "I love you. Please, I am begging for your forgiveness. I felt inferior because you had more attractive and powerful qualities. You look like a glamor model."

"Thanks, and no need to be sorry. I want to have a new face on this psychotic planet." Anna pressed and jerked her face with her hands as if she kneaded clay. Her face became young and fair. Red lipstick and an eye makeup palette appeared in her hand. After painting her thin lips and eyes, she asked Hintocha to come close to her. Hintocha tiptoed forward, and Anna tore off her dress, revealing her underwear. "I forgive you because I love every bit of you. Thanks for looking after my niece." She wanted to kiss her, but a cell phone beeped. "Yes."

"Hi, Angela. How are you, love?"

"I am fine, honey. Thanks."

"What happened to your voice?"

"Do you like it?"

"Yeah, it is sexy. Listen, I want to see you. Is that OK?"

"Wonderful. When are you coming?"

"Next week."

"Honey, can you come after two weeks? I have work to do outside Toronto."

"Yes, love, no problem. I will text you about my flight. Bye, sweetheart."

"Bye, love. Take care."

Anna kissed and fondled Hintocha. "We need to see my mom, and I want to spend more time with you and travel around and help our people."

"Will your niece come back here?"

"I don't think so. My niece will not be in Canada. Gayadosha says she will reappear in the Seneca land when the Eagle Goddess glorifies the world. Let us go."

"As you wish."

Anna and Hintocha showed up in Nina's house. "Stay here and don't make a noise." Anna sneaked into her mother's bedroom. She kissed her hand, awakening her. "Who are you? How did you enter the house?"

"Mom, I am Awehitecha."

She switched on a table lamp and leaned her back on the headboard. "You don't look like her."

"I changed my body."

"Can you prove what you say?"

Anna warbled, and a bald eagle landed on her left arm. "Oh, sweetheart." Nina hugged her and kissed her face with tearful eyes. "I believe you and miss you so much. I haven't seen you for a hundred years. Where have you been?"

"I inhabited the forests of Northern Canada and fought the Flying Heads and the Monster Bears. I killed them all, and we need to find Tawiscara and kill him."

"Where is Angela?"

"I don't know. She got rid of the eagle's eye nineteen years ago. So, I stopped seeing her and hearing her voice. However, a twirling water sucked her down in a deep black hole. Who would make that and take her away?"

"Only Winona and the Holder of the Sky would do that. Did you see anyone of them?"

"No. I saw a goddess's hand pulling her down. Where is my sister?"

"In her house."

"Her house is empty. Where is Amitola?"

"I don't know. Where would she and her mom go?"

"I have no information. But Gayadosha says my sister and her daughters will appear when the Eagle Goddess reigns over the Northern Land. You should go up to the sky and ask our goddesses about them. You have a guest in the living room."

Nina greeted Hintocha with a hug and kisses and ascended to the sky. Anna and Hintocha returned to Angela's house. The wrecked walls and furniture brought back memories of the turbulent incidents they faced. The air hung with the acrid scent of gas, a sign of the dangers lurking beneath the surface.

"I smell gas," Hintocha said. Her brows furrowed, and her eyes gazed at Anna with concern. "Should we fix the house before we go away?"

"We will do that later. Fixing the house is not our priority. Let us go."

After turning the black FBI car into a silver Land Rover, they wore aboriginal costumes and ponchos and visited forty-three First Nations reserves in Ontario, Manitoba, and Saskatchewan, where they performed wonders and supernatural acts. On one occasion, they immersed their hands in Lake Winnipeg and caught twenty-two walleyes in eight minutes. They barbecued the fish on burning driftwood and fed a community on the eastern side of the Lake. On another day, they blew a whirling, misty gust, erecting four cottages for indigent families near Cross Lake.

Later, Elisha called when they were in Thunder Bay. "Don't forget to meet me tomorrow at the airport. I will arrive at two-twenty pm."

The next day, on their way on Indian Road, Anna and Hintocha saw a cluster of police and fire brigade vehicles forming a barrier that blocked off the southern part of the road. Hintocha stopped the car at a sidewalk, and Anna left the car. As she drew closer, she discerned the frantic activity of the police, forensic detectives, and firefighters who coordinated their efforts to guarantee the safety of the area and its residents. Anna asked people standing in silence at a crime scene tape. "What happened?"

A woman shook her head. "A colossal explosion took place in a house."

"Which house?"

"A house owned by an Italian American woman?"

"Do you know her name?"

"Yes. She was Angela Lucciano."

Anna wiped her lower lip and sat in the car. "There was a blast in Angela's house, and people say it killed her. Do you believe that? I feel Tawiscara has caused the explosion to avenge the death of his last wife and monsters. What do you want to do?"

"Let us get a hotel room."

They got a room in Hotel X. Anna switched on the TV. "The news of the devastating explosion, leveling a mansion and claiming the lives of a woman and two men, has shocked the city. Reports say the woman was a wealthy US citizen. Neighbors say her name was

Angela Lucciano," a news anchor said.

"Did you hear that? The police and the crazy media think my niece is dead."

"We know this is nonsense. Let them say what they like. No one can interrogate us and say we caused the death of anybody."

In New York, Emily Singer called Elisha. "Have you watched the news?"

"No. What is going on?"

"The news says an explosion has killed your mom in Toronto. I am sorry...."

"Are you sure? I am about to go to the airport and get a flight to Toronto."

"Yes, I am sure."

"My God! Thanks. I will watch the news. Talk to you later." Elisha wept, called, and sent texts to Angela's phone.

"It is Elisha. I do not want to confuse her with our affairs. I am going to let her know the truth about my niece when I meet her at the airport."

Elisha switched on the TV and listened to the news, which said an explosion had occurred in a Toronto house owned by a rich woman called Angela Lucciano. She got a taxi to the airport. On her way, she called her mother. "Mom, where are you?"

"I am at the airport waiting for you."

"I will be there in a few minutes."

Caitlyn met her daughter. "Your eyes are red. Are you OK?"

"Yeah. We are running late. Let us take the flight. I will tell you something later."

As they settled into their seats on the airplane, Elisha felt a storm of anxiety washing over her, like high waves crashing against the shore. The hum of the plane's engines echoed the turmoil in her heart, and her breaths became rapid and shallow. "I am very sad," she confessed, her voice trembling with emotion. Her hand grasped her mother's arm, as if holding on to an anchor amid a storm. Tears welled up in her eyes, threatening to spill over the edge of her emotion. "Please, forgive me," she pleaded, her words choked with sorrow.

Her mother enfolded her in a gentle embrace. "There is nothing to forgive. It is okay to feel sad. Emotions are a part of who we are, and it is alright to let them out."

"It is not about me. Angela...." She cried.

"What's wrong, honey?"

"A bomb has killed her in her house."

"Oh, my God!" Tears streamed down her cheeks, and she struggled hard to hold the flood of emotions overwhelming her. Her hands covered her face, as if seeking shelter from the sudden storm that had engulfed her heart. "When did that happen? Why didn't you tell me about it before coming to the airport?"

"It happened three hours ago. Emily told me about Angela just ten minutes before I left the house."

"My gosh. Poor Angela. What a shame. I got an engagement ring and wanted to do intimate things with her. Any news about the Lucciano family?"

"I don't know. No one has texted me. But I am sure many Sicilians will come to Toronto. Angela was their godmother."

"What will we do in Canada?"

"We will go to the hotel and wait for the Luccianos. I guess I should talk to the authorities and say I am Angela's official daughter?"

"Do what you like, though I don't want the law enforcement agencies to interrogate you. Wait until we know the truth."

In Toronto, Hintocha groomed Anna's sandy blonde side-swept bangs. "What will you tell Elisha about Angela?"

"I will tell her the truth. We are not going back. This is not a game. My responsibility to our people begins here and now. What about you? Are you coming with me?"

"No. I will wait for you here."

Anna wore a belted halter dress and appeared in Terminal Three. Her eyes ran with two tears, and her lips beamed when she saw Elisha and Caitlyn. She moved toward them, but explosions, gunshots, and rowdy shouts of *Allahu Akbar* had frightened them. Four camouflaged, masked terrorists stormed into the arrival hall and shot in all directions. Caitlyn embraced Elisha and cried out. They crouched and crawled on the smooth floor, yelping and quivering. Anna enwrapped them, and a white cloud of smoke emanated out of her mouth. "Caitlyn, Elisha, listen to me. Stay down and do not leave the smoke area because it will protect you. I have a job to finish. See you later." With angry fists, Anna bounded toward the terrorists. A terrorist froze when his bullets did not penetrate her body. She grabbed his belly and cast him up to the ceiling, smashing the glass grid roof. When his crippled body fell to the floor, her bald eagles attacked him, dunking his body in a pool of blood. Anna tilted her frowny face toward the other attackers. "Stop and put your guns down." Their automatic rifles turned into plastic toys. She punched, kicked, and gripped the waists of two terrorists, flinging them to the front glass. Their flown bodies shattered the windows of an airport bus outside the arrival hall. A moment later, Anna scowled at the fourth terrorist. "Surrender, piggy, or I will send you to hell."

"*Ya kafirah. Ya rih al-Jannah* [O' infidel. O' the wind of Paradise]," the infuriated terrorist yowled. When Anna grappled him around the throat, the terrorist pulled a Rambo knife and tried to slit her chest. The blade slashed her dress and displayed her red padded bra and firm breasts. The attacker paused and gawked at her breasts. "*Ya ilahi. Astagfiro Allah* [Oh, my God. I ask Allah for forgiveness]."

"Yeah, I am a woman, dingbat. I will show you what this woman can do." She drubbed him and twisted a steel trolley around him, placing them on a baggage carousel. Helmeted soldiers pointed their machine guns at her. "Hands up."

She raised her hands over her head. Five bald eagles attacked the soldiers. "*Sawa dedi* [Go back]," she said. The eagles flew away, and an officer cuffed her wrists behind her back. When another officer noticed her half-bare breasts, he covered them with his jacket. Later, Anna found herself at a police station in Brampton.

An officer pulled her into the interrogation room. "Who are you?"

"I am Anna Awehitecha."

"Are you a Canadian citizen?"

"No. I am a citizen of the third sky."

"Interesting. What do you do on earth?"

"I am a tourist."

"A tourist from the sky? We have never seen a female tourist who fights like Jean Grey. Do you have any official documents?"

"We don't use documents in the sky."

"Are you a human being?"

"No, and yes. You can check my blood and skin if you can. Why am I here? You should thank me. I have taken care of hundreds of lives at the airport."

"You know that is our business. You damaged official properties and acted like Superwoman."

"I am more powerful than Superwoman."

The officer scratched his head and simpered. "Do you have a mental health problem?"

"I am not a wacko. Believe me. I am a goddess and can do superhuman things." Her voice carried a hint of confidence and merriment, and her disclosure offered a glimpse into her profound level of self-confidence.

"Like what?" Her bold proclamation had piqued his curiosity. His eyes held a mixture of amusement and intrigue, as he awaited her response, ready to delve into the realm of her extraordinary claims.

A mischievous smile danced on her lips as she leaned in closer, as if sharing a coveted secret. "Like asking the stars to shift their patterns for me. Or ordering the winds to carry my words to far-off lands."

He chuckled, charmed by her fanciful notions. "And

what else?"

She broke the wrist shackles and clenched her hands, gripping both sides of the steel table with a vise-like grip. Inch by inch, the table buckled under her immense power, bending and twisting until it reached a right angle. Six primeval women warriors holding boar spears and colored eagle shields stood behind her. "Come on, thank me for saving people's lives. You should treat me as a hero, not like a felon."

The officer gasped in awe and disbelief and shrank away. "Excuse me." He exited the room and met his colleagues. His rasping voice sounded astonished and incredulous. "This madwoman is a witch and out of this world. She broke the handcuffs and bent the table." His words tumbled out, a rapid succession of amazement and disbelief. What he saw had defied all rational explanations, an odd spectacle that left him struggling for words. His gaze searched for further evidence of the inexplicable. "Crazy warriors are in the room."

Anna raised her head and stared at a surveillance camera. "Delete." She stepped through a two-way mirror and a wall and faced officers standing in a circle and discussing the city's security situation. "When are you going to release me? My family is worried."

A policeman removed his hat. "How did you walk through the wall?" His question sought to unravel the mysteries of the impossible, and his eyes searched for clues that might shed light on the enigma before him. "Are you an alien?" His skepticism colored his tone.

She delivered her response with a serene smile. "I am a goddess." Her voice carried a muted authority that seemed to resonate with a reality beyond the ordinary. "Look at me. I am a divine woman with supernatural power." Her simple words were a gentle assertion of her unhuman identity, a testament to the extraordinary nature of her being. "You cannot put me in jail, and your walls or bars cannot stop me. No army or a police force can kill me."

A gasp of disbelief rippled through the air as her foot kicked the solid floor. The thud of her foot was like a gunshot, sharp and resonant, yet it was the aftermath that sent shockwaves through the corridors. A floor tile cracked and broke, its fragments scattered like fallen stars. A tremor radiated in all directions, rippling through the foundation of the police station. Desks quivered, papers fluttered, and the air was heavy with a sense of unease.

Horror gripped the police officers, who watched the scene with wonderment. Their faces paled, and their expressions mirrored the seismic shift that had occurred. "OK. You can go now. An officer will give you a ride."

"Thanks. I have sturdy legs. I prefer to walk alone. Here are a thousand dollars to fix the floor." She left the police station and clapped. Her frock turned into a backless maxi dress. A bald eagle landed on her left arm, and she rubbed her head. "Where are Caitlyn and Elisha?"

The eagle screaked. "Thanks. You are amazing." She flew to the Sheraton Gateway Hotel and knocked on a door on the third floor. Elisha looked through the round peephole. "Oh no! My God. This is the airport superwoman. How does she know we are here?"

"Stay away from the door."

Anna walked through the closed door and entered their room. "I can't wait. I am happy to see you."

Caitlyn sat on a bed, with her hands between her legs. "Who are you? How did you come here?"

"I am Anna Awehitecha. I am Nina's daughter?"

Elisha gaped and rested her cheek on her hand. "I remember your voice. How did you get Angela's phone? Angela is dead."

"Angela, or the person who loved both of you, is my niece."

"What?"

"Angela is my niece. You met her mother, who is my twin sister." A thread of revelation wove into her words. The disclosure of a shared lineage added another layer of complexity to the narrative, a twist that hinted at a deeper truth beneath the surface. She paused, a moment of comprehension passing between them. "I know it is hard for you to understand our divine nature. I am the Eagle Goddess." She whistled, and a bald eagle flew through a window and landed on her arm. Caitlyn and Elisha moved behind a chair. "Don't be afraid of my friend. This eagle is my eyes and ears. She will not harm you. As I have said, I am Angela's aunt for reasons you won't understand now. Angela is not in Canada, and I must protect you. I don't know where she had gone. She disappeared two weeks before the explosion."

"Who died in the explosion?"

"I don't know. No one can kill my niece because she is a goddess."

"Your niece was a human like us, and you don't look like a goddess."

A sense of wonder filled the room as a ball of light appeared in her right hand. Its luminous glow cast an ethereal sheen across her features. Caitlyn and Elisha watched, their eyes widening with amazement, as the ball of light danced like a captured star within Anna's grasp.

With a swift motion, Anna threw the ball at them. The ball streaked through the air, leaving a linear trail of brilliance before contacting its intended targets. Caitlyn's and Elisha's clothes turned into red low-back cami dresses; a sudden shift that left them stunned. The room shimmered with the aftermath of the beguiling performance, as if it had charged the air with a touch of magic. "That is better. Both of you are gorgeous. Come and hug me. I am here to look after you."

"My God. We cried for hours because of Angela or your niece." They embraced her. "Where is she?"

"No one knows, though I believe she is in a safe place because our sacred book says she will rule the world after my return."

Caitlyn smiled. "How? She couldn't rule me, let alone rule the world."

"You saw her human side."

"Why do you say she is in a safe place?"

"Because the boss of the Flying Heads wants to kill her."

"Who is this guy?"

"He is a horrid, brainless monster. I killed his gods and devils because they murdered innocent people."

"Angela had never mentioned her mother has a sister."

"That's true. My mom erased her memory when she turned her into an egg and put her in Bella's womb. As I said, Nina is my mother."

"Oh, my God. Is she a goddess?"

"Yes, she is a supreme goddess. She descended to this planet to search for her mother and me. And according to our holy book, Angela will be the protector of humanity for forty years."

Caitlyn sat on a chair arm. "Forty years? Are you serious?"

"Yes, I am serious."

"You look twenty years younger than my mom." Elisha touched her new dress. "Angela told me that Nina is her grandmother and mentioned your name, but she had never said you were her aunt."

"She didn't want to reveal herself and shock you. You were lucky to fall in love with a sweet goddess."

"Interesting. Your mother has never changed. She looks thirty years old."

"Yes. She does not change because she is from heaven. She is the Mother of the Oceans and Seas."

"What is the Mother of the Oceans and Seas?"

"Before the existence of life on earth, my mother made the Atlantic and Pacific oceans, and I created the whales and the fish."

"Unbelievable. Are there more goddesses with us?"

"Yes. The caring goddesses are back."

"You are powerful. We saw what you did in the airport."

"I am a goddess. What do you expect?"

"Amazing. Thanks for saving our lives. We are happy to meet you. You are stunning. How did you get this gorgeous body?"

"Believe in miracles. Well, aren't you hungry? Let us have dinner."

Caitlyn entered the restroom, and Elisha touched Anna's hair and scanned her body. "You look so young and attractive."

"I eat healthy, natural food and exercise every day." She laughed. "Honey, I am a goddess and can do anything with my body." She touched Elisha's hair, turning it into curtain bangs. "Look."

Elisha looked in a mirror. "You are incredible. Ah, I miss your niece. She was my true love. When will we find her?"

"I wish to know the answer. I had never talked to her. She was born after I came down to the earth. My hunch is that she is far away from here."

Elisha hugged her and wept for a moment.

"Honey, I don't like to see these diamond tears. What's bothering you, love?"

"I guess this is the end of my life with Angela. I miss her so much."

"Why do you say that? She will always love you, and someday you will see the actual goddess, but I don't know when and where."

In the restaurant, Anna narrated legends and how evil monsters wanted to massacre indigenous tribes. "What I have told you is confidential. Do not tell anybody about it, or awful things will happen to you."

She touched Caitlyn's hand. "I know you got a ring for my niece. Keep it all the time in your purse. I will see you in New York."

Caitlyn and Elisha went up to their room, and Anna moved back to her hotel. A breaking news story had disturbed and befuddled all of them. "We have received a video clip showing the last moments of the life of billionaire Angelo Lucciano. The abductors took the video clip in Angela Lucciano's house in Toronto at the time of today's explosion. Warning. The clip contains flashing images and disturbing scenes of violence. Viewer discretion is advised," a news anchor said.

The video clip showed a handsome, beardless man tied up with a thick sisal rope to a chair. A husky male voice said, "Where is the code?"

"Which code?"

"The code in the eagle's eye."

"What are you talking about? I am a businessman of technology. I don't deal with eagle eyes."

"We know the Eagle Goddess had given you the eagle's eyes and the code. Where are they?"

"Is this a game? Who are you, people? What do you want from me? Do you want money?"

"Where is Angela?"

"Who is she?"

A dark cloud descended upon them, and a symphony of loud groans and screams reverberated through the house. When the recording camera panned outside the house and positioned itself across the road, it captured a scene of unimaginable destruction. An enormous explosion created a pall of thick, black smoke and catapulted the debris and remnants of furniture into the air.

"Oh, my God! That was the real Angelo. He is an actual human person. Who was Angela?" Elisha said to her mother.

"I am confused. I don't know what to say."

Anna and Hintocha watched the video clip. "My Goddess! How did the abductors know about the eagle's eye and the code? Who is this man Angelo Lucciano?" Anna said.

"He looked like the real Angelo who was with me."

In Ottawa, Dinah Hansson watched the video in her house and sobbed. In New York, the adult members of the Lucciano family had disputed with each other about the identities of Angela and Angelo. "Angela flew in the air and killed the Russian, Ukrainian, and Polish Mafia bosses, but this Angelo is an ordinary, nice person. Why did the kidnapers take him to Angela's house? Why don't we know anything about him?" Franco said.

The next day, Dinah traveled to Toronto and visited Louise Lee, a chief criminal investigator. "I am Dinah Hansson and Angelo Lucciano's wife."

"Oh, sorry to know about your loss? Do you have any proof?"

"Yes." She opened her handbag. "Here are photos of Angelo with me and the family. Do you know anything about his abductors?"

"No. We are at the beginning of our investigation."

"He has been missing for four days. Last night's video showed him alive in Angela Lucciano's house. Why did the abductors take him there?"

"We don't know. What else can you tell me?"

"Angelo owned the biggest high-tech company and a mansion in Ottawa, and we have a daughter and a son." Dinah picked up a key from her bag. "This is the key to Angelo's private house."

"Where is this house?"

"At Southampton Beach."

"I see. First, I need to see your house in Ottawa. Can I see it tomorrow morning?"

"Yes, you can."

"Write the address and your phone number." She gave Dinah a paper and a pen.

Dinah wrote the address and the phone number. "Good. I will see in the morning."

Louise and two assistants visited Dinah's house at Winding Way. "This is my daughter Mia, and this is my son Jack." Louise shook their hands and looked at a wall portrait. "Was that your father?"

"Yes. He was a businessman."

"What did he do?"

"He owned the Eagle's Eye high-tech company. He was a billionaire."

"Why don't we know much about him? Why didn't the media interview him?"

"He was a very private person. He worked sixteen hours a day and refused to attend interviews and parties."

"Do you have photos of your father's mother?"

"Yes." Jack opened the drawer of a console table and picked up photos. "This is my dad's mom."

"She is beautiful. Who is her husband?"

"Leonardo Lucciano. He and our grandmother lived in New York."

"Where are they now?"

"They are dead."

"Sorry to know that." She gazed at Dinah. "Official documents show that your husband owned the house in Toronto when he was a student. How did Angela Lucciano become the owner of the house?"

"I don't know. My husband lived only here and had never mentioned a house in Toronto."

"But your husband was with an American student called Caitlyn and with a daughter called Elisha. How did he leave them with Angela and marry you?"

"My husband was the only Angelo Lucciano in America and Canada. He loved only me. We thought the Toronto Angelo was an imposter."

"But people say Angelo was in Toronto before the coming of Angela."

"That's not true. Angelo lived only in Ottawa, and I was in touch with him all the time."

"Did he have enemies?"

"No. He disappeared five days ago. His father, Leonardo Lucciano, was the godfather of the Italians in New York. Two FBI agents, affiliated with a European Mafia, killed him and his wife. So, we think a Mafia group has also killed my husband."

"Why would a Mafia group kill him in Toronto? Why did his kidnapers take him to Angela's house?"

"I don't know."

"Did you inform the police?"

"Yes, we informed them. They searched ten places,

including Angela's deserted house."

"What do you mean Angela's deserted house?"

"The police entered her house and found damaged walls and furniture. No one was in the house."

"Why did they search Angela's house?"

"We use a location map app which tracks our movements. Angelo's last destination was at Angela's house."

Louise looked at her watch. "Can you see me on Monday, at ten o'clock in the morning? I need to see the other house."

"No problem."

On Monday, Dinah and Louise moved north-west to Southampton Beach and entered Angelo's vacation house. Louise wore protective gloves and examined the framed photos of Angelo with Dinah and their children. Dinah gazed at the photos and wept, and Louise embraced her. "Please, don't touch anything. We may get fingerprints. Can you give me the key for a couple of days?"

"Yes, of course."

In the evening, Dinah entered the Hilton Toronto hotel's restaurant to see the Lucciano cousins and Martina. "Hello, everyone. Sorry to interrupt. I am Dinah Hansson. Angelo was my husband and the father of our children. Here are photos of me with Angelo and Leonardo and Bella and our children. Leonardo was my father-in-law, and Bella was my mother-in-law."

Nicolo stood and shook her hand. "Nice to meet you. Please, have a seat. I think I saw you on Forty-Eight Hours and Sixty Minutes shows."

"Yes. I am an investigative journalist."

"You said Angelo was your husband. This is weird because Angela was Leonardo's only son Angelo before she became a woman. The Angelo we know was with an Irish woman. Their daughter, Elisha, is a famous model."

"Angelo had never become a woman. He was my partner since he was thirteen."

Martina looked at the photos. "When did you marry him?"

"Twenty years ago. Leonardo and Bella were with us when we got married in St. Lucia. They visited us in Canada every three or four months."

"We thought they came here to see Angela who was Angelo, their only son."

"How could this be possible? Please, do not conflate Angelo with Angela. Angelo was Angelo. He was a man, a husband, and a father, and he had never become a woman. He worked seven days a week and founded the largest tech company in Canada." Her voice carried a sense of admiration and pride, and her husband's achievements had infused her words with reverence. "With due respect," she continued in a measured and polite tone, "no one knows him as I do."

"How do we know nothing about your husband and children? Why didn't you visit us in New York? Why didn't Leonardo and Bella tell us about you?"

"It is too late to ask them, but I think they didn't want to tell you his son married a Swedish Mormon. Leonardo and Bella asked us to stay away from your family and not to tell you about our relationship. That is why we couldn't attend their funeral."

"Strange. Where do you live?"

"I and the kids live in Ottawa."

"What about Bella?"

"As I have said, she attended our wedding party in St. Lucia and visited us many times."

"We are confused. If your Angelo was Bella's only child, how was Angela her daughter?"

"Angelo had never said he had a sister."

"But Leonardo and Bella told us that Angela was Angelo. She was our godmother, though we still don't know how she was a super powerful woman."

"Maybe she was an alien pretending to be a human. Angelo was humble and kind. What do you want to do?"

Franco guzzled red wine. "We asked the Canadian authorities to give us what remained of Angela's body. But now, you have surprised us. We can't do much about your Angelo without your permission. We hope you don't want long investigations and procedures."

"Don't you want to know who killed Angelo?"

"We and the cops don't know who abducted and killed him. There was a gas explosion in the house, and the cops didn't find any evidence. So, we think the explosion was an accident because it is not possible that the abductors killed themselves."

"But Angelo disappeared three days before the explosion. I think a hoaxer impersonated Angelo and claimed to be your cousin."

"You might be true because Angela was not an ordinary woman. She flew in the air and killed tough gangsters without using a gun."

A week later, the Lucciano family had persuaded Dinah to bring another coffin from Canada and said they would bury Angelo and Angela beside each other and close to Leonardo's and Bella's graves. Dinah went to the cemetery in Brooklyn and met Martina. "This is Mia, and this is Jack."

Martina hugged them. "This is Elisha Lucciano, whom we know as Angela's daughter, and this is her mother, Caitlyn. This is Dinah Hansson. She was Angelo's wife, and these are Angelo's daughter and son. You need to sit and talk to each other to sort out the puzzlement." Dinah removed her dark glasses and hugged Caitlyn and Elisha.

Elisha pushed her hair back. "When did you meet Angelo?"

"He was my partner since we were in the eighth grade. We got married twenty years ago, and I moved to his house in Ottawa. What about you?"

"I was born in Toronto when Angelo was with my mom. All the Luccianos knew my dad was Leonardo's only son. How was he with you and us?"

"That's what I am trying to unravel."

After returning home, Elisha removed her black jacket and shoes and sipped orange juice. "I don't believe Angela had betrayed all of us. How did she claim to be Angelo? Why didn't she tell us about Dinah and her children?"

Caitlyn held her coffee cup. "I don't know what to say. Heaven's goddesses don't follow our rules."

"What do you think of Anna?"

"She is another shocking surprise. How would

anyone believe there are goddesses on earth? What would we tell people about her?"

The doorbell rang. Elisha opened the door. "Hello. How is everybody?"

"We are fine. We were in the cemetery."

"Hi, Anna. Please, come in. Tea or coffee?"

"Tea, please."

Caitlyn made a cup of tea and sat next to her daughter. "What have you been doing today?"

"I was with my mom. She is upset about my sister and nieces. We chose not to go to the cemetery to avoid people's questions."

"Do you know Angela has a human sister?"

"Who is she?"

"Martina Lucciano. Leonardo had an affair with her mom, who was his secretary in New Jersey."

"I should pay her a visit to get to know her."

"There was another surprise about your niece. We met a woman who said she was Angelo's wife. Her name is Dinah. We met their daughter and son. She said she was Angelo's girlfriend since he was thirteen and they got married twenty years ago. How was Angelo with her and us at the same time? Angela had never talked about another guy called Angelo."

"My family knows Dinah was Angelo's girlfriend when they were in school. But we know nothing about Angelo who lived in Ottawa. How do you feel about that?"

"Disappointed and betrayed."

Anna sat beside her and rested her arm on her shoulders. "Don't think of the past. You are young and attractive. I am here for you."

The next day, Martina entered her office and saw Anna sitting in her chair. "Excuse me. Who are you?"

"I am Angela's aunt, and my name is Anna."

"Who are your parents?"

"I am Anohitecha's sister."

"Oh, my God. Are you also a goddess?"

"Yes. Please, sit down."

Martina sat on a chair and rubbed her thighs. "Who killed Angela?"

"No one. Angela will never die."

"How?"

"She is a goddess."

"What about Dinah's Angelo? Who was he?"

"I have no idea. I know nothing about him and his family."

"Whom we buried yesterday?"

"Stupid devils."

"Are you telling me the truth?"

Nina popped up. "Yes, my daughter is telling you the truth."

"Oh, my God. Is Anna your daughter?"

"Yes."

"You looked after Angelo before his departure to Canada and were his mother's secret lover. Who was Dinah's boyfriend and husband?"

"We have many questions. As I know, Dinah was Angelo's girlfriend when he was in school and before he fell in love with Caitlyn. Angelo became Angela in my house. So, I don't know how Dinah married a guy called Angelo. Angela had never mentioned him."

"So, Dinah is telling us the truth. Why didn't she invite you or our family to her wedding party or to her house if Leonardo and Bella knew her and treated her husband as their son? Why didn't Angela tell us anything about her?"

"This is a mystery. I wish to know the truth."

"What do you want from me?"

Anna smiled. "I will run for the presidency, and I want you to be my spokesperson. What do you think?"

"This is a surprise. But you are a goddess. How will you win the election and run the country?"

"That's the simple part. Think of the matter and let me know soon. I need to go now. Here is my phone number. I left cash in your drawers. Give some of it to the poor. Happy to meet you. Take care." Anna and Nina hugged her and disappeared. Martina sat in her chair and opened the top drawer of her desk. "Holy Mary." She opened the other drawers and found millions of dollars.

Caitlyn visited Anna every two or three days for six weeks. One evening, she invited her to dinner at her house. "I think what I want to say would sound weird. You know your niece was my girlfriend for nineteen years, and I am bisexual or ninety-five percent lesbian. I ... I have feelings for you. I mean, I love you. You have been generous and kind to Elisha and me. I wonder, would you like to be my girlfriend?"

Anna smiled and touched Caitlyn's face. "Yes, and something else. I would like to be your friend, but I cannot have an official committed relationship with you because of our different natures."

"That's fine with me. I need a buddy, and I am afraid of being alone because of personal traumas. Not to mention the shocking surprise about Angela and Angelo. You can live with me in my house."

"Don't be afraid. I am here to protect you and your daughter." They made love and vacationed for a week in Santa Barbara to set the terms and conditions for their friendship. Anna changed her hairstyle to a silver gray balayage bob and declined to reveal her occasional dalliance with Hintocha.

Chapter 7

Anna and Caitlyn lived together in a luxury house at Washington Square Park. Caitlyn worked as a professor of anthropology at New York University, and Anna interacted with her mother and indigenous tribes and published books. One morning, Anna had a succinct, numinous conversation with the Goddess Winona. "The time has come for the Supreme Goddess of Creation to exalt the Eagle Goddess. You are the Eternal Word and the chosen emissary of the Supreme Goddesses. My people are waiting for their liberator. Use your power to perform miracles for prosperity and security. Remember, you are the Supreme Goddess of war and wisdom and the interpreter of Gayadosha. Desires are not your reason for being in the human world. Use your wisdom for the wider good of our land.

Be a voice for the voiceless and the poor."

"Advise me what to do."

"See how people live. Help the needy and give shelter and food to the homeless. Heal the sick and give money to the poor, regardless of their race and religion. Avert natural disasters and cure diseases. There are many beneficial things you can do. Listen to your deep spirit and let your imagination lead you. Care and love are what people need."

"Praise be to you, our Holy Goddess. I will do my best for the inhabitants of the earth."

After switching on the kitchen TV, Anna sat next to Caitlyn. "Did you hear that tacky trash? Politics is turning people against each other. Americans are dividing the country with no sense of orientation and purpose."

"The Founding Fathers founded the country on theft and murder. We are reaping their harvest."

"And the media is brainwashing the greedy and the gullible. He is conservative. She is radical. The left. The alt-right. The libertarians. The socialists. Antifa. Hate speech. Me Too. Black Lives Matter. White Lives Matter. Immigrants are welcome. Refugees go home. Build the wall. Defund the police. Why can't politicians and groups work together to make things better for all citizens?"

Caitlyn swigged tea and rubbed the back of her neck. "Because they are not wise goddesses like you. Politics is a dirty game for men, and we are stuck with the two-party system. This system bans the truth and makes lies headlines. And social media is full of morons and trolls.

What can we do?"

"We need to fix the corrupt system."

"How? The deep state controls our politicians and the military."

"I want to be the next president because I can't stand this narcissistic, homophobic president."

Caitlyn gazed at Anna's face and chortled. "You are hilarious this morning. The Eagle Goddess of war is the President of the United States of America." She giggled. "Finish your breakfast and let us do useful things today."

"Believe me. I am honest about what I say. I will solve the country's troubles if I become president."

"Honey, you are honest. But as a goddess, you can solve any problem without being involved in politics. What about your nature and power? Think of your indigenous people and their security. The corrupt media will say we are lesbian perverts. The churches will hate you because your people call you the Incarnate Goddess. Why do you want to be a president? You are not a human being or a member of any party."

"Imagine you and me in the White House."

"A political fantasy is not something I would like to imagine. I am happy where I am and with what I do. Please, stop your celestial imagination and wear a nice dress. I want to move my stiffened legs and get fresh air."

Anna entered the closet room and wore a long maroon pleated skirt. Caitlyn kissed her shoulder. "I am worried about Elisha. She is depressed. It had been hard for her to forget what she had done with Angela. I hope she finds a girlfriend to cheer her up. I like this skirt on you."

"Thanks. Elisha will always be a special girl. I will do something for her."

After exiting their home, Anna stooped beside a homeless, unkempt woman, reaching out for aid. "Do you have an empty mug?"

The woman raised her eyes and gave her a cup. Anna placed her palm on the carton cup and blew. "Take the cup and hide it."

The woman looked in the cup and found a thick bundle of hundred-dollar notes. She stared at Anna and quivered. "Oh, my God. Who are you?"

"I am Anna, the Eagle Woman." Anna gave her a gold eagle necklace. "Find a pleasant place and get healthy food. Have a lovely day. Bye."

Caitlyn kissed Anna's head. "You are wonderful, and everything you do is awesome."

They ambled through Washington Square Park. A Democratic Congresswoman scolded and accused the President of breaking the Constitution and obstructing justice. "Stay here." Anna flitted to the Congresswoman and hypnotized her eyes with her sight. "Hello. Please, give me the mic."

She smiled and handed over the mic. With a soft voice filled with warmth and encouragement, Anna addressed her audience. "Dear friends, have faith in yourselves, and miracles will happen to every one of you." She raised her sight and directed her eyes toward a solitary cloud drifting across the sky. "Have hope, and this cloud above you will rain money."

As if touched by the enchantment of her words, the cloud heeded her call. A gentle shimmer spun in the air, and the cloud released a cascade of money notes, fluttering down like snowflakes. The listeners became a flurry of motion. Their eyes widened with delight and stupefaction as they beheld the surreal scene unfolding before them. In a quick instant, they transformed themselves from passive, indolent observers to eager participants in the unexpected symphony of wealth. Laughter and excitement filled the air as the money notes tumbled from the sky. Like children chasing butterflies, the listeners reached out, their hands grasping at the flying money with awe and exhilaration.

Anna moved amidst the joyful chaos, with a serene smile gracing her red lips. A journalist took photos. "Who are you?"

"I am Anna, the Eagle Woman." She pointed at her eagle pendant. "Excuse me. My partner is waiting for me. Have a wonderful day."

In the evening, Caitlyn and Anna visited Elisha in her home. A playful glint danced in Anna's eyes as she cast a quick glance at Elisha's flannel shirt and jeans before a mischievous smile curved her lips. She raised her right fingers in a subtle gesture, and with a faint tick, she started a transformation that defied the ordinary. "What about this dress?"

Elisha's reaction was nothing short of astonishing. An elegant off-the-shoulder maxi gown had replaced her casual attire. The change was so sudden and dramatic that Elisha could not help but spring back with her eyes widening with surprise and delight.

"Wow!" She twirled, and the flowing fabric of the gown swirled around her as if it had swept her into a fairytale scene.

With a playful grin, Anna beckoned Elisha closer with her eyes gleaming with a spark. "Come here. You need a new trendy hairstyle." As Elisha complied and stepped closer, Anna reached out with a light touch, her fingers dancing through the tousled locks. With a deft and swift motion, she ruffled the hair, and the strands responded to her touch like pliable threads of silk. And in the blink of an eye, the transformation was complete. The tousled hair had evolved into crisp, wispy bangs that framed Elisha's face.

Elisha's reflection in the mirror revealed the fresh look, and a gasp of surprise mingled with delight had eluded her lips. Her eyes gaped as she took in the change with her fingers reaching up to touch the new hairstyle.

"This is more attractive. Wait here." Anna stepped into the kitchen and waved her right hand around, causing the oak cabinets, sturdy and warm in their natural hue, to undergo a gradual transformation. The rich tones of the wood shifted and faded, giving way to a new palette. The surface of the cabinets adopted an elegant off-white color, imbuing the space with a fresh and timeless ambiance.

When Elisha saw the new cabinets and the long marble breakfast bar, she hugged Anna. "Oh, my God. How did you do that?"

"There is a goddess in the house. Come with me. I have a special thing for you."

They went out to the car park. Anna picked up a key from her purse. "Find your new car."

Elisha pressed the key, and an expensive Audi car beeped. "It is bulletproof. Get in and try it."

Elisha perched herself in the driver's snug seat, glancing around and scanning the interior. Her eyes surveyed the controls, the dashboard, and the array of instruments. "Wow! Amazing! Thank you." She left the car and kissed Anna's lips. "I love you so much." She winked at her mother. "Sorry for the kiss. I don't know how to thank Anna. We are lucky to be with her."

"Kiss her as much as you can."

Local newspapers published photos of the flying money and called Anna the "Money Magician." To get more public involvement, popularity, and recognition, Anna dawdled through the busy streets of Manhattan to help disadvantaged people. One morning, she visited the American Museum of Natural History and met a young girl clomping with elbow crutches and wearing front leg splints. "Hello, sweetheart. What happened to you?"

"Had a car accident three weeks ago."

Anna kneeled and brushed the splints. "Give me the sticks and walk."

The girl walked to a wall. "Jump."

The girl hopped. "I can walk now. How did you do that? Who are you?"

"I am Anna, the Eagle Woman." Anna gave her an eagle necklace. The girl hared off to a restroom to see her mother. "Mom, look at me. A woman touched my legs and healed them. I can walk."

"Great, honey. Who is this woman?"

"She looks like a supermodel. Her name is Anna. Come and talk to her." The girl turned around and found no trace of Anna. "She is not here. I don't know where she's gone."

"You said her name is Anna. Are you sure?"

"Yeah, I am sure. That's what she said. She also said she is the Eagle Woman. Look. She gave me this gold necklace."

In the afternoon, Anna sat in a French-style café on Broadway to drink coffee. After a while, she rushed out, her spirit guiding her toward a woman in peril. With lightning speed, she extended her arms, catching a falling woman moments before she would have met the unforgiving ground below.

The sight left the three police officers who had been standing nearby in awe, their mouths agape as they saw the astonishing display of heroism and power. The officer closest to her couldn't help but reach out, with his hand patting her shoulder in admiration and astonishment. "You are incredible. How did you do that? Are your arms OK?"

"Yeah, they are fine. Please, let me ask the woman about her suicide attempt. I can support her."

"OK. You have a minute."

The rescued woman, her heart still pounding from the near-fatal fall, clung to Anna. Her gratitude had manifested in her tear-filed eyes. Anna touched her shoulder. "Why did you want to kill yourself?"

"How could you save me with these two arms? I jumped from the tenth floor. Who are you?"

"I am Anna, the Eagle Woman."

"How are you the Eagle Woman?"

"You did not answer my question."

"I am a schoolteacher and don't have money to pay the medical bills."

"Do not worry about money. I will pay the bills. I will get your name and address from the police. Take care and eat nature's food. See you soon."

A policeman snapped photos of Anna and asked her to visit his police station. In the evening, local news said the Eagle Woman had saved a woman's life. A news anchor beamed. "We wish to interview this mysterious woman who calls herself Anna and the Eagle Woman."

The next day, Anna flew to the city of Homestead to deal with a large hurricane sweeping toward Florida. She hired a car and drove to Key Largo, where she stayed in a modest beach hotel.

Amidst the gathering storm and the presence of news reporters and camera operators, she found herself engaging in a conversation with the media personnel who had arrived to cover the impending hurricane. As they approached her, their equipment in hand, she couldn't help but inquire about their purpose. "Why are you here?"

A journalist smirked in response to her question, assuming her lack of awareness, and seemed eager to shed some light on the situation. "Strange indeed," he replied. "Haven't you seen the weather warnings and watched the news? A catastrophic hurricane is heading toward this state, and we are here to document its impact and relay essential information to the public.

Where are you from?"

"From New York."

"You shouldn't be here. The hurricane will cause life-threatening storm surges and destruction."

"When will the storm come?"

"Tomorrow afternoon."

She smiled. "Go back to your homes because there will be no hurricane but little rain. I promise. You will see a shocking surprise tomorrow. Good luck."

In the morning, she drove on Andros Road until she reached the metal fence of a villa. She skipped out of the car and set foot on the sprawling front lawn of the magnificent mansion. A mustached man opened the main door and stood on the top step. "Excuse me, ma'am. This land is a private property. What do you want?"

"I am sorry for venturing into your land without permission. Please, I wish to look at the beach for a minute."

"A massive storm is coming. You need to hurry."

"I know. Thank you."

Anna leaned against a swaying palm tree. Her eyes gazed over the island of Rattlesnake Key, and with a humble voice that carried veneration and a plea for harmony, she prayed. "Dear Winona, please order the hurricane to return to the ocean. Holder of the Sky, take the storm away and slow the winds. We love Mother Nature and want peace with her. Forgive people's sins and cleanse them from wickedness. Amen."

She turned back and waved to the landowner. The next day, she spooned Caitlyn on a couch. "Let us watch the news and see what they say about the weather."

The news channels and meteorologists scrambled to make sense of the bewildering turn of events. They couldn't explain the rapid retreat of the hurricane. Confusion and astonishment had manifested through their reports and discussions as they grappled with the sudden change in the storm's trajectory. A Florida reporter ambled along Coral Way. "We met a peculiar New Yorker who told us there would be a surprise about the storm." The villa owner called a TV news channel and said an attractive woman prayed and asked the hurricane to return to the ocean. "She is like the Virgin Mary."

Anna held Caitlyn's hand. "You see what your heavenly friend can do?"

"I am proud of you. Keep doing the good things."

Later, Anna switched to another channel and watched the news of volcanic eruptions in Hawaii. "I have to go there and stop the disaster." She took off to Kailua-Kona and stayed overnight in the Royal Kona Resort. In the morning, she hired a jeep and drove to Pahoa in the District of Puna in Hawaii County. When the car stopped beside a pizza restaurant on Pahoa Village Road, she heard booming sounds and looked at a large plume of ashes rising into the gray sky. She moved on Makamae Street until she met a police officer standing close to a crawling lava. After getting off the jeep, she strode toward the massive magma.

"Ma'am, where are you going?"

"I want to stop this mad beast."

"Funny. Please, move back."

In a moment of defiance and command, she stood her ground before the raging inferno. With a serious expression, she spat on the blazing lava. The molten fury shuddered and cooled, and the scorching heat yielded to a transformative power.

When her spit met the searing semi-fluid, a remarkable alchemy occurred. The lava, once a torrent of destruction, underwent a dramatic change. It solidified, morphing into a colossal chunk of sludge. The officer quavered in awe and disbelief. His eyes remained fixed on her, blurring the boundaries of reality as he grappled with the impossible becoming possible before his him. "Gee. I don't believe that. Who are you? How did you do that? Are you a magician?"

"I am Anna, the Eagle Woman." She gave him an eagle pendant and returned to her vehicle.

Her next stopping place was a little area called Glenwood. She parked the car beside a tree and walked uphill for ninety yards until she saw Kilauea's volcanic crater. Her knees touched the moist ground with her eyes closed. She invoked Pele's grace. "My dear love Pele, I am the Goddess Anna Awehitecha. I know you are indignant because of people's undue transgressions and American occupation, but this is the island you created. There are sinless plants, worms, and animals in the soil. The fish in the ocean are innocent. Your tremendous forgiveness extends to all living things in this glorious land. Have mercy upon your people. I ask you this in the name of the Great Spirit. Amen." She prostrated and kissed a coarse stone. A moment later, a thunderstorm struck the violent volcano and stopped its eruption. "Thank you, Pele. Did I forget to say I love your black hair and charming eyes? You are gorgeous. I love you."

"I love you too," a female voice replied.

When Anna rose and turned her back, she wiped her hands and knees with a foulard and greeted a rotund indigenous man wearing wide jeans and a T-shirt. "I followed you after you parked the car. I heard you talking to the Goddess Pele. How do you know her? How did you stop the eruption of Kilauea?"

"Ask Pele. I am a woman."

"You are more than an ordinary woman. I feel your divine spirit and connection to the Goddess Laka. You must come to my store."

The man took her to Hirano Store, between the volcano and Mountain View. "My name is Eamon Inouye. I have prepared this special food today." He gave her a chili bowl with rice.

She chewed a bite of the food. "It is piquant. Thank you so much."

"Please, tell me, how did you talk to the Goddess Pele? You must be a special person."

"I love our goddesses. There is a spiritual bond between them and me. I am related to the First Nations, who lived in North America for two million years. Our merciful goddesses love me and listen to my prayers. The Creator of Hawaii loves us and can help us, but we need to praise her and do good things. Faith is about the things we cannot see. Hope is about the things we do not have." She blew at an empty glass jar and filled it with paper money. "Give this money to the poor people in this island."

The next day, she flew back. As she soared above California's hazy coast, her eyes opened in shock and sorrow. Below her, a harrowing scene unfolded– uncontrolled wildfires raging across the state, painting the landscape in shades of orange and red. The size of the devastation was overwhelming, and the acrid scent of smoke filled the air. She landed in Sacramento and called Caitlyn. "The wildfires are ravaging California, and I must snuff them out. I will see you on Saturday."

After securing a room and changing her everyday clothes in Hyatt Regency Sacramento, she strolled to the California State Capitol Museum. She entered the building and spoke to a female secretary sitting at a mahogany desk. "I need to talk to the Governor about the wildfires."

"Do you have an appointment?"

"No. The matter is urgent."

"Sorry. The Governor is busy, and you need to get a formal invitation from our office. Here are the Governor's emails and phone numbers. Call or send a message." The secretary gave her a business card.

"Thank you. Where is the restroom?"

"Over there to the right."

The moment she stepped into the restroom, she vanished from sight. She walked out and got into an elevator. On the first floor, she passed through a wall and walked into an office. Her right hand tapped on the Governor's desk. The Governor closed his phone. "Excuse me. Who the hell are you? How did you enter my office?"

"From that wall."

"Jesus Christ. Get the hell out of here, or I will call the guards."

Anna stared at the office door. The door lock clicked, and the Governor's shaky finger touched a phone button. "Don't move." His fingers froze.

"Please, what do you want?"

"I need help to quench the flames in your state."

"Huh! Ridiculous. Eight thousand firefighters are risking their lives, and you are here to tell me a joke. Thanks. We do not need your help. What a young woman like you would do?"

"Listen to me. I need a copter to douse the fires."

"No. No. Period. Please, leave my office."

Anna's face darkened. "Nobody in this land dares to say no to the Eagle Woman. I am the Supreme Goddess Anna Awehitecha. Do you hear me?" She lifted her right arm, and the Governor and his chair rose to the ceiling. "Listen, man. I order you to get me a chopper, and you must come with me to see what I can do. I do not need to repeat myself."

"OK, please, please, get me down. I will do what you want." The Governor descended to the floor and made a call. "Hi, Julie. Cancel today's appointments and get me a helicopter. I want to be with the firefighters." The Governor looked daggers at Anna. "Who are you, for God's sake? Are you a magician?"

"No. My people call me the Eagle Goddess. I am not bluffing, and you must trust me. You will see something you have never seen in your entire life." A bald eagle entered the room and landed on her left arm. "I told you

I am the Eagle Goddess."

"OK. Let us go."

"Tell your colleagues I am a businesswoman."

They moved to Sacramento Executive Airport and jumped into a green helicopter. When they flew over Stockton, Anna implored the Great Spirit with her hands under her chin. "Wakan Tanka, bring down rain and preserve your nature. We praise you forever and ever. Amen." After saying these words, gloomy clouds gathered like mountains and poured heavy rain.

"Please, take us to Sierra National Forest," Anna said to the helmeted pilot. The helicopter hovered over Oakhurst, and Anna bowed forward, calling on the Holder of the Sky. "Tarachiawagon, send down water and quell the fires. We need your bountiful grace and mercy. Amen." Moments later, thundering clouds spilled torrents of water, and the fires died out.

The helicopter moved west, and large wildfires blazed in Madera and Mariposa counties. Anna prayed. "Great Spirit, this is your territory. Stamp out the fires of hell. We love you. Amen." Squalling rain fell over the slopes and wiped out the flames.

The pilot looked back. "I need to go to Fresno Airport to get fuel."

The helicopter settled on the airport highway. The Governor gazed at Anna with a flicker of hope. "Where do you want us to go?"

"We will inspect San Jose, San Francisco, Santa Rosa, and Redding, and go to a special place for the final praise."

After flying over the four cities, Anna said to the

pilot, "Please, take me to Mount Shasta. I need to calm down the angry spirits."

"Please, do what she says," the Governor said.

As the helicopter moved northward, the vast landscape had transformed into a breathtaking vista of majestic mountains. Among them, one peak stood out, rising high in the sky with an aura of mystery and allure. It was to this pinnacle that Anna directed the pilot. When the pilot poised his helicopter above the mountain, Anna requested him to drop her on its zenith. "Come back after five minutes." She removed her suede shoes, and with a firm grip on her eagle, she jumped off the helicopter and into the open air. The wind rushed past her, whipping her hair as she and the eagle landed on the mountain peak. Thick smoke masked the northern counties. With closed eyes, Anna kneeled and wiped her forehead with dry snowflakes. "My love, the Goddess Winona, bestow your mercy upon us and grant us forgiveness. Guide and use us for the just things in the world. Guard us against the evil spirits that want to wreck your precious nature. I praise and love you. Amen."

The pilot picked her up, and the Governor patted her shoulder. "How do you know this isolated place?"

"The Creator of this land has guided me to this place and let me see beyond what my eyes can see. We need to go back as soon as possible."

"Why? What is in your mind?"

"Wonderful things will take place in your state. Wait to see miracles."

They disembarked in Redding to get fuel, and the

Governor shivered. "It is drizzling and getting cold."

They took off, and the Governor's gaze fixed on the captivating sight outside his window, where snowflakes danced and twirled in the air, descending upon the barren peaks and ridges in a delicate flurry. "My God! Snow in summer? Impossible. How do you do that?"

"It is not me. I am here. The clouds are doing their perfect work."

"I listened to your invocations. Why did you not mention God or Jesus Christ?"

"God is an English word, and it is not even a name. This vast land belonged to the indigenous peoples who settled here before our immigrant ancestors. The aboriginal spirits have given me power, not Jesus Christ or the church. Shouldn't I be thankful to them?"

They arrived in Sacramento. The Governor took her to the Firehouse restaurant. After eating, they attended a press conference in the State Capitol and met the Lieutenant Governor, the Mayor, the Chief of the Police Department, the District Attorney, the Secretary of State, the Fire Chief, the City Controller, and other official figures. The Governor rubbed his hands and delivered the following brief statement.

"On behalf of the people of California, I want to thank our brave firefighters for their extraordinary diligence and sacrifices. I also want to thank our communities for their resilience. I have a confession for you. When I attended the school in Irvine, I questioned the reality of biblical myths and miracles. Today, I have changed my mind. I have seen fascinating miracles performed by this incredible woman, Anna, or the

Eagle Woman, who called for the forces of nature to bring down rain and snow. You saw the rain and the blizzard. Yes, it snows in summer. Thank you, Anna, for your superb service. May God bless you and your family."

The Governor hugged her, and the officials offered a round of applause. "Anna, please, you can say a few words."

Anna stood. "Thank you, Mr. Governor, for the remarkable work you and your amazing team do in California. I am one of you, and I will do my best to protect and serve this country." She picked up a piece of paper from her jacket pocket. "Here is a modest check of twenty million dollars to the firefighters and their families. Love will win. Hate will fail. I love you."

Back home, Anna got hugs and kisses from Caitlyn. "I am very proud of you. You are my best goddess."

As the news of Anna's astounding story spread like a tropical storm, it reverberated through the political community, capturing the attention of politicians, citizens, and media outlets alike. Her remarkable work became the prevailing talk of the city, sparking intrigue, fascination, and a sense of wonder.

The political parties got engaged in discussions and deliberations, pondering with wonder over Anna's exceptional personality and the unexpected wave of popularity that went with her story. They recognized the impact she would have on the political landscape, with her story resonating with people from all the levels of society.

Internet and social media platforms had become a

battleground of opinions and debates as users shared her story everywhere. Memes, hashtags, and viral videos had surfaced, amplifying her narrative, and fueling arguments among the online community.

One day, five Democratic Representatives visited her in her residence. "I am Senator Kirsten Maloney, and I am the leader of the Democratic Party in the city. It is our pleasure to thank you for the impressive work you do for this country and to tell you we are honored to select you as our presidential candidate. Our political party supports the LGBTQ community and their human rights. Our country is yearning for change, for a new direction that would bring about progress, unity, and a sense of hope. So, we need a resolute and intelligent woman like you. What do you say?"

"This is a pleasant surprise. Thank you so much. Your kindness is unparalleled. I will decide nothing before I get my partner's consent."

Caitlyn caressed her hand and beamed at her face. "Honey, go for it. I know you can do it."

"The boss has spoken."

"Fantastic. We will make an official statement about your nomination."

"Do what is good for the country."

When the delegates exited the house, Caitlyn threw herself on Anna's knees and wiped her face with her lips. "I love you, Ms. President."

"No one has allowed you to sit on the president's legs."

"Shut it. I can do anything I want."

"Do you say shut it to your goddess?" Anna opened

her hands, and Caitlyn dangled in the air. "Please, get me down. I am sorry."

Anna laughed. "Come down." Caitlyn landed on her lap. Anna gazed into her eyes and touched her lips. "Thanks for your wonderful love and support. It will be an added responsibility, and I need you by my side to get through what I must do in this world."

"I will always be with you." Caitlyn kissed her. "I am in love with you. Do you want to marry me?"

"Marry?" She closed her mouth and put the tips of her fingers on Caitlyn's rouged lips. With her eyes closed, she nodded and remained silent. Caitlyn rested her head on her thigh, staring at her pensive face. "Honey, I am so sorry to upset you. I know I can't marry a goddess, but I am so happy for you. Please, forgive me."

Anna's fingers massaged Caitlyn's auburn hair. Her tears ran down her sober face. "Love, what happened? Why are you crying? Did I cause you distress when I mentioned marriage?"

Anna turned her face to the right and placed her hand on Caitlyn's chest, saying nothing.

"Are you worried about exposing yourself when you get involved in human politics? It won't be easy for a goddess to liberate the indigenous peoples from the white hegemony and challenge the status quo and behave like a human president."

"Ah, Caitlyn. It is not about matrimony, politics, or the presidency. I want to be honest with you. Although I behave like a woman, I am not like you. The divine cannot become profane. I wish you know the real me and what is in my essence. I am over two-hundred million years old. Yes, I am with you like a normal woman, but do you think an average goddess can go up to the third sky in a few seconds and stop tornadoes, hurricanes, volcanos, and wildfires?"

"I have no idea what sky goddesses can and cannot do. You need to tell me."

"I fought the devils of fire and their macho gods for thousands of years. One day, my girlfriend and I heard about the Great War and wished to see it. So, my girlfriend violated our divine law and made a hole in the lower sky to watch the senseless men who killed each other. We didn't know why men hated each other and made wars instead of enjoying the beauty of nature. My girlfriend bobbed up and down and pushed me down for fun. I fell through the hole and couldn't fly up or stop my fall because of the hole's power of suction. So, I landed on this planet and made myself an ordinary woman to assimilate with the people and experience human life. I lived with indigenous tribes and wild animals in cold forests and ate simple food to acquaint myself with the human lifestyle. Later, my girlfriend came down and caused a deadly blizzard in Canada and New England to punish the psychopaths who assaulted women. Sad to say, the snowstorm killed innocent people. So, her mother imprisoned her in this world to punish her and guard my niece."

"Why your niece?"

"Because she will be the goddess of kindness and the protector of humanity."

"I had never sensed your niece's divine nature. She

even authored a book called *The Lesbian*."

"You saw her human side, not her divine essence. Her mother and I lived a happy life when the world was without animals and people. We were lovers."

"Lovers? Do goddesses allow incest?"

"We don't practice incest, though my sister and I shared intimate moments together. It is not like your earthly sex and orgasm."

"What else do you want to say?"

"I want to say two things. First, my sister killed your father."

"Oh, my God! Why?"

"Because he wanted to kill Angela."

"I know he was a wicked man, but why did he want to kill her?"

"Because she threw a knife at him when he wanted to kill Sandro Lucciano."

"Your niece had never told me that. What is the other thing you want to tell me?"

"I am in love with my eternal girlfriend. My true love is here." She placed her right hand on her chest. Hintocha cried. "I love you. I will always love you."

"Who is she?"

"She is the angelic woman inside me." More tears ran down her face, and her wet lips kissed Caitlyn's hand. "You love me, and I love you, but as I told you once, I cannot have a matrimonial relationship with you because I am a supreme goddess, and our sacred book says I must marry the goddess of love who lives in me. I am here to safeguard you and your daughter, not to marry you. I have a relationship with someone else."

Caitlyn slid off the couch and glared at Anna. "Do you have an affair with another woman? Do you have sex with Elisha?"

"No. I have an affair with the lesbian goddess who is in me."

She laughed, and her manicured fingers touched her lips. "Phew. Oh, dear. Are you in a dream? So, there is a lesbian goddess inside your body, and you have sex with her. Right? What kind of sex? The lovely lap dance? Wake up, honey. I thought you had an affair with a real woman."

"The goddess inside me looks like a woman like you. She kisses me and makes love to me, even when you are with me."

"Even when I am with you. Why haven't I seen her or your sex with her? Is this another fictional story of your imagination?"

"The goddess inside me has been my lover for thousands of years. Her name is Hintocha. She made love to Angela when you lived with her in Canada. She thought I had vanished forever. Hintocha, come out. Caitlyn wants to see you and know the truth about us." She dozed, twitching left and right, and moaning like a wailing ghost. Caitlyn stood beside a window, staring at Anna's quivering body. A strident racket came out of her mouth, and Caitlyn hid behind a drape. Hintocha glided out of Anna's chest and stood on her feet. Caitlyn fainted on the floor.

"Poor little woman." Hintocha squatted beside her and snapped her fingers. "Wake up." Caitlyn opened her eyes. "Hello, Caitlyn. Surprise."

Caitlyn squirmed, and Hintocha's glowing light had given her a jolt. "Oh, my God. Who are you? What are you doing here?"

"Do you no longer recognize me?"

Caitlyn raised her head. "I remember you. You are the indigenous woman who was in the bank. What happened to your height?"

"This is my normal size with the people I love."

"Can I touch you?"

"Yes, you can."

Caitlyn touched her left arm and hand. "You are real. How did you enter Anna's body?"

"I am a goddess made of eternal light. I can do and be anything I want."

She moved back. "Goddess?"

"Yes. I am the goddess of love and romance. My name is Hintocha."

"Why were you in Anna's body?"

"My mother asked me to assist her."

"Your mother?"

"Yes. My mother is the Supreme Goddess who created the Americas and the First Nations."

"Oh, my God. Did you listen to my private talks and watch my foreplay with Anna?"

"I tried to close my eyes and ears."

"Gosh."

"Anna will be the leader of the First Nations."

"Why her?"

"Because she is the greatest and most courageous daughter of our supreme goddesses. Mother Nature and the animals love her. The indigenous people know she is their supreme goddess and liberator.”

“How did you meet her?”

“Her grandma and my mom were best friends. I came into being when Anna and her sister were a hundred solar years old. We were a threesome and the youngest goddesses in our sky.”

“Threesome?”

“Yes. Anna was the lover, and her sister was the charmer.”

“What do you want from me?”

“Nothing. You are a part of the divine will, and no one can change it. My mom will decide the time for our political revolution on earth.”

“Your mom?”

“Yeah.”

“I see. For how long you can remain out of Anna’s body?”

“Forever. I entered her body to hide from you. Please, my intimacy with Anna is not like your sex with a woman. Goddesses do not have sexual organs and don’t get aroused. Be content because we are here to protect you. Come and give me a hug. Do not be afraid.”

Caitlyn hugged her. “Good to see you again. Thanks for saving my life. What do you want to do?”

“I can be your maid and security guard.”

“But you are a goddess and superior to me.”

“My mom asked me to be with Anna and you. We love both of you because we know what is in your hearts.”

“May I ask, how do you have sex with her if you don’t have sexual organs?”

"Our euphoria is not like your biological orgasm. We fondle and kiss and do what goddesses do with spiritual depth and liberty. We can merge in one being and make love in the air, under the oceans, and in forests. For your information, Anna arranged your first meeting with her niece."

"How did she do that?"

"Do you recall the whisper that awakened you in Toronto? Anna inspired you to go to High Park and asked Angela to go there to meet you. Anna also forced Leonardo Lucciano to kill your rapist."

Caitlyn shivered. "Leonardo? Oh, my God."

"Yes. Leonardo killed the rapist and gave you money for your living and education in Canada. So, wasn't it wonderful to be the girlfriend of Anna's niece?"

"More than wonderful, I guess. Am I supposed to live with goddesses for the rest of my life?"

"Maybe. Anna loves you for your honest love for her and Angela. That is all you need to know now. Do you want dinner?"

Caitlyn flexed her arms. "Yeah. Why not? Let us go to the kitchen and make dinner."

"Stay here with Anna."

Hintocha brought three plates of grilled fish and green leaf salads sprinkled with roasted pine nuts and cashews. "How could you make all this food in a minute? How did you get avocado and nuts?"

"That is what true goddesses can do. What about a glass of wine?" She put the plates on a table and clicked her left fingers. A white wine bottle and three crystal glasses appeared in her hands. "You are amazing. No wonder Anna loves you." She stroked Anna's knee. "Anna, Anna, wake up."

"What happened?"

"Dinner is ready. Thanks to Hintocha."

Anna washed her face and had a few cuts. "I have an idea for my presidential campaign."

"What is it?"

"Because we cannot say Hintocha is a goddess, I suggest she becomes my vice president."

"Yeah, that's fantastic, but Hintocha wears these aboriginal clothes."

Hintocha rose and twirled on her toes. "What about this sexy dress?"

Anna and Caitlyn ogled her silver tight bodycon dress. "No. No, darling. You cannot wear this mini dress and show your legs when you are with Anna."

Hintocha put two fingers in her mouth. "What about this maxi one?"

"No. No. You cannot show your bare shoulders and cleavage. Can you put on a dress like mine?"

"No problem. That is very easy to do." Hintocha pirouetted and wrapped her body with a collar blouse and a suit.

"Yeah. That is proper."

"Anything else you want me to do?"

"Remove the orange paint around your eyes and change your hairstyle."

Hintocha twirled and got an asymmetrical bob with side bangs, and the paint around her eyes faded.

"Wow. Impressive. Now you are Anna's official vice president. Oh, my God. Imagine the goddess of war is the President, and the goddess of love is the Vice President of the United States. I can't wait. Yee-haw."

Later, Caitlyn kissed Hintocha's face and asked her to come to her bedroom. "Do you sleep?"

"No, because I look after my universe, but I can close my eyes and catnap."

"Please, stay with us." Caitlyn touched her face and pointed at her bed. "You can sleep with us."

"And watch you?"

"We can have fun together, and you can show me how goddesses love each other."

"You will know that later. But now, have fun with Anna. I will stay in the other room."

The next day, Anna parted the silk curtains of the living room, unveiling a scene that crackled with energy and anticipation. Beyond the glass, a bustling crowd had gathered, a sea of reporters and camera operators who had converged at her building.

As the curtains fell aside, the sunlight poured into the room, illuminating the space, and casting a warm glow over Anna's figure. Her expression remained composed, a mask of poise that belied the whirlwind of attention. She reclined on a couch and switched on the TV. There was a brief report on her presidential nomination by the Democratic Party. Caitlyn and Hintocha came and rested beside her. The Republican President told journalists he would win the next election. When a reporter asked him about Anna, he replied, "I have never heard of her." Another journalist informed him that Anna calls herself the Eagle Woman. The President winced and squinched his eyes. "This means the sleepy radical socialist Democrats want the witches to run the country, which means more illegal immigrants and rapists who would bring crime into the US."

"What a moron." Caitlyn threw a soft cushion at the TV screen.

The doorbell rang. Anna opened the door, and nine of Caitlyn's Irish relatives swarmed into the entryway and gave her hugs and kisses.

"Make me the Secretary of Defense so I can blow up the arse of North Korea," one said.

"Let me be the Secretary of State because I want to go to Ireland and see the family," another man said.

One of them ogled Hintocha's body. "Who is that sexy woman?"

"Shut up. Don't you ever talk about her like that. She can kick your ass."

"Did you hear what the doofus said about you?"

"That is his opinion."

"He is a bozo and an ass...."

"No need to swear."

"Chill out, woman. We are a family. Do you have Guinness?"

"Yes. In the fridge."

"Let us order Irish food."

"You will eat what Caitlyn and I want to eat."

After lunch, Anna gave them a sports bag. "This is for you."

One of them opened the bag. "It is empty."

"Open it again." The bag fell on the floor. He opened it and found it full of cash. "This money is for you and your families. I don't want to see poor Irish people, and I want you to vote for me. OK?"

"Of course. We will vote for you, and we want you and our cousin to be in the White House."

"Good. Be kind to each other and don't make troubles." She asked them to leave. A Democratic representative called, requesting her to start the presidential campaign the next day at Madison Square Garden in Midtown Manhattan.

In the early evening, the President made a brief statement in the Oval Office. "We have realized that Anna's girlfriend is the last granddaughter of Cian McManus, the godfather of the Irish mob. The ruthless Irish Mafia wants to take over America and our economy. I will defeat my foes and make America great again."

In the morning, Anna and Hintocha met a flock of reporters outside their home. "What is your first response to the President's statement about your partner and the Irish Mafia?"

"I support the First Amendment and believe in the freedom of speech. The President can say what he likes, and the valiant Irish know how to respond."

"But the President says you want the Mafia to rule the country."

"Do you believe that? I am a lesbian, and I don't think the Catholic Mafia likes lesbians. For God's sake, look at me. Do I look like a Mafia yakuza?"

"Aren't you angry at the President?"

"No. I do not know anger because my mind and body are in harmony with Mother Nature."

"Do you believe in God?"

"I believe a Creator or Creators had made our universe. Our existence is not a fluke."

"Are you open to debate with the President?"

"I am open to talking with any American citizen. I have no prejudice against anyone."

"Do you consider yourself a liberal?"

"I consider myself a reformist woman. Let our deeds, not labels, speak."

"If you become the President, what would be your policy on immigration?"

"You and all the citizens who live in this land are immigrants, or descendants of immigrant settlers. This country will always welcome legal immigrants."

"What do you say about the illegal workers in the country?"

"If they are civilized people, they should become US citizens and pay taxes."

"There are anti-racist riots in Chicago, Seattle, and Portland. What is your opinion on the Black Lives Matter movement?"

"I don't like the ideologies of the Left and the Right. I believe all human lives matter, including the lives of the indigenous peoples."

"If you become the President, will you support Israel?"

"I will support all the peacemakers."

"Do you believe in global warming and climate change?"

"We must work together to preserve the earth, our only homeland."

"Do you support abortion and birth control?"

"Let us stop the war on women's bodies. Men have no right to tell women how they should treat their wombs and bodies, though I stress all human lives matter."

"Why are you gorgeous?"

She beamed. "Why are your ears small? I mean, the Creator has made us different."

After the news meeting, Anna and Hintocha headed to Madison Square Garden to meet Martina and their supporters. They stood on a stage. Senator Kirsten Maloney introduced Anna as "an incredible advocate" and "a woman of wonders."

Anna held a mic. "Dear friends. I want to thank the Democratic Party for choosing me, though many people are more qualified than me. To be fair, I am not a politician, but I have a big heart that cares for every one of you. My policy is the policy of care, love, and prosperity. I promise you there will be no homeless mendicants. My government will help the citizens who cannot pay their medical bills. Education will be free, and medicine will be free. There will be no wars, and there will be no guns and shootings on our streets. The death penalty is unethical. There will be no drought, wildfires, tornadoes, or hurricanes. If I become the President, I will open the White House's doors to the public and allow you to come on certain days to talk to me about your problems. Hintocha Sakokete will be my vice president, and the adorable Martina Lucciano will be our campaign manager and spokesperson."

In the evening, the President commented. "Did you

hear what Anna said? She says education will be free. Who will pay for our teachers and schools if education is free? She also says health care will be free. So, if you think Obamacare is bad, Anna's idea of free medicine is worse. She says there will be no guns to defend ourselves. I tell you this misandrist woman wants to abolish our Constitution and the Second Amendment. I didn't lie when I warned you about the Catholic Mafia's plan to take over America and steal your money. Anna's official spokesperson is Martina Lucciano. We all know the Lucciano family's reign of terror in New York and elsewhere. And before I leave, do the Americans want a president who looks like Martha Hunt, or what is her name that bikini woman, Candice Swanepoel?"

Anna began her official campaign with visits to children's hospitals in Manhattan. Doctors, nurses, and parents felt stupefied when she healed injuries, fractured limbs, and disabled kids. "Who needs doctors and drugs when I am here?"

In the next morning, a newspaper headline said, "Virgin Mary in the Town." Local media published photos showing Anna's healing phenomenon. A wave of awe and wonder swept through the country. People from all social classes viewed her as more than a politician. Many perceived her as a holy figure, believing that the Divine had inspired her presence and actions. They saw in her a beacon of hope, a channel through which their prayers and troubles could find sympathy.

Text messages and printed letters flooded in, each

carrying a personal story of struggle, pain, and hope. People poured out their hearts, showing their profound fears, desires, and challenges, and seeking guidance and healing from someone they saw as a superhuman.

With unfeigned compassion and humility, Anna read and absorbed each message, recognizing the weight of trust given to her. Within four weeks, there were no homeless people in New York.

Anna and Hintocha toured the country's states. One fateful day, news reached their ears of the devastating tornadoes that had ravaged through Alabama, leaving a trail of destruction and loss in their wake. The weight of the tragedy pressed upon their hearts, and with a sense of purpose, they set out to bear witness to the aftermath. Their steps led them to Lee County, where the extent of the devastation became clear.

Surveying the damaged area, they navigated through the debris and destruction, each piece of wreckage bearing witness to the force of nature's wrath. Amid the chaos, they noticed a lonely woman perched on a rough heap of broken furniture, a solitary figure among the ruins. Her presence radiated a feeling of despair and loss.

Moved by sympathy, they approached the woman. With a touch as soft as a whisper, Anna reached out and placed her hand on the woman's shoulder, a gesture that conveyed an understanding of the pain that had befallen the community. She squatted, allowing herself to be at eye level with the woman. "What happened?"

"I lost my husband and two kids."

"Oh, dear. We are sorry for your loss. We don't know

how you feel, but we are here to help in every way. Where are their bodies?”

“In a mortuary in Opelika.”

“What is your name?”

“Rebecca Jones.”

“Where is your home?”

A moment of poignant stillness followed before the response came, tinged with a sense of sorrow and displacement. “I have no home. The storm plucked it from the ground and tossed it in the air like a toy.” This vivid presentation had painted a bleak picture of the devastation wrought by the tornadoes, as if nature had become an indiscriminate force, tearing the very fabric of life.

“Sometimes nature gets angry. I vow to do my best for you. Where was it?”

She pointed her finger at a pulverized, flattened house. “Over here.”

“Where do you stay?”

“With my sister.”

“Where does she live?”

“On Lee Road.”

“What is the number of her house?”

“Two-nine-zero.”

In the late evening, Anna and Hintocha puffed out white smoke and made everyone in the area fall asleep. They made new houses and parks and cleared piles of the wreckage, touching nothing. In the early morning, they visited Rebecca and her sister. “Come with us in the car. We have a surprise for you.”

Rebecca and her sister visited the new homes. “My

God! Who built the houses? Who cleaned all the mess in one night? It is a modern town." She entered a new house. "Wow! I had a small house, but this one is huge. The kitchen is fantastic." She looked through a window. "I do not see workers and equipment. Who made the homes and cleaned the streets?"

"Nature destroys, and nature builds."

Rebecca embraced Anna and bawled. "You are an angel. I want you to be my president."

"Thank you. I have another surprise for you. Let us go upstairs."

They went upstairs. "Open this door." Rebecca opened the door and shrieked after seeing her husband and two kids sitting on a bed. She sobbed. "My God! My God! This is impossible. How did you do that? You are like God."

"Be happy and enjoy your time together. I left some money for you in this wardrobe. We must go."

Rebecca and her family and the media said Anna had performed a supernatural miracle.

Chapter 8

Anna's journey took an unexpected turn as her story resonated everywhere, touching the hearts of people from all levels of society. The unassuming individual had transformed into a celebrity and influencer, with her presence radiating a magnetic allure that drew people toward her.

Radio and TV channels sought her out, eager to share her unmatched experiences and insights with their audiences. Her interviews became a platform for inspiration, a chance to delve into the depths of her wisdom and the resilience that had propelled her forward. Her voice echoed through the airwaves, leaving an indelible mark upon those who listened.

Her influence extended beyond the realm of the media, and her story captivated artists, channeling her popular involvements into works of creativity that resonated with the human spirit. Musicians wove melodies inspired by her journey, each note carrying a fragment of her courage and intentness. Activists embraced her as a symbol of hope, a testament to the power of individual action to spark change. Athletes admired her perseverance, finding a kindred spirit in the unwavering dedication that had moved her forward through challenges.

As her popularity soared and her charismatic presence continued to capture the attention of many, the President and his zealous supporters, fueled by envy and apprehension, had harnessed the power of the conservative media to launch a campaign against her. Like a storm gathering strength, they delved into her past, seeking to uncover any vulnerabilities that could tarnish her image.

Accusations, some grounded in truth and others distorted or exaggerated, had surfaced like wavelets in a pond. The media networks, once drawn to her inspirational stories, now became a battleground where they thrust all sorts of allegations into the spotlight. Sensationalism and speculation filled the airwaves, as the opponents sought to chip away at the pedestal on which she stood.

Allegations flooded, creating a perpetual cacophony of noise, a dizzying blend of truths, half-truths, and outright fabrications that threatened to obscure the essence of her journey. The narrative became muddied as the focus shifted from Anna's message of hope and resilience to the drama of scandal and controversy. The

Republican rhetoric of fear and hate had reached a momentum as it honed in on what it perceived as unquestionable vulnerabilities in her behavior and background. It contended that her obvious lack of prior involvement in politics had left her ill-equipped to navigate the complex landscape of domestic policies and international relations. The absence of a political and social record became a focal point of their criticism, a perceived weakness that they aimed to exploit.

The arguments of the Republicans gained weight they as they delved into the various facets of Anna's life. They pointed to specific gaps in public knowledge, highlighting what they claimed was a serious lack of transparencies about her family, education, work history, and experiences. The unknowns became fodder for speculation, casting suspicion over her narrative style and raising questions about her qualifications and suitability for the role she seemed to embrace.

Her foes aimed to cast doubt on her credibility, leveraging the public's appetite for information and transparency. They tried to weaken her bond with the citizens by insinuating that her past was still obscure and that she lacked a deep comprehension of the intricacies of governance.

Anna defended her nomination by talking about her upbringing in a multicultural home. "For the last three centuries, my clan supplied this state and New England with food, minerals, and wood from across the border. Our artisans crafted the decorations and interiors of famous houses and structures in New York. My partner is an acclaimed professor and a best-selling author of over fifteen books. Our diligent communities, driven by their unswerving tenacity and resilience, have achieved notable success and earned prestige, despite enduring the hardships of racial discrimination. Their positive contributions played a pivotal role in shaping the nation's infrastructures, industries, arts, politics, and culture."

Critics derided her, saying the US citizens do not know her parents and siblings. In addition, Caitlyn, they pointed out, is a descendant of the most notorious Irish family that smuggled guns, drugs, and alcohol, owned illegal brothels, murdered rivals and police officers, and terrorized the nation for two centuries. News networks published graphic photos of terrible crimes conducted by the Irish mob, confirming that Caitlyn's father, grandfather, great-grandfather, and uncles were notorious serial killers. "If Anna cares about people and peace, as she says, why is her Irish partner a member of the most brutal Mafia family?" a conservative commentator said.

Journalists and news analysts uploaded news photos and FBI and police documents, proving Caitlyn's and Martina's ancestors were the original architects of the Mafia in America. They used these documents to accuse Anna of wanting the Catholic Mafia and its clandestine businesses to govern the country with total disregard to the Constitution.

The public's fascination with Anna had taken on an added dimension, fueled by the rumors that swirled around her supernatural powers and deeds. These rumors, often whispered in hushed tones and shared with wonder and skepticism, had gained a life of their own.

Tales of her abilities had spread like wildfire, passed from person to person like cherished secrets. People spoke of the times she had altered reality to her will, turning ordinary situations into extraordinary displays of power. The stories ranged from the mundane to the fantastical, each one adding to the mystique that surrounded her. In some accounts, people said she had healed the sick with a single touch. Others recounted instances where she had quelled storms with a mere gesture or causing flowers to bloom out of season. "Anna is nobody but a cunning manipulator of black magic," a news analyst said. Republican magicians performed outstanding tricks, such as making tall buildings and airplanes disappear, and told the press that Anna's acts were fake and illusions. Their explicit statements had contributed to the rampant gossip about Anna's plot to exploit her magic to control people and rig the election and the political system.

Other opponents reminded people that Anna was a radical lesbian feminist who expressed an emphatic aversion to men and an enthusiastic love for liberal lesbians. Legislators and TV hosts spent days and months exchanging sarcasm and satirical jokes about a lesbian in the White House. A commentator said, "If Anna wins the election, she will be the first man-hating president." A political cartoonist mocked. "If Anna becomes the President, she will wear a rainbow gown and call the White House the Pink House." Other satirists compared her to porn celebrities and Victoria's Secret models.

Tabloids added complexity to the situation with their publication of Elisha's sensual photos. "Anna will entertain Caitlyn's daughter and turn the Oval Office into the Orgy Office," a Virginia tabloid said. "Elisha's lesbian mother is a substandard role model for decent daughters," a Chicago tabloid said.

That media defamation was not enough for the partisan conservatives. During his extensive travels in the country, the President attacked Anna's candidacy by sowing seeds of fear and provoking concerns about a seizure of power that the country had never seen before. In an interview with a TV channel, he disparaged. "Anna and Caitlyn are two desperate socialist puppets for the LGBT fanatics. They want to promote the woke and cancel culture and impose communism and Marxism in our country and undermine the First Amendment, the freedom of speech, and the right to keep and bear arms." The channel showed photos of their lesbian romance and derided the LGBTQ organizations for their unequivocal support for Anna.

The constant vilification of Anna took on another serious dimension when Dinah Hansson conducted and funded her own investigation. With the help of an army of private investigators, she followed the news and documented images of Anna's touring campaign and public speeches. One day, her close friend Pamela Ryan, also a famed investigative journalist, visited her in a New York apartment to inform her of matters affecting her investigation. "Look at Anna's face. She has ivory skin, gray eyes, light-brown thin eyebrows, a narrow forehead, and low cheekbones. In contrast, her alleged mother has golden skin, dark hair, brown eyes, a broad forehead, and high cheekbones."

Dinah had a sip of coffee. "She is a liar. What about the other liar Elisha? The modeling world, the media, and the Irish and Italian families say she is Caitlyn's and the impostor's daughter. My husband had never met her or mentioned her name. Besides, I inspected photos and fashion magazines. Elisha has blonde hair and blue eyes. I checked out her YouTube channel, where she says the color of her blonde hair is natural."

"She said she was the daughter of the hoodwinker who had red hair."

"She lies. She doesn't resemble anyone in the Lucciano family. Do you know why Anna looks like a supermodel and twenty years younger than Caitlyn?"

"I am not a biologist. By the way, Hintocha lives in their house. No vice-presidential candidate had ever lived with a presidential candidate."

"Why does she live with them?"

"She is their housekeeper."

"But why did they hire a Native American?"

"I think they are a lesbian threesome. I have never seen the three women with men."

"Who is Anna's family? Is her father alive? Does she have siblings?"

"That's a mystery."

"Where did she grow up?"

"We don't know where she was born, though she

hints she belongs to the indigenous people in New York and Ontario. The Cayuga actor Jenna Halftown said to me Anna is a holy woman, and the Native Americans revere her for religious reasons.”

“What do you mean?”

“The Native Americans believe a sky goddess had fallen to the earth and incarnated in her body. They say only a goddess can perform Anna’s miracles.”

“Anna doesn’t work. How is she a billionaire? How did she pay twenty million dollars for her house? She donated over thirty million dollars in the last month. She also funds her campaign.”

“That is another conundrum. What happened to Leonardo’s wealth? Did Angelo get any money from his inheritance?”

“No. The mountebank got two hundred million dollars from his inheritance.”

They had a break and a snack with a cup of tea, and after turning on the TV and watching an interview with Anna and Hintocha, they moved to the study room. As Pamela walked around the room, her eyes examined the photos that covered the walls. “Where is Hintocha? I don’t see her.”

“That puzzles me.” Dinah inspected images on her camera and phone. “Hintocha is always invisible. I don’t have any photos of her. Do you know why she disappears for three days every month?”

“God knows. No one sees her when she leaves the city. You should see Rachel Harris, who works with the Social Security Administration.”

Dinah contacted official records and met Rachel at a

coffee shop on Eighth Avenue. "What do you know about Anna and Hintocha?"

"We don't have any official documents about them. Didn't the Democratic Party check their papers and identities before nominating them?"

"That's weird. I will talk to the party's leaders."

"You should go back to Canada. Caitlyn got her degrees from Toronto, and her daughter was born there."

Dinah traveled to Toronto and talked to officials, journalists, academics, and ex-students. "Caitlyn was hyperintelligent. She earned three first-rate degrees in humanities. She was an astute and sedulous student," a professor said. "Caitlyn was a fashion model and Angelo Lucciano's partner," a lecturer said. "We don't know what happened to Angelo. A woman called Angela became Caitlyn's second girlfriend. Her stories were about lesbian love. Her famous book is called *The Lesbian*," an arts journalist said.

On a different day, she visited the Toronto Public Library and embarked on a quest for information and knowledge. Her fingers traced spines of books, and her eyes skimmed over titles. News clips lay before her like fragments of a mystery. She pored over articles that were windows into the past. Pages turned under her fingers, revealing a treasure trove of information.

Later, in the quiet solitude of her hotel room, the remnants of history spread before her like pieces of a jigsaw puzzle. With a meticulous focus, she sifted through copies of old papers. The rustling of papers seemed to echo through the room as her fingers walked across headlines and paragraphs. Her search extended beyond the tangible papers. With a laptop, she navigated official websites and social media platforms. As her cursor clicked and keystrokes danced, she uncovered pieces of data that painted a clearer picture. Facts, figures, and records formed a mosaic of information. With each click and turn of a page, she moved closer to unraveling the threads that wove her narrative that had become intertwined with the stories of those who had come before her. In the morning, she called Louise Lee, the criminal investigator who probed the explosion of Angela's house. "Good morning. This is Dinah Hansson."

"What a lovely surprise. I have been thinking of you. Where are you?"

"In Toronto. Do you have time to continue our conversation about the charlatans? I have gathered interesting information about them."

"That is great. Can you see me today after five pm in my office?"

"Yes. See you then."

Dinah met Louise in her office at Coxwell Avenue. "What do you have?" Louise asked.

"I believe the presidential candidate Anna and her partner, Caitlyn McManus, had plotted the death of Angelo and Angela. They met in Toronto on the same day when the blast happened. Do you know why they visited the city on that day?"

"No. But we know that Caitlyn lived with Angelo Lucciano in Toronto for four years before she became Angela's partner for fourteen years. Her Angelo looked very much like your Angelo. Elisha's first birth certificate says Angelo Lucciano was her father, though she was called Elisha McManus. When she was four, her father disappeared, and Angela Lucciano became her new parent. The connection between Angelo and Angela is still a mystery. At twenty-one, Elisha called herself Elisha Lucciano and told the world that she was Angela's daughter. She and her mother are persons of interest because they didn't contact us or the FBI to talk about the explosion or even about Angela, who lived fifteen years with them."

"The FBI should have interrogated them because Angela and Angelo were US citizens."

"That is true, and I do not know why the FBI didn't interview them." She opened a file and gave Dinah three photos. "This Native American woman was the last person with Angela in the United States and Canada. The Canada Border Services Agency and the US CBP have no evidence that they had crossed the border."

"That's strange." Dinah scrutinized the photos. "This woman is Hintocha. She is the Democratic vice-presidential candidate. She changed her traditional dress and hairstyle. How did she know Angela? Why did she put Angela in the FBI car?"

"We don't know. We also don't know why Angela's mother and family didn't ask about her."

"Who was her mother?"

"The FBI told us her mother was unknown. Her house in Manhattan is vacant. No one knows her name or what happened to her."

"How could she get a house in Manhattan without showing legal documents?"

"We couldn't find any document about her or about her house, though we got photos of her with Angela."

"This means Bella Lucciano was not Angela's mom."

"Correct, though Bella treated her as her daughter. Anyway, there is a proof that the FBI car was in Canada, yet we don't know how it crossed the border. We don't think Hintocha killed Angela before or after crossing the border. Look at these images." She gave Dinah four photos.

"These photos prove Hintocha and Angela were lovers."

"That might be true, but we still don't know how they crossed the border. The romantic kisses on the lips and holding hands show Angela was Hintocha's lover, yet Angela's relatives and friends said they had never met Hintocha, and Angela's diaries do not say a word about her."

"Angela looks very much like Anna. Do you think there is a relationship between them?"

"That's possible because they have the same body shape and skin color. What is intriguing is that the First Nations people say Anna and Hintocha had performed miracles for them, walked on water, built homes, caught fish with their hands, and healed their sick. They also say grizzly bears, wolves, lynxes, and moose licked their hands and legs because they are holy goddesses." Louise gave Dinah seven photos. "They roamed across three provinces before the explosion and stayed together in a Toronto hotel room after the explosion. People saw them holding hands and kissing each other."

"So, no wonder they and Caitlyn live in one house. They are lesbian freaks and partners in crime."

"That's possible, but we need evidence." She gave Dinah two photos of Anna holding a bald eagle. "Interesting. Anna calls herself the Eagle Woman, and she and Hintocha do supernatural things. Any scientific explanation?"

"Legendary stories among the First Nations say their aggrieved goddesses will come down to earth to liberate them and rule their occupied lands, despite God's objections. In the Cree language, Anna's family name, Awehitecha, means the warrior-savior who fell from the sky. We do not know any Canadian citizen who has that family name."

"Does anyone say she is their daughter or sister?"

This question hung in the air, and the response came with a sense of finality, a confession of the limits of official knowledge. "No," came the answer, a simple word that held with it a world of indecision. "We know nothing about her family."

"Will there be an apocalyptic war between the goddesses and God and the human beings?"

"That would happen if actual goddesses and gods exist."

"Considering what you have said, do you think Anna and Hintocha are aliens?"

"You know me. As a scientist, I do not believe in superstitions, though the weird actions of these two women are out of this world, and I cannot explain them in a lab. Look at this video." Louise played a video on her laptop. She paused at the beginning of the video to show the faces of Caitlyn and Elisha at the airport.

"What were they doing with Anna at the airport? Why did Anna hug them, and how did she blow that white smoke?"

"We don't know why Anna met them at the airport. The white smoke was a part of Anna's weird magic."

Dinah checked the date of the video. "Can I get a copy of the video?"

"Yes."

"Again, why were Caitlyn and Elisha in Toronto on the day when the explosion took place?"

"As I said, we don't know. Official documents say Elisha is Angela's daughter. So, maybe they came here to know about Angela's fate."

"Where is this Angela? My husband had never mentioned her or Elisha."

"As a fact, Elisha doesn't look like Angela."

"That's obvious. Did Angela adopt her?"

"There is no evidence for that."

"Back to Hintocha. If she was the last person to see Angela in the United States and Canada, why didn't your office or the FBI interrogate her?"

"Dealing with the traditions of the First Nations in Canada or in America is a sensitive matter. How can we question her if the First Nations and their animals think she is a holy goddess? We arrested a suspect. His name is Norman Wilson. He said a tall man with a dark red face and fiery hands and a muscular, brown man had forced him and his brother into conducting the abduction in Ottawa and bringing your husband to Angela's house."

Dinah's heart pounded fast, and a jolt of fear and anger had shocked her body. Her mind raced, trying to process the added information. "Who were these men? What were their motives?"

"We don't know their motives. Norman said there were piles of damaged walls and furniture in Angela's house and he smelled a gas leak. According to his confession, he and his brother Martin tied your husband to a chair, and the red man asked him about Angela and got angry when he found a burned skeleton and a huge dead body."

"What about the camera and the explosion?"

"We couldn't find the camera that recorded the explosion, and we don't know who used it and sent the video to the media. Norman said three female warriors threw black smoke bombs and killed his brother and the muscular man with tomahawk axes when they tried to torture and execute Angelo. When these women seized your husband, the red man swore to blow them up. Norman said he sprinted to the back garden and hid behind a tree before the explosion took place. We found a female skeleton and three male skeletons and couldn't find the big dead body."

"So, who died in the explosion?"

"We are not a hundred percent sure. You and the Lucciano family took two charred skeletons, and we suspect the other two skeletons were for Norman's brother and the muscular man."

"I still don't understand why the abductors took my

husband to Angela's house."

"My theory is that Angela was the prime target of the abductors. The red man, the muscular man, Norman, and Martin abducted your husband to force Angela to tell them about a secret code. But they felt frustrated when they couldn't find her. So, they asked your husband about the code because they thought he was related to Angela, who was very wealthy."

"But why did the abductors ask for a code instead of money? As you know, they asked my husband to give them the eagle's eye or the code. What did they mean by that?"

"The Eagle's Eye is the name of your husband's company. I wonder if the name has something to do with Anna, who calls herself the Eagle Woman. We found Norman's van, which took your husband from Ottawa to Angela's house. We still don't know why the abductors asked your husband about a secret code that has nothing to do with money. I assume the code has something to do with your husband's artificial intelligence technology."

"I think you are right. My husband said to me he named his company the Eagle's Eye because he saw a birthmark that looked like an eagle's eye."

"We still don't know the identity of the red man and the three mysterious women. We couldn't find bullet casings or murder instruments."

"Whom we buried in New York?"

"We think they were your husband and Angela because the height of the skeletons and the shape of the skulls match their bodies. What still amazes me is that your husband and Angela had never been to doctors or dentists in Canada."

"I know nothing about Angela's health, but Angelo was healthy. He had never been sick."

"There are no medical records for them, and my forensic team couldn't do a thorough examination because the explosion incinerated the bodies, and the Sicilians in Canada and the US were furious. They forced our government to give them the female skeleton, and we expected a Mafia war against us. Italian insiders told us that Angela Lucciano was the godmother of the Italian Mafia in New York and Canada. So, the Italians took her burned body and buried it in Brooklyn. After the burial, their hitmen assassinated three Irish Mafia bosses in Quebec and Ontario. Then, an Irish assassin killed Kathy Swain, the investigative journalist who said the Irish Mafia had killed Angela and Angelo, because the Godfather Sandro Lucciano wiped out the Irish mob in America. However, we became perplexed when an American informant told us that Nina is Angela's grandmother."

"But Angela was white and had red, orange hair, while Nina is a brown Native American from the Seneca tribe in New York. I have known her for twenty-five years." She paused for ten seconds. "Oh, my God."

"What's the matter?"

"An FBI agent told me Anna lived in Nina's home for three or four months before moving with Caitlyn to her new house. He heard her calling Nina mom. So, if Angela was Nina's granddaughter, Anna would be her mother or aunt. Anna's spokesperson, Martina, is

Angela's half-sister, and her mom was Leonardo's secret lover. So, it is an organized family Mafia business, and Leonardo had multiple secret affairs."

"Brilliant observation. However, someone still uses Angela's bank accounts and visa cards, but we could not trace him or her."

The admission that an unknown person was running Angela's financial affairs had deepened the sense of mystery, leaving questions unanswered and casting doubts. "Where did the transactions take place?"

"In Ontario and New York."

"Strange. Who would withdraw money from her bank accounts?"

"We don't know. The surveillance cameras inside and outside the banks didn't record any irregular activities. Credit cards did the transactions. The law doesn't allow us to seize the money. The interesting thing about Angela's wealth is that no one had asked for it, not even her alleged daughter Elisha."

"Is it possible that one of Angela's girlfriends uses the credit cards?"

"That is possible. Why did you say girlfriends?"

"Because Angela was a polyamorous lesbian and loved only girls. Do you think Hintocha disappears three days a month to use Angela's bank cards to give Anna money?"

"I have no proof of that. Anyway, we examined Angela's official documents and realized that she and your husband had the same date and place of birth. So, if Angela's parents were Leonardo and Bella, and Angelo's parents were also Leonardo and Bella, and they were born at the same time and place, this means they were twins."

"But Angelo had never mentioned a sister. All the Luccianos know Bella gave birth only to a son. She didn't have a daughter."

"But Bella and Leonardo treated Angela as their daughter, and the Lucciano family made her their godmother. Maybe Bella gave birth to twins, and the Lucciano family hid the girl."

"That is not possible because Angelo was my boyfriend when we were in school. He told me many secrets about his family, but nothing about a sister."

"Again. If Angela was Nina's granddaughter and Anna's daughter or niece, how do the Luccianos say she was Leonardo's daughter and their godmother? Do you understand the paradox?"

"Nina was Angelo's caregiver and his mother's secret lover. She had never talked about a girl when I saw Angelo in her house."

"Correct. So, the only possibility is that Angela and your husband were separated twins for unknown reasons. How they died at the same time and place is another riddle. The Canadian and US authorities say they did not cross the border except in the coffins. Anyway, what are you doing tonight?"

"Nothing important."

"Have dinner with me. I have a new kitchen."

Back in New York, Dinah reviewed the Canadian video and asked Hu Yang, a private forensic expert, to analyze photos of Leonardo, Bella, Angela, Angelo, Anna, Hintocha, Nina, Caitlyn, Martina, and Elisha. Hu used artificial intelligence photo editing software tools and image manipulation programs. Later, he called her. "I examined the parietal, frontal, and zygomatic bones and available DNA samples. I can say your husband was of Sicilian and English-Irish descent. He and Angela were not siblings or first cousins. So, I don't know how the Sicilian Luccianos considered Angela one of them. The other thing I should mention is that it is impossible for Caitlyn's Angelo to become Angela. Gender transitioning can't change a person's hair color, height, and bone structure. Angela was five-ten, and Angelo was six-two. This means Angela was not Caitlyn's Angelo, who was a hermaphrodite. However, it is difficult to know why the kidnappers took your Angelo to Angela's house and asked him about a secret code. I think they thought Angelo and Angela were siblings and business partners because of their wealth and the family name."

"That's interesting. What else?"

"Elisha is ninety-five percent Irish and Caitlyn's true daughter. This means that her father was Irish. So, she cannot be Angelo's or Angela's biological daughter. Nina's DNA is mysterious, and considering Angela's pheomelanin and head shape, she cannot be her grandmother, while Hintocha is her niece or cousin because they have the same DNA, and they belong to the same Native American tribe. Anna's mandible is not the same, meaning she doesn't relate to anyone of them."

"Are you sure?"

"Yes, I am sure. Nina and Hintocha have a tan

square face shape, while Anna has pale skin and an oval face. She is different."

"What about Martina?"

"The DNA test says she is forty percent Sicilian, thirty-five Scandinavian, twelve percent French, and five percent Icelandic."

"You are amazing."

A month later, Dinah published a book entitled *The Extraterrestrial Lesbian President*. The book said Anna and Hintocha were alien beings. "Their ensuing mission is to rule the Earth with force and deceit and make the United States of America their operational headquarters," she wrote. "To achieve their aim, they and Caitlyn killed my husband and Angela Lucciano to steal their wealth and secret codes related to their businesses," she concluded. Influential newspapers, such as *The New York Times*, *the Washington Post*, and *Los Angeles Times*, quoted chapters and excerpts and published sensual photos of Caitlyn when she was a glamor model and actor. Dinah's compelling evidence and the media's constant furor had impelled the Democratic Party to spurn Anna and Hintocha and select new candidates. In response, Anna threatened to form an independent party, telling the Party's directors that she would speak the truth and refute Dinah Hansson's allegations.

Elisha defended herself and her mother and dismissed Dinah's arguments in interviews with TV channels. "Dinah's book is full of childish fantasies and fictional conspiracy theories. My official name is Elisha Lucciano. Here is my original birth certificate, which proves I am the only daughter of Angelo who was intersexual before he became Angela. My mom has blue eyes and blonde hair, and her father had blue eyes and ginger hair. That is why I have blonde hair and blue eyes. Here are photos of me with my mom and Angelo in the hospital after my birth. Here are photos of me with Leonardo, Bella, and the Lucciano family when I was a girl. My mom was Angelo's and Angela's partner for nineteen years, and it was Angela who saved my model friends and me when the Polish guys abducted us. So, how does Dinah say Angelo was her husband and my mom killed him and Angela and stole their money? My mom was a poor orphan in New York, but Leonardo Lucciano sent her to Canada and paid for her living and education. My mom and I went to Toronto because we loved Angela. We also love Anna because she saved our life when the terrorists attacked the Toronto airport...."

To negate Elisha's response, Dinah conversed with journalists. "I challenge Elisha to check her DNA. No one in the Lucciano family looks like her. My husband, Angelo, was with me for eight or nine years before we got married. Angela was a lesbian with a vagina all her life. So, how does Elisha claim to be her biological daughter? My husband had never lived in Toronto and with her mother. He became a billionaire because of his super intelligence and Leonardo Lucciano's generous support."

Journalists met Martina to find out her reaction to Dinah's criticism. "It seems Dinah is my sister-in-law. She should know that we discuss our problems only with the family. Angela loved all the members of the family, including Caitlyn and Elisha. And whether Dinah likes it or not, Elisha is my favorite niece, and the Lucciano family loves her. We respect and support Anna and Caitlyn. Dinah's claim that Anna is my biological aunt is absurd. She lies when she says Anna, Hintocha, and Caitlyn killed my sister to steal her money. No one had touched my sister's money."

After Martina's statement, juvenile members of the Irish community had unleashed a wave of aggression against Dinah. They pelted her Lincoln car with bricks and smashed its windows. Later, Dinah asked a nearby restaurant to deliver two pizzas to her eighth-floor apartment on Madison Avenue. When a delivery driver rang her doorbell, four Irish men, posing as her brothers and cousins, had ordered him to give them the pizzas and leave the building. Dinah opened the door, and the intruders burst into her apartment. She leaned on a wall and tried to reason with them, but one of them put his hand on her mouth. "Keep your mouth shut. We do not want to hurt you. Just be quiet."

They entered her study room, grabbed her laptop, and collected photos and papers related to Anna and her family. "Look at this sicko. She drew penises on Anna's photos," one said. On their way out, a capped man turned his face toward Dinah and punched the wall behind her. "This is our last warning. We will kill you if you continue to accuse Anna and her partner of your crap. Don't be a fool."

In the aftermath of the disturbing incidents, Dinah tried to restore a sense of order to the chaos that had occurred. She called upon the authorities, reaching out to the police to report the damage that the offenders had inflicted on her car and the intrusion into her home.

As the dust settled, a news anchor arrived to interview her. A camera focused on her, capturing the weariness in her eyes and the determination in her voice. "What happened today?"

Her response was unequivocal. "Caitlyn's ruffians damaged my car and ransacked my house. They stole my laptop and documents and threatened to kill me."

The implications were chilling, a sign to the lengths some people will go to suppress the alleged facts she represented. Her voice remained consistent as she continued. "They fear the truth." Her words were a declaration that a fear of the revelations she brought to light had driven the actions of those who targeted her.

"That's horrible. What do you say about Martina Lucciano's statement?"

"Martina is afraid of Anna's and Hintocha's alien witchcraft. She also doesn't want the media to know she is the daughter of Leonardo's secretary. Angelo told me his father had a long affair with his secretary in New Jersey when he was married to an English woman. Please, play the video that shows Hintocha holding Angela on her shoulder."

The TV channel played the video. "Look at the vice-presidential candidate. She is not a human being. See her power and strength. She was the last person with Angela. Where did she take her? Witnesses in the bank said she came out of Angela's body like a ghost and bullets couldn't touch her body. Normal women don't do these things. Can she tell us anything about her family?"

The Lucciano family summoned Martina to the Brooklyn house. "Our father taught us that what we do and say should be in the family. We do not talk to the media about our plans and politics. Why do you defend Anna and Hintocha?" Viola said.

"They are good people."

"How do you know that? They caused the death of Angela and Angelo."

"I am their spokesperson. What do you want me to do?"

Franco fetched a piece of cake. "We do not trust the corrupt system and the media. We will talk to Hintocha and ask her questions."

"Be careful. She is not an ordinary woman."

In the evening, a woman visited Anna and gave her an envelope. Anna held the envelope and sat beside Caitlyn on the bed. "What is this envelope?"

"Your cousin, Niamh, gave it to me. She said your cousins got documents and photos from Dinah's house." Anna opened the envelope and glanced at Dinah's insulting comments and erotic drawings. "What is this? Why Does she hate us so much?"

"Because of her love for her husband. She thinks we killed him."

In the morning, Hintocha gave Anna papers and photos. "Fight fire with fire, as people say."

CBS This Morning hosts Tracey Werner and Erika Lanto welcomed Anna, who placed a folder on a glass table. "First, Dinah Hansson says you are an alien from outer space. Is this true?" Tracey asked.

A quizzical expression crossed Anna's face as she considered an answer. "In the beginning, I condemn the despicable attack on Dinah's car and the malicious incursion into her home. I believe in peace and freedom, yet Dinah's calumny is ridiculous and contrary to logic and science. An extraterrestrial being would not have a New York accent and a US passport. Do cosmic aliens drink smoothies and eat cooked food? Do aliens author books and pay taxes? I am here with you. Do you sense I am a spooky outlander from another planet? Let me show you some material." She opened her folder and selected photos and three pieces of paper. "This is my mother, Thalia, holding me soon after giving birth. This photo shows me with my paternal grandparents after my birth. Here is a picture of the midwife, Kasa Inuksuk. This birth certificate mentions the names of my parents and the date of my birth." Anna gave Tracey and Erika the certificate.

"But Dinah and other people say you do not look like the Native Americans," Erika said.

"That is true. I have never said I am a Native American, but I said I defend the human rights of the Native Americans. I have a fair skin, and my partner is a white Irish American, not a Native American."

"But we have seen photos of you with the Native American tribes."

"Doing what? Am I not allowed to see them? My Nunavik grandmother was one of them."

"You look different from the Native Americans."

"Look again. My father, Owen, and my mother, Lucy, were white people. Here is the marriage document, which verifies my point."

"Why do the Native Americans revere and worship you?"

"As Buddhists believe in reincarnation, the First Nations say a sky goddess had fallen and incarnated in me. Any medical doctor can check my blood and see I am a true woman."

"Dinah says you are an extraterrestrial invader disguising as a lesbian woman," Tracey said.

"It is weird that I get misogynic and homophobic comments from the woman who has an affair with the Canadian detective who fabricated stories about my partner and me." Anna showed them two erotic photos of Dinah with Louise Lee. "Is it a crime to be a young and healthy lesbian? I love women, and that is why I write lesbian stories."

"It is not a crime, but the video, which shows you fighting the terrorists in Toronto, proves you are a phenomenal woman."

Anna unbuttoned her shirt and let Tracey and Erika gaze at her white brassiere and bosom. "These are real female breasts, and I am not an alien, as Dinah says. You can say I am phenomenal, but this does not mean I am not like you. Please, give me your cup."

Tracey pushed her mug toward her, and Anna blew on it, turning the black tea into cream. "You see? This white magic is what I do. I stopped crimes, volcanoes, twisters, and wildfires because Mother Nature made me a gifted person. Can the bragging magicians who insulted me and called me illusionist stop tornadoes, hurricanes, and forest fires? I am not a space alien who wants to rule America and the Earth, as Dinah says."

"What about your partner, who belongs to a notorious Irish family? How did you meet her?"

"My partner was born in this city, and I met her in Toronto when the terrorists attacked the airport. She fell in love with me because I saved her life. As a successful model, she graced the pages of fashion and lifestyle magazines. Her talents and natural beauty had also landed her in three movies, displaying her adept versatility as an actor."

"People wish to know the truth about your vice-presidential candidate Hintocha. Who is she? Why does she live in your home?" Erika asked.

"Are we going to ask the indigenous people to prove they are true patriotic Americans? Shame. Questioning Hintocha's racial background is a total disgrace. I feel peeved at the mainstream media and the far-right bigots who question the identity of the indigenous people, who have been in America for thousands of years." Anna paused and picked up a paper. "Here is a birth certificate which says Hintocha was born in New York."

"She looks like twenty-five," Erika said.

"Because she exercises and does not eat junk and processed food. She was our housemaid and chef. We do not have kids in our home, and there is no need for her to rent a costly house in the most expensive city in the world."

"But do you want a maid to be the Vice-President?"

"Hintocha is super intelligent. She got six degrees in science and social sciences. How many guys in the US Congress have earned six degrees?"

"Dinah says Hintocha is intangible, and cameras cannot take photos of her," Erika said.

Anna fingered her hair and guffawed. "This is a lie. Dinah should get new spectacles and a good camera. Hintocha's images are all over the place. The media, like your TV and radio networks, has interviewed her, and she gave over twenty public speeches." Anna stood and gave Tracey and Erika photos. "These are photos of Hintocha with my family and me."

After the twenty-minute interview, Anna moved to the Democratic Party's office on Third Avenue and exchanged heated viewpoints with official delegates. "No one of you can stop me, and I will form a new political party. I threaten nobody, but I am the only person who can figure out our country's problems and wipe out political corruption. So, stay away from me. Do not provoke my anger and do not let me come up here again."

The turmoil and uncertainty that surrounded Anna had taken on a new dimension, as Democratic leaders, recognizing the implications of their actions, sought to mend the fractures that they had exposed. Worries about her unbeatable indignation and the potential repercussions had prompted a change of heart. The leaders, realizing their hasty misjudgment, had extended a peaceful olive branch as an apology. The acknowledgment of their actions was a step toward reconciliation, a recognition of the need to address the wrongs they had committed.

The olive branch carried an added promise. The offer to make Anna a member of the Cabinet, contingent on their candidate's victory in the election, had represented a pivot in the narrative. It was an implicit acknowledgment of her influence and the impact she had on the public's perception. She refused their offer and founded the Freedom and Love Party. So, over five hundred indigenous tribes had agreed to vote for her. Their publicized backing had made it difficult for federal courts, political parties, and media to censor Anna's untested party, fearing accusations of colonization and racism.

With a sad face, Dinah sat on her bed, surrounded by the magazines and newspapers that depicted her alleged romantic relationship with Louise Lee. She reached for her cell phone and made a call. "You have disappointed me. I have never thought you would betray me."

"What leads you to that conclusion? I have never betrayed you."

"How did Anna get photos of us in your house? Do you have surveillance cameras in your home?"

"No. Do you think I would discredit myself and damage my career? You know, we are not involved in any romantic relationship. What I recall is a friendly kiss, nothing more."

"I think the evil witches had photoshopped photos from a porn site. What should we do?"

"We stay calm and say the photos are fake."

"I have enough money to sue Anna, but I am afraid

of her. She is powerful and cunning.”

“Ignore her. We need to keep our reputation and dignity. I will make a public statement and confute the allegations. Don’t worry.”

“Thank you. I am glad we are on the same page.”

On the other side of the political spectrum, heads of twenty-two white supremacist groups met at a wood cabin in the Talladega National Forest in Alabama. They agreed to transfer assault rifles and explosives to New York and assassinate Anna and Hintocha. “Our mission is to defend our Christian identity, nation, and the interests of the white people. Our free, promised land is not for atheists, socialists, abortionists, Jews, Muslims, illegal immigrants, and gay and third-sex people. With God’s will, we will fight the corrupt vamps who want to revive the heathen religion of the pagan people and eradicate our great Aryan Nation,” their manifesto said.

When they had lunch, a slender man with a super wizard beard appeared with a granite box in his hands. A bristly militant stared up at the stranger’s furrowed face. “Who are you, ruddy man? How did you come here?”

“Do not call me that again. I am a Babylonian fallen angel, and my name is Tawiscara Mupacata. Your bullets cannot kill Anna and Hintocha because they are goddesses from the sky. I have known them for thousands of years.”

“Who buys this bullshit, idiot?”

Tawiscara swung his right hand, and an orange fireball hit the man’s chest, throwing him out of a window. He screamed in pain, trying to put out his burning fleece jacket with his hands. His friends pulled their guns. "Do not be stupid like him, or I will burn you in hell. You need this Blutonite." He opened the box, and a blue substance emitted lambent rays.

"Who are you?"

"I am the leader of the invisible world. Trust me. These homosexual and perverted goddesses want to destroy your country and rule your people. Come out with me. I want to show you something." They exited the cottage. "Shoot that tree."

A man used a rifle and fired a bullet at a tree. The shot made a scratch on the tree. "Give me a bullet."

The shooter gave him a bullet. Tawiscara put the tip of the shell in the gluey blue substance. "Use it now, and you stay away from the tree."

The shooter loaded the bullet in his rifle and shot at the tree trunk. The tree exploded into thousands of pieces. "Holy shit! Oh, my God. How did you make that, man?"

"That is a long story. Take the box and use the blue stuff to kill the tramps and their jerks. Don't touch it with your bare skin and don't forget to wear these to prevent their witchcraft." He placed a dozen carved obsidian necklaces on a picnic table and disappeared.

They touched the necklaces. "I believe the guy is Satan or the Anti-Christ," one of them said.

On a syndicated radio program, Anna said she would not take part in the presidential debates. "They are a waste of time and a babble of ludicrous words by men. I will give a speech at Bryant Park on the sixth of

November, a day before the election."

After the announcement, eight white supremacists had agreed to conduct the armed operation against Anna and Hintocha. They placed three cello cases and four hiking backpacks full of ammunition and rifles in trunks and under seats in three trucks and moved northeast to New York City. On the third day of November, they arrived at a car park on Park Avenue and wore fashionable clothes and New York Yankees caps before getting four bedrooms in Park Terrace Hotel on West Fortieth Street. They spent the next two days exploring the nearby areas and planning their shooting operations.

On the sixth day of November, organizers and technicians filled Bryant Park with folding chairs and set up a stage and a wide TV screen on the upper terrace. The eight supremacists left the hotel at eleven o'clock and walked to Park Avenue. After sitting in a red Ford Raptor, one of them unfolded a colored map of Manhattan. "Let me repeat. Mason and I will take the MSR guns, and enter the Park from West Forty-Second Street, and sit in the Grill. James and Alfred will take the AR-Ten rifles, and get into the Park from West Fortieth Street, and sit at a separate table in the Grill. I will wait for a call from Owen when the cars are ready. Andrew, drive this truck and wait for me near the FedEx Office on West Fortieth Street. Daniel will take the gray car and wait for Mason and James at the Books Store on Sixth Avenue. Jonathan will get the black truck and wait for Alfred near the State University of New York on West Forty-Second Street. We will shoot for five minutes. Keep guns in the cars. Is this clear? Any question?" he said and folded the map.

"No, brother Jack. The fags and the dykes will not rule us. One God, one country, one flag. We will protect the existence of our white people and the future of our children. The race mixers have conquered our country. They will not replace us. God will save us, and we will defend America and die for our free land because we are right. America first and forever," Owen said, shaking the hands of his friends.

Jack and Mason carried two cello cases and trod to Forty-Second Street-Bryant Park Subway Station. James and Alfred hefted their hiking backpacks and drifted to West Fortieth Street. Owen, Andrew, Daniel, and Jonathan remained in their vehicles in the car park.

News operators positioned cameras at the upper terrace's steps, over Gertrude Stein Statue and Goethe Statue, and beside Josephine Shaw Lowell Memorial Fountain and Southwest Porch. Jack and Mason entered Bryant Park Grill and ordered lemon chicken, shrimp Cobb salad, and American lager. James and Alfred got into the restaurant five minutes later and sat at a table after asking for steak frites and Budweiser beer. At twelve-forty-five, Anna, Caitlyn, Hintocha, Martina, and Elisha got out of a limousine car near Bryant Park Hotel, entered Bryant Park, and rested on the front seats. After a brief introduction by a female party member, Anna stood on the stage and spoke with gratitude to her supporters. Jack called Owen. "Move. The call girl is puking."

A minute later, Owen called back. "We are ready. Good luck, brother."

Jack stood and waved to James and Alfred. "Come on, guys. Let us kick the pussy's hell ass." They opened their cases and pulled out their machine guns and grenades. A waiter screamed. "Shut the hell up and stay here, and you too," Jack said.

Two seconds later, Jack swore, threw a grenade, and fired bullets at Anna's back. Anna pressed her fingers on her legs and fell on her face. Her fingers moved and scratched the surface of the stage, and white and aqua blue fluid spilled out of her body and flowed beneath and around her. Hintocha got shots in her head and left chest after erecting a bullet-proof glass around Caitlyn, Martina, and Elisha. Jack's friends threw grenades and fired tens of bullets at guards and the crowds who scooted in all directions. Jack fired a blue shot at the protective glass, shattering it into thousands of tiny pieces. Caitlyn, Martina, and Elisha screamed, getting down low and clinging to each other. Hintocha covered them with her arms and body and huffed, making them disappear. She turned her face and roared like a tiger. "Stay still, asshats."

The attackers shot at her, and blue bullets hit her thighs, ripping off her pants and flesh and forcing her to crouch down. Xiola appeared behind Jack and slew him by cutting off his neck with a carving knife. Three female warriors threw javelins at the other attackers. The javelins perforated their upper bodies, and a dozen bald eagles descended and slashed their faces and chests. Xiola and her warriors flew away, and Hintocha slithered to Anna, turning her body on her back and blowing white mist into her drooling mouth. "Love, what happened to us? What happened to our power? Do not leave me. I love you. You will never die. I promise. I promise." She wept streams of tears and kissed Anna's lips.

Anna fizzled. "Love ... you. Love ... you."

Crows cawed, dogs barked, and the mammal animals in the New York zoos howled, splashed water, and jumped on fences. Furious monkeys and gorillas threw stones and pieces of wood at people. Zookeepers asked the visitors to leave.

Stains covered Anna's head, and Hintocha's eyes turned red and full of fire. She writhed on the ground, and her blazing face scowled at the dead attackers. "I will cut you into pieces." She crawled forward with a tomahawk in her hand. An ominous thunder quaked the grounds of Manhattan, and a bombastic voice came from the sky. "*Yadogweh! Yadogweh!* [Stop! Stop!]." Hintocha gazed up at Nina and Jodasiya and their Alaskan malamute. Jodasiya adjusted her bow and a leather quiver full of long arrows, and the dog bit the attackers' legs.

Hintocha waved. "Nina. Jodasiya."

"Stay where you are. It is my turn. Anna is my daughter." Nina kneeled and cried when she saw her daughter's face and hands covered with sticky liquid. Her fingers touched the liquid and smelled it. "Anna, your mother is here. I will give you my spirit, my beloved girl." She wiped her eyes. Anna opened an eye. "Mom. Mom. Stay with me."

"The guys used Blutonite. How did they get it from the planet Blutonica?"

"Tawiscara." She dropped her head on Nina's thigh and closed her eyes.

Jodasiya touched Nina's shoulder. "I will come back." She got up with an angry face and asked the eagles to carry off the attackers. When the attackers soared high in the air, she fired eight arrows. The handcrafted arrows penetrated their chests and toted them to the top floor of the Bryant Park Hotel.

A shrill blast lightened the sky and rocked the area. Nina, Hintocha, and Jodasiya looked up at the gloomy clouds. An eight-foot-tall woman and a white, furry wolf landed and walloped the ground. "Mom. Mom. Yonih," Hintocha said. Her mother stroked her hair, and the wolf licked her hand.

"*Yagwaiyehsoh* [Wait]." Winona elevated her arms, and the attackers' three trucks flew over the park. She breathed a whooshing firestorm, incinerating the vehicles and the four conspirators. She turned her face toward her daughter and wiped the open wounds with her hand and healed her. "*Yagwaiyeh gyuyo* [Stay with her]."

"*Sehne hodoye ogwao* [She is the best friend]."

Winona looked at Nina and Anna. "*Sehne gohonyoh gedo* [She is taking care of her]. *Yahnohsehdeya geye* [We will revenge]. *Geye yadado noos hohodeya geye* [I will go and fight the boar]." She and her wolf flew and disappeared.

Jodasiya carried Anna and took off, and Nina, Hintocha, and the eagles followed her.

News cameras recorded the grisly events in Bryant Park. Citizens and political parties did not know the identity of the attackers or what happened to Anna after being shot and flown by an enigmatic woman who wore a feathered headband and brown moccasins. The national and international media issued speculative statements about Anna's fate and relationship with the women who flew and performed preternatural acts. Dinah interacted with two TV newsreaders. "This gory massacre is a despicable act of terrorism. My thoughts and prayers are with the victims and their families. However, I was right when I said Anna is not a woman. The far-right terrorists threw bombs at her and shot her with tons of bullets. Nothing happened to her body, and we have not seen red blood but white and blue liquid. Who are those antediluvian and draconian women who fly without wings and breathe fire? Even Hintocha and a dog and a wolf know how to fly and disappear. You have seen the wild red-haired woman who slaughtered the first attacker. Did you see the mysterious women warriors and their ancient clothes and spears? Did you see the ferocious eagles? I didn't lie when I said Anna and Hintocha are extraterrestrial lovers. Have you seen the luscious kiss on the lips despite the horrendous murder of many innocent citizens? Hintocha is the heartless Wonder Woman, or Elektra, who abducted Angela Lucciano and killed the guys who tried to rob Chase Bank in Manhattan. Wake up, please. We are dealing with menacing aliens. Who can stop them? What would our armed forces do to save the country from those barbaric aliens? Anna and her callous varmints want to rule America and the world."

The President declared a national emergency and asked the armed forces to protect the country from the alien enemies. "This is a black day for America. I feel sorry for the victims of the horrific tragedy in New York and condemn this heinous and cowardly terrorist attack on innocent people. I also feel sorry for Anna but think of it. Do the American people want to vote for the woman who speaks to flying women? Have you seen that crazy giant woman and her flying wolf? My American people, there will be unprecedented and dangerous consequences if you vote for the draconian women."

After the President's statement, Winona and her wolf arrived at the Washington Monument. The wolf lowered her head and drank from the waveless Lincoln Memorial Reflecting Pool. Winona stared up at the marble capstone of the pyramidion and made herself taller than the obelisk. Her wolf became twenty feet long. Stunned visitors and tourists took photos of her and the gigantic wolf. Ten seconds later, she and the wolf landed on the North Lawn of the White House. Secret Service guards fired at her, but she smiled. The guards escaped behind trees and the White House. Winona asked her wolf to go inside the White House. The wolf dashed into the White House, and security bodyguards shot at her. "I do not want to harm anybody. I just want the President to meet my goddess." The guards ran off and holed up behind closed doors, and the Secret Service chairman asked an army captain to send military helicopters and special forces troops. The wolf passed through a wall and entered the Oval Office, forcing the President to get out to the North Lawn. Winona glared at him. "Hello, white man. Did you say I am crazy? I am the Supreme Goddess of this continent and the First Nations." She pointed her forefinger at him. "Kneel. You are a guest in my motherland."

Two Apache helicopters swooped over the White House and fired three missiles at Winona's chest. She shrugged and dabbed her chest and shoulders with her fingertips. Her hands broke up a helicopter's tail boom, forcing the pilot to make a safe landing on the South Lawn. "Go home, boy." Her wolf jumped high, and her teeth grabbed the rudder of the other helicopter, impelling the pilot to land in the First Lady's Garden. Troops surrounded the White House complex, and a soldier fired an anti-tank missile at Winona. The rocket moved through her body and damaged the roof of the White House. Winona made herself three hundred feet tall and threw lightning bolts on the surrounding streets, forcing troops and spectators to escape as if wild tigers had chased them. The President tried to flee, but the wolf howled and brought him back.

"White man, bow before me, or my wrath will burn the ground under your feet." The horrified President kowtowed. "Listen, little man. I created this land and my chosen nation. You and your people are guests in my land. Do you hear my words? This holy land belongs to me. Anna will be the new president, and you will go back to your home. It is my divine will to see my nation in the fullness of glory." She stared at the White House.

"This building behind you will be the Orange House, and my people's eagle flag will replace that striped cloth."

She and her wolf vanished. The President turned his back and gaped at the White House that turned orange. With an eagle image, a brown-yellow flag waved on the rooftop flagpole.

When Jodasiya descended twelve feet above Chautauqua Lake, she dropped Anna's body into the water and dived like a sea lion. Anna's static body rested on the floor of the lake. Nina and Hintocha sat beside her, touching her head. Nine muskellunge fish enclosed Nina, and Jodasiya plucked watermilfoil stems and pondweeds and inserted them into Anna's mouth and nostrils. A blue, viscous paste came out of her open wounds. "Your Highness, please, go inside her to keep her energy circulating."

Hintocha merged with Anna's inert body. The body shivered, and Jodasiya carried it out of the water and entered a wood cottage shaded by trees in Bemus Point. After placing Anna on a bed, she removed her stained clothes and covered her body with a wool blanket. Nina kissed her pale face, and Winona and her wolf appeared beside her. When Nina bowed, Jodasiya lay prone on the floor. "My Great High Goodness, please, keep Anna alive."

"Get up and sit on the chair. Anna is our sublime war goddess and my daughter's eternal lover. She will never die. Hintocha, come out."

Hintocha rose from Anna's motionless body and settled cross-legged on the bed, with her left hand on her head. The wolf tongued her right hand and face.

"Anna suffers from exhaustion and memory loss because the depraved assailants used Blutonite. Only Tawiscara and his diabolic god know how to get it from Blutonica. We won't let any god shield them from us. They must die. I will remove the Blutonite elements that cause pain and reset her spirit to the primordial times. What do you say?"

"Your Great Highness, you are all-wise. Do what you please. I am grateful," Nina said.

"Your daughter lost her recollections. You will fix her memory because you made her. Do that piece by piece for three or four months, and I will restore her power of creation and war. And since you are here, I have a personal proposal. My daughter wants to marry Anna and be a wife and a mother. What do you think?"

"As you will, our Glorious Supreme Goddess. Your Highness, can you tell me anything about my mother, Anohitecha, Angela, and Amitola? Do you know what happened to them?"

"Our goddesses and I know nothing about them. We don't even know if they are alive. Sorry for saying that. Let me heal Anna." She inserted her hand into Anna's body and threw away a ball of blue tissues. After that, she pressed Anna's cheeks and opened her mouth. Her forefinger gleamed and disgorged white fluid into it. Her right hand moved over Anna's body and made it fresh and gleamy. "This will be her body for another epoch, and people will never harm it." Nina hugged her, and Jodasiya left her chair and kissed her socked feet.

Anna moved her eyes to a bright, double-framed

window and sneezed two times. "Yuck. What is this green stuff in my mouth and nose?" She turned her face to the right. "Who are you?"

"I am your mother." Nina inserted a globule of light into her forehead.

"Hi, mom. Nice to see you. Jodasiya, what are you doing on the floor? Hi, Hintocha. What is this wolf doing here? Who is that tall woman?"

"Happy to hear your lovely voice. Get up and show reverence to the Supreme Goddess Winona."

Anna lurched backward and palpitated. "I am honored to see you on earth. I love you." She jumped off the bed and hugged Winona around her waist. Nina, Hintocha, and Jodasiya gazed at her round bottom cheeks and smiled.

Anna covered her private parts with a hand and hid her bosom with an arm. "Oops. I am sorry. Where are my clothes? I feel cold."

"Here they are." Winona hissed, and a light-brown costume covered Anna's body.

Winona touched her daughter's face and smiled. "Sit on the table."

She sat on a wobbly table. Winona burned three dry leaves in her left hand and put two vertical lines of ashes on her daughter's forehead. "You are now free. Love my people as you love yourself and do no evil." She turned her face to Anna. "I have one more thing to say before I leave. I could not come down before the shootings because our Mother Goddess had asked me not to interfere. She knows what we do not know. Maybe She didn't want me to cause a galactic war with the belligerent gods. I love you and choose you, with my full blessing, as the leader of the First Nations because you are a wonderful goddess, like your mother. Your mother and I have decreed that you shall marry my daughter and make her a wife and a mother. I expect you to agree. You will see me again soon. I have willed to go." She and the wolf faded away.

Hintocha clapped and kissed Anna's lips. "After all these turbulent millennia, I will be so delighted to be your devoted wife."

Anna remained unamused. "Your mother said you are free. What does she mean?"

"She means I am free to do what I want here and in the sky within the limits of our law."

"What about Caitlyn? What should we tell her?"

"Don't you love me?"

"I love you. Does your mother want me to leave her? I can't break her heart. She loves me and reminds me of Angela."

"We are not leaving Caitlyn, and everything from and for us is a virtue and a divine will. You are gorgeous like your mom. Forget this thing now. We must go back and tell the world you are alive."

"How will we go back? Jodasiya, do you have a cell phone?"

"Did you forget you are a goddess? Come and let me remind you of what you can do. Walk through this wall without my help."

Anna stood on her bare feet and walked through a wall like a ghost.

Hintocha brought a bowl of water. "Blow on this

water and think of freezing it."

Anna breathed out on the water and turned it into ice. "Amazing."

"Let us go out." They exited the cottage. "Look up and jump with confidence."

Anna sprang and flew forty feet. "How can I come down?"

"Just come down, you lovely girl." Anna looked down and landed on her feet. "OK, let us say goodbye to Jodasiya and return to New York."

After hugging and thanking Jodasiya, Nina and Hintocha held Anna's hand. "Say, Caitlyn, New York City."

"Caitlyn, New York City."

They arrived at Caitlyn's house. Anna knocked on the door. "Caitlyn, that is me."

Caitlyn opened the door. "Oh, my God. You are alive." She hugged her, and Elisha left her room. "Gosh. The entire country thinks you are dead. How are you alive?"

"Miracles happen. We are not alone in this world. Where is Martina?"

"She went home." She gazed at Anna's body. "How did you get this dress?"

"I got it from our Supreme Goddess."

"I am so happy to see you active. What do you want to do now? The election is tomorrow."

"I need to tell the people I am well. I will see you later. Watch the news. I love you."

Anna and Hintocha held each other's hands and exited the house. "CBS Building." In a seamless transition, they got new dresses and shoes while flying and landed at the iconic CBS Building on West Fifty-Second Street. Their surprising landing had garnered a reaction that mirrored the complete astonishment that went with their presence. A receptionist, surprised by their sudden appearance, had stammered in shock. "Wha, what, what can we do for you?"

"We need a quick interview right now."

A news anchor interviewed them on-air for twenty minutes. Anna kept the shroud of mystery that had enveloped her encounter with paranormal women and refused to divulge the details of her healing. Her message extended beyond the veil of the unknown. With a call to action, she urged the citizens to cast their votes in her favor and against "the racist misogynists and enemies of freedom."

After the interview, Anna and Hintocha moved to CNN's New York office at Columbus Circle. They declined to analyze the attack and requested the people to "vote for the person who would bring about freedom, justice, peace, and prosperity."

They returned to their house. Anna kissed Hintocha's lips. "Good night, love. Thanks for being with me. See you tomorrow."

Hintocha entered her room, and Anna and Caitlyn went to their bedroom and sat on the bed. "Do you love Hintocha?"

"Of course. Hintocha has been my best friend for thousands of years."

"I know that, but do you love her?"

"You have asked me this question. You know my

story with her."

"I know you have an occasional affair with her, but you were different today. There is more than a fling and a one-night stand. She caressed your hand and kissed your lips five times after your, I should say, resurrection. I watched the news. When you fell unconscious or dead in the park, Hintocha cried and said intimate words, which only true lovers say. What's going on between her and you? How are you alive? I saw what happened to you?"

"Honey, thank God you and Elisha are breathing. The terrorists killed sixty-nine people, and it has been a horrible day for all of us. I do not remember the day's events and don't know what happened to me. People say I am a goddess, and goddesses do not die. I hope we will know the truth after tomorrow." She took off her outer clothes and stared at a mirror. "How did I get this new body? Do you feel I am me?"

"Yes, you are you, but with a new body."

"I feel I am not the woman we knew. I do not know how to explain myself. Horse. Deer." A horse and a deer appeared beside the bed.

"Oh, my God. Why did you do that?"

"I am like a wraith from another world. Give me your hand." She blew on Caitlyn's hand and made it golden. "I can do anything."

"I do not want these animals here."

"Go away." The horse and the deer dissipated. "Let us close our eyes and sleep. We have endured a tough day, and tomorrow will be a long day full of surprises. I hope the good-hearted people will give me their vote."

In the morning, she met Hintocha. "Are you ready to go?"

"No. I want to stay here today."

"Why?"

"To be sure we win the election. I also want to prepare myself for the big day."

Reporters followed Anna, Caitlyn, Martina, and Elisha, who cast their votes at a public school in Midtown Manhattan. When a reporter asked Anna about her recovery and comeback, she simpered. "I don't remember what happened. A bulletproof vest saved my life. The indigenous people use red cedar, sweetgrass, and sage to heal wounds."

"What wounds? A salvo of bullets and bombs hit your body. What sort of body do you have?"

"I don't know what you say. As I see, my body is perfect."

"Who are those women and animals who came down from the sky?"

"Heaven knows. Did you see them? I guess there is a life outside our planet."

"Where is Hintocha? Why isn't she with you?"

"She had a rough day. She voted by mail. So, she is resting today and looking after her health."

After leaving the voting place, Anna returned to her house and watched the news on the TV and her phone. In the morning, the news networks declared she won sixty-one percent of the electoral votes, the highest in US history. Anna and Caitlyn rejoiced and thanked Hintocha for her meticulous work. "I want to make a public statement and thank the voters." She moved to

Madison Square Garden and made a brief speech, thanking her supporters, and promising to resurrect the dead victims and create a high-quality life for all citizens.

After the speech, Hintocha took her aside and whispered. "Our mothers want us to get married tomorrow."

"Can we delay it?"

"No. What happened to you? Mother goddesses do not change their times and plans."

"What about Caitlyn and Elisha?"

"We do not invite people to our celebrations. So, tell Caitlyn and Elisha that we want to go away and thank our people."

"What about my mom?"

"Your memory is jiggling. Your mother is one of us and she will come to our wedding party."

"Are we getting married in heaven?"

Hintocha cackled long and loud. "Which heaven? You are hilarious. You have lost your thought. We will get married on earth."

Anna returned home and talked to Caitlyn. "I want to see our tribes to thank them for supporting me. Let us have a party and celebrate our victory."

In the morning, she and Hintocha found themselves in Adirondack Park, New York. "Where are we?" Anna asked.

"This is Heart Lake."

Anna turned her face around. "Nobody is here. There are no houses. Are we getting married here?"

"Be patient for a while."

Jodasiya appeared from behind a pine tree with a feather crown on her head and hugged them. "What a joy it is to see the two of you again."

A misty light descended upon them. A charming woman appeared with an oak walking stick and an eagle on her arm. Jodasiya and Hintocha bowed in respect.

"Anna, how are you, my love?"

"Who are you?"

"I am your mother, Achiqueta, Nina."

"Oh, mom, I didn't recognize you because of the bright makeup. I am sorry for leaving you. I do not know what happened to my being. Something is wriggling in my head."

"Come with me. I want to give you a dose of medication, and you need to wear a wedding dress."

"Where? There are no stores here."

"Listen to your mother."

They walked through a thick forest. "Stay here and don't talk." Anna stopped, and her mother crushed green leaves in her hands and put them in a glass of water. "Drink this medicine."

Anna drank the green water, and an energetic power bounced her body like an electric current. Nina put her gleaming right palm on her head and recited obscure words. "How is your memory now?"

"Better. There are a few things I remember. I love you, mom. I am happy to be with you again."

Nina brought a tree branch and swept it over Anna's body. Anna touched her new gold dress, and her mother put a three-color feather headdress on her head. "What about Hintocha?"

"That is not our concern. Let us go back. You look fabulous."

They moved back. Anna halted her slow steps, shedding quiet tears. She licked her lips and leered at Hintocha's brilliant face, feather fascinator, and white dress. "Oh, my Goddess. I have never seen a stunning goddess like her. She is like a diamond star."

"You are right. Remember, she will be your equal after the wedding, and you won't be her superior in our divine kingdom. So, you must respect her. Stand on her left side with gentility and reverence." Anna beamed and stood next to Hintocha, trying to hide her tears.

As a soft melody resonated from above, twenty-one well-groomed, perfumed women marched with staid solemnity toward them. Their graceful and deliberate movements had synchronized their steps. An aura of elegance and mystery filled the air as they approached. Their attire exuded sophistication, with flowing gowns adorned with intricate patterns and embellishment. The colors were vibrant, reflecting their dominion and charisma.

"I am happy to rejoin the supreme goddesses of the First Nations. Where is your mom?"

"Be silent. This is a holy ceremony."

The goddesses stood in dignified silence next to Hintocha. They spoke nothing until a light breeze swirled around them. Winona, in a golden-brown dress, and her snowy wolf landed before them. The goddesses bowed with the dazzling palms of their hands together. Hintocha elbowed Anna. "Bow." Anna inclined her head.

"*Gaweneh geya genoh yegenyenye woh* [Thanks for your kindness toward me]." She gazed at her daughter. "*Gede geneyo, nesda dawi. Gahnohe gwesenyowo odenye. Gahno lagwe yodano* [My beloved family, she is in good health. They love each other. They are like twins]." They smiled.

"*Gegowe deeno genoh sow genogoh. Gahnohe gwesenyowo genogoh* [I will take care of you. We love each other]." She eyed Anna. "*Gegowe deeno eyow genoh. Gegowe hedohse geo nyosa* [I have adopted her. I should speak the English language]." With a colorful crochet shawl on her left shoulder, she held five chestnut eagle feathers and swung them over Anna's and Hintocha's bowed heads. A gold chalice of grape, blueberry, and cranberry juice appeared in her glowing right hand. "Drink with my full grace to you." They sipped from it. "Love, in our essence, is eternal. What I do, others cannot undo. With the gracious blessings of our noble goddesses, I make you a wife and a wife forever. Hold each other's hands and offer the sign of love." They kissed, and Winona and Nina draped a large white blanket over their shoulders. The smiling goddesses clapped and tossed red roses at them. "I have prepared a meal for you. *Gegowe heh geno* [Let us eat]."

Anna held Hintocha's hand and glanced at a long oak table surrounded by fancy chairs and covered with fruits, corn soups, and juices. "I feel happy when our goddesses eat their nature's food."

"They want us to feel snuggly."

A sudden ear-splitting shriek pierced through the air, causing heads to turn and spirits to race. The goddesses gazed up, looking for the source of the scream. A shadowy figure plummeted from the sky, hurtling toward the ground with great speed.

With a resounding thud, the creature crashed on the earth, shaking the ground beneath it. The force of the impact created a shallow pit, with the solid soil exploding into a brown dusty cloud that obscured the creature from view. Silence prevailed over the area as the dust settled, revealing the fallen being.

Anna dropped her posy on the ground. "That's Tawiscara. I will kill him."

"Shush!" Winona raised her arms in front of the goddesses. A charming woman, wearing a luminous long gown and a golden diadem, landed next to Tawiscara and tied his hands behind his back with steel handcuffs. Flaming sparks from her gilded scepter kindled a pyre. She seized Tawiscara's neck and cast him in the roaring fire. Tawiscara stood and chuckled. "You cannot burn me. I am a fallen angel made of fire and light. I will come back and kill you."

The woman threw a drawstring pouch on the fire. The fire sputtered and flared up high, and Tawiscara screamed, trying to extinguish his burning legs with his hands. Xiola appeared and shot a blue arrow at his chest. An explosion blew him up into pieces, rocking the area. The enigmatic woman raised her scepter, sending showers of colorful sparks up to the sky. Bowing before her, the goddesses murmured recondite words. Pink petals and flowers showered them when the woman ascended to heaven.

Anna looked upward at the sky. "Who was that?"

Winona waved. "That was our Holy Creator, the Supreme Mother Goddess. Killing Tawiscara was her gift for both of you."

Xiola kissed Anna and Hintocha and vanished after giving them corsages. Winona cheered, and the goddesses applauded and followed her in silence. After drinking, eating, and conversing with joy, Winona's affection gleamed in her hazel eyes, and her hands landed on Anna's shoulders. "I have made a seraphic house for you." She twinkled at the other goddesses. "*Dyagoda geye* [Now I will go]." She and her wolf disappeared. The goddesses and Jodasiya offered their warm wishes to Anna and Hintocha and dispersed.

Anna held Hintocha's hand. "That's it? Are we now a wife and a wife?"

"Yes. I am overjoyed to be your wife after all the labor we have undertaken."

"Me too. I am ecstatic to be a wife. What should we do in this lonely place?"

"We will go to the house, which my mom made."

"Where is it?"

"Give me your hand."

They popped up at a white house overlooking a lake. "Where are we?"

"In Indian Lake State Park in Michigan. Come inside the house and make love to me. I want to be a mother."

"Why are you in a hurry?"

"Listen to your darling wife. Our daughter will do wonderful things for us."

"Daughter?"

"Yes, daughter. Married lesbian goddesses make only majestic goddesses. Our lucky daughter will get more than our combined powers."

They entered the house and found themselves in a colorful fantasyland. "Your mother has an incredible imagination."

"I know." Hintocha put Anna's right forefinger in her mouth and sucked in a viscid honey liquid. "Come to the bedroom." In the utopian, hazy room, Anna put her head under Hintocha's wedding dress. "*Gahnohe gwesenyowo genogoh* [We love each other]." After saying these words, a white vapor emitted from her mouth and entered Hintocha's body.

Hintocha pulled her head up and kissed her. "Thanks, honey. I can't wait to be a mother." They spent the rest of the day making love and talking about their marriage and life. In the morning, they returned to New York.

A day later, Caitlyn noticed Hintocha's bloated belly. "What? Are you pregnant?"

"I think so."

"Great. Who is the lucky guy or god?"

"Must be one of us."

The next day, Hintocha got an apartment on West End Avenue and informed Anna and Caitlyn about her desire to be alone.

On the following day, Anna visited her. "Why did you leave us? We love your company."

"I will give birth in two days."

Anna pouted her lips. "How?"

"My pregnancy is for a week, and we will have a gorgeous girl to give us a purpose in life."

"Oh, dear. Do you want to go to the hospital?"

Hintocha shook her head. "No. Are you getting dementia? Have you ever seen a sky goddess in a hospital? Our child is not a human being. My mom will be here to help me."

Two days later, Winona brought a pottery vase and anointed Hintocha's abdomen with corn oil. Within a minute, Hintocha pressed her belly and gave birth to a honey-skinned girl. Anna gaped at the immaculate conception of her daughter. There was no blood or an umbilical cord. The baby was clean and did not cry. "How was that?"

"How many times do I need to remind you we are goddesses? Hold your daughter."

"She is gorgeous as you and your mom. What do you want to call her?"

Winona rested her arm on her shoulders. "Your daughter will be the supreme goddess of harvest and revenge. So, what about the Goddess Onatah?"

"Goddess?"

"Yes. Your daughter is a goddess, like her moms and grandmothers."

"How would she live with people? How would we register her name and make her a US citizen?"

Hintocha cuddled her daughter. "Goddesses do not need earthly citizenships and birth certificates. Leave this matter to me."

Winona held Anna's right hand. "Sit here and contemplate what I want to say." Anna sat in a chair with her lips closed. Winona placed a hand on her shoulder. "I will refresh your memory, but promise to tell the truth. Lying is not good. There was no need for a courageous goddess like you to say a bulletproof vest saved your life. No need to say a tribe healed your bullet wounds and bleeding by using herbs. I know you lost your memory. But try to be honest with yourself. If people ask you about me, say I am Winona, the Supreme Goddess. If you do not want to reveal your divine nature, say you do not want to talk about it. The leader of the Former Nations and my daughter-in-law must speak the truth all the time. You are Awehitecha, and you should know what your name means. You are our people's first divine leader. Be an exemplary mother and honor the Earth. Care for the poor and the elderly. Be a voice for the oppressed. I love you." She kissed and massaged Anna's temple with oil. An orb of rainbow lights appeared in her hand. "Close your eyes." Winona injected the ball into her head.

Anna opened her eyes wide. "Wow. I remember my past. I promise to speak the truth. Praise be to you, our Glorious Goddess."

"I half-smiled when Hintocha changed the results of the election. I forgive you both, but from this time forward, I don't want to see fraud. With the truth, I created my command, and with the truth, I sent my will down."

Later, Hintocha and Onatah visited Anna and Caitlyn. Onatah sat on a baby chair and played with a toy. "Mom, I want a glass of water."

Caitlyn gaped at her and placed her hand on her

chest. "Oh, my God. Onatah speaks. How is that?"

Hintocha smiled. "She is a minor goddess."

When they sat at the dining table, Onatah looked at Anna. "Mom, give me a carrot."

"OK, darling."

The doorbell rang. Onatah opened her hands. "Door, open." The door opened. Elisha entered the foyer and looked around. "Who opened the door?"

"The holy goddesses of the house. Come in and see your new cousin."

Elisha winked. "Hi."

Onatah jiggled her hand. "Hi, Elisha. How are you, gorgeous?"

Elisha quivered and moved backward. "Oh, my God. Do you talk? How old are you?"

"One week."

"What is your name?"

"Baby Goddess Onatah."

"I told you the house is full of goddesses. Your cousin is a goddess and can do anything for you. What else do you want?" When Hintocha, Elisha, and Onatah left the house, Caitlyn gripped Anna's hand. "Are you Onatah's mom?"

"Yes. I am her mom."

"How?"

"I made love to Hintocha."

"When?"

"Two weeks ago."

"Where?"

"In Michigan."

"Bitch." She slapped her arm. Xiola showed up and

hurled Caitlyn on a couch. "Don't you ever hit my goddess, or I will crush your bones."

Caitlyn stared at her black hood, hazel eyes, and painted face. "I am sorry. Please, don't hurt me."

"Xiola, leave her." Xiola disappeared, and Anna lowered at Caitlyn. "What did you say?"

Caitlyn shivered. "Sorry. I didn't mean to swear and hit you, but you live with me, and I have the right to know what you do. I feel you are using me."

"How am I using you? I can create anything I want. Why are you jealous? Did you forget your sex with Hintocha?"

"No. But we are a threesome. I am your partner and expect you to tell me about your shenanigans with Hintocha. Why didn't you tell me about your plan to be a mother?"

"You are right if I am a human like you, but I am not. I told you several times I cannot have an official committed relationship with you because I am a goddess, and you know my love for Hintocha."

"I know that. But why didn't you tell me the truth? How could you make Hintocha pregnant without that thing?"

Anna laughed. "Goddesses don't need penises. I am also a goddess of femininity and fertility. It was my divine fate to marry and impregnate Hintocha."

"Is Hintocha your wife?"

"Yes. She is my wife forever."

"What happened to you? Why do you keep it a secret? Am I not your lover?"

"Love, listen to me. I do not belong to your world. I

am on earth for a reason. We don't know why our Mother Goddess involved you in our matter. You and all the peoples of the world cannot challenge our divine will. We can destroy the world in ten seconds. I love you, honey, and Hintocha worships you. I will never leave you, and Hintocha will never take me away from you. We can make a thousand lovers, but we are with you because we love you and you are an amazing woman. I will do anything for you." She clapped, and Caitlyn found herself in a pink satin nightgown in their bedroom. "That's what I mean."

On the nineteenth of January, Anna and her family flew to Washington, D.C., and stayed in Mandarin Oriental. In the early evening, they sat in the hotel restaurant, and a stubbly man derided Anna and Hintocha, accusing them of being in league with the devil. Onatah lifted her fork. "Hit his head on the wall." The man flew and banged his head on a wall.

Hintocha seized her hand. "Listen to me. Listen. Do not do that again."

"He said bad things to you and mom."

"We know how to respond."

Anna smiled. "Onatah got your impatient genes."

In the morning, a limousine took Anna, Caitlyn, and Elisha to the Capitol Building. Hintocha and Onatah preferred to use their supernatural power to transfer themselves.

At eleven-thirty, a Republican Senator stood and began the presidential inauguration ceremony on the West Front, commenting on the country's notable practice of a peaceful transition of political power.

Indigenous, Christian, Jewish, Muslim, Hindu, and Buddhist representatives delivered quick prayers. A Republican Senate leader ended a hasty speech by asking the audience to stand for the swearing-in ceremony.

Associate Justice Oliver Williams stood and swore in Hintocha as the new Vice President, with her left hand on an old copy of the Book of Wisdom. Onatah clapped. "Mommy, mommy." An indigenous choir performed *Yeha Noha* for a minute. A rainbow flash appeared in the sky, and snowflakes fell on Hintocha. "Thank you, mom."

At noon, Chief Justice Clarence Roberts swore in Anna as the new President. Anna used the Bible, the Vedas, and the Quran, which Caitlyn held with calm delight. The Marine Band performed "Hail to the Chief," and a military band conducted the twenty-one-gun presidential salute. Prismatic lightning brightened the gray sky, and the atmosphere in the capital was of celebration and tranquility as the city came together to honor the new president. Colorful decorations adorned the streets, and people filled the air with mild chatter. Anna stood on a stage to deliver a speech, but a sudden, deafening squeal shattered the serenity of the moment. Startled gasps and alarmed whispers spread as the piercing noise reverberated through the streets. Anna's words faltered, and a concerned expression crossed her face as she scanned the surroundings, looking for the source of disturbance. Bodyguards surrounded her and her entourage and asked them to leave.

"Wait." Anna pointed up at the sky. "That's the

Supreme Goddess Winona."

Winona landed in the United States Botanic Garden. Her hand halted a rocket fired from the roof of a hotel near the National Air and Space Museum. She raised her right hand and howled like a nightly wolf. As a dumpy man, carrying an anti-tank rocket launcher, hovered over Independence Avenue, Winona puffed fire and turned him into ashes. A second later, she stood in front of the Capitol Building. People took fright, and Anna and Hintocha bowed. Winona touched the head of her wolf and held a microphone. "People of the Earth. Listen to my words. I created this land millions of years before your existence, and you are temporary visitors to my territory. I decreed Anna must lead the First Nations and rule this country because I want to see love and peace. If you intend to harm her, I will wipe you out and create new people. Do not cut down trees and do not kill animals for fun. Do not pollute my rivers. This land is sacred. Live in peace and give kindness to all the creation. Anna and Hintocha, come down here. It is the time for my protocol."

Anna and Hintocha descended to the front yard and bowed. Winona covered them with a wool cape, and they vanished. Seconds later, they landed beside a waterfall. "What is this forest?"

Hintocha dropped a stone in the stream. "This is Shenandoah National Park in Virginia. It was a sacred place for the First Nations."

Winona sat on a rock. Her wolf drank from the running freshwater. "Come here beside me. I want to say something to you."

Anna and Hintocha kneeled, and Winona put her right, glowing hand on her daughter's head. "I am giving you my powers, except the powers of creation and omniscience. Protect your family and the First Nations in my land. I love you." A lambent light flashed from her hand.

"My honor, my holy mother."

Winona touched Anna's left shoulder. "I have appointed you the leader of the First Nations in my northern land, which people call North America. No physical harm will happen to you after I give you the ultimate power of heaven. I will reward Caitlyn for her faithfulness and honest love for you. Remember, my land does not belong to you, but you belong to my land when you are here. Be humble and listen to your heart. Make my land green. Love is power." A black bear appeared and rested next to her. She rubbed her back and gave her a fish. "Let us go back."

After returning to Capitol Hill, Winona held a microphone. "Congratulations, people of the earth. I will watch you, and you have my blessings. *Yagwiye gae nah yusooh. Geniyo ogwe niyawehs* [That is how it happened. I love you]."

She and her wolf left, and Caitlyn held Anna's hand. "What happened? Where did you go?"

"To a sacred place." She rested her right arm on her shoulders. "What a life I have endured on earth. Who thought the Goddess of war and wisdom would become the leader of the First Nations and the President of the United States? Who imagined the Goddess of love would be the Vice-President? Have you ever dreamed of becoming the First Lady? Our life is a miracle if we understand it. Let us do the best we can. I love you...."

Chapter 9

Anna moved to the White House, and Hintocha settled in the Number One Observatory Circle. They worked day and night, visiting cities and towns to bolster confidence, trust, and efficiency. Caitlyn resigned from her university position and enjoyed being the First Lady. Elisha quit her modeling job and set up a fashion foundation to train female designers.

The Republican and Democratic parties and their media had dismissed the election results and said Anna used her paranormal power to rig the ballot and deceive the citizens. Outspoken members of the US Congress looked for legal and moral excuses to impeach her and remove her from office, though they feared Winona's rage. "What practical steps should we take to impeach the Venusian President? The gigantic necromancer said she would obliterate us if we offended her," a congresswoman said.

After internal debates over the impeachment, the two political parties had chosen Dinah Hansson to besmirch Anna and expose illegal violations to avoid direct confrontation with her.

The supremacist leaders in the Bible Belt states mourned the death of their comrades in New York and swore to avenge. They met in a detached house at Cardinal Drive in Knoxville, Tennessee, and agreed to conduct a covert military operation and use remote explosive devices.

One day in the first week of March, the Director of Oval Office Operations, Freda Kanoska, entered the Oval Office. "Good morning, Madam President. I have an urgent matter."

"Good morning. What is it?"

"Tornadoes rolled through Tennessee, Alabama, Missouri, and Kentucky, leveling neighborhoods, and knocking out power for thousands of homes. The first reports say the deadly storms have killed over two hundred individuals and injured three thousand people and devastated Northern Nashville."

"Oh, dear! That is awful and tragic. Why didn't the National Weather Service inform me about the tornadoes? We promised our citizens to protect them from natural disasters."

"I will investigate the matter."

"I should make calls and offer our condolences and support. Please, ask my secretary to get me the phone numbers of the governors and mayors of the affected states and cities."

"Yes, ma'am."

Secretary Gloria Romero gave Anna a printed paper. "These are the emails and phone numbers of four governors and three mayors."

"Thank you. I should visit the devastated states. What do you think?"

"That is a sensible thing to do, but I am afraid you cannot go there this week. You have meetings today and tomorrow with the British Prime Minister and the Russian, Chinese, and Cuban presidents. You also need to be in New York on Wednesday to meet other world leaders and deliver a keynote speech on climate change."

"I see. Keep me posted. Thanks." Anna left the Oval Office and went upstairs to her second-floor bedroom. Caitlyn touched her face. "Honey, your face is red. What is the matter?"

"Windstorms damaged many areas in Tennessee and other states and killed three hundred people. I feel sorry for the victims."

"Plagues, wars, earthquakes, and volcanos killed millions of people, and the sky gods did nothing. This is our fate on earth. So, don't worry. Things will get better."

"I wish to visit the devastated areas, but I have meetings with heads of state. I also need to go to New York and give a speech at the UN."

"That is why we have governors, mayors, and civil servants. You and the Federal Government cannot do everything. I can visit the damaged counties and talk to the officials there if you wish."

"That would be wonderful, but first, I want to call governors and mayors." Anna called the Governor of Tennessee Lee Cannon and talked to Ivan Ewing, the Mayor of Nashville. "I am sorry to hear about the deadly tornadoes in your city. My sympathy goes out to the victims and their families. Please, let me know if your city needs any assistance from the Federal Government and me."

"Thank you, Madam President. I hope you and the First Lady will visit us to see the devastation in the city's northern neighborhoods. Over three hundred twenty people have died, and the deadly storms have destroyed hundreds of homes. We will appreciate any help from your side."

Anna paused for a moment. "Today is Monday. I will see you on Friday. What do you think?"

"Wonderful, Madam President. It will delight us very much to welcome you here."

Anna went downstairs and asked Gloria to prepare for her flight on Friday morning. She also requested Elisha to go with her.

The mayor of Nashville left his office and met a white leader in the Hyatt Place hotel at Rudy Circle. "The dyke pigs are coming to the city on Friday. We need a clean operation."

"What do you suggest?"

"The Gorgons will be in a bullet-proof car, and their bodyguards will be everywhere. So, we need more than guns and pistols. The only way I see it is to use anti-tank guided missiles or place explosives under her motorcade and the road. Do you have enough rockets and explosives?"

"Yeah. Which road will Anna's motorcade take?"

"The Seventh Avenue because she will come to the State Capitol to meet the Governor and me. Do your best."

On Friday, at five o'clock in the morning, Anna's bedroom phone rang. She wiped her eyes and sat on the edge of her bed. "Yes."

"Sorry to disturb you, Madam President. North Korea has fired ballistic missiles at our airbase in Seongnam city in South Korea. The missiles killed sixteen Americans and forty-two South Koreans," the Secretary of Defense, Owen Carter, said.

"Dammit. I am sorry to hear that. I want you and the Secretary of State to be in my office as soon as possible. We must do something about the deranged maniac in North Korea."

Anna pressed her head with her hands. Caitlyn touched her back. "Honey, what's going on?"

"The tyrant of North Korea fired missiles at our airbase and killed Americans and Koreans."

"What about our flight to Tennessee?"

"I cannot go. Can you and Elisha go without me?"

"Yes, no problem."

Anna changed her nightie and went downstairs to her office. She called Hintocha. "Come to my office. We have a global problem."

"I will come soon."

Anna met her cabinet to discuss the situation in the Korean Peninsula. At nine o'clock, Caitlyn and Elisha boarded a Marine One, which took them to Ronald Reagan Washington National Airport. After landing, they got a private flight to Nashville International Airport. The Governor and his wife welcomed them. "Where is the President?"

"The President apologizes for not coming. There is an international crisis in Korea." Caitlyn looked at a cluster of journalists standing behind steel barriers and security guards. "May I make a statement on behalf of the President?"

"Of course, you can."

Caitlyn and three armed bodyguards moved to the journalists. "Good morning, everyone. I want to say the President is so sad to know about the tornado-ravaged areas and the death of innocent citizens. She planned to come today, but North Korea has killed and injured many of our servicemen and women in South Korea. The President promises to come here as soon as possible. Thank you."

The Governor and his wife sat in a Chevrolet Suburban car, and Caitlyn and Elisha rested in the backseat of a black limousine, followed by three security vehicles. When the motorcade slowed down on Seventh Avenue North, and in front of the State Library and Archives building, two parking cars and a drainage hole exploded, damaging the vehicles and the front windows of the library. The explosions were so powerful that the limousine flew fifteen feet and landed on the opposite rocky slope behind the Tennessee State Capitol. A masked man with an RPG gun appeared on the roof of the library and fired a grenade at the limousine. The grenade hit the roof of the vehicle, which slid to its side and fell on the damaged road. Security officers at a nearby checkpoint made calls. Three helicopters, six police cars, four fire engines, and five ambulances arrived at the grubby scene. After quenching the fires, firefighters and medics rushed to the toppled limousine. They used heavy hydraulic tools and opened the back door of the car. The explosions had concussed Caitlyn and Elisha, with flowing blood running over their faces and clothes. Two firefighters pulled Caitlyn out of the car, and two medics put her on a folding stretcher. A female physician checked her pulse and wept. "Oh, my God. She is dead. The First Lady is dead." Another medic examined Elisha's pulse. "She is alive. I need an oxygen tank and a stretcher." An ambulance took her to Nashville General Hospital.

The Director of Oval Office Operations got a phone call from the Governor's office in Nashville. "We regret to inform you that a terrorist attack has killed the Governor and the First Lady near the State Capitol. The First Lady's daughter is in an intensive care unit...."

The Director rushed to the Cabinet Room in the West Wing of the White House and opened the door. "Madam President, I need to talk to you right now. There is an emergency."

The Room fell into a hushed silence as the advisors and secretaries had paused to talk in the gravity of the Director's words. "Excuse me." Anna closed the door behind her. "What is going on?"

Two tears ran down the Director's face. "I am so sorry to inform you that a terrorist attack has killed the

First Lady in Nashville."

"What? How?"

"We don't have many details, but a powerful blast has destroyed the First Lady's vehicle and killed her."

Anna hugged her, sobbing on her shoulder. "Oh, my Goddess. I planned to be with her. What about Elisha?"

"She is alive in an intensive care unit."

"What happened to the stupid world? Korea and my family. The enemies of love will never win. I will make a statement to the nation after ten or fifteen minutes. Make things ready." She returned to the Cabinet Room, gazing at her secretaries and advisors. "Please, put the TV on."

A secretary turned on the TV. "Oh, Christ. Oh, my God." Hintocha's eyes burned like a blaze of fire. The Secretary of Defense pushed his chair back and stood. "Madam President, we are so sorry to hear the sad news. What can we do?"

"We must declare a national emergency. Alert the security agencies and the armed forces. Today's attacks are a blatant war on America. I want to make a public statement right now."

She moved to James S. Brady Press Briefing Room with a handkerchief in her hand. After wiping her eyes, she frowned. "My dear fellow Americans. The United States is mourning today. I have never felt so sad and outraged in my life as I do now. The bestial gang in North Korea has killed Americans in South Korea, and the local terrorists have murdered the First Lady, my beloved partner. I do not know how I would live without her ample love. But I have one message to the devils in and outside our country. You will never win, and none of you will stop me from doing the right things. Jesus Christ and other sages had asked us to love our enemies, but you are not enemies. You are the evil psychopaths. The righteous people and I will annihilate you forever from the face of the earth. You have committed a big mistake. This mistake is me. You will see what I can do."

After her statement, she met Hintocha and could not say a word. "I am sorry. What happened to us? Why couldn't we know about Caitlyn's fate? I believe my mom has a plan. Stay here. Do not go anywhere. Ask officials to bring Caitlyn's body here. We will do something after we bury her. Yes, we are goddesses, but we are not omniscient about every person. Oh, love. I swear I knew nothing about what happened to Caitlyn."

"Your mother said she would reward Caitlyn for her love and dedication. Is this how she rewards our best human friend?"

"My mother is our Supreme Goddess, and we don't know what she wants to do."

Anna declared a three-day mourning period and spent most of her time alone in her White House bedroom. Irish spokespersons told the media that their community would bury Caitlyn in Green-Wood Cemetery in Brooklyn.

Caitlyn's flag-draped coffin arrived at Joint Base Anacostia-Bolling. Anna kissed the casket with eyes filled with tears and hugged Elisha, who wore black glasses and sat paralyzed in a wheelchair, with a cervical collar on her neck and elastic bandages around her hands and forearms. When military officers put the coffin on a table, Anna insisted on seeing Caitlyn's face. An officer opened the casket. Anna kissed Caitlyn's pasty forehead with streams of tears. Two days later, Caitlyn's relatives and officials went to the cemetery. Anna stood between Elisha and Nina, and Onatah held the hands of Hintocha and Martina. When four pallbearers lowered the coffin into the grave, Anna fell to her knees and wept like a hungry child. Nina and Martina bowed forward and rubbed her back and shoulders. Elisha cried, and Onatah embraced her hand.

In the evening, Anna met Hintocha. "We need to do things our way, even if we must fight the macho God. And before we avenge Caitlyn's death, we need to execute the punk in North Korea."

"What do you want to do?"

"We will go to North Korea. Elisha and Onatah can stay with my mom."

They dematerialized. When they flew over the Sea of Japan, a bald eagle made a low-pitched sound in Anna's ear.

"What does she say?"

"She says the drunk dictator is in Ryongsong Residence, north of Pyongyang."

The eagle showed them the North Korean leader's palatial residence. They landed in the backyard of the fortified mansion. The Korean leader stood on the tiled edge of a swimming pool, holding a glass of soju cocktail. Anna threw a twig at him. "Hello, Ki-woo."

The Korean leader shouted and dropped his glass in

the swimming pool. Bodyguards came out of adjoining rooms and fired multiple shots at Anna and Hintocha. They quivered and surrounded their leader with fearful expressions, and Anna and Hintocha made funny faces and sneered at them. Hintocha raised her arms and began a swift motion, moving them around with an air of command. A powerful swirling gust materialized around her, growing in strength with each passing moment.

Unaware of what was about to happen, the horrified bodyguards stood their ground, bracing themselves against the mounting force of the wind. But their efforts proved futile as the gust intensified, catching them off guard and hurling them backward with great force. The powerful current swept through the complex, tossing outside anything in its disastrous path, including the screaming bodyguards.

The North Korean leader's arms flailed as he tried to stay calm. Anna lolled out her tongue. "Do you know who I am?"

"Yes, I know who you are. You are the biggest American prostitute. You made a terrible mistake coming to my country. How will you go back?"

"You tell me, bighead. You murdered innocent people in South Korea, and you will pay for your crimes. I will not touch you because you are a dirty pig, but my ferocious army will tear you up." Anna shrilled. Bald eagles, a pack of six gray wolves, and two Amur leopards attacked Ki-woo and ripped up his body, causing him to die. "*Yadogweh. Genoha wahyeh* [Stop. Go inside]." Hintocha took photos of the tortured, lifeless North Korean leader.

The animals entered the capacious palace, tearing up furniture and killing bodyguards hiding in cellar rooms. Troops fired three intercontinental ballistic missiles from a northern forest. Hintocha flew and blew fire, burning the long missiles over the Taedong River. When she returned, Anna suggested they should knock down the main military installations and nuclear arsenal. They ascended four thousand feet before blasting two nuclear sites and seven missile facilities by sending down lightning strikes and large asteroids. Later, they appeared in military uniforms at the US embassy in Seoul. Anna greeted the staff. "Please, call the South Korean president and tell him I want to meet him now." She winked at a secretary. "Ask the major media outlets to come here. I want to make a statement after I talk to the president." An hour later, the South Korean president came and greeted Anna, Hintocha, the ambassador, and the embassy staff before moving to a vacant room. Anna held his hand. "Sorry for turning up in your country without letting you know. The Vice-President and I have conducted a secret mission in North Korea. We executed the tyrant and avenged the recent death of the innocent Koreans. We also destroyed the major military bases, so your country can live in peace."

"Ms. President, I do not know what to say to you. I admire your great fortitude and stamina in bringing justice and peace to the Korean Peninsula. We are very much indebted to your valuable efforts. On a personal note, my wife and I feel saddened and sorry to hear of the tragic passing of the First Lady. What can we do for you?"

"We need to strengthen the diplomatic relations between our countries. But before that, I want to make a statement and tell the world about what we have done in North Korea. You can join us."

They entered a square hall. Anna stood at a press conference podium and thanked the President and his government and the people of South Korea. "As the Commander-in-Chief of the Army and Navy of the United States, I conducted a secret military mission in North Korea. Unlike the earlier timid presidents who stayed at home and sent our troops abroad, I, the courageous Vice-President, and our special forces sneaked into North Korea. We killed the despot and his murderers and destroyed their key military sites. You will see photos after a while. I warn all the dictators in the world that the United States will not tolerate aggression and oppression. Yes, my country committed heinous war crimes in the past. But from now on, there will be no overseas wars under my leadership. However, I will punish all the cruel totalitarians who persecute their peaceful citizens and suppress freedom. I give them a month to stop their tyranny, or I am going to root them out from the face of the earth. Their nuclear bombs and ballistic missiles will not stop me from doing the right thing. The oppressed peoples of the world want freedom and dignity. I am for them...."

In New York City, a scruffy man tracked Dinah Hansson's movements. One night, he hid a silenced pistol in his ski jacket and waited near an elevator door in a building on Madison Avenue. When Dinah left the elevator, he pointed his handgun at her head. "Get in. We need to talk."

Dinah opened the door of her apartment. The man pushed her forward. "Sit here. Why did you kill my cousin, Caitlyn?"

"How do you say that? I didn't kill her. I swear."

"Why did you hate her and her partner?"

"I am a journalist. I hate no one."

"You slandered them even after my cousin's death. Why?"

"I loathe corrupt criminals. The vicious lesbians killed my husband."

"So, you think the President killed your husband? Who believes this crap?"

"I have my evidence."

He pointed his gun at her, and she cowered back. "No. Please. I will give you anything you want."

"Sorry, but I have to do it." Xiola popped up and threw him against a wall. "Liam, get out of here. You said what you wanted to say."

He moaned. "How do you know my name?" He fired three bullets at her. She flung a stone tomahawk at his arm, dropping his gun on the floor. With the speed of light, she pressed his face to a wall and twisted his arm behind his back. "I said, get out. Don't let me kill you." She kneed him in the stomach.

He ran out of the apartment. Dinah stared at her with frightened eyes. "Who are you?"

"I am a sky warrior. I have saved you because of your love for Angelo. But listen to me." Her forefinger touched Dinah's chin. "I will annihilate you if you continue to smear Anna. So, be an amiable woman and write positive things about her. Understood?"

"Yes. Thanks for saving my life."

"Call the police and tell them Liam McManus has tried to kill you. Don't touch his gun."

The next day, Anna and her secretaries gathered in the White House to discuss political and security situations. The Secretary of Defense put a closed dossier on the meeting table. "Madam President, you said our special forces have engaged in the military operation in North Korea. May I know why you didn't inform me?"

"Because the special forces are not US citizens. Do you like to see them?"

"Yes, ma'am."

She whistled. Two bald eagles, three wolves, and a tiger appeared behind her. The secretaries quivered and jumped off their seats. Anna laughed. "Sit and don't be afraid. My warriors fight only the bad guys." The animals disappeared.

"Animals don't bomb military installations. Who destroyed the military bases?"

"Hintocha and I. We used our magic."

Dinah couldn't sleep after her terrifying encounter with Liam and Xiola. In the early morning, she left an envelope on the dining table and called Pamela Ryan. "I am going away for a few weeks."

"Where are you going?"

"Where I can have peace with nature."

"And?"

"To have time for myself. We live in a lousy and stupid country. The Irish barbarians want to kill me, and we have a President and a Vice-President who can fly for thousands of miles and blow up the military nuclear stations in North Korea without firing a bullet. Don't people see the danger of allowing aliens to run our country?"

"Our people are gullible. They are obsessed with eating anything and shopping and gossiping about trivial matters. As long as Anna gives them free money, they won't care."

"I love you, Pam. You are my best friend. I wish I could stay with you, but I can't bear the mighty weight of hopelessness, loneliness, and sadness. It makes me sad to tell you about my last feelings because it will hurt you the most. Look after Mia and Jack. Bye, love." She switched off her phone and left the city.

Meanwhile, Onatah sneaked out of her house. At a cabin northwest of Wears Valley in Tennessee, she made herself six feet tall before climbing five wooden steps and knocking on a door. A bearded man opened the door and leered at her bra and breast cleavage. "Yes."

"Do you have a map? I think I lost my way."

The man looked around. "Please, come in."

She entered the cabin and found twelve men loitering near the windows. "How can I help you?"

"I need a map."

A man opened a drawer. "Here is one. How did you come to this place? Where is your car?"

"I don't have a car. Somebody told me a secret about

you. So, I am here to congratulate you for killing the First Lady.”

They panicked and picked up their guns. “How did you come here?”

“I have two legs. I walked. Who blew up the First Lady’s ass? I want to have sex with him.”

“You bitch.”

“Bitch? Good people do not use that rude word. Let me see.” Her eyes examined the men and stared at a capped man. “Now, I know the truth. You killed her when you detonated the explosives in the State Library. Hooray! You are a genius.” She unbuttoned her shirt. “Do you like to have sex with me?”

The man flushed and aimed his gun at her face. She smiled. “Shoot me here.” She pointed at her chest.

When the man touched her hair, she grabbed his rifle and put its muzzle into his mouth, blowing his fauces and the backside of his head. His friends fired a barrage of bullets at her. She laughed. “You missed, morons.”

A man discharged his gun at her. “Shit. She is one of them. She is a witch.”

A meat cleaver appeared in her right hand. “Don’t move.” She slashed the cleaver at a man’s chest and killed him. She got his machine gun and executed the other men in ten seconds. A cell phone flew into her hand. She called nine-one-one and changed her voice. “Hello, lazy guys. I have executed the evil scum who murdered the First Lady. Get their rotten bodies at an oak cabin on Chamberlain Lane in Tennessee. Catch me if you can.”

She left the cabin and blasted it with a gust from her mouth. The house fell into a forested valley. She flew and popped up in the Nashville mayor's office. The mayor shivered. "Who are you? Why are you here?"

"For one thing. Surprise! I have come to kill you because you murdered the First Lady, who was my mother's girlfriend."

He pressed the alarm button. "Send the guards."

She cackled. "Please, call the cops and the army to get me." Her eyes emitted rays at the office door and turned it into a cement wall. "Stand at that wall."

The quivering mayor stood at the wall, and she saw leather pen holders on his desk. She held pens and pencils and threw them at him, piercing his chest and legs and making him scream. "What do you want from me?" He heard noises outside his office. "Help, help."

"Help. Help. Keep shouting, stupid man. Call the National Guard and the Marines if you can." A tomahawk appeared in her right hand. "My people use the tomahawk. Do you know why? That is why." She pitched the sharp instrument at his brow and killed him. Her hands held him and hurtled his body through a window, dropping it on an adjacent street. With her feet on the mayor's desk, she called nine-one-one. "Hello again. I have killed the mayor of Nashville because he planned the murder of the First Lady. His dead body is on the street. Catch me if you can, and do not forget to clean up the mess." After that, she held the mayor's desk and chucked it out of the office. "I hate desks. People live in cages like rats."

Anna went up to her bedroom to loosen up. After

taking off her jacket and shoes, she sat in bed and switched on the TV. There were breaking news reports about the murder of the mayor of Nashville and the assassination of the New York publisher who published Dinah's book. "Oh, dear. Mad country, and dumb people, and insane gods." Onatah appeared beside her. "Hello, mommy."

"Who are you?"

"I am Onatah."

"Wow. You are a big woman now."

"Yes, I grow up fast."

Hintocha passed into the room with a scowling face and a pouting mouth. "Can't I have privacy?"

"Which privacy? I am your wife. Did you forget that?" She glared at Onatah, who stood beside the curtains. "Come here. Come here."

Onatah hugged Anna. "Mom, protect me."

"From what?"

"From that cranky mom."

"Are you serious? Do we need a war between two goddesses? What do you expect me to do?"

"Why didn't you talk to me about your plan? Tell your mom what you have done."

Anna touched Onatah's long hair. "What have you done?"

"A few things to make you happy."

Hintocha grabbed the back of her neck. "My mom imprisoned me in this nasty world for forty years because of a mistake. I can put you in a pig all your life. Don't you ever, ever do anything before you talk to me. Do you understand?"

"A mother in action. What did Onatah do?"

"She massacred the people who killed Caitlyn and slew the mayor of Nashville because he organized the plot."

"I wanted to do something good for my mom. The mayor's dad planned the murder of Martin Luther King, and no one had arrested him. Do you think the cops would catch the killers? The mayor and his dogs are a bunch of racist murderers. I didn't kill innocent people."

"We understand how you feel, but don't you ever do dangerous things before talking to us. I will ground you for a month in your bedroom. But before I do that, how did you know who killed Caitlyn?"

Winona appeared between them. "I told her about the supremacists. She did an excellent job, and I liked it. I want her to be our family's secret assassin."

"Mom." She bowed.

"Grandma, grandma, I love you." She embraced her grandmother.

"Yes, sweetheart."

Anna rested her arms on her body. "Interesting. The holy family is in the White House."

Hintocha tossed a towel at her. "Behave. Don't talk to the Supreme Goddess like that."

Winona smiled. "Only the Goddess Awehitecha can talk to me as she wishes because I love her."

"Mom, why didn't you tell us about the crime against Caitlyn? We could have saved her. Anna cried for days, and Elisha is blind and paralyzed and cannot move. Give Nina the power of healing so she can hail Elisha."

"That was my divine will. I wrote two thousand years ago that the Eagle Goddess would marry my daughter and become the President. I also wrote something else. You will know it before the end of this day." She whispered in Onatah's ear. "Do your best."

Onatah disappeared. "Where did she go?"

"I asked her to do something for me. Go back to your offices. I will be back at six o'clock. Wait for me here."

She disappeared, and Anna asked Hintocha to sit beside her. "And you, how did you know Onatah has killed the criminals?"

She pulled a piece of paper from her pocket. "Xiola told me about our daughter. She is upset because she is the boss of our covert assassination squad. This is her official complaint. We need to take the case to the Court of Goddesses."

"But your mother is superior to Xiola, and she who ordered Onatah to do the killing. Our Goddesses cannot sue her in the Court because of human affairs. Only the Supreme Mother of the Goddesses can reprimand her."

Onatah appeared at Nina's apartment and rang the doorbell. Nina opened the door. "Grandma."

"Who are you?"

"Don't you recognize me? I am Onatah."

"My Goddess. You are a woman now."

"Yup. Where is Elisha?"

"In the guest room?"

"Wear a chic party dress. We are having a family reunion."

"Where?"

"In the Seneca land."

Onatah entered a dim bedroom and stood beside a bed. She ogled Elisha's face and kissed her lips.

Elisha's lips twitched. "Who is this?"

"I am your sweetheart, Onatah."

"Sweetheart? You are six months old."

"I am a big goddess now. I can do anything."

"Yeah, I forgot."

"Do you like to be my girlfriend? I love you."

Elisha trembled. "Oh, my God. What are you talking about? You are a baby."

"I am not a baby anymore. Don't you like to live forever with the goddess who can make you the most gorgeous woman in the world?"

"Do I have a choice? I cannot even see and walk."

Onatah inclined her head and rested her chin on her fingers. "From a human perspective, you have no choice. I am an omnipotent goddess, and you are a weak woman from this miserable planet. But I love you, and I am a lesbian like you. Not very much like you, but you should know what I mean."

"What do you want from me?"

"Be my lover, and I will make you live forever and do marvelous things for you. I will let you fly in the sky and see the world in a minute."

"But I am blind and disabled."

"You are not, my dear." Onatah wiped her eyes with her hands and made her see. She removed the bed cover and walked her fingers over Elisha's bare legs. "Get up and walk."

She slid off the bed and walked. "You are amazing. This is unbelievable." She looked in a mirror and touched the dark scars on her neck and face. Onatah embraced her and licked her neck, and the wounds faded. "What do you think? Do you like to be my girlfriend?"

"What would I lose? I have no parents. Yeah. We live in a crazy world."

Onatah kissed her crisp lips, and a shimmering diamond ring appeared in her hand. "This is for you, love."

Elisha placed the ring on her middle finger. "It is elegant. Thank you."

"Have a shower and wear a sexy dress. I want to take you and grandma to a special party."

After bathing and wearing a red cowl-neck-knee-length dress, Elisha left the room and met Nina, who wore a green sheath dress. "Oh, Great Spirit. You can see and walk now. Where are the bandages and the scars?"

"Gone. As Anna says, who needs a doctor when a goddess is in the house?"

"Sorry for not helping you heal. I wished my mother had given me the power of healing."

"No problem. I have the power of healing." Onatah grinned. "Hold my hands." They held her hands and vanished.

At six, Winona entered Anna's bedroom, and Hintocha sat on a couch. "Get up and touch my hands. We will go to the house of nirvana."

Anna and Hintocha gripped her glowing hands and evanesced. Three minutes later, they landed at a river. "Where are we?" Anna asked.

"This is Ohiio, or the Allegheny River, which I created sixty million years ago."

"It is idyllic." Anna turned her face back. "That's Colestah's house."

"Yes, we are having a party with our friend."

"Why? What do we want from her?"

"We want to thank her for doing many good things for our people."

They crossed Front Avenue, and Anna knocked on the white door. "Who is that?" Colestah asked.

"Open the door. This is the President of the United States of America."

Colestah's daughter, Talisa, opened the door. "Good evening, Madam President. It is an honor to welcome you and the Vice-President to our humble home." She hugged her and greeted Winona and Hintocha. "Your Highnesses, I am so overjoyed."

Anna entered the house. "Hi, mom. Lovely dress. When did you come here?"

"An hour ago. Onatah brought me here."

"Where is she?"

"I am in the kitchen."

Jodasiya came out of a room with a red flower in her hand. "Hello, Ms. President. This is for you. How are you doing in Washington?"

"I am fine. What is going on here?"

"It is the day of reckoning. We are having a family reunion party. Our goddesses are in the house."

"I am delighted to see you and have a break from work." She kissed Colestah's forehead and sat at a dining table surrounded by ordinary wood chairs. Two tears ran down her face.

"Come here, love." Winona placed a hand on her shoulder and let a finger wipe her tears. "What's going on in your head?"

"Nothing. I ...."

Onatah interrupted. "Moms, I have a girlfriend."

"A girlfriend? You are six months old."

"I look like you. I am not six months old. Do you like to see my girlfriend?"

"Yes. Where is she?"

Elisha left the kitchen. "Hi, Anna. Hi, Hintocha. Surprise. I am the girlfriend."

Anna left her seat and hugged her, kissing her face. "How are you, honey?"

"I am good. I can see and walk now, and the scars disappeared. Thanks to the goddess-girlfriend."

They sat at the table, and Anna noticed nine empty chairs beside her. More tears ran down her face. Winona touched her hand. "Life on earth has affected your emotions. Why do I see tears on your face?"

"I miss my sister and Caitlyn. They should be with us. I miss them so much."

Two hands landed on her shoulders. "Do you miss me?"

Hintocha yelled, and Anna shivered and leaped from her chair. She turned her face. "My Goddess. Caitlyn, Caitlyn. This is impossible."

"Nothing is impossible. I am here."

Anna kissed her lips and embraced her. "I don't believe my eyes. We buried you in New York. How are you alive?"

"Ask your gorgeous Goddess Winona."

Hintocha embraced Caitlyn and Anna genuflected, kissing Winona's hands and knees. "My Glorious Goddess, praise be to you. I will never forget your grace. I love you."

"Get up. You are the President." They laughed. "I had a tough argument with Caitlyn's God over the seventh sky, and He agreed to resurrect her because of her pure heart. After dinner, I will change her face and hair so she can travel around and meet you. She will live with your mother until I arrange something for all of you. We must also consider Elisha's new relationship with Onatah. Elisha needs all of us."

Anna gazed into Hintocha's eyes. "What about my wife?"

"You will marry her again in public. So, look for a new Vice-President. And yes, I want another pretty, powerful granddaughter." She raised her arms. "This is what the divine providence has done for our holy family. This providence is incomplete without the indispensable presence of the Supreme Mother of the Goddess, who wrote Gayadosha before our existence, created our divine families, and ordained our laws. Dear Colestah, can you tell us something about her?"

Colestah left her wheelchair and stood, leaning on her stick. Anna looked at her wrist. "I remember this blue bracelet. Who are you? Oh, my Goddess. Are you...?"

"Be quiet. It is the time for the first revelation." She peeled off the sagging skin of her face and arms, and became a charming young woman with a golden jeweled tiara on her head and a radiant scepter in her right hand. Her wheelchair turned into a golden throne encircled by four brunette fantasy warrior goddesses. Talisa stood and removed the outer skin of her face. The glowing radiance of their luminous bodies had turned the house into a paradise decorated with clean rivers, tall trees, and stars. Nina, Jodasiya, Anna, Hintocha, Caitlyn, Elisha, and Onatah passed out, dropping their heads on the table. Winona's hand rested on Talisa's shoulder. "What happened to our family?"

Colestah struck the scepter on the table. "They need more training."

Nina opened her eyes and bowed. "Who are you, our Holiest Supreme Goddess?"

"I am your mother, my beloved one."

"My Goddess. Mom. Mom. What have you done? I missed you so much." She wept and kissed her face.

"Yes, my beloved daughter. Now you know the truth about Colestah."

"Why did you leave us for so long?"

"For my way has no alteration, and I have fulfilled my promise." She touched Talisa. "Talisa is your sister, the Goddess Yakama."

When Nina hugged her sister, Anna opened her eyes and stood. "What happened?"

"Bow to the Mother of the Supreme Goddesses. She is your grandmother," Nina said.

She bowed. "Grandma, you are unbelievable. I am so happy to see you. How did you fool us?"

"I do not fool. When the time of my command comes, the truth prevails, and the hoaxers lose."

Hintocha, Caitlyn, Jodasiya, Elisha, and Onatah opened their eyes and remained wordless. Winona bowed before Colestah and rested on a red royal throne. Colestah grinned. "My family, listen to what I want to reveal to you. I am the Beginning, and I am the End. I am the Outside, and I am the Inside. Before place and time, I was the First Goddess. I was the One when my throne was on the water of heaven. Before the creation of things, I authored Gayadosha and preserved it under my throne above all the skies. It tells all the events in the universe and your stories. In the beginning, I made Winona from my indefinite spirit and gave her the powers of omnipotence, omniscience, and creation. Then, I created Achiqueta, who produced the twins Awehitecha and Anohitecha when she was three-thousand years old. A hundred years later, Winona created Hintocha.

When Winona made the First Nations, the gods and their devils became envious and resentful. They wanted to subdue our people and make them serfs. Their actions incited hatred and wars in the world.

Although I love you and appreciate what you do, you have disappointed me over ten times. Let me start with the Supreme Spirit, Winona. Winona, you violated our divine law when you turned Hintocha into a girl and imprisoned her in Angela without consulting her mother, Anohitecha. You should have grounded your daughter on a planet or in a place beside you. I forgive you. Do not do that again, for Gayadosha says a goddess must not contravene the rights of another goddess's being and impose her will on her. Second, you revealed yourself in a supercilious way in this mundane world. Since when does a supreme goddess show herself off and threaten to exterminate God's people? I order you to feed three hundred poor families for one year."

Winona nodded. "I repent."

"Nina, you committed a grievous sin when you erased your granddaughter's memory and turned her into an ovum and put her in a human body we did not create. Although you didn't know that Angela had made herself like her mother, you should have rejected Bella's request and asked her to get an egg from another woman. Or you could have made a baby boy for her. Angela suffered immense emotional and physical stress. Besides, you committed another sin when you engaged in an unchaste affair with a married woman. Do not do that again. I forgive you."

"Mom, I am sorry. I will not do like that again."

"Anna Awehitecha, our goddesses are proud of you. You protected them and fought the evil gods and their devils for three million years. However, I want to say straightforward words to you and Hintocha. I can destroy the continents of the earth in a jiff, but I want the change to be gradual and based on the natural laws of the universe. You should not have displayed your divine power. You committed a grave sin when you and Hintocha rigged the presidential election and forged certificates and photos of fake families. People know in their hearts you are not human, but they are afraid of you. The shootings in the park were terrible, but there was no need for Winona, Nina, and Jodasiya to do supernatural acts. You might say you had no choice but to save Awehitecha, Hintocha, and the innocent people. You could have landed on high roofs and uttered divine words instead of flying in front of people and cameras as if you were in a Hollywood action movie.

The mission of our divine family is to restore justice and peace in the universe. It will not be easy when gods and demons are against us."

She gazed at Caitlyn. "Our dear friend, we love you. You have been an amazing companion. It is unfair that Anna remarries Hintocha, and you suppress your true emotions and feelings. So please, open the main door. I have a prize for you."

Caitlyn got up and opened the door. "Oh, my God. Oh, my God. My love, come and give me a big hug."

Nina and Anna pushed their chairs back and dashed to the door. "Angela." They embraced and kissed with tearful eyes. "Hi, grandma. Hi, Anna. How are you doing?" They sobbed, and Anna carried her and kissed her face. Hintocha gaped and stood. "My Holy Goddess. I am so happy to see you again. Where have you been, my prison officer?"

"Here with my great-grandma. I have special guests with me."

Anohitecha and Amitola entered the utopian house. Nina and Anna gasped. "My Goddess. Come here, my sweethearts." Nina kissed their faces and clapped. "This is the happiest day in my life. I am so delighted to be with my family."

Anna stood still with eyes filled with quiet tears. "My sister, my love, my warrior. You are always charming and brave. Happy to see you."

"Thanks, honey. I beg you not to leave us again." They hugged, and their tears flowed down their cheeks.

Hintocha stood and embraced them before she looked at Colestah. "Your Great Holiness, why didn't you tell us about Anohitecha?"

"You do not wish except what I will."

Angela held Elisha and gave her a warm hug. "How are you doing, sweetheart?"

"I am like Alice in Wonderland. I don't believe I am with real goddesses. My words cannot express how I feel when I am with you. I missed you so much."

Onatah pushed her plate away, frowning and leaning her arms on the table. "Why did Elisha kiss her? She is my girlfriend."

Anna looked at her. "Are you jealous now? Get up and say hello to your aunt and cousins."

Angela hugged Onatah and kissed her head. After that, she kneeled before Caitlyn and opened a box. "Cat Hen, do you like to marry me?"

"No, because you still don't know how to spell my name." They laughed. "Yes, sweetheart, I want to marry you, and we will get married and live in New York. So please, no more arguments, and no more brawling."

"As you wish, my lovely goddess. I want to be close to everyone in the family."

"Listen to me. You need to do nothing but get a wedding dress. We have arranged everything for the wedding. Something else." She touched her Native American costume. "With my due respect to everyone, I do not want you to wear this dress on our wedding day. OK?"

"More orders, my queen?"

"That's enough for tonight." Her gaze swept across the room, landing on each face. "You are my new family. I don't believe I am now a deity like you."

They cheered and had a glass of wine.

Anna touched her mother's hand. "I am blissful because Gayadosha says the Eagle Goddess will rule the North Land when her twin sister comes back."

"One minute." Colestah rushed to a ghostly room and closed its door. A black shadow appeared in the middle of the room. "Go now and don't be late."

The shadow melted away, and she returned to her throne. "There are six empty chairs at the table. One will be for a new member of the family. Who will be the new Vice-President?" They gazed at each other and didn't know what to say. "Don't you know the answer?" She smiled. "Yakama, open the door."

Yakama opened the main door. "Hi, Martina. Happy to see you."

Martina gaped when she entered the heaven-like mansion. She bowed. Colestah kissed her forehead, and Anna embraced her. "Why are you here?"

"To see my president."

Yakama kissed Martina's lips. "Martina is my fiancée. We got engaged two months ago."

"How? Where?"

"In New York. Your sister introduced us to each other."

Colestah tapped her glass with a fork. "Hintocha will be the First Lady, and Martina will be the Vice-President. After that, we will have six public wedding parties in two weeks. Angela will marry Caitlyn, Anna will remarry Hintocha, and Yakama will marry Martina."

"These are three marriages, not six," Anna said.

"Do you know better than me?"

Nina rested her right arm on Jodasiya's shoulders. "Listen, my family. I have an announcement to make. Jodasiya and I are getting married, and we invite you. No gifts, please."

"Jodasiya, you have been a remarkable woman. You are now a goddess. You will no longer live in a lake water," Colestah said.

"Praise be to you, our Holy Mother."

Onatah licked her fork. "What about me? Am I not getting married?"

"You need to speak to Elisha and appreciate her feelings. Maybe you should make her a powerful goddess like you," Anna replied, glancing at her grandmother. "What is the fifth wedding?"

With a sword in her hand, Xiola appeared from the back door and greeted them. Winona stood and held her hand. "Xiola and I will get married in ten days. She is my secret lover and intrepid fighter."

"Good. But next time, don't ask Onatah to do a violent act without permission from Xiola. Xiola is the head of the covert operations and superior to your granddaughter." Colestah gave Onatah a cluster of grapes. "Before you do any serious action against our opponents, you must talk to Xiola and get permission from her. Understood?"

"Yes, I understand."

Anna smiled. "What about you, our holy grandma? Do you have a partner?"

"That's one of the greatest mysteries I will never disclose."

"How will Angela become the commander of the human world?"

"Angela will not become the leader of anyone."

"But Gayadosha says Angelo will be the Supreme God of humanity."

"You tell the truth, but your niece is not Angelo. Angelo is the most beneficent and most merciful God and the son of a special goddess."

"Who is this god and who is his mother?"

"You will know that later. But now, Angela, tell us your story."

"Thanks, Your Holiness. My grandmother came down to earth to search for her mother and Anna and left my mother alone for many years. That was reasonable in the beginning. But my mother felt upset when her mother got involved in a sexual relationship with Bella. She wondered how a supreme goddess would have an affair with a married human woman and thought she loved Bella more than her. So, my mother moved to a new galaxy in the second sky and created me and Amitola to keep her company. Five years later, my grandmother came back, not to give my mother hugs and kisses, but to turn her into an egg to save Bella's marriage. My mom asked her to give her a day to think about it. I saw my mother concerned. She told me about her mother's urgent request. So, I made myself look like my mother without her knowledge. My grandmother seized me and turned me into an egg after erasing my memory."

Nina, Anna, Hintocha, and Caitlyn shuddered, gaping at her. "What happened after that?"

"Jodasiya installed her human spirit in me to let me develop like a normal human embryo in Bella's womb. Five hours after that, Leonardo made love to Bella. His sperm fertilized and split me, creating a boy with me, and his male chromosomes penetrated me, making me a mix of a boy and a girl. A minute before Bella gave birth to the boy, my mother caused everyone in the delivery room in the Brooklyn house to sleep. Bella delivered a baby boy, and my mother took him to her house. I was born thirteen seconds after the boy, and Sandro called me Angelo. When Leonardo and Bella wanted to apply for a birth certificate, my mother hypnotized them, forcing them to apply for two birth certificates. When the Health Department sent the two certificates that had the name Angelo, my mother got a certificate before it arrived at the Brooklyn house. My mother looked after the boy because she knew he would be the Merciful God of humanity, and when I was seven, she introduced herself to me and let me see Angelo in her house. It shocked me to see a person who looked like me. We thought we were identical twins. So, he and I had agreed to swap our roles because of our similar features. Neither my grandma Nina nor anyone in the Lucciano family had noticed the difference between Angelo and me. At thirteen, I asked Angelo to love Dinah Hansson and be her boyfriend, though my grandma thought he was me.

After graduation, I traveled to Toronto to study humanities, and Angelo went to Ottawa to study technology and computer sciences. At twenty-one, my grandma restored my omniscient memory, and I realized Angelo was my son."

"Son?"

"Yes, Angelo and I are one soul in two bodies. He is my son, and Leonardo is his biological father. I kept the matter a secret to protect him. However, the Mother Goddess removed the male organs and made me a female woman when I was in my grandma's bathroom, though human elements remained in my body to prevent any suspicion. Next day, I told Leonardo about his son and warned him about revealing the secret. So, he and Bella met Angelo in a secret place and flew to St. Lucia to attend his and Dinah's wedding party. They and Dinah's family kept their relationship a secret. On my fortieth birthday, the devil Dagwano wanted to kill me in Toronto, but my mother and sister rescued me and got rid of my human skeleton and elements before taking me up to my new house in the fourth sky. That's why the detective found a female skeleton."

Anna took a piece of melon. "What about Angelo and the explosion in your house?"

"Tawiscara and his evil god Hagwedatah abducted Angelo when they found his name floating in the East River, nineteen years after I threw the eagle's eye in a toilet. That is why they asked him about the eagle's eye and the secret code which were on my leg. When they wanted to kill him because of his unawareness of the matter, I and my mother and sister rescued him and caused the explosion that killed Tawiscara's god and a man."

"What happened to Angelo?"

"Our Supreme Mother Goddess made him a full god equipped with all the divine powers and took him up to her kingdom, which most of us had not seen. Dinah was right when she said Angelo was her husband and Leonardo's only son. As I have said, after I became a woman, I told Leonardo about his son in Ottawa and forced him and Bella to keep the matter a secret. That's all, my sweethearts. Let us eat and drink and celebrate our company."

In Ontario, Dinah had a hot shower in Angelo's vacation house. Her eyes fixed upon the tranquil waters of Lake Huron, seeking solace and a moment of silent reflection. Her hand brushed through her hair, a soothing gesture that concealed her despair.

As the evening approached, casting its golden tinge on the serene surroundings, she made her way to the bedroom. With a contemplative expression, she closed the curtains.

Choosing a red lace satin nightdress, she donned the garment, its delicate fabric embracing her body. The choice of color, bold and passionate, hinted at a side of her hidden from public view. With meticulous care, she painted her lips a soft shade of pink.

A wave of emotion overcame her and tears welled up in her eyes. She reached for a photograph of Angelo, holding it with tender care and pressing her lips against it. "Bye, love. I hope to see you in heaven." She picked up a pistol and inserted its muzzle in her mouth. A hand grabbed the gun and put it on a side table. "People eat food, not guns."

She quivered. "Oh, my God. Angelo, Angelo. You are alive. How are you here?"

"This is my house."

"How are you alive?"

"I am alive because I didn't die."

"I saw the explosion."

"Did you see my body? My mother and her family caused the explosion to kill the abductors."

"Your mother's family is in England. Where have you been?"

"My mother, grandmother, and aunt rescued me from the abductors, and the Mother Goddess kept me in Her kingdom."

"What are you talking about? Who is the Mother Goddess?"

"It is a long story. Aren't you excited to see me?"

"How did you come in?"

"From here."

"From this wall?"

"Yes, I came from this wall because you locked the doors. I can move through anything."

She snatched the gun and pointed it at him. "Who are you?"

"Honey, I am Angelo. What, sweetheart? Do you want to shoot your hubby? Please, put the gun down and come here."

"Not before I get all the answers right now. Tell me the truth. Who are you? Who is your family?"

"Honey, I love you."

"Don't lie to me."

"Believe me. I don't lie to you or to anyone else. A god and his devil and two men had abducted me in Ottawa to get a mysterious code related to the future of the earth. Angela Lucciano is my mother. She and her mother and sister had rescued me and destroyed the house to kill the abductors."

"Your mother is dead."

"She will never die."

"Nonsense. Stop playing games with me."

"I don't play games with you. Bella gave birth to me, but she was not my biological mom. The egg in Bella's womb was Angela's. Leonardo was my biological father. That's why I am called the Son of the Man. I am the promised God of humanity."

"What is this nonsense? Do you want me to believe that?"

"I didn't know I am God before I met my mom and her family after the explosion."

"What about Mia and Jack?"

"Mia is a demigoddess, and Jack is a demigod."

"What about Leonardo and Bella? They treated you as their son."

"That's true. As I have said, Angela is my mother, and Leonardo was my father. My mother made a secret deal with Leonardo and Bella after you agreed to marry me."

She threw a shoe at him. "Why didn't you tell me the truth after we got married?"

"My mom and I and your family had promised to keep quiet. Honey, come on. You kissed my photo and said you love me before you wanted to kill yourself. Why are you upset now?"

"How do you know I kissed your photo?"

"I am an omniscient god. I liked your book. You are right in one thing. Nina, Anna, and Hintocha are divine goddesses from the sky." He raised his hand and elevated her, forcing her to come to bed. "Give me the gun. Do you want to kiss me or what?"

She kissed him. "Oh, my God. What happened? I wanted to kill myself because of you. How are you alive? Everybody thinks you are dead."

"Well, I am here. I won't die." He caressed and made love to her. She touched his arms and chest. "You have firm muscles?"

"I worked hard during my rehabilitation. Let us have a shower. I want to make you a goddess and take you to a special place to let you know the truth about me and my divine family."

In the shower room, Angelo recited recondite words and covered her body with coruscating light. She shivered and gleamed. After the shower, he got her a crimson mini-dress and exited the house. "Where do you want to take me?"

"We need to see our kids. Close your eyes and hold my hand." They flew and landed at their house in Ottawa. He called Jack. "Hi, son. Your mom and I are back. Open the door."

Jack exclaimed. "Mia, Mia. Mom and dad are here." They opened the door and embraced them. "Where have you been?"

"Long story short. Wear nice clothes. We want to

take you to our new family."

"What do you mean?"

"Listen to your mom and dad. We are going to a family party."

"Where do you want to take us?"

"Gosh. Stop talking and be ready in five minutes."

When they became ready, Dinah hugged her daughter, and Angelo embraced his son. "Are you ready? Close your eyes." They closed their eyes and flew. Ten minutes later, they descended to Colestah's house. Angelo rang the bell and Angela opened the door. "Good evening, mom. This is my wife, Dinah Hansson, and these are our children, Jack and Mia."

"Please, come in. Happy to see you all."

Dinah held Angelo's hand and trudged into the earthly heaven. "What is this place? Is this a house or a forest?" She hid her face in his arms.

"This is heaven on earth."

When everyone stood, she grabbed Angelo's chest. Angelo's fingertips grazed the back of her hair. "This is my divine family. My mother is the Goddess Angela, and my aunt is the Goddess Amitola. My grandmother is the Goddess Anohitecha, and the Goddess Anna Awehitecha is her twin sister. Nina is the Goddess Achiqueta and my great grandma. She created the oceans and the seas. The Goddess Hintocha is Anna's wife. The Goddess Kotyanga, you can call her Colestah, is Nina's mother who kept me in her heavenly kingdom. This Goddess is Winona. She is Hintocha's mother and the Creator of the Americas and the First Nations. You know Caitlyn McManus and her daughter Elisha."

Dinah shook Caitlyn's hand. "Oh, my God. You were dead. What happened?"

"The Goddess Winona has restored my life."

Angelo rested his arm on Dinah's shoulders. "You know Martina. This is the Goddess Onatah, Anna's and Hintocha's daughter. This lovely, ancient woman is Jodasiya. She is Nina's sweetheart. Xiola is the war goddess who saved you from the Irish psycho. She is Winona's partner. That goddess is called Yakama. She is Nina's sister."

Dinah smiled. "What should I say? I am pleased to know the truth about all of you."

They sat around the dining table except Anna. "Dear Dinah, I and Hintocha and our divine family want to apologize to you for causing so much stress to you and your family. You were right when you said we are not humans. You were also right about rigging the election. We shouldn't have exposed ourselves and interfered in the human affairs of this country. We did not intend to defame you, but to do justice for the indigenous peoples who lost their livelihood and lands, which we created. I will be the President for one term to allow fair elections. I do not speak on everyone's behalf, but I assure you we are the kindest family and goddesses in this universe. We will do anything for you and your children and make you immortal beings. Please forgive us. We love you and we welcome you to our divine family."

Dinah wiped her tears. "I love you too. Angelo is the best gift you have given me. I and my family promise to do our best for your people."

Angelo stood. "Dinah and I will renew our vows on a

hot beach in Mexico and introduce you to Jack and Mia. We invite you to join us."

Colestah got up. "This is the best conclusion, and I have fulfilled my promise. I will make all of you omniscient and omnipotent, so no one will hurt you. Some of you will have new bodies and names, and I will teach you how to deal with the human beings in the next era without exposing yourselves. What you did in this world was a test, and I hope you have learned a lesson. I am not an oppressor or a dictator. I want you to outline a comprehensive plan to implement the promise embodied in Gayadosha about making Angelo the Merciful God of humanity. What I suggest now is Xiola, Anna, Anohitecha, Amitola, and Onatah oversee the war and assassination operations. Nina, Angela, Caitlyn, and Elisha should guide our creativity and innovation. Jodasiya will be our principal negotiator with the First Nations and the indigenous peoples. Martina and Yakama should manage our business and finance. Winona and Hintocha will provide you with intelligence information. I request Dinah to continue her investigative journalism. Remember that our next struggle will be with God, who wants Jesus Christ and his believers to rule the world. And since you are going to live in separate homes, I have selected a special aide to organize the logistics that you will need in the next phase."

"What do you mean?" Anna asked.

"The Seneca Nation expects me to die soon. So, we will have a funeral after a month, and I will change my appearance and make myself a normal woman. We need an assistant to coordinate our work to make it look more human and natural."

"Who is the assistant?"

Colestah walked to a foggy staircase and raised her eyes. "Come downstairs."

A masked woman in a white dress came downstairs and bowed. Colestah held her hand and moved to the dining table. "Remove the mask."

"Hello, everyone."

Everyone stood in astonishment. "Bella, Bella. Oh, my Goddess." They hugged her.

"I resurrected Bella because she bore Angela and Angelo and loved my daughter. She will stay with me until we leave this planet. It was my will, and it will be my order. Peace be with you..."